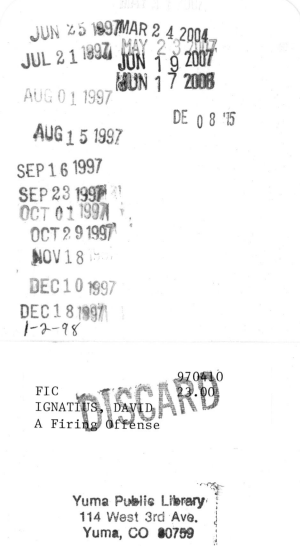

A Firing Offense

A FIRING OFFENSE

David Ignatius

RANDOM HOUSE   NEW YORK

970410

Grateful acknowledgment is made to A. P. Watt Ltd. for permission to reprint
two lines from "The Municipal Gallery Revisited" from
The Collected Poems of William Butler Yeats.
Reprinted by permission of A. P. Watt Ltd. on behalf of Michael Yeats.

Library of Congress Cataloging-in-Publication Data
Ignatius, David.
A firing offense / David Ignatius.—1st ed.
ISBN 0-679-44860-8
I. Title.
PS3559.G54F57 1997
813'.54—dc21 96-29518

Random House website address: http://www.randomhouse.com/

Printed in the United States of America on acid-free paper

24689753

Book design by Lilly Langotsky

For my parents, Paul and Nancy Ignatius

Reporters should not ordinarily engage in outside activities and jobs. That is especially true of connections with government, which compromise the newspaper's fundamental mission of independence and objectivity. Any deliberate violation of this policy will be regarded as a firing offense.

—*The New York Mirror Handbook on Style*

Prologue

❖❖

A FUNERAL

MAY 1996

Arthur Bowman's funeral was a Washington event, as finely choreographed as Bowman could have wished. It was held at St. John's Church, an austere structure across Lafayette Square from the White House. The church was almost full. The vice president was there, along with four members of the cabinet and several dozen senators and congressmen. They were sitting up front near the family, but for once they were the passive observers, and we, the journalists, were the real actors. The whole of the newspaper seemed to have gathered. The publisher and the executive editor and the demigods had flown down from New York, but hundreds of others had come, too—reporters, copy editors, assignment editors, news aides—all the ranks in our newspaper army.

I was sitting in the front row between Edwin Weiss, the executive editor, and Philip Sellinger, the publisher. Weiss had asked me to read something at the funeral. I was the last person from the newspaper to have seen Arthur Bowman before he died in Beijing, and I had accompanied his body back to Washington. The executive editor said it would symbolize continuity at the paper: a beloved colleague departing, the younger generation ready to take over.

As we waited for the service to start, you could hear a low buzz in the church, gaining in intensity as the minutes passed, as people leaned toward each other to share bits of Washington gossip, trade information, discuss the personalities who were there and those who weren't. By the time the rector rose from his chair and walked to the lectern, the sound was almost a roar.

" 'I am the resurrection and the life, saith the Lord,' " he began, and the buzz of voices suddenly died away. The mourners fumbled in their prayer books for the Order for the Burial of the Dead. Who knew Arthur Bowman was an Episcopalian? That was another of his secrets. I looked over my shoulder at the congregation. All the people I cared about in the world seemed to be gathered under the dome of the church. Several rows back was Annie Baron, my ex-girlfriend, already dabbing at her nose with a handkerchief. When she saw me, she tried to smile, but a tear rolled down her cheek. She arched that long neck away from me and, in the same motion, swept a few strands of hair back from her forehead. She was an actress, even in her grief. The rector continued his intonation: " 'We brought nothing into this world, and it is certain we can carry nothing out.' "

There was an overwhelming silence. It was my turn to speak. The rector nodded to me, and I rose and walked to the lectern. I had dressed soberly for the funeral—in a blue suit, white shirt and blue tie—but I suspect I still looked like a California kid: skinny, just under six feet tall, sandy brown hair combed over the top of my head. I was thirty-seven years old; I didn't yet look damaged or unhealthy enough to be a reporter.

I had expected that I would feel nervous about speaking before so many famous people, but I felt a perfect, unworldly calm. A part of me was still back in China, kneeling over Arthur's broken body, wiping the blood from his mouth as he gasped for words and breath before he died. The ringing in my ears was the ambulance siren on Chang'an, the Boulevard of Eternal Peace, sent by the men who had murdered him.

Philip Sellinger looked up at me expectantly. There was an odd sparkle in the publisher's eyes. His best friend had died, but his newspaper survived. I cleared my throat. For that moment I stood on the bridge of this ship of the dead, which was carrying all of us—Arthur and me and our hundreds of colleagues—into our vision of the afterlife. We journalists were the last believers in the god of history. We were its secret priesthood, and though we liked to pretend otherwise, we really did think we were better than ordinary people. We struggled to maintain a divine impartiality, but so often, as in Arthur's case, we got corrupted somewhere along the journey—caught up in the events we tried to cover.

"For those who don't know me," I began, "my name is Eric Truell. I accompanied Arthur to China on his last reporting trip, and I was with him when he died." I paused. That was enough to say. Any more and I would begin to tell lies. "The Bowman family has asked that I read a favorite psalm, which Arthur had marked in his Bible at home. It is Psalm One Hundred and Two."

I cleared my throat again and began speaking—slowly, evenly, the way the rector had told me to do. Like so much of Arthur Bowman's life, the funeral was a form of theater, and I wanted to play my assigned role as well as I could. " 'Hear my prayer, O Lord; let my cry come unto you. Do not hide your face from me in the day of my distress.' " My voice was strong, clear, unreal. People's faces were turned toward me with attention and expectation. "Incline your ear to me; answer me speedily in the day when I call. For my days pass away like smoke, and my bones burn like a furnace. My heart is stricken and withered like grass; I am too wasted to eat my bread.' "

I had practiced reading the psalm over a dozen times, but until I spoke the words aloud I hadn't fully understood what a sad, desperate passage it was. The members of the congregation didn't seem troubled. They mostly had the blank, tolerant looks of irreligious people waiting for the mumbo jumbo to be over. " 'I lie awake; I am like a lonely bird on the housetop. All day long my enemies taunt me; those who deride me use my name for a curse. For I eat ashes like bread, and mingle tears with my drink.' " I stopped for a moment and looked at the audience. I wondered if I was the only one who could hear Arthur's voice speaking these desperate words. There were a few more verses—happier ones with the boilerplate about God smiting enemies and tormentors—and then I was done.

I returned to my seat. Ed Weiss squeezed my arm as he made his way up to deliver his eulogy. When he reached the lectern, he gripped it tightly on either side and gazed out at the audience. Even at sixty, he was a man of sharp edges—hard cheekbones, a nose that hooked slightly like an Indian chief's, all that gray hair, swept back on his head—and then the surprise, that lovely, soft smile. He was smiling now, in a way that could only reassure the audience of mourners. This was his flock, more than the rector's. He removed a written text from his pocket but laid it down, unopened, and began to speak.

"Here is how I remember my friend Arthur," he began. "It's a hot afternoon in Phnom Penh, during the height of the war in Cambodia. A group of us have gone to the airport to try to catch a flight out to Thailand. We're sitting on the floor of the terminal behind the sandbags, smoking cigarettes. Every few minutes, a shell lands near the airport. We're tired, dispirited, feeling sorry for ourselves. After a while a two-engine plane circles the airport and lands. It's the weekly flight from Bangkok, the one we've been waiting for. They open the door and out walks a guy in a white linen suit—the most beautiful suit you've ever seen—carrying a bottle of champagne.

And, of course, it's Arthur. He walks straight across the tarmac, ignoring the screech of an incoming round that lands a few hundred yards away. When he gets to the terminal, he looks at all of us, peering out over the sandbags at him like a bunch of gophers. 'Hello, lads!' he says. 'Don't tell me you're leaving.' He pops the cork and hands the bottle of champagne around.

"Needless to say, none of us left Phnom Penh that day. How could we, once Arthur Bowman had arrived? Our editors would have just sent us back, once his stories began to appear in the *Times*. I can imagine the cables we would have received from the foreign desk: 'Times fronting Khmer Rouge massacre. Why we unhave?' " There was a ripple of laughter from the back of the church, where the old-timers were sitting. "There was a lot the *Mirror* unhad in those days, but we wanted to be a great newspaper. So the first thing I did when I came home to become foreign editor was to conspire with Phil Sellinger to woo Arthur from the *Times*. It was the best hire we ever made.

"Nobody was a better war reporter than Arthur, because nobody was a better reporter, period. He breathed a story in whole, swallowed it, devoured it. There was something overwhelming about his energy and appetite. It might be after midnight and long past time to go to bed, but Arthur would still be there at the bar, wanting to share one more story, throw down one more drink. You'd stay in bed the next morning until ten trying to sleep it off, and when you finally got downstairs and looked for Arthur, the desk clerk would say he left at seven-thirty to go interview the prime minister—an interview he had somehow forgotten to mention the night before, when he was telling you his life story."

Weiss stopped speaking and looked up at the perfect white rounded arches of the church, and down at Bowman's black coffin. He shook his head sadly and muttered something under his breath that sounded like "Shit." He took a white handkerchief out of his pocket, blew his nose and then continued.

"People told Arthur so many things over the years. Too many things, I sometimes suspect. Especially after he came back to Washington to be our diplomatic correspondent. I look out at the distinguished officials who have come to pay their respects to Arthur, and I ask you: Was there anything that Arthur Bowman didn't know? Was there any policy position, internal power struggle, or personality clash that Arthur hadn't heard about? Most of what he knew wound up in the *Mirror*, where it belonged. Not all of it. But most of it."

The executive editor smiled. The publisher, sitting two seats away, laughed and shook his head, and other people chuckled, too. That was one thing Arthur was famous for: he knew all the secrets. I seemed to be the only one who didn't think it was funny, but that was my problem.

"Arthur Bowman was a great man. He deserved better than what he got. To die like that, so far away . . ." Ed Weiss paused, and I thought he was just catching his breath. But he looked down at the coffin, choking back tears that had suddenly come to him, and put his fist in the air. "Good-bye, dear friend!" he said gruffly, biting his lip to keep from crying any more.

All around the room, people were weeping now. I think I was the only dry-eyed person in the church. But I knew too much.

Philip Sellinger, the publisher, spoke next. He was a thin man, with tightly curled silver hair and those sparkling blue eyes. There was so much emotion in the room, I wondered what he would say. Arthur had been his best friend since college. He had cried on the phone when I called from Beijing with the news. But he was perfectly calm now, talking about his friend as if he were sitting in the next room.

"I would like to share with you a letter Arthur Bowman sent me several years ago," he began. "I had so many communications with Arthur over the years, but of all of them I think this was my favorite.

" 'Dear Philip,' he wrote, 'I hate to bother you about something as trivial as this, but the accounting department is refusing to reimburse me for some expenses on my recent trip to Europe. They seem particularly unhappy about a bill at Mirabelle's restaurant in London that came to approximately two thousand three hundred dollars.' " He paused, and a few of the mourners began to laugh. " 'Between us, Philip, let me explain what happened. My guests on this occasion were two very senior members of the British Foreign Office and their wives. Because of their immense value to the newspaper over the years, I wanted to show them an especially good time. As always with the Brits, it was the wines that caused the problem. We had a good white Burgundy with the fish course, a Bâtard-Montrachet, I think. And a particularly good claret, a 1982 Léoville-Las-Cases. My guests suggested a Sauternes with dessert, and the inevitable bottle of port, and it all added up. I'm embarrassed that the final bill was so large, Philip, but I don't have to tell you the importance of maintaining relationships like this. I wish it could be done inexpensively, but good journalism costs money. As ever, Arthur.' "

Sellinger stopped and smiled. By now the whole of the church was laughing. This was a side of Bowman people had gossiped about for years, but rarely discussed. "Here is my esteem for Arthur Bowman," the publisher continued. "I took the expense form and wrote a note to the accounting department in the margin: 'Charge this to publisher's account. Mr. Bowman is worth every penny.' I'm not sure anyone but me will ever know how profoundly true that was. My debt to him is incalculable. I miss him more than I can say."

When Sellinger finished, we sang an old Anglican hymn—"Time like an ever-rolling stream bears all its sons away"—and there were some final prayers. They asked the pallbearers to come forward, and we carried Bowman's coffin to the hearse outside. Ed Weiss took me by the arm after we had laid the coffin in the long black Cadillac and spoke in my ear. "It was like a torch being passed, watching you read that psalm," he said. "That was my only consolation today."

We turned back toward the church. It was a spring afternoon, and the air was soft and fragrant. Colleagues from the newsroom were coming toward me, to shake my hand. For the first time all day, I felt like crying. Not for Arthur, but for myself. Looking at this gathering of my dearest friends—all grieving over a man who, they devoutly believed in their hearts, represented the great traditions of our newspaper—I could not imagine ever telling them the truth, about Arthur or about me.

But so much has taken place in the months since Arthur Bowman's funeral, I realize now that I have no alternative but to tell the story as it really happened. And the truth here will be disturbing to many people.

I

PARIS

MAY–JULY 1994

1

❖

At the time I now regard as the beginning of this story, I was working as the *Mirror*'s bureau chief in Paris. I had been there two years and I
was getting bored. I think that may have been a factor in what happened
later. Boredom is ordinarily the fuel of journalism; it is the dry powder
that, under the right circumstances, ignites into the flame of curiosity that
connects a reporter with his story. We need that burst of energy, because
despite what people think, journalism is often quite dull. Reporters spend
most of their time waiting for things to happen: for a meeting to end; for
one of the cops to give you a fill; for the shelling to stop so you can go outside and see what's left of the city. And we usually accept the waiting and
the passivity; it's like a launchpad before liftoff. But too much boredom can
spark too much heat—creating a passion to connect with the story that is
consuming, unbounded, uncontrollable. And I suspect that's what happened in this case.

It was May 1994, two years before the funeral in Lafayette Square. I was
driving to a suburban town east of Paris along the Marne River to interview a French scientist named Roger Navarre. The press spokesman for his
company had called me a few days before, claiming that their man had discovered a new technique for regenerating brain cells. He made it sound like
a new polio vaccine—something that could cure Alzheimer's disease, pre-
vent Lou Gehrig's disease, mend severed spinal cords. Our science editor
said it would certainly be newsworthy if true—though he doubted it, since
the findings hadn't been published in any of the U.S. medical journals
yet—but he wanted to make sure nobody else scooped us. That's a strange
idea when you think about it—the notion of "scooping" another newspa-

per about a lifesaving scientific breakthrough—but that's the way the news business works. At the very least, the science editor said, I would get a nice drive in the country and a feature story about the French biotechnology industry. And I was happy enough to do it; there wasn't much real news in France that the paper cared about anymore. I had been spending most of my time looking for Lifestyle stories about food and wine and French movie stars—and waiting for a plane to crash or a ferryboat to sink, which would at least get me on the front page for a day.

It was a bright spring afternoon, the kind that reminds you that France is still worth the trouble. And I was on the road, which in itself was a small antidote to my boredom. I had the window of my Renault down—the Paris bureau still had a car, even though we didn't have any news—and I was sailing along through the Bois de Vincennes, past the tall shade trees that guarded the edge of the park. On the seat next to me was a stack of scientific papers my news aide had gathered, summarizing the latest developments in neurobiology. Forty-eight hours before, I had known absolutely nothing about these subjects. I still knew nothing, really, but over the years I had developed a powerful ability to fake it, if given the smallest amount of raw material. We journalists are skilled impostors; that is one of our trade secrets.

The car radio was on; the French announcer was rattling away the day's news. Sports scores, the latest from the Balkans, a bulletin about police being summoned to deal with a disturbance in the Rue Lamennais, off the Champs-Élysées. All of it sounded far away. I was driving too fast, which is almost required in France, and I was feeling a sensation I often have when I'm on the way to a story—a sense of possibility, a sense that the familiar is about to give way to the unexpected. The chance of such encounters—even when becalmed on the glassy sea of boredom—was what made my job bearable. That was the game of journalism—waiting patiently for your shot, and then nailing it—and I had always been proficient at games, ever since I was a boy in northern California.

We're all shaped and misshaped by the experiences of our childhoods. Mine was happy and uncomplicated, which was itself a kind of burden— the burden of lightness. People with emotional scars know they have to be wary; they learn to ration their passions; they know what will hurt them. Nothing in my childhood taught me those lessons. My father was a professor of medicine at the University of California at Davis, and I grew up in the never-again idyll of California in the 1960s and '70s. We had a big house and a pool, a horse for my sister and a tennis court for me. And what I mostly did until my eighteenth year was to hit tennis balls. Thousands of them, pounding them down the line, crosscourt, forehand, backhand, slice, topspin. Over and over, *boom-boom-boom-boom,* until I could place a tennis-ball can anywhere across the net and stand a reasonable chance of hitting it. That was how I spent my youth. Haight-Ashbury and its convulsions were over the mountains and into another solar system. I lived in the sun-kissed Sacramento Valley, hitting yellow tennis balls and picking oranges off the trees in our backyard.

My first great adventure was going away to college—all the way to Stanford, ninety miles across the bay. The university accepted me partly because of my tennis, but I also tested well, and they wanted to be nice to my father, who had gone to Stanford Medical School and still lectured there occasionally. The day I arrived in 1977 to begin freshman year all I was really thinking about was making the tennis team and playing in national tournaments. But I was like so many kid athletes—I had been wound so tight for so many years, I was ready to pop.

And so I did. By the spring of freshman year, it was clear that life had more to offer than hitting small yellow balls. My internal spring went unsprung with amazing suddenness—certainly amazing to my parents when I told them in April that I had dropped off the freshman team. But it was the right thing to do. I had realized in those first few months at Stanford that while I was an adequate college player, I would never be a superstar. And, in truth, I was ready for bigger challenges than hitting those damned tennis-ball cans.

Like all college students, I read poetry—do we ever really read poetry again, after college?—and I cried with my girlfriend, Annie, every time we read "Ariel" together. But men do not live by poetry alone, except when they're trying to get laid, and I began to realize that I missed sports—not playing them, but being around them—so by the end of sophomore year I had begun writing sports stories for the *Stanford Daily,* and then regular news stories, which I loved more than anything I had ever done. There was a cleanness to newswriting, a directness that reminded me of what I enjoyed about tennis. One night when I was sitting in the *Daily* office, the president of Stanford had a heart attack, and I was asked to cover it because I was fast and didn't make mistakes, and we were approaching deadline. And I nailed the story. I was totally, completely, in the zone. I worked the next summer for a small newspaper in the Bay area, the *Santa Rosa News-Herald*. By the time I graduated, I knew precisely what I wanted to do, which was to work for a great newspaper and write stories forever. *Boom-boom-boom-boom*. Set them up and knock them down. I applied for internships at the *Times, Post, Journal* and *Mirror*; the first offer I got came from the *Mirror*.

I was a good reporter, but more important than that, I was lucky. I started in Metro, like everybody else. I had been covering Long Island for two months when a black teenager was beaten to death in a white neighborhood. I was a twenty-one-year-old white guy from California—too new to New York not to ask everybody the obvious questions—and the minute you read my stories, you knew exactly what had happened. The folks in that neighborhood just hated black people, and they had pounded that poor kid until he was a bloody pulp. My stories ran on the front page for a week. There were more good assignments after that: a corruption scandal in Long Island City; a fabulous homicide in which a state court judge strangled his wife with a garter belt and nylons she'd gotten as a gift from her lover; a series about bad cops in the New York City police department.

And then in 1983, the paper needed someone to go to Beirut in a hurry, and I volunteered, and suddenly I was covering a war where they were putting pieces of U.S. marines in body bags. I was as lucky as those dead marines were unlucky. I was writing, doing, being—no gap between thought and action—and the paper was putting it all on page one. I was just twenty-four, much too young to be a foreign correspondent, but I was doing the job, and they let me stay. After four years in the Middle East, they sent me to Hong Kong, and four years after that to Paris. It wasn't until I finally got to Paris—which was supposedly the great prize for having done so well—that I began to feel ordinary and bored. I was out of the zone, thinking too much about what I was doing. I had this feeling I'd already done all the French stories before: Algerian immigrants in Marseilles; trade wars with the United States; French politicians and their mistresses; the arrival of the Beaujolais Nouveau. It was a nonjob, really.

I missed the old days in Beirut and Hong Kong, where every morning there was the strong likelihood that someone completely bizarre would walk in off the street, unburdening me from the ordinariness of my life and introducing me to the strangeness of his or hers. That ever-present possibility of release had drawn me to the news business in the first place, and sustained me ever since. It was the perfect job: it offered a chance to consort with people at the far edges of life—people who broke all the rules—without actually having to break any myself.

After a forty-five minute drive, I approached the walled complex of the research center where Roger Navarre worked. Looming above the barbed wire was a sign displaying the words UNETAT, S.A., the name of the French conglomerate that owned the biotechnology facility. Unetat was the hottest company in France that year. It had been privatized in the late 1980s and was devouring every high-tech business it could find. The company was headed by a charismatic man named Alain Peyron. The press said that he was making business "sexy," which in France was a reliable proxy for success.

At the gate a uniformed guard asked for identification; after checking my name in his computer, he gave me a Unetat security pass. The French were obsessive about security, especially where technology was involved. I suspected they were flattering themselves—who would want to steal anything from France?—but it was part of the intense conservatism of that society. For all their supposed liberality, the French loved rules. Inside the building I was stopped again, asked once more for identification, and finally cleared to meet the press officer, a fussy-looking man who was dressed in a wool sweater, despite the warm spring day.

Navarre was waiting for me in his lab. He was dark and thin, with the bright eyes and sallow complexion of a man who lived indoors. He shook hands shyly, and seemed embarrassed by his keeper, the press officer, who was already blathering about how the doctor was "a miracle worker" whose research was going to save the world. When the press man began talking about Wall Street's potential interest in the lab's discoveries, the scientist raised his hand and cut him off. He was a gentle man who didn't like being marketed. When I asked to see some of his experiments, he looked very relieved.

Navarre led me into an adjoining lab and pointed to several cages of mice along the wall. On their heads you could see the remnants of surgery—red wax sealing the holes that had been drilled in their skulls. "*These* are the miracles," he said, gesturing to the rodents. "A few weeks ago, they had no memories. We had cut a pathway of neurons in their brains. They were like people with Alzheimer's disease, who suffer degeneration of this pathway. They could not perform the simplest memory test."

I jotted down some notes on my pad. I wanted him to think I was paying close attention, but my mind was wandering. His description of the
mice with no memories reminded me of a visit I had paid to a nursing
home in California several years ago to visit an aging aunt. All those faces
staring up dumbly, shipwrecked in an eternal present. At first you wanted
to smile or say something nice, but after a while you just wanted to get
away.

Dr. Navarre beckoned me toward an experimental apparatus: a large vat
about the size of a wine barrel, filled with a milky white liquid, with a small
platform in the center just below the surface. In the experiment, the mice
were allowed to splash around until they found the platform. Normal mice
remembered how to find it, but those with severed brain pathways were
lost. They had to search for the platform randomly each time.

"So we gave these poor mice our treatment," Navarre explained, "and
after several months, their memories returned, every one. Here, I will
show you."

Navarre brought a cage containing one of the treated mice to the table.
He opened the cage door, removed the mouse and placed him gently on
the edge of the vat. The mouse swam very deliberately toward the hidden
platform. When this first mouse was safe on its perch, Navarre took him
back to the cage and plucked another, who performed the test just as well,
then repeated it with a third. "You see!" he said when the last mouse was
back in the cage. "They are cured."

"How did you do it?" I asked. I wanted to be interested. I wanted to listen to this cloistered little man all afternoon, and then write a story about
how his mice would change the world. I didn't want to slip back into ordinariness.

"We gave them a substance called a neurotrophin—a nerve-growth factor—which allowed the severed brain pathway to rebuild itself. This is my
cure." He explained the basic science for me. Neurotrophins were the essential tools of the nervous system. They fed the axons in the brain and
spinal cord: without neurotropins, the axons died; with them, even the
axons of a severed spinal cord could grow and regenerate. But the brain had
a horrible counterpart to these neurotrophins. They were known as "suicide genes," and they destroyed brain cells and their connections. That was
what made Alzheimer's disease so debilitating, according to Dr. Navarre.
But a treatment that could get the life-giving neurotrophins into the brain
might rebuild the damaged pathway, and cure Alzheimer's.

I was nodding, but my concentration had been interrupted. Out in the corridor someone was shouting. A door opened at the other end of the lab, and a security man summoned the press officer. He scurried away, leaving me alone with Dr. Navarre.

"But how did you do it?" I asked again. "How did you get the neurotrophins into the brain? I thought there was a barrier that blocked things from getting in." In reading my crib sheets over the past twenty-four hours, I had discovered something called the blood-brain barrier, which allowed glucose and some proteins to enter, but prevented passage of most other substances. That was why doctors found it so tricky to treat some brain diseases with drugs.

"This is my discovery," said Navarre quietly. "I have found a chaperone, which can escort the neurotrophins into the brain."

"What's the chaperone's name?" I asked, still jotting down notes. I wanted this to be a great story, but it was so complicated, and although I was good at pretending, I wasn't sure I really understood what he was talking about.

"My chaperone is a very unusual protein, known as a prion. No one knows precisely why, but these prions are capable of getting past the blood-brain barrier. So if we can tether a virus that will make neurotrophin to the prion, we may be able to slip it into the brain in large enough quantities to cure these horrible diseases—just as we have cured the mice." He lowered his voice. "But I must tell you the truth: there is a problem with my solution."

Dr. Navarre glanced toward the door to make sure the press officer was still outside the room. "My colleagues at Unetat do not seem interested in understanding this problem—they are dreaming of the billions of dollars they will make with a cure for Alzheimer's disease—but it is quite real. These prions may be lifesaving chaperones, as I hope. But mutant forms also seem to cause the worst brain diseases of all—the spongiform encephalopathies—which can leave the brain riddled with holes. These diseases are quite terrible. The victims suffer loss of coordination and then dementia. My colleagues would be very angry if they knew I had told you this. But it will help you to understand why we are far from having a cure for anything."

A dark cloud of ordinariness had suddenly descended. Dr. Navarre hadn't found a miracle, after all. I asked him a few more questions about how his treatment would work, assuming the prion-chaperone idea turned out to be safe. He answered with careful explanations I didn't entirely understand, and gave me several scientific papers he had written that he said would clarify certain points—which I suspected I also wouldn't understand. My hopes of getting a story on the front page—or even on the front of the science section—were vanishing. I was actually grateful when the press officer returned.

"I'm sorry," he said. He had lost his earlier officious self-assurance; his face was flushed and his hand movements were agitated. "We must end the interview. There is a problem in Paris. The police are warning people. Something has happened near the Champs-Élysées."

"But he is our guest," protested Dr. Navarre. "He may have more questions."

"What's going on in Paris?" I asked. It sounded like actual news. I didn't want to be disrespectful to my new friend the scientist, but he and his halfway cure for Alzheimer's could wait. They were not yet a story, at least not for *The New York Mirror*.

"I don't have any details," said the press officer. "Our people in Paris say it's serious. They have issued a security alert, I don't know why. I'm sure it will be on the radio. I'm very sorry. Perhaps you will come back and finish the interview another time."

I shook Dr. Navarre's hand, certain that we would never meet again. By the time he solved his prion problem and had a real cure I would be long gone from Paris and onto another assignment. He looked so sad as I walked away, I realized that his laboratory must feel like a kind of prison. I felt sorry for him, left alone with his mice and his keepers. But as my Arab friends used to say, the camel train must move on.

As I was walking back to my car the cellular phone in my briefcase began to ring. It was Pascale, my news aide in the Paris bureau. Her voice was shaky. She said she wanted to read me a bulletin that had just moved on the Reuters wire. A dozen hostages had been seized on the Rue Lamennais at Taillevent, perhaps the most famous three-star restaurant in Paris. The hostages included members of the restaurant staff, as well as some diners who had lingered too long over lunch. Police had surrounded the building. The identity of the hostage takers and their demands were unknown.

I told Pascale I would be back in the bureau as soon as I could get there. She asked if she could go home early, and I said yes. She was frightened; she had a young daughter—we weren't paying her enough money to ask her to take any risks.

2

All the traffic was going the other way, out of the city. Even in the Bois de Vincennes, the outbound traffic had spilled over into three lanes, leaving just one in my direction. They were fancy cars, mostly—Mercedes and big Citroëns. The radio news was still upbeat—the police had surrounded the building, the situation was under control—but Parisians seemed to know instinctively that this version couldn't possibly be right. Something dangerous was happening in the center of the city; only fools and poor people would stay in harm's way and risk the consequences. The traffic jam in this manicured park was a reminder that France, behind its neat hedgerows, remained a Mediterranean country—a place where people knew things without being told, where the official version of events was assumed to be a lie. It was like Beirut in that way; the Lebanese warlords always seemed to know which part of the city would be shelled on a particular evening, and managed to stay away. The rich people who knew things never got killed in that war, or in any war.

By the time I was back inside the gates of Paris, it was 3:30 in the afternoon—9:30 A.M. in New York—which meant that the foreign editor, Lynn Frenzel, was probably in her office. I pressed the buttons for the foreign desk, expecting the news aide to answer, but Frenzel picked it up herself.

"I may have a story here today, Lynn," I said. "Wanted to give you a heads up. It could be interesting." Never oversell a story. That was part of the code.

"Yeah, I know," she answered matter-of-factly. "It's on the wires." Frenzel had been in a bad mood lately. Her husband had walked out on her, leaving her with a baby at home, plus all the babies on the *Mirror*'s foreign staff.

"What do the wires say?" I asked. "I'm not back in the office yet."

"I'm aware of that. I've been trying to reach you. Pascale said you were out doing that bullshit story for the science section." She was really in a bad mood.

"What about the wires?" I repeated. That was another rule among foreign correspondents. Steal everything you can from the wire services. Arriving in a strange city, the first stop for a correspondent was always the local AP or Reuters bureau. It was like connecting to the central nervous system.

"Reuters says there are fifteen hostages inside the restaurant. They're being held by five people who claim to represent a group called Vert/Vertu, which Reuters translates as Green/Virtue. Can that be right? It sounds better in French. AP doesn't have the name of the group, but they're quoting someone who escaped from the restaurant who says that two of the five people holding the hostages are blacks, and that they're protesting French weapons tests in West Africa. Agence France-Presse is useless. They're only putting out the police bulletins. Do we know anything about French weapons tests in West Africa? That's a new one on me."

"Nope. At least I don't. I thought they tested their weapons in the South Pacific."

"Well, I'm sure you'll find out by deadline. Unless you botch the writing, it stands a chance of making the front."

"Maybe you should just run the wire story," I said sarcastically. But she had already hung up.

The first police roadblock was on the Rue de Rivoli, near the Louvre. The officer was wearing the dark jumpsuit and shit-kicker boots of the Police Nationale. I showed him my residency permit and my press card and explained that I needed to get to my office on the Rue du Faubourg-St.-Honoré, a mile away. He gave me a pass that said PRESSE in bright red letters and told me to put it on my windshield. That got me past another checkpoint at the Place de la Concorde, but I was stopped again along the Champs-Élysées, several blocks from my office. By now, there were few people on the street, except for hundreds of these paramilitary police in their black uniforms.

"Journaliste américain," I said, waving my press credentials. In many countries, that's actually enough to get you past a checkpoint. But the French officer shook his head; he ordered me out of my car while his colleagues checked with the Foreign Ministry press department. Someone there must have vouched for me because he wrote me a special *laissez-passer* that gave me permission to go to my office—which was technically within the forbidden zone because it was near the Rue Lamennais.

When I got to my office, I turned on the television. CNN was showing a live shot of the building. You could see the black metal awning, with its neat crenulated edges and the name "Taillevent" over the door of the restaurant. A few police were moving in the foreground, but otherwise the narrow street was empty. The French television networks were showing the same picture. The commentary on all the channels was garbage. Nobody really knew anything.

Pascale had gathered the wires and put them in a neat pile on my desk. Next to them was a stack of clips from the French press about weapons testing in the South Pacific. She hadn't been able to find anything on the group called Vert/Vertu, and she said in a note that her girlfriend who worked at AFP couldn't find any record of the group in their files, either. Sweet Pascale. I was glad I had let her go home.

A little before 7:00, another bulletin moved on Reuters summarizing the demands that had been made by Vert/Vertu in a fax sent a few minutes earlier to its bureau in Paris. First, the group demanded that France acknowledge that it had been testing nuclear weapons secretly during the past two years in the deserts of Niger. Second, they wanted the French government to pay ten billion francs in reparations to Niger and the other former French colonies in West Africa. Third, they demanded safe passage from France for the hostage takers. If the demands weren't met, Vert/Vertu said, it would expose the hostages to radioactive materials it had gathered in the deserts of Niger and brought to the restaurant.

Frenzel called me thirty seconds after Reuters moved its bulletin. "This *is* a pretty good story," she said. "Bowman is hearing that the State Department may evacuate the embassy. Weiss says you can have all the space you want. So let it rip." She sounded almost excited. "This restaurant is near the bureau, isn't it?"

"A few blocks. The police have closed off the quarter. They gave me a pass to get to the office."

"Well, keep your head down." Frenzel was allowed to say that. She had taken a bullet in the leg ten years earlier while covering the civil war in El Salvador.

The French government issued a statement at 7:30 that was broadcast live on radio and television. A spokesman said the charges made by Vert/Vertu were "groundless," "laughable" and "completely untrue." The statement said the French government was prepared to negotiate only the surrender of the "enviro-terrorists" and warned that unless they agreed immediately to leave the building, they would "pay a heavy price."

The French statement elicited a quick response. At 7:45, the door of the restaurant opened and a man in a white outfit was pushed out the door. I watched it live, on television. The man turned out to be an Algerian busboy. He was carrying a written message from Vert/Vertu. He had been told that unless it was read immediately on television, the sommelier of the restaurant would be shot. The Algerian stood before the camera and nervously read from the piece of paper in his hands. The message said that if the French government didn't meet its demands by midnight, Vert/Vertu would begin exposing the hostages to the radioactive materials it had brought from Africa. "The death of the hostages will prove the truth of what we are saying," the statement concluded.

This was a *hell* of a story. I sat down at my computer and began trying to pull something together for the first edition. I cribbed from the wires, from the French and Vert/Vertu statements, from the television coverage, from the clips Pascale had found me. I even threw in a paragraph describing the main dining room where the hostages were being held, based on my one visit to Taillevent. I tried to reach my best contact at the French Foreign Ministry, but he wouldn't take my call, and the press officer at the American embassy was useless. He sounded nervous about being in the office at all. So I typed—to call it writing would be generous—throwing together shards and snippets of other people's work, casting an eye occasionally at the live picture of Taillevent on television. That was as close as I came to reality. I finished up my story and filed it for the first edition.

I sat back in my chair and closed my eyes, waiting for that pleasant buzz that comes after filing. But I had a bad feeling in my gut—empty, uncomfortable. I had written a reasonable enough piece of work, certainly no worse than what would appear in the competition. But it was entirely derivative; it had no life. A few blocks away from me a great story was unfolding, and I had covered it passively, from a distance, as if it were taking place on another continent. What had happened to me, in my thirty-fifth year, that I had become so lazy?

I rose from my desk and walked to the windows. My office was on the seventh floor, overlooking the rooftops of the neighborhood. One window looked east down the Rue du Faubourg-St.-Honoré, perhaps the most fashionable shopping street in Paris, housing the boutiques of Versace and Hermès and Yves St. Laurent. It was deserted now. Nobody was "licking the windows," as the French call window-shopping; no cars were on the street. My other window looked southwest across the rooftops to the Eiffel Tower. There was a ghostly glow in that direction, and I realized it must be the floodlights trained on the small *hôtel particulier* on the Rue Lamennais—housing the fifteen hostages and the unknown terrorists who had seized them. The image of the Taillevent awning was still flickering on my television screen. Surely it was of at least passing interest to the world to know who these people were.

It took only a moment more of self-disgust for the dry tinder to ignite. This was a real story—the kind that offered a chance, as Ed Weiss loved to say, to "cover yourself in glory." It was worth a little effort. At the very least, I needed to see the building for myself, rather than watch it on the damned television set.

It was dark outside when I emerged a little after 8:00 P.M. The café across the street, Le Saint-Philippe, was empty and locked up tight. So was Le Griffon, the fancier place a few doors up. The street had a gentle, upward slope about a quarter mile to the Avenue de Friedland, a grand tree-lined boulevard that led to the Arc de Triomphe. I had hoped to approach the restaurant that way. But after walking a hundred yards, I saw a cluster of armored vehicles and black-uniformed police gathered at the top of the street. The police were talking, leaning against their buses, smoking cigarettes, waiting for action. It was obvious that route wouldn't work.

But I knew the neighborhood. I turned left onto the Rue de Berri, just past the fancy art galleries and antiques stores, and walked one short block to the Rue d'Artois. It rose steeply, past my sometime tailor, Filippo Anselmo, who claimed to make the best suit in Paris for just three thousand francs—unless you were an Arab, in which case he charged you four thousand. I was hugging the walls as I moved up the street, trying to stay in the shadows, but I still hadn't seen any police. The quarter had emptied out hours ago. At the top of that block, I came to the Rue de Washington, a bigger street that ran parallel to the Avenue de Friedland. Everything was called "Élysées" now, as we neared the famous thoroughfare. A hairstylist called "Nuances Élysées." A Chinese restaurant called "Mandarin Élysées Chinois."

I was almost there. I needed to be very careful now. I crossed the cobblestones to the far side of the Rue de Washington and crept up a long block to the corner of the Rue Lamennais. As I neared that corner I saw again the glow of the police floodlights and heard the squawk of their radios. The corner building was a modern stone-and-concrete box housing a private bank; As I neared the edge I heard voices on the other side and smelled cigarette smoke. The voices were chatting about people they knew, and about expensive bars and restaurants, and trips to the United States. They didn't sound like cops.

I turned the corner. Fifty yards away was the floodlit awning of Taillevent. Just ten yards from me, gathered in a knot with a police escort, was a group of French reporters. One of them looked familiar—a woman named Fabienne from *Le Figaro*. She spotted me and waved, but the policeman was quicker. He told me I was in a forbidden zone and demanded to see my identification. I showed him my press card and the *laissez-passer,* but he said they weren't valid there. He seemed serious about kicking me out when Fabienne and one of her French colleagues came up behind.

"He's okay," said Fabienne. "We know him." The policeman shook his head no, but the other French reporter—an older man who had the official Yves Montand putty face and nicotine-stained fingers—said into the policeman's ear that it was all right, I could stay, and that was it. So I joined the little circle of hacks and hackettes, and listened in on their gossip. They were talking about a recently resigned Socialist minister of education, who was said to be sleeping with a woman reporter at *Figaro*—not Fabienne, but a friend of hers. That led to a conversation about another reporter at *Le Nouvel Observateur* who had been propositioned a few years before by King Hussein, no less. I listened with half an ear, keeping my eyes on the police farther down the street. There were sharpshooters on top of each of the buildings across from the restaurant, and it looked as if a small army was assembling on the Avenue de Friedland. The reporter gossip continued. It wasn't what I had come for.

"Has anyone tried to get inside and talk to the people holding the hostages?" I asked. The group looked at me quizzically.

"Of course not," said the older French reporter. He examined me as if I were a bumpkin, just off the bus and in the big city for the first time. "The police don't want anyone to talk to the terrorists."

"But I don't work for the police," I said. "I work for *The New York Mirror.*" It sounded even more arrogant in French than in English.

Several of the reporters frowned and motioned with their hands, up and down, in a gesture that translated roughly as "big fucking deal." I stood back from the group and let them continue with their chatter. More police were continuing to arrive at the far end of the street. It was obvious that at some point something was going to go down. The time to cover this story was running out.

How could I get inside the restaurant? I scanned the row of buildings that adjoined Taillevent. They were all the same height, about six stories, except for the last one, the corner building across from where I stood, which was one story taller. It housed a modeling agency—called, inevitably, "Élysées Models." If I could get to the roof of that building, there might be a way to slip down one floor to the common rooftop that led up the street to Taillevent. I had no idea how I would get inside the restaurant from there, but it seemed like the only possibility.

I ambled away from the French reporters and their cop friends, back toward the Rue de Washington. I crossed the street and walked to the far corner of the Élysées Models building. The windows along the Rue de Washington were decorated with the faces of winsome, come-hither women, but the front door was locked. Just past the building was a tiny alley, not much bigger than a walkway, where trash was dumped. It ran only about thirty feet. I looked behind me, back toward the Rue Lamennais. Nobody was watching.

Do it! I told myself. I darted into the alleyway and looked for a fire escape. Toward the back of the building was a small metal ladder. I began climbing, waiting for someone to shout for me to stop. But the only sound was the muffled clanking of the metal ladder against the wall of the building. I was frightened, but there was a liberating feeling about taking a chance to get a good story. It was like waking up from a long dream. I had done something like this only once before that I could remember. It was more than ten years ago when I was covering a closed police-corruption hearing in New York City. I had sneaked up to the floor above the hearing room and listened to the proceedings through an air shaft. That story had driven the investigators crazy; they had never been able to figure out my source.

I paused after four stories to catch my breath, then continued the rest of the way. As I neared the top I remembered the police marksmen who were posted on the rooftops across the street. I moved very carefully, pulling myself gently onto the roof and crawling across it toward the end of the

Élysées Models building. The light was even stranger up here, a bluish glow from the floodlights, reflected off the streets and the sides of the buildings. I continued my crawl, splayed out on the rooftop. From my vantage, I could look down to the rooftop of the Taillevent building. I saw a large air vent in the middle of the roof and a door that led downstairs. At least there appeared to be a way down toward the restaurant, if I could get that far. I crawled a few more feet to the edge of my building, rose to a crouch and prepared to jump.

In that moment I saw the policeman on the next roof, and he saw me. "Oh, shit," I said aloud. A spotlight was trained on me instantly, blinding me briefly, and when I could see again, a half-dozen police were moving toward me, putting ladders against the wall of my building—shouting at me to freeze, put down my weapons. *"Journaliste!"* I cried out. It sounded so limp.

When the first police officer reached me, he hit me with a wooden club and knocked me back down to the roof, which was unnecessary, and when I tried to get up, he did it again. The second blow hurt. I reached up to touch the wound and felt it wet with blood. A more senior officer arrived a few moments later, demanding to know who I was and what I was doing. When I told him I was a reporter and handed him my press card, he studied it for a moment and then laughed derisively. *"Connard!"* he muttered, a vulgar expression that translates roughly as "Stupid cunt!"

The police officer didn't know what to do with me, so he radioed his boss, who was in the command post across from the restaurant. This gentleman, in turn, apparently wanted to swear at me himself. So the French police sent me back down the metal ladder to the alleyway, and then back along the Rue Lamennais. The little knot of French reporters was still in the same place. As they saw me walk past with my police escort, they shrugged and shook their heads. Several of them actually looked pleased—like trained poodles watching a stray dog carted off to the pound. Fuck them, I thought. At least I wouldn't end up like *that.*

I was led up the street, past the restaurant, to a mobile command post that was parked on the Avenue de Friedland. I tried to look inside Taillevent as we passed, but the curtains were all drawn. Except for the floodlights and the cops outside, it might have been just another evening of three-star dining. Inside the police trailer sat a dark little man in plain clothes, who was barking orders into a telephone. He had the intense, Mediterranean features of the Corsicans who were said to dominate the French security services. He glanced at me and the press card I was waving at him, muttered an oath and told one of his aides to take care of my head wound. It was duly cleaned and bandaged in a medical trailer.

After twenty minutes I was returned to the Corsican commander. He was alone in his trailer now, smoking a cigarette. He asked for my identification.

"I should arrest you," he said after studying the documents. "You are interfering with the police."

"I should sue you," I answered. "My head hurts from where your man hit me."

"What were you doing on the roof of that building?"

"I was doing my job. I wanted to get into the restaurant to interview the hostages and the people holding them."

"Fous le camp," he said, shaking his head. Get the fuck out of here. He told me to wait outside until they found a policeman to escort me back to my office.

I stood in the doorway of an optometrist's shop on the corner of the Rue Lamennais, just outside the command post, waiting for my police escort to accompany me home. It was demeaning. The hostages and their captors were only a few dozen yards away from me now. It embarrassed me, all over again, to be so close to the story and yet so powerless to do anything about it. As the seconds passed I thought again of how I might get inside. The only possible way in, it was now obvious, was through the front door—as a guest of the terrorists. But how could I do that?

A mental spark fired in my reporter brain. Inside my coat was the pocket *Guide Michelin,* which I, like every Paris-based reporter, kept handy to make reservations for the appropriate expense-account meals. I stepped back into the shadows and opened the little red book to the page for Taillevent. I removed my cellular phone gently from my other pocket and punched in the phone number. I waited, trying to think of what I would say if anyone answered. But an instant later I heard a recording saying that the line had been disconnected. I looked in the pocket guide again and found a fax number. I pressed the buttons and waited. From my perch in the doorway of the optometrist's shop, I was almost invisible. My police escort still hadn't arrived. The phone rang once, twice.

On the third ring a voice answered. He said he was the sommelier, and he sounded absolutely terrified. I asked to speak to the man who was holding the hostages, and he handed over the phone to someone else.

"Who is this?" asked a deep voice in heavily accented French.

"I'm an American reporter," I answered. "I'm nearby. I would like to come interview you, to hear about French weapons tests in Africa. You tell me, and I will tell the world."

"Are you police?" He sounded suspicious, but also curious.

"No. I'm a reporter. And if you don't decide quickly, you'll lose the chance to tell your story."

I could hear him talking to someone else, in quick, frantic bursts of French.

"It's okay," he said. "When will you come?"

"Right now," I said. "I'm fifteen meters away. Go open the door." I really didn't have time to think about what I was saying, it happened so quickly.

"Now?" the voice repeated. But the line had gone dead.

Now. I stood in the shadows for another instant. I had that sweet-sickness in my gut that every reporter feels before going into a combat zone. You know it's a great story, you're pumped with adrenaline, but you're also terrified. I was poised in the doorway like a cocked gun, knowing that if I didn't move quickly, the police would take me away.

Go! It was like jumping off a high dive. You either did it, or you didn't. A jolt of electricity shot through my legs as I bolted from the shadows and turned the corner into the Rue Lamennais. The black awning was fifteen yards away, ten, five. The French police were screaming at me to stop, a siren behind me was sounding, and I heard a gun go off—a warning shot, thank God, and then another. I kept running. The heavy glass door of the restaurant was opening, the screams and sirens outside were getting louder. In a moment, I was inside the door.

"Bravo!" came a voice from inside the restaurant, and then another, and some cheers. The reaction of the people inside—hostage takers and hostages alike—was that I was very brave and very stupid.

3

The man who opened the door was a heavyset West African, with skin as dark as a bar of unsweetened chocolate. He escorted me down a paneled hallway into the main dining room, where the hostages were still shouting about my sudden visit. They were gathered in a circle on the floor, their hands tied behind their backs. The group was split about evenly between members of the restaurant staff—dressed in tuxedos or white coats, depending on their station—and diners who had been unlucky enough to have booked a table for a late lunch that afternoon. Facing them on three sides were men holding guns—a spindly black man, an Arab with sunken cheeks and pockmarked skin and a wild-eyed European who looked as if he were auditioning for the part of Jesus Christ.

"Quiet!" shouted the long-haired European guard, and the hostages immediately fell silent. They looked up at me now imploringly, desperately—imagining that I was somehow going to deliver them from their fate.

I surveyed the dining room. It had the feel of a wealthy gentleman's library, paneled in dark wood with blue banquettes and crisp white tablecloths. The decorations were an eclectic mix that might have come from a French estate: Chinese lamps, dark oil paintings of French lords and ladies, fine old porcelain displayed in wooden cabinets, fresh-cut daisies on each table, and at each place a profusion of china, wine goblets and silver flatware. On a few of the plates you could still see the remnants of the exquisite meals these poor diners had been eating before the terrorists burst in the door and seized control of the place. A silver dustpan and brush, normally used to sweep up crumbs from the white tablecloths, lay askew on one of the tables.

The heavyset African man looked nervously at his watch. A pistol was tucked into his pants, half hidden by the bulge of his stomach. "Now you are here, my friend, what do you want?"

"My name is Eric Truell." Fear was in my voice. I paused and took a few deep breaths. "I work for a newspaper in the United States called *The New York Mirror.* I want to interview you. My paper is very powerful. It is read by the president. Here's my card." I took a business card from my wallet and handed it to him. My hand was shaking slightly. He looked it over and handed it to a man with light brown skin—he might have been a North African or a Frenchman, it was hard to tell—who had emerged from the back room. He was neatly dressed in a gray business suit and a fine silk tie. He looked at the card dubiously, and then at me. I guessed he and the darker man with the pistol were the group's leaders. He gave a nod, and then retreated back to the foyer.

"Ask your questions," said the African.

My mind went blank for a moment. "What is Vert/Vertu?"

"We are a global movement!" answered the big man. His voice boomed like a loudspeaker. "We have many thousands of members. We want radical action to save the environment. Africa is the last frontier. We are the wretched of the earth. We have been colonized, victimized, patronized. Our lakes and forests have been poisoned. We want to save Africa before it is destroyed."

I was scribbling notes in the reporter's notebook I had put in my back pocket that morning, as I did every morning. I wrote down what he had said, but it had all the spontaneity of a canned recording. "Why hasn't anyone ever heard of your group, if you have thousands of members?"

"Because we are secret. We want radical action to save the environment. Africa is the last frontier. We are the wretched of the earth. We have been colonized, victimized, patronized—"

"I understand all that," I said, stopping him before he repeated the whole speech. "Where are you from, personally?"

"From Africa." He smiled.

"And what is your name?"

"I have no name; I have every name. You can call me Monsieur Afrique. I am the spokesman for Vert/Vertu. I speak for my continent."

I was still writing it all down, but inwardly cursing my stupidity. This interview was not worth the risks involved. So far, he had said less than what was in the statement the group had faxed to Reuters a few hours ago. I should at least get the ultimatum in his own words.

"What are your demands, Monsieur Afrique? Tell the world. What will it take to get you to release the hostages?"

"The French must pay reparations to their African brothers. Some of the money they have stolen from us. It is billions of dollars."

"Ten billion. Is that right?"

He flicked his hand, as if he were brushing away a fly. "The French know how much. Now they must pay."

"What if they don't pay?"

"We will kill the hostages. Too bad. Very bad. But the French know. They will pay." He tried to laugh, as if it were all a joke. I looked down at the poor folks on the floor. I hated to add to their misery, but I had to do my job.

"How will you kill them?"

"We will make them eat what our brothers and sisters in the jungles must eat. The wastes of French nuclear weapons tests. We have brought them from the desert. These wastes have been killing our people, and now they will kill yours, too, unless the French pay us the money."

At this, one of the hostages—a woman in her fifties, dressed in a Chanel suit and an Hermès scarf—started to moan softly. Her husband began moaning, too, pleading for her life. The captors appeared unmoved, except for the thin black man who had been helping guard the hostages. He moved away from the group and toward me. Monsieur Afrique tried to wave him away, but he was intent.

"I will explain more about Vert/Vertu, sir, so you will understand us better," he said. "My name is Dr. Obado. I am a professor of biology. I don't care if you know that. Come with me into the other room, where we can talk." He beckoned for me to follow. Monsieur Afrique wasn't happy, but he didn't stop him.

Dr. Obado sat me down in the outer dining area, a brighter room decorated with beige curtains. He had a wispy, unkempt beard and sharp eyes that were shielded by thick glasses. Where Monsieur Afrique had the easy, languid movements of a man who enjoyed the pleasures of the world, Obado had the austere intensity of an ideologue, a man who believed in abstractions.

"I am the *founder* of Vert/Vertu," he said ceremoniously. "I am from Abidjan, in the Ivory Coast. My colleague, who calls himself Monsieur Afrique, is from Gabon. He and these other men asked to join me in Vert/Vertu. They know far more about the world than I do, so I agreed. They are the muscle. I am the brain, and the soul. We do not have thousands of members, unfortunately, but we have the strength of our ideas!"

I scribbled notes as fast as I could. This was what I had come for. Dr. Obado explained that for the past two years, the French government had been conducting secret weapons tests in remote areas of West Africa. Most of these tests had been in the deserts of Niger, hundreds of miles east of the capital, Niamey. Before, the French had always conducted their tests in the South Pacific, but now they had decided to use their former colonies in Africa, where the political leaders were compliant and the danger of public protest was less. But the nuclear testing was killing the wildlife, Obado said. Women in nomadic tribes who wandered through the test zone were giving birth to deformed babies. Obado had tried to protest quietly, but the French hadn't listened. So he had formed Vert/Vertu. "And then I met these other gentlemen," he said, "who convinced me it was time for action."

"What will you do to the hostages?" I asked. "That's what the world wants to know."

"Sir, we have brought here to Paris, to the finest restaurant in all the world, a meal of radioactive poison. It is water drawn from aquifers near the test site. We have brought it in a lead container, so it is harmless for now. But unless the French admit they are conducting the tests—and agree to stop them—we will make the diners and staff of Taillevent drink the radioactive wastes."

"What about money? Monsieur Afrique said he wouldn't release the hostages unless the French government paid billions of francs."

"That is their demand. They are men of the world. I only want the tests stopped."

I wrote it all down, just as he said it. I looked at my watch and saw that it was already 9:30. If I was going to get something in the next morning's paper, I needed to finish my interview soon and get back to the office.

"Dr. Obado, I need to ask one more favor. Could I interview some of the hostages, please?"

"Yes, why not." He led me back into the wood-paneled dining room and the knot of people on the floor. They looked wretched. The elegant woman in the Chanel suit was sobbing quietly. Her husband was pleading with the Arab guard, offering to pay millions of francs if they would let him and his wife go. It was a sorry little lifeboat. Obado spoke to his colleagues and told them he had given me permission to interview some of the hostages.

"Five minutes only," said Monsieur Afrique. He put his hand on his pistol, to remind himself and me that it was there.

"I'm sorry, folks," I said in English. "I don't have much time. Are any of you here from the United States?"

"Yes," spoke up a man from the center of the circle. I hadn't noticed him before. He had a round, gentle face, with a fringe of unruly curly hair encircling a large bald spot. He was well dressed, in a linen suit, wearing large tortoiseshell glasses.

"What's your name and where are you from?"

"George Frankheimer. I'm a lawyer, from Washington, D.C. I'm in Paris on business."

"How did you happen to come to Taillevent today?"

"Just lucky," he said with a thin smile. "It's my birthday. I thought I would give myself a treat."

"What did you have for lunch?" It was a gruesome detail, given the circumstances, but I thought it would interest readers.

"Poached asparagus with truffle juice and rack of lamb with a purée of green beans. Accompanied by a half-bottle of Gevrey-Chambertin."

"And for dessert?"

"I was just about to order dessert when these gentlemen arrived. I think I would have had the *crème brûlée*. But I hadn't decided yet."

I wrote it all down. There were moments, even in extremis, when a journalist got to hear the sound of one hand clapping.

"How was the food?" I asked.

"Very good. One of the best meals I've ever had, actually."

I briefly interviewed the wealthy French couple, because they demanded it. He was an industrialist from Lyons and still seemed convinced that he could bribe his way out of there; he even offered me cash to get him out. I also tried to interview the Taillevent sommelier, Henri, who was the ranking employee of the restaurant and was wearing his pin of grapes on his lapel, but he was trembling, poor man, and not up to it. A tuxedoed captain spoke up for the employees. He said stoically that the restaurant was very sorry for the inconvenience its guests had experienced—as if this were all the management's fault—and that he was also sorry for all the people whose dinner reservations for that night had of necessity been canceled.

I looked at my watch again. More than my allotted five minutes had passed. I asked all the hostages to give me their names and addresses, and wrote down all fifteen very carefully. I promised that someone would contact their families to let them know they were safe. That was the least I could do. Then it was time to go.

Dr. Obado led me toward the door, but on the way out the man with the *café au lait* skin emerged again from wherever he had been hiding.

"Should we let him go?" he asked. "He knows what we look like. He will tell the police."

"No, I won't," I said emphatically. "I don't work for the police. I work for *The New York Mirror.* The only people I'm going to talk to are the readers of my newspaper."

"Bosh!" he said. "What a fairy tale."

I turned to Dr. Obado. "Unless you release me, nobody will know your story. The French can tell whatever lies they want about Vert/Vertu. They can kill you like dogs, and nobody will know the truth." Dr. Obado nodded. He wanted me to make him and his loony group famous.

"My friends, listen to me." It was the genial face of Monsieur Afrique. "We should let this newspaper boy go. The French will pay us the money, and they will let us go free. I'm telling you. So what does it matter?" He waited for someone to contradict him, and when no one did, he took me by the elbow and steered me back down the long, beige-paneled entrance hall.

"Go on, boy," he said, pushing me out the heavy glass door onto the Rue Lamennais.

As I stumbled forward in the glare of the lights, a team of men in black uniforms rushed toward me. I cried out my ritual protest—*"Journaliste!"*—but the police continued their surge and knocked me to the ground. As I fell, my hand moved instinctively to shield my crotch—just before a boot landed there. A knee went into my side, and a gloved fist pounded the soft tissue under my eye. I kept shouting that I was a reporter—as if that would do any good—until an officer finally pulled me up, put my arm around his shoulder and dragged me away from the restaurant to a waiting police van.

I retained a faint hope they might be taking me back to my office or to the American embassy, but the van roared off in the other direction, around the Arc de Triomphe and down the Avenue Marceau. We crossed the Seine to the Left Bank and raced along the river, siren wailing, past the Eiffel Tower. I had no idea where we were going; none of the familiar government buildings was anywhere near here. The van turned into a narrow street called the Rue Nélaton and stopped in front of a plain office block with a black marble façade. Above the door were the words MINISTÈRE DE L'INTÉRIEUR. I later learned that this was the headquarters of the French in-

ternal security service, known as the Direction du Surveillance de Terri-
toire, or DST. Two men in plain clothes escorted me from the van to one
of the upper floors of the building, where they put me in a small, windowless room and closed the door.

I hurt all over, but my biggest worry at that point, honestly, was how to
get back to the bureau in time to file. There is nothing worse—absolutely
nothing—than having a great story, for which you have taken considerable
risks, and being unable to get it out. Back in Beirut, I used to save my
biggest bribes for the hotel telex operator and, when necessary, I would
punch the tape myself, my martini glass rattling on top of the telex con-
sole.

They held me all night on the Rue Nélaton. A tired-looking cop with
big jowls and a dumpy suit came into the room after a few minutes, looked
at me and shook his head. *"Tu es vraiment dans la merde,"* he said, which
meant, more or less, "You are up to your eyeballs in shit."

I gave him the list of hostages—which seemed only fair—but that just
whetted his appetite. He questioned me for hours about what I had seen
and heard inside the building. When I wouldn't answer, he accused me of
being part of the terrorist group and told me that the penalty for such
crimes in France was death by guillotine, which presumably was meant to
frighten me but sounded, in the moment, entirely absurd and caused me
to laugh aloud. He asked me a long string of specific questions about Monsieur Afrique and Dr. Obado and what subject the doctor taught in the
Ivory Coast, and it gradually dawned on me that they must have planted a
microphone inside, and that they probably already had a transcript of
everything I'd said. The only question I answered was whether I had actually seen the radioactive material they supposedly were going to use to poison the hostages, and that was easy. I said "No."

Midnight, the deadline set by the terrorists, came and went. My inter-
rogator wouldn't answer my questions about what was happening back at
Taillevent. I pleaded with him to let me file something—anything—for
the paper or at least call New York and let them know I was all right. He
found my notion that I had any rights in this situation contemptible. *"Tu
me fais chier,"* he said. "You make me shit."

They finally released me just after noon. I was taken downstairs to a
magistrate, who said the authorities had concluded that I was not a terrorist, and that therefore the charges against me were being dropped. He
wanted me to sign some papers, but I refused to sign anything unless I

could talk to a lawyer, so he just let me go. It was obvious they wanted me out of there. I was a potential embarrassment.

I walked across the street and ordered a sandwich at a little bistro called the Restaurant Nélaton, which was filled with square-jawed guys who looked like cops. They were bantering and joking as they drank their wine and smoked cigarettes. That was the first moment I realized what must have happened. I asked the waiter what was going on at Taillevent restaurant and he looked at me curiously, as if I had just landed from the moon. *"Mais, c'est fini!"* he said. It's over.

It had all happened in the dark. After I got back to the office, I pieced together what had occurred from the wires and a call to my French journalist friend Olivier at *Libération.* Around 9:00 P.M., even before I made my dash into the restaurant, the French had ordered the television cameras away from the building to the other side of the Avenue de Friedland, preventing any direct shots of the restaurant. Two hours later, as the deadline approached, the cameras had been unplugged entirely. With the area sealed off from public view, a French antiterrorist squad had taken the building. The hostages had all been released. The terrorists had all vanished—the government said they were being held at an undisclosed location—except for Dr. Obado. He had been killed in the rescue—the only fatality—and a picture of his dead body had been flashed around the world. The wires said he was the leader of the group and had masterminded the operation.

The French government was claiming a great triumph. They announced that they had routed the terrorists from the building without paying them any money or acceding to any of their other demands. The president and the prime minister were on television, taking credit for their brilliant handling of the crisis. The French news media were joining in the applause. They reported, uncritically, the government's denial that it had been testing any weapons in Africa. I was tired and dirty, but I had a story that would be worth reading, even if it was a day late.

4

I called Ed Weiss at home at 8:00 A.M. New York time. He was my boss, and he was also the person who had given me my first real chance, ten years before, when as foreign editor he had sent me overseas to Beirut. I was so tired and strung out after my night on the Rue Nélaton, I don't know what I expected him to say. But it wasn't this.

"Where the fuck were you last night, junior?" He was crunching on his breakfast cereal as he spoke. "We tried to get you all night. A rather big story happened last night on your patch of turf—the biggest goddamn story in the world, as a matter of fact. The sort of thing we thought our Paris correspondent might deign to cover for the late editions. It would have been nice to lead our page with something other than a frigging wire story, don't you think? Bowman had to write a news analysis from Washington. Where the hell were you, anyway?"

"I got arrested outside Taillevent. I was held all night by the Interior Ministry. They wouldn't let me call anyone."

"Cut the shit. Who were you banging? I'd rather have the truth."

"I'm telling you the truth, Ed. They arrested me because I snuck into the restaurant. I was inside the place! I interviewed the terrorists and the hostages. I had the whole thing—the story of my life—and these pricks arrested me."

"You're serious, aren't you?"

"Yes, sir. Totally serious. They released me an hour and a half ago."

"How the hell did you sneak in?" His voice had a sudden enthusiasm. This was the sort of newspaper escapade that warmed Weiss's heart. Somehow, over the years, he had not lost sight of the essential mischievousness of the news business.

"First I tried to go across the rooftops, but they caught me and were going to send me back to the bureau. So while I was waiting, I just called the damned restaurant and spoke to one of these crazy Africans and told him I was a reporter, and that I was going to make a run for the door in five seconds, and that he had to let me in. And he did. I stayed about forty-five minutes. I have fabulous stuff."

"I love it! Love it, love it, love it." He was absolutely gushing now. "You are a devious prick, Truell, you know that? And after those heroics, they arrested you?"

"Yup. They jumped me as I was leaving the restaurant. They beat the crap out of me, as a matter of fact."

"God damn it!" he roared. "We'll sue them. We'll protest to the Foreign Ministry. We'll get Sellinger to raise hell with his French business friends. If these bastards think they can assault a staff reporter for *The New York Mirror*, they're wrong. They have picked a fight with the wrong damn newspaper!"

You had to love Weiss. He played the role so perfectly, he *was* the role. His voice returned to its normal register.

"Listen, Eric, we are going to kick some serious ass in tomorrow's paper. You write up your story and file it. I want you to get one of the AP photographers to take a picture of you right now, while you still look like shit, so we can run it with the story. MIRROR MAN ATTACKED AFTER BRAVING TERRORISTS' LAIR. I mean, *holy shit!* Is that a headline, or what?"

I sat down at the computer and typed like a zombie for three hours. I wrote a main news story, which led with the allegations Dr. Obado had made about French nuclear testing and quoted the repeated assurances of "Monsieur Afrique" from Gabon that the French would pay the ransom that had been demanded. Without saying so outright, the story implicitly questioned the official French account. I wrote a sidebar on the hostages, which led with the Washington lawyer George Frankheimer, talking about the wonderful lunch he had been eating before the terrorists arrived. I tried to find Frankheimer to ask him how it felt now to be a free man, but he was already on a plane back to the United States. Finally, I wrote a first-person color piece about my own adventures in reporting the story.

The *Mirror* ran all three pieces the next morning on the front page, above the fold. I had, indeed, covered myself in glory. Weiss told me so himself. We sat back to wait for the rest of the news media to chase our scoop. We had challenged the French denials that they were nuclear testing in Africa! But the reaction instead was a vast silence. The French media ignored my story, which I expected, but so did the other American news-papers. The local hacks acted as if I had done something wrong in pursu-ing it so aggressively. The buzz was that I had been a "hot dog," and thereby violated the journalistic code of nonchalance. I felt sorry for my colleagues, I really did. They were sleepwalking.

Weiss's plans to declare war on the government of France didn't fare much better. The *Mirror* filed an official protest with the prime minister's office at the Hôtel Matignon, protesting my detention and demanding an apology. The French responded tartly that I had been in the area without authorization, that I had repeatedly been warned to leave, that I had es-caped police custody, and that the authorities therefore had good reason to arrest me on suspicion that I was working with the terrorists.

Weiss was furious and wanted to take the case to the United Nations or the International Court of Justice or *somebody*. But the State Department called Phil Sellinger, the publisher, and advised him that the French had technically been within their rights, and that we would probably be wise to drop the matter. Our own lawyers concurred. In the end, we negotiated a mutual exchange of letters between *The New York Mirror* and the French Interior Ministry that said absolutely nothing except that I would be al-lowed to remain in Paris and keep my press credentials.

"Don't worry about it," said Weiss. "These people are professional ass-holes. As far as I'm concerned, you did everything right. I like your hustle. I like your pizzazz. So don't feel bad. Get some sleep. We love you."

But I did feel bad. I was convinced that the French government was lying about what had happened that night on the Rue Lamennais, and that they were getting away with it. I tried to contact some of the French hostages, but none of them would agree to be interviewed. Henri, the som-melier, said they had been warned by the DST not to talk to any journal-ists. What were they hiding? If the hostage rescue was such a glorious triumph, why wouldn't they let the hostages talk? And for that matter, where were the terrorists themselves? Nobody had seen them, and a rumor was circulating among the Paris press corps that they had secretly been flown back to Africa to "stand trial" there. And finally, what about the money—the billions the terrorists had demanded as the price of surrender?

These mysteries were part of what the French like to call *le brouillard*, "the fog." To resolve them, I needed the sort of person known colloquially as *un débrouillard*—a defogger, literally—a fixer, we would say.

I knew one man in France who fit that description. His name was Ali

Aziz. I had met him a decade before in Lebanon, and had maintained regular contact with him ever since. Because of the nature of his business, he knew things that ordinary people didn't know, especially about West Africa, where he had spent his early years. He lived now in a villa in Cap Ferrat, perhaps the wealthiest enclave on the Riviera. And at that moment, I felt I deserved a vacation in the south of France.

5

Ali Aziz was waiting for me by the pool. He had the studied good looks of a man who had been sanded, buffed and polished by professionals. The skin on his face was tanned to a deep honey-gold. There were no bags under his eyes or wrinkles on his forehead, no signs of the stress of ordinary life. His only resistance to vanity was that he no longer wore a toupee to cover his bald spot. He looked much better without it, actually. He was so rich now that he didn't need to pretend about anything.

Ali's villa was an immense place, surrounded on three sides by the azure of the Mediterranean. A long driveway wound up the hill, past a tennis court, to a kind of plateau of green lawns and flower gardens carved out of the hillside. Modern sculpture graced the grounds, and there was a faint sound of orchestral music coming from speakers hidden in the trees. The house itself was magnificent—painted a creamy white, with sumptuous furniture and huge picture windows looking out on the sea. Between the main residence and a lavish guesthouse was a large pool shaped like an elongated figure eight, with fountains and a waterfall and small islands of green. Rising from a pool chair to greet me, one hand outstretched and the other grasping a cellular phone, was my host.

"My dear Eric," he said, ignoring the man on the other end of the cell phone who continued to babble away. "What a pleasure it is to see you. Put on some trunks and have a swim. I will be with you in an instant." He rolled his eyes, as if to say that the telephone conversation was mere business, whereas I represented that most precious thing on earth, which was friendship.

Ali Aziz liked to think of himself as an investment banker, and in many ways he was. The chief difference was that his deals generally involved the payment of bribes to politicians, abroad and in France, but they were no less complicated for that. They required networks of offshore accounts, sophisticated legal services, careful money management. Above all, they required absolute discretion and reliability in sharing out the spoils among the parties to the transaction.

In all these tasks Ali Aziz was a master. He regarded himself as the Lazard Frères of corruption. Suppose a French state-owned company was selling tanks to one of the oil kingdoms of the Persian Gulf. A complex set of transactions was necessary to provide funds to the local participants in the deal—say, the senior princes who headed the key ministries and, of course, the representatives of the king himself. But that was only the beginning. The more complex aspects involved the return of some of those funds to France—to the defense minister and other senior representatives of his political party. There were perhaps ten men in France who were capable of handling deals on this scale, and of those, Ali Aziz was among the very best. He had only one failing, for a man in his line of work, and that was his friendship with me.

I had first met Ali in Beirut in 1983, while I was writing a profile of his village in southern Lebanon. It was called Jouaya, and it had come to be known in Beirut as "the village of the millionaires" because so many of its sons had gone off to Africa and become rich. West Africa in those days was a kind of apprentice school for young Lebanese Shiite businessmen who wanted to make their way in the world. Ali himself had recently returned from Abidjan with a small fortune. His first big score had been a scheme to sell uniforms to the Nigerian army through a company he had created for the benefit of the man who was purchasing the uniforms, the Nigerian chief of staff.

Ali was articulate and friendly, and I had quoted him at length about the Arab businessman's special knack for "making business." Somehow, the article came to the attention of a Saudi prince, who had known the Aziz family and decided that young Ali was the right sort of chap to invest a small amount of his capital.

That Saudi connection, Ali said, was the beginning of his real success, and he always attributed his subsequent vast wealth to my article about "the village of the millionaires." He had even offered to buy me a car—a red Mercedes convertible—as a token of his thanks. I refused, but we had stayed in touch over the years, even when I was in Hong Kong and Ali was starting to do business in Asia. My only compensation—the only one I wanted—was the opportunity to ask Ali's help when I needed a particular kind of information.

I took my swim in Ali's perfect pool, shimmering with the intense sunlight of the Côte d'Azur, while he finished up his business on the telephone. Eventually he joined me in the water. He swam a few laps and then relaxed in the shallow end, calling to one of his servants to bring us glasses of fresh lemonade.

"So how can I help you, my friend?" he said as we bobbed in the water. "You were not very communicative on the phone."

I explained that I was investigating what had really happened at Taillevent. I said I didn't believe the official French version. I suspected it was a lie.

"Of course it's a lie," he said amiably. He was resting his head on a rubber float, slowly treading water with his feet. "A complete lie."

"So what happened to the terrorists? Where are they now?"

"They were paid off, my dear Eric. That is the way all problems in France are solved. The government paid these people to go away, and they did. That's what the French *do*—with the Iranians, the Syrians, the Lebanese and now the Africans. It's always the same. And some of the money always sticks to the hands of the Frenchmen who made the payoffs."

Ali confided that the Taillevent hostage incident had been a fraud. It had been staged by a group of African politicians and middlemen who thought they were being shortchanged and wanted more money. Vert/Vertu didn't exist, except for the bizarre science professor Obado, who had been so loquacious in his interview with me. That was why he had been killed, Ali said. He had talked too much.

To understand the Taillevent affair, Ali said, you needed to understand the depth of French corruption in Africa. The French had sent many billions of francs in aid to its former colonies on the understanding that some of the money would come back home—in kickbacks to the French political parties, to middlemen and to the politicians themselves.

"Here is the real secret," said Ali in his softest, most conspiratorial voice. "The Africa network was operated by a clever old gentleman who is one of France's most senior politicians. The money he gathered from Africa was part of the glue of French politics. It was the *caisse noire,* the 'black fund,' from which people could draw when they needed cash."

"Who is he?" I was as eager as a dog in heat.

"My dear Eric, don't ask me that."

"Why not? Don't you know his name?"

"Of course I do. That is why you should not ask me. The man is one of my clients. That is the one thing I cannot tell you. The rest, I don't care. I can tell you his advisers—people like Jacques Daghestani and Michel Bézy—names you have never heard of. But not the man himself. Please." He held up his hand, plaintively, as if I were trying to pick his pocket.

But Ali loved to gossip. This, for him, was the equivalent of an ordinary investment banker explaining how a leveraged buyout had been put together. Ali explained how the feud had begun with a dispute about an oil deal in Gabon. One of the French nationalized oil companies had been buying oil cheaply there for years, and sharing the spoils with local politicians. But the Gabonese had recently discovered that they were being diddled—part of their share was going to pay huge commissions to middlemen in Switzerland—so they got angry. They talked to other Africans and realized that the French were cheating them, too, so they decided to get even. And that's what had led to Taillevent. The crisis had been resolved only when the French had agreed to give the Africans a bigger slice of the *gâteau*.

"Everyone is happy," said Ali. "The Africans and their agents will get a larger percentage, the French will get a bit less. The so-called terrorists disappear back into the shadows; several of them are probably on the Riviera at this very moment, enjoying the weather. But the system survives."

"How much will the Africans take away from the deal?" If I was going to write a story, I needed the number.

"In the short run, a billion francs, about two hundred million dollars. Over the next five years, more than one billion dollars."

We talked awhile longer. Ali gave me lunch: fresh fish that had been caught that morning and fried whole, a salad of fresh tomatoes and fresh figs for dessert. The meal reminded me of Beirut; indeed, everything about that day reminded me of Beirut. I felt alive as a reporter, on the track of a story that mattered. But I still didn't have everything I needed. As I was preparing to leave for the airport late that afternoon, I brought the conversation back to the events at Taillevent.

"I want to know the French politician's name, Ali," I said. "The one who runs the network. I've never asked you for anything valuable before. You've offered me things in the past, and I've always said no. This time I'm asking you for a favor. I need his name."

Ali Aziz gave me a look that was less reproach than surprise. In the code of the East, he owed me. He took out a piece of paper, wrote something on it, folded it up and handed it to me.

"I am giving this to you, Eric, because you are my friend and you have asked for it. But I know you will not be able to publish a story about it, because if you do, they will kill you. So it will remain a secret."

I didn't open the piece of paper until I was in the car, heading back to Nice airport. On it was written the name of the French minister of defense, Maurice Costa.

When I returned to Paris, I did something unusual. I called the U.S. embassy and asked to speak to a man named Tom Rubino, who I had always suspected was the CIA chief of station in Paris. We'd had lunch once, at the suggestion of a mutual friend who was the Paris correspondent for one of the British newspapers, and we'd had a pleasant enough time. He was looser than the usual diplomat, more self-confident, and we had polished off a bottle of wine at lunch. I'd asked him for help once after that, on a story about U.S. covert action in Bosnia, and while he hadn't said much, he hadn't lied either. But I didn't like dealing with CIA people. There was an unspoken rule among American foreign correspondents that the agency was off-limits. The potential cost of any information outweighed the benefit.

But the calculus in this case seemed different. I was working on a potentially explosive story. Even discounting Ali's warning, the risk of a libel suit was still substantial. I needed a second source before I could even consider publishing it. And I couldn't think of where to turn for hard information about such a sensitive topic other than the U.S. government. So I called Rubino, and he was surprisingly warm on the telephone.

"I liked your reporting from Taillevent," he said. "Keep at it! You've just scratched the surface." Funny enough, I said, that was the reason for my call. I told him I was working on a follow-up story, and before I could say any more, he suggested that we meet for coffee in thirty minutes at a café near the embassy.

Rubino arrived wearing a knit sports shirt and a pair of slacks. He suggested we take a table outside. He was a handsome man, with dark, close-cropped hair and an ex-athlete's body. He reminded me of the kind of people I used to meet in tennis tournaments—very focused during matches, very loose off the court. I commented on the fact that he wasn't wearing a suit and tie. "Today is casual day," he said. "The ambassador is visiting a computer factory in Lyons. There's nobody I need to impress."

He asked what I was working on, and I explained. A source had told me that the French had paid $200 million—as a first installment on an eventual $1 billion—to the intermediaries who represented prominent African politicians. The architect of the deal had been none other than the French defense minister, Maurice Costa. Rubino studied me intently as I talked. He took in every word, but let out nothing of his own.

"What do you want from me?" he asked when I was done.

"Confirmation. I can't go with what I have. I need another source. I have to know it's true."

I waited for him to respond, but he just sat there staring off into space for maybe thirty seconds, which is a long time when you're waiting for an answer.

"I can't do it," Rubino said finally. "I'm sorry. I don't know enough, and if I make inquiries, it would be dangerous for both of us. The French are all over me. But I know someone who's quite an expert on this sort of thing. Maybe he can assist you."

"Help me out!" I felt a sudden surge of anger at the calm, controlled man across from me. I was out on a limb, and he was just sitting there watching. "You're playing games. I need some sign from you whether this is worth pursuing."

"Hold on!" he said sharply, and then lowered his voice. "You're not listening. I just offered to help you, by putting you in touch with someone who really knows things. I wouldn't have done that if I didn't think the story was worth pursuing."

"Sorry. I was out of line. How will I find your expert, then?" I was still miffed that Rubino was refusing to help me personally, but a part of me was also relieved. The CIA was poison; every journalist knew that.

"Don't worry about it," said Rubino. "If he can help, he'll find you. But don't come back and see me on this one. You're on your own."

6

My first encounter with Rupert Cohen is fixed in my mind, like a birthday or a funeral or some other ritual event that takes on increasing significance with the passage of time. It started innocuously enough. I was in the Saint-Philippe, across the street from my office, drinking the morning cappuccino with three spoons of sugar and reading the French papers. It was a Friday, the day after my encounter with Tom Rubino. I was hoping to get out of Paris that weekend and visit some friends who had rented an old mill in the Loire Valley.

I was sitting there in a pleasant daze when a stranger approached me with an eager smile, as if he had just spotted a long-lost friend. He was dressed like a German filmmaker, in a fuzzy black sweater, black pants and a black leather jacket. He was about my age, maybe thirty-five, medium height, hair short except for a tuft at the top. And he had a subversive gleam in his eye that I eventually came to understand was the mark of a man who—whatever other ideology he professed—was an anarchist, a professional troublemaker.

"Am I late?" he asked cheerily. He settled down next to me and took a sip from my coffee.

"Who are you?" I asked.

"Cohen, Rupert." He had an eager tone of voice, like those people who do car ads on TV. "I'm the fellow a mutual friend said would be looking you up."

"Are you, now? Well, sit down. Or we can go up to my office and talk."

"That would not be wise, *illustrissimo,* I assure you." He lowered his voice to a whisper. "I was hoping we could meet later today, actually, for lunch. You pick the restaurant, because you will be picking up the tab. I would offer to pay, but that would require me to submit operational paperwork that would defeat the purpose of our discussion. Is that acceptable?"

I thought a moment, but no more than that. He was strange, but that was hardly a disqualification. "Sure," I said.

I suggested that we meet at an out-of-the-way place on Avenue Jean-Jaurès called Au Cochon d'Or, out near the old stockyards in the humble nineteenth arrondissement. It was one of my favorite spots in Paris: it had a rough, workingman's atmosphere, without the pretensions of the fancy expense-account places. Rupert said he would meet me there at 2:00. It was that simple—like a fish, swimming into an open net. I was quite sure, back then, that Rupert Cohen was the fish.

As he got up from the table he took another sip of my coffee. *"Ciao, professore!"* he said, giving me a little salute and disappearing into the Paris morning.

Rupert Cohen was still wearing his black leather jacket when he arrived at the restaurant. I had made the reservation, from a pay phone, under a false name—already, I was playing Rupert's game—and asked for a quiet table in the back. Rupert insisted that we order a bottle of wine, straightaway. Before we got to drinking, an activity at which I suspected he was more proficient than I, there were several things I wanted to know.

"Excuse me for being blunt," I said, "but who are you? Where do you work?"

"I am a foreign service officer," he said serenely. "Until recently, I worked at the American embassy in Rome, in the commercial section. I am now here in Paris, as one of the U.S. representatives to UNESCO. A fine organization. I help them with things."

"Help them with what?" He didn't look much like a diplomat, and he certainly didn't look like a UN bureaucrat.

"Security problems. It's not a very demanding job, frankly. It leaves me time for other things."

"So how long have you been in the, uh . . ." I paused.

"Foreign service," he said, finishing my sentence. "Eight years. Before Rome, I was in Belgrade. Before that, in Beijing."

I looked down at his wrist as he spoke. He was wearing a most peculiar timepiece. Displayed on the dial was a portrait of Mao Tse-tung. As the seconds ticked off, Mao waved his hand to an imaginary crowd.

"Quite a watch," I said.

He gave me a goofy grin. "China is what's happening, my man. Even the French realize that. China *is* the twenty-first century."

Cohen didn't fit any image I'd ever had of a CIA officer. I was intrigued. "What did you do before you joined the foreign service?" I ventured.

"How nice of you to ask. I studied Italian renaissance history at Berkeley." He paused, wondering if I cared to know more, and pressed on when he saw that I did. "I was writing my dissertation on the governance of the Venetian city-state in the fifteenth century. A worthy topic, but my professors could see that I was miserable. One of them suggested government work. I took the exams, and it seemed I had a certain *aptitude*."

"So you abandoned the Venetians?"

"Not at all. The good citizens of *La Serenissima* are with me every day. Venice is my inspiration: founded on an island in a swampy lagoon; sustained by bribery, trickery and political assassination; sponsor of the finest intelligence service the world has ever seen, and arguably the finest flowering of art, as well. In short, the place where heaven and earth meet. No, sir! I will never abandon my beloved Venetians. They are my *illuminati*."

The wine had arrived, and Cohen took a long drink. He had a curious twinkle in his eye, as if he were playing some kind of practical joke that only he understood. He was in every respect an unlikely civil servant.

"Tell *me* something about the newspaper business," he said. "What's it like? It must be fabulous. You get to talk to interesting people, attack evildoers. And your work is all *out there*. If a reporter is incompetent, you know it instantly, just by reading his story. Not like government work, where it can take years to realize that someone is an idiot."

"Journalism has its moments," I allowed, "but a lot of the time it's a bore." I looked at my watch—it was nearly 2:30 and we were still getting acquainted. "Maybe we should get down to business," I said. "I assume that Rubino told you what I'm after."

"More or less. He said you're chasing Maurice Costa and his dreaded network, and how they paid two hundred million dollars to make the Taillevent hostage problem go away." He drained his glass of wine and turned toward me. The mischievous look in his eye had focused into something sharper, almost lethal.

"My information comes from a very good source," I said, "but I need corroboration. What do you know?"

"Hold on, *dottore*. First, let's talk about ground rules. That's what you reporters say, isn't it?"

"Yes. That's what we say."

"For starters, I assume you know what I do. Beyond that 'foreign service' business. I mean, you have doped that out already."

"I assume you work for the CIA."

"I didn't tell you that. You figured it out, so what could I do? That's what I'll say, if anyone ever asks. And this is all off the record. My role in telling you any of this has to be completely secret. Otherwise, I'd do it myself as a covert action—leak it to the French press, destabilize the government—and save you the trouble. Assuming I could get approval in Washington, which I can't, because the lawyers and congressional committees and the other nannies would have a fit. So there you are."

"The ground rules sound fine. But what do you actually *know*? I'm hungry for information."

"Me, I'm hungry for food. Then information, but first food."

So we summoned the waiter. Rupert Cohen looked to see what the most expensive items on the menu were, and then ordered them: snails and a huge *filet de boeuf* for two, which he said we would have to share. When the waiter was gone, he launched quite suddenly into the heart of what I had wanted to know, sending me scrambling for my notebook.

"Have you ever heard of La Puissance Occulte?" he began. "The Secret Power."

"Never. What is it?"

"It's an organization that doesn't exist. But it's there, just the same, like the Cosa Nostra, which also doesn't exist. It's the power behind the power. When a car bomb explodes in Lebanon and kills the prime minister, nobody knows who did it. But *somebody* knows, and that person is often in France. When hostages are taken in the Middle East and someone has to go get them, that person is often French. When a bribe is paid to win a big trade deal for a European company, the place where you'll find the man who paid the bribe—and perhaps also the recipient—is France. These are things that don't happen. But they happen."

I looked at him skeptically. "And the organization that makes all these things happen is La Puissance Occulte?"

"Don't be so literal. You're thinking about an organization with a flow-chart. I'm talking about an *affinity*. There isn't a single network, but dozens of them. The Secret Power includes businessmen, spies, politicians. It is a loose collection of the people who really run things in France, as opposed to the people who *appear* to run things. These people with the real, secret power have an affinity for each other. And they all have an affinity for the old fox, Maurice Costa. It's pointless to look for an organization—as I said, it doesn't exist—but here's a clue. Many of these people you are looking for are Freemasons."

I shook my head. "You're kidding. The guys who wear fezzes and organize children's benefits? That can't be. Those people are clowns."

"Not *them*. Here in France there are very old and secret Masonic orders. They are a kind of hidden thread that runs through French life. They recruit people who want to share in the secret power—people who are ambitious, outgoing, want to make connections. People who are prepared to ignore public laws for the sake of the private network. There is a security brotherhood, for example, in which you will find senior members of French intelligence and the police. There are left-wing Masonic orders that began as a kind of anti-Catholic underground. The members of these orders aren't in it simply for money. They see themselves as part of the secret order that holds society together against the forces of disorder—the barbarians, the Americans, the forces that would destroy France.

"And that is especially true of Maurice Costa. He is the only one who knows *all* the secrets. He is an austere man, tall and thin like de Gaulle, who for many years lived with his mother in a simple apartment near the Luxembourg Gardens. Though he has gathered many billions of dollars in bribes over the years, he has no personal interest in money. He has been a Socialist Party member all his life, and his only personal extravagance has been a private airplane, to fly him on weekends to his family farm near Toulouse. The money is all for his network. Costa has contacts in every city and town in France. His people are in every ministry, in every big corporation, in the intelligence agencies. They are the power behind the power."

He leaned toward me. "Do you begin to see what I'm talking about here, Eric? Mmmmm? Do you?" His eyes were radiating light and energy. Listening to him was like hearing a tale by Scheherazade. It was so intriguing, it cast its own spell. But I needed to focus on the facts that could go into a newspaper article.

"Let me see if I understand," I said. "The French network in Africa was part of this loose affinity group you're calling La Puissance Occulte. Is that right?"

"Correct." He nodded.

"So when the Africans got upset and wanted more money, the various elements of the network came together to find a way out—the security brotherhood, the oil-company brotherhood, the nuclear-weapons brotherhood, and all the intermediaries and dealmakers. And they all agreed to change the payoff formulas for Africa and rejiggered the secret accounts. Do I have it right?"

"Correct," he said again.

"And then they sent in the police to free the hostages—and more important, free the hostage takers. And it was all blessed by Maurice Costa."

"You have it, *illustrissimo!*" He was smiling from ear to ear, like a naughty boy who has just built something diabolical with his chemistry set.

I shook my head. The information was so powerful, it took a while for me to register its potential effect. It could bring down the government if it was true. "How do you know that it's right, Rupert?"

"That is an epistemological question, Eric. How do we know anything? How does our brain confirm the validity of what our eyes see and our ears hear? It could all be an illusion. I know it because I *know* it."

"Cut the bullshit. This isn't an academic exercise. My career is on the line with this story. I have already been arrested and beaten by the French government. I've had somebody tell me I'll get killed if I pursue the story. Now I'm trying to decide whether I can publish anything. I need *facts*. Not Venetian ghost stories."

Rupert pulled back from the table. "That was unnecessary," he said.

"I'm sorry. But I want you to understand the stakes. If I can confirm this story, I'm going to put it in the paper. And all hell is going to break loose."

Rupert closed his eyes. "God, I wish I were a journalist." He said it quietly, reverently. I realized in that moment that he would never, in a lifetime in the CIA, have as much power as I did now. And it was obvious that he realized it, too.

"I understand what you need," he said. He looked carefully around the restaurant, to make sure that nobody was eavesdropping on our conversation, and then dropped his voice to a whisper. "There is a category of information that is known to my colleagues as Special Intelligence, or 'SI.' It consists of communications intercepts, telephone taps, surreptitious monitoring of conversations. There are very few things that the United States cannot listen into if it wants. And that is true even inside a friendly allied country, like France.

"So when I say I *know* things, I am referring to this category of infor-

mation. It is possible that a record exists that would give you the confirmation you need. Not certain, but possible. But this information is *never*
made available to journalists."

Then he gave me one of those strange smiles that marked him as a born
troublemaker, and suggested that it was time to enjoy the meal.

7

The next Monday, after I had put out a few queries to try to confirm parts of what Ali Aziz and Rupert Cohen had told me, I received a call from my friend Olivier at *Libération*. He asked me to come see him at the paper and said it was urgent. Although I had many other things to do that afternoon, I said I would come right over. It was a half hour by metro to the paper's offices on Rue Béranger, just off the Place de la République.

Olivier took me to the newspaper's rooftop terrace, which embodied the scruffy, leftist chic of the place. It was a simple canteen, with soft-drink machines and rickety garden furniture and a Ping-Pong table, yet it commanded one of the best views in Paris. A visitor gazed out over the city to the Eiffel Tower, Montmartre and the Beaubourg, with the sound of Ping-Pong balls clicking in his ear. Olivier had a disturbing message to pass along. He said a friend in the DST had told him that I was working on a story about Maurice Costa. The friend had said that I should drop the story, now. Otherwise, my life could be in danger. Olivier wouldn't identify his source, but he did name the man from whom his source had heard the warning. He was a former Justice Ministry official named Jacques Daghestani—one of the names that Ali Aziz had mentioned.

"I know these people, Eric," said Olivier. He gazed out over the rooftops of Paris and looked back at me. "They are dangerous. This is France, not America."

I thanked Olivier for his information. At that point I still thought it was bullshit. A decade as a journalist had taught me that however angry people may get at reporters, they don't kill them. It only creates more trouble, and guarantees precisely the outcome they want to avoid, which is publicity. I left the meeting with Olivier concerned that Costa's people were trying so hard to intimidate me, but more convinced than ever that I was onto a great story.

Tuesday morning I was back in the office, making more calls, when I received another summons. This time it was a man who identified himself as the regional security officer at the U.S. embassy, someone I had not only never met but never heard of. He sounded extremely serious. It was normally a fifteen-minute walk from my office to the Avenue Gabriel, but that morning I made it in ten.

The regional security officer—his name was Chuck, I think—said he had been asked by Washington to deliver a message. The United States government had information that a threat had been made against my life. He wouldn't say what their sources were, or who was doing the threatening. But he said that the State Department regarded the threat as credible. "I cannot force you to leave France," he said, "but I would strongly advise you to do so."

Now I began to worry. There is something about the power and authority of the U.S. government that gives information a different status. It "reifies" it, as the philosophers like to say—it turns it into a *thing* that feels harder and more concrete. I wanted to go down the hall and find Tom Rubino, but I knew that would be unwise. He had warned me specifically not to contact him again about the Costa business. My point of contact was Rupert Cohen, but I'd heard nothing from him since our meeting the previous Friday, and I found that silence ominous. I was out on the firing line by myself.

I thought about my options. The first thing I needed to do was call the *Mirror* to let them know what was happening. I hadn't briefed my editors about what I was working on, except to say that I was following up my earlier Taillevent reporting. I waited until 4:00 P.M. Paris time—10:00 A.M. in New York—and then called Lynn Frenzel, the foreign editor. I gave her a bare-bones version of the story and told her about the death threats, and then went through the whole thing again while Ed Weiss listened on the other line.

Frenzel spoke up first. She thought I should leave Paris. "No story is worth getting killed over," she said. "I learned that in Central America."

I waited for Weiss to speak. Before giving me any advice of his own, he asked me what I wanted to do. There was a long pause while I thought. I cleared my throat.

"Here's the way I feel," I said. "If I really thought I was in danger, I'd want to leave, obviously. I'm not crazy. But I don't think anyone really intends to kill me. They just want to scare me. And I hate to give in to that kind of pressure. So I guess that means I want to stay."

"I love you, Eric," said Weiss. It was spontaneous, but he meant it. Journalism for Weiss was a love affair. "But that's the wrong answer. The right answer is that you should leave Paris for a while. Go to London. See a show. Let things settle. Then come back and write whatever the fuck you want."

"That sounds like the official line," I said.

"Yes. But it's also the unofficial line. I'm not going to order you to leave. You should do what you think is right. But like the lady said, no story is worth getting killed over."

I said I would think about it and let them know what I had decided. Thirty minutes later, a telex arrived from the communications center in New York. That was strange in itself, since we usually sent messages by computer. The telex was from Weiss, who apparently wanted a formal record of his cautionary advice: "Pro Truell Ex Weiss. Assume you will be uncrazy and leave Paris ASAP. That is an order. I mean it. All bests."

Honestly, I don't know what I would have done if the messenger hadn't arrived that afternoon. I was sitting in my office, staring blankly out the window down the Rue du Faubourg-St.-Honoré, wondering what I should do. I had already sent Pascale home to her kid. There was a sharp knock at the door, which scared the shit out of me, frankly. But it was just this odd messenger. He didn't identify himself or ask me to sign anything; he looked at me, as if comparing me with a picture he'd studied, and handed me an envelope. And then he was gone, out the door and back down the elevator.

I opened the envelope. Inside was a single sheet of paper with a yellow Post-it sticker attached. The page was part of a transcript of a telephone conversation. The two speakers were identified as "Daghestani" and "Costa." The original French text came first, followed by a translation:

Daghestani: On est bien d'accord: Il faut payer un milliard de francs pour en finir avec cette histoire. We agree that we must pay a billion francs [$200 million] to finish with this problem.

Costa: Et si nous payons, c'est fini. Les otages sont libres, les voyous disparaissent dans la nature. C'est ça? And if we pay, it's over. The hostages are free, these lying hooligans disappear. That's it?

Daghestani: Oui, bien sûr. Nous avons une garantie. Yes, of course, it's guaranteed.

Costa: Alors, payez. Then pay.

A message had been handwritten in ink on the yellow sticker attached to the transcript. It read: "Knowledge is power. Use this *very* carefully." It was unsigned, but I knew who it was from. This was Special Intelligence, the kind that allowed people to know things, with moral certainty, so that they could act upon them. And now I knew. I had my second source, confirming what Ali had told me. I reread Ed Weiss's telex message, ordering me to leave Paris. Then I sat down at the keyboard and banged out a brief telex of my own, addressed to Weiss. It read: "Message unreceived. Truell."

It took only a few hours to write the story. I had been gathering string for nearly a week, so I already had most of the information I needed. And I figured that time was now working against me. The longer I waited before putting the information in print, the more vulnerable I would be. I started by calling United Airlines and booking two seats for their flight to New York the next day; I also made a reservation at a hotel in Manhattan for the following night. I hoped these steps would mislead the DST officers who were undoubtedly listening in on my phone calls into believing that I was bailing out. Then I sat down at my laptop computer and wrote a lead.

> Paris, May 28—French defense minister Maurice Costa personally authorized a $200 million payment to associates of the Vert/Vertu terrorist group that seized Taillevent restaurant two weeks ago as part of a secret deal to release 15 hostages, according to authoritative sources.
>
> The payment was part of a broader financial package that will provide prominent West African political figures who sponsored the Vert/Vertu terrorist operation with at least $1 billion in secret funds over the next five years, another informed source said.

The story went on like that for another two thousand words. It wrote itself. The top of a newspaper story is like a hanger in a closet. If it's weak or off center, it won't support anything. But if it's solid, you can hang a ton of information on it, and it will all lie flat and straight.

I spent that night back at my apartment, fact-checking the story—going over every detail and thinking how we would defend ourselves against any libel claims that might be brought against the paper. Lawsuits were probably the least of my worries, but they were the only ones I could protect against. When I was done with the checking, I printed out a copy of the story. I then composed a long memo for Weiss, summarizing in detail my sourcing for the story. I attached a copy of the transcript of the phone conversation between Costa and Daghestani, and put everything in an envelope with Weiss's name on it. Finally I deleted the files from the hard drive of my computer, so that there would be no other record of them.

The next morning at 7:00 A.M., I called Pascale at home and asked if she would like to take her daughter on a quick vacation to New York. *Bien sûr!* Of course she would. I picked her up at home, drove her to the airport and escorted her to the United departure gate. I didn't want to leave her unprotected for a moment. When they called the flight, I gave her the sealed envelope and told her that when she arrived at Kennedy, she should take a taxi directly to the *Mirror*'s offices. She should give the envelope to Ed Weiss, the executive editor—delivering it personally, to him only, no matter who offered to help or demanded to see it. And then she could do whatever she liked.

The story created an uproar in France when it was published two days later, stripped across the top of our front page. Paris is a gossipy town, and many French reporters had known I was working on something hot. They knew I had been threatened, and when nothing had appeared in print, they had assumed we had caved in to the intimidation—just as the French reporters had done for so many years. When we dared to publish, despite the threats, we shamed the French press into action.

Maurice Costa issued a statement denouncing the story soon after it hit the streets in New York. He scheduled a news conference at the Ministry of Defense for that afternoon. My friend Olivier, full of congratulations that we had published despite the threats, said he'd heard that Costa intended to denounce me as a CIA spy. He would wrap himself in the tricolor, claiming that the story was part of an American plot to destabilize France.

But shortly before Costa's press conference was scheduled to begin, official Paris began reading the first editions of France's hyperserious afternoon paper, *Le Monde*. It carried a detailed, independent account of the Taillevent disaster, based on its own sources in Paris, confirming the essential details of what I had written. Costa's briefing was delayed for an hour and then canceled outright. It was clear that the French Establishment was having second thoughts about going to the wall to defend Costa and his gang—especially when *Le Monde* appeared to be backing the other side. The defense minister and his murky network were relics of the past. They had suddenly become an embarrassment. With the grace and precision of a ballet dancer, France Inc. was moving in a new direction.

I spent that night in a hotel room, which I had booked under a false name. I wasn't really frightened anymore, but there was something to be said for staying out of harm's way. And I truly wanted to hide. In all the great events of my life, from winning my first big tennis tournament to graduating from college, my way of celebrating has been to disappear. My own satisfaction in those moments is sweeter than any words I might hear from others.

Libération chimed in the next morning, with its own detailed dossier of what was now being called *L'Affaire Costa*. The other French newspapers and magazines followed, as did the American press. By that weekend the *Mirror* had lots of company. The next week, the crisis was resolved in a characteristic French way. Maurice Costa resigned as minister of defense. Thereupon, he was immediately appointed by the Élysée Palace to head a new commission to be called France 2000 that would plan for the twenty-first century. His first trip would be to visit old friends in Africa, and then he would travel on to Beijing.

8

❖❖❖

I was a hero. It is immodest to say so, but it was true. My story had toppled a powerful French politician and altered, in at least a minor way, the
conduct of French politics. Because of my reportorial antics, I had also become part of the story. With my editors' blessing, I appeared on *Nightline*
and was profiled in the press sections of both *Time* and *Newsweek*. *People*
magazine sent out a photographer, but they were running their special
"High School Sweethearts" issue that week—with pictures of Hollywood
stars and the people they took to the senior prom—so they never ran the
article about me.

Ed Weiss was happy as the proverbial pig in shit. He gloried in moments
like this. He embraced any opportunity to talk about the *Mirror*'s big
scoop, and made a point of showing reporters who came calling the two
now famous cables—his ordering me home and my "message unreceived"
response—which he had framed and put on the wall of his office. Weiss
said he planned to nominate me for a Pulitzer Prize and a George Polk
award. As things turned out, the Pulitzer was a long shot—that was the
year the world learned the truth about Bosnian death camps, and it was assumed the prize would go to the reporter who did the most to uncover
them—but Weiss said I had a lock on the Polk, which was named for a
journalist who had gotten killed in the line of duty. I seemed to be their
kind of guy.

Through the month of June, I took a long victory lap. I came back to
New York and addressed a *Mirror* staff meeting. So many people wanted to
come that they had to hold it in the ballroom of a nearby hotel. I recounted
my story, yet again—emphasizing the silly parts like getting busted on the

roof of the Élysées Models building and spending the night in the slammer on the Rue Nélaton—and answering gee-whiz questions from friends and colleagues. I did it all happily. This was a ritual of self-love, for the newspaper as much as for me. Afterward I had visitations from several of the younger women reporters, who previously had never given me the time of day when I was on home leave. I brought one of them back to my hotel room after a glorious night of dancing and drinking. We made love exuberantly through the night and woke up bleary-eyed the next morning. I had hit the jackpot. The quarters were tumbling out of the machine into my lap. The day before I left, Sellinger gave me the monthly Publisher's Award, which came with a five-thousand-dollar bonus, and promised he would raise my salary next year to eighty thousand dollars, which was more money than I had ever dreamed I would make as a journalist.

Yet when I finally returned to Paris, a sense of unease began to grow in me, like mold in a remote corner of a bathroom. At the core of my great scoop were events I didn't understand. We had been able to publish the exposé of Maurice Costa only because of information provided by an anonymous source. I was certain I knew who had given me this information, but I didn't know why. I tried to find Rupert Cohen at UNESCO, where he supposedly worked, but they had never heard of him. That added to my disorientation. Had I been used in a covert campaign by the U.S. government, deliberately plotted in Washington, to change French politics? Or had a source in Paris—a weirdo in a black leather jacket—slipped me the information on his own? Had I been the active player in this drama or simply the object of other people's designs? I didn't know the answers to these questions, and that was the source of my unease.

Arthur Bowman called me in early July. He was coming to Paris in a few days with the secretary of state, and he had a free evening, and would I like to join him for dinner at Taillevent? I thought he must be joking, but he said he had already made the reservation. The invitation surprised me. At that time I barely knew our legendary chief diplomatic correspondent, and I wasn't sure why, with all of Paris to choose from, the visiting pasha had chosen to bestow his expense-account largess on me. But I was so accustomed to being celebrated at that point that I readily said yes.

The owner of Taillevent, who luckily had been away the day it was seized, greeted me warmly when I arrived. He summoned the sommelier, Henri, who was wearing the same gray coat he had worn that wretched evening, with the grape pin on the lapel. Henri kissed me on both cheeks and embraced me, and I thought for a moment he might start crying. I had not realized that earlier evening how intimate and soothing the restaurant was. Everything in the room—the Chinese lamps, the porcelain, the absurd arsenal of silverware—now conveyed a spirit of timeless luxury. As the owner walked me to the table there was a smattering of applause from other diners and several of the restaurant staff. That month I was still famous in Paris.

Bowman was already seated at the blue banquette when I arrived. He immediately struck up a conversation with the owner. They seemed to be old friends. Bowman had a magisterial air, especially that night. He was dressed in one of the perfect suits he ordered every year from his tailor at the Mandarin Hotel in Hong Kong—a deep charcoal gray, accompanied by a crisp white shirt and an Hermès tie with a pattern of gold braid on a field of lustrous blue. In the soft light of the restaurant his graying hair appeared to be dappled silver.

"Of course you know Jean-Claude," he said, after our host had left.

"I've never met him before, to tell you the truth," I said. "My expense account is not as robust as yours."

"Nobody's is. I am the last of a breed. But now that you're such a star, you may be eligible to join, so I'll tell you my secret. Whenever you're in New York, try to do favors for the business side of the paper. Talk to advertisers, give a speech at the accounting department's annual retreat, be nice to the publisher. Then, if anyone ever tries to question you about expenses, you'll have friends in the right places." I nodded at what sounded like sage advice.

Bowman seemed to know the menu intimately. "You'll never go wrong with the house specialties here," he advised. I put myself in his hands and ordered what he suggested—a seafood sausage to start, and then a ragout of pigeon.

"And for wines, what do you think? Let's start with a bottle of Meursault 'Les Luchets,' 1987. And with the pigeon, a nice Burgundy." He scanned the list. "A 1985 Vosne-Romanée, I would say."

My head was spinning. Bowman had just spent three hundred dollars of Philip Sellinger's money on the wines alone. He looked as happy as a man could possibly be. I don't know what I had expected from Bowman. He was such a senior correspondent, such a legend among younger people at the paper, that he had always been a kind of cardboard cutout for me.

What I hadn't fathomed was his raw charm, the way he drew you irresistibly into his conspiracy of good food, wine and talk.

When the sommelier had poured the wine, Bowman lifted his glass in my direction. "Here's to the Paris bureau chief of *The New York Mirror*. You have what is quite possibly the best job in the world, and you've done brilliantly with it. I hope you're enjoying it."

"I'm having fun," I answered, "but I won't be unhappy when the silver carriage turns back into a pumpkin. Celebrity and journalism don't coexist very well." That was the truth, and I wanted to be honest with Bowman that night, to connect, to establish a relationship.

"Enjoy it, Eric. You wrote a great story. A bigger story, maybe, than you realize."

"What do you mean? I'm not following you."

Bowman looked at his glass. "This '87 is actually very good, isn't it? Jean-Claude only gives it a 'thirteen' on his vintage chart, but I think it's better than the '88, which gets a 'sixteen.' *De gustibus, non est disputandum.* Am I right?"

I had no views whatsoever on the relative merits of the '87 versus the '88. I asked my question again. "What did you mean about the story being bigger than I realized? It feels pretty big already."

"Hmmm," he said, turning his gaze from the glass of Meursault back toward me. "Let me ask you a question about that story, if you don't mind. It was obvious to any sensitive reader that you were in possession of a telephone intercept from the National Security Agency. That's about the most sensitive information the U.S. government can obtain. The mere fact that we can intercept internal communications in France is a very big secret in itself, I suspect. Which raises the obvious question: Why was that transcript given to you?"

Bowman came right at you. That was part of the power of his personality. He breached your defenses and was behind your lines before you knew it. He left you no choice but to be honest. "I don't know why I got the intercept," I said. "I've wondered about that question myself. What do you think?"

"I can't really answer without knowing who your source was, and I don't intend to ask you that. That's between you and Ed Weiss. But I can give you some background that may be helpful. For the past eighteen months, since the new administration took office, the CIA has quietly embarked on a new cold war. The enemies this time are our principal trade competitors—France and Japan, but especially France. The new administration is obsessed with global economic competition, and the bureaucrats at Langley know very well how to read the prevailing winds. The clandestine service has been mobilized around the world to gather information about French trading practices—where they play games, whom they bribe. The goal supposedly is to 'level the playing field'—that marvelous American metaphor—as if the playing field could ever be level between the world's only remaining superpower and a relatively small European nation. But that's the new Zeitgeist in Washington. Level the playing field. Bash the French. And who do you suppose is the leading protector of French markets—the man who secretly closes all the big deals from Saudi Arabia to Taiwan? Who might that be?"

"Maurice Costa," I said.

"Just so. His resignation was a setback for the French in international trade, without question. They'll recover. They'll regroup their forces and create new networks, and they'll probably be better for it in the end. But it was undeniably a win for Uncle Sugar."

"So I was set up by the CIA, in this effort to bash the French and 'level the playing field.' That's what you're saying, isn't it? I'm not offended. I've certainly wondered the same thing myself."

"You weren't set up. What you did was very brave. But there's a larger game going on, that's all. Who do you think gave you the NSA stuff? Don't tell me his name, for God's sake. But was it someone from the embassy, do you think?"

"No," I answered. He was my colleague, and he knew things. I wanted to be open with him. "He was a strange guy, actually. He looked like he was auditioning for a Werner Herzog film. I shouldn't say any more about him, but I knew he was CIA. He said so."

The waiter came to refill Bowman's wineglass, and he took another fond drink. "You have to feel sorry for them," he said, addressing the crystal goblet. "They're looking for work."

"Who's looking for work?" For all I knew, he was referring to the vintners of France.

"The underemployed gentlemen at the CIA. They have a serious problem, now that the cold war is over. They are selling raincoats in Saudi Arabia. Nobody's buying. So they have to look for new product lines. Two years ago the hot item was drugs. This year it seems to be economic espionage. Combating the wily Frog."

"Maybe the French *are* a threat. Costa's network was real. It was dangerous."

"Perhaps to Frenchmen, but surely not to the United States. However sordid a character Maurice Costa may be, it's a problem for the French to resolve. Costa has been doing more or less the same things since the 1950s, and nobody in Washington gave a damn. He was actually something of a favorite out at Langley because he despised the Russians so much. Now Costa and his network are suddenly a three-alarm fire. What does that tell you?"

"That I've been an unwitting lobbyist for the CIA Full Employment Act."

"Precisely." Bowman swept his silver-gray hair back from his forehead. "The agency is out beating the bushes for new business. It is inventing new roles for itself. This whole mania about economic espionage is dangerous nonsense, if you ask me. But then, what do I know?"

"You know everything, Arthur. That's what everyone says."

The seafood sausage arrived. At the touch of my knife, it released the most fragrant perfume of truffles and buttery shrimps, lobster and scallops. We finished off the white Burgundy; instantly the waiter brought the red to accompany the pigeon ragout, rich with the flavors of wild game. I was so full that I couldn't imagine ordering dessert. But Bowman said that if I didn't, he would never invite me to dinner again.

"Imagine a man coming to a great restaurant and not ordering dessert," he said. "It's appalling. This is their artistry. It's like going to the Louvre and refusing to look at the *Mona Lisa*." He studied the menu.

"There is only one possible choice," he concluded, "and that is the *Marquise au chocolat*." That turned out to be an intensely rich chocolate cake, more mousse than cake, topped with crème anglaise that had been mixed with ground pistachios. The owner insisted that we have a glass of Sauternes, on the house.

I was a sensualist that night. I had never eaten so well or been so thoroughly charmed. Bowman had one more question for me.

"What are you going to do when your tour in Paris is up, young Truell?"

"I hadn't really thought about it," I answered. "I have another year here, possibly two. I'd love another tour overseas. Maybe Moscow. I'll worry about it when the time comes."

"You should go back home. Come to the Washington bureau for a while. Learn the ropes. Then you ought to go to New York and become an editor. They need you."

"Who says?" The last thing I wanted to do at that point was become an editor. It sounded too much like a real job.

"Ed Weiss," he answered. He had lit a cigarette and was drawing the smoke back into his nostrils. I sensed that night, really for the first time, that my career was being shaped by forces over which I had only limited control.

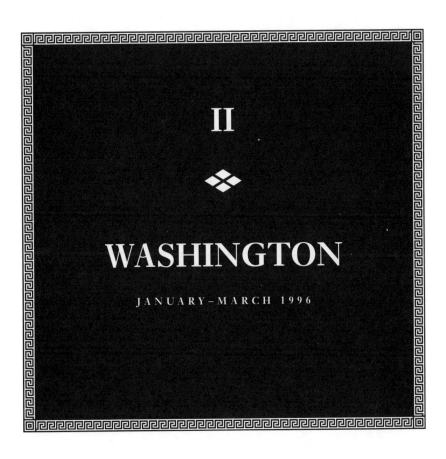

II

WASHINGTON

JANUARY–MARCH 1996

9

I returned home the next year, to take a reporting job in the *Mirror*'s Washington bureau. It was a summons. Ed Weiss phoned me one day in Paris to say that the Moscow bureau would be opening up soon. "You can have it if you want it," he said, "but I hope you won't. You shouldn't stay overseas any longer. You've done that. You'd do fine in Moscow, but so what? We need you in Washington. Come home and do great things." And so I did. Weiss could have told me to open a new bureau in Seward, Alaska, and I would have done it.

I was more than ready to leave Paris. It had become a lonely existence. My American colleagues envied me, and my French sources were scared of me. Journalists are essentially parasites. They insert themselves into the life of a community and draw nourishment from it. But I'd lost my camouflage in Paris. I had become radioactive. That was evident to me the day I paid a call on Ali Aziz. He was cold and distant, and it was clear he'd paid a dear price, at last, for the favor I'd done him years before in Beirut. "You should leave France," he said, and he was right.

My new position in Washington was "special projects reporter." It turned out that meant I could do pretty much as I wanted, so long as I kept busy. The Washington bureau chief, Bob Marcus, was deferential. He sensed that I had been anointed in some mysterious way he didn't understand, and that his own career interests would be enhanced if he maintained a good relationship with me. I made it easy for him: my first project was a series about a slumlord in Baltimore who had purchased a magnificent villa on the French Riviera with his loot. I'd heard about him back in Paris, so I basically arrived with the story in my pocket. Marcus thought I was a genius.

The Washington bureau into which I settled was a monument to the *Mirror*'s ambitions. The *Times* and the *Journal* had large Washington bureaus, and they were great newspapers, so we would have one, too. It took up a whole floor of one of those elaborately ugly office buildings on lower Connecticut Avenue. The bureau chief's office might have belonged to the undersecretary of commerce, or the chairman of the Export-Import Bank. It was a vast room, with an enormous cherrywood desk, heavy green drapes and a thick carpet in a luminous shade of blue. There were so many chairs and couches placed about the room that reporters summoned for conferences with Marcus never knew where to sit.

From his office, Marcus could survey the long row of desks along the Connecticut Avenue windows. The Corridor of the Gods, we called it. At these desks sat the grandees of the bureau: Amory Small, who had covered Congress since Carl Albert was Speaker, and still sported the same crew cut he had worn when he joined the bureau in the early 1960s; Noel Rosengarten, the Pentagon correspondent who was always about to land a job with one of the TV networks but never did; Susan Geekas, the White House correspondent, who had covered three presidents and prided herself on never, ever, having attended a White House social event.

The only reporter who had his own office was Arthur Bowman, the chief diplomatic correspondent. It was at the other end of the corridor from the bureau chief's office, and almost as grand.

The rest of the reporters were arrayed in the interior of the room, back from the windows. One of those banished to the hinterland was my best friend at the paper, George Dirk. Like me, he had started on the Metro desk in New York in 1981, and like me, he had dreamed of going overseas. But it had never happened for him. He had gotten married and had kids, and the arc of his career had turned down. He now worked as an investigative reporter for the Business Today section, producing a steady stream of good stories. But his fortunes had continued to sink at the paper, for reasons that were never clear to me. As a result, George Dirk was consumed with envy for other, more successful reporters—attributing their progress to deceit and double-dealing. He particularly disliked Rosengarten, whom he regarded as a shill for the military-industrial complex. Dirk still liked me, despite my success, but he was visibly upset when I was given a desk along the windows, midway between Marcus's office and Bowman's. To Dirk, the fact that I now occupied this prime real estate was evidence of a moral shortcoming on my part.

The newspaper, I gradually discovered, was a different place from what it was when I had set sail on my first foreign assignment ten years before. It was more careful, more bureaucratic, more frightened, more vulnerable. These changes had been taking place over many years, but I hadn't fully grasped them. When you're overseas, you don't really understand what's going on back at headquarters. People tell you, but you don't get it. Now I could see how much things had changed. The great explosion of journalistic energy of the 1970s—when reporters were emblems of America's revolt against authority—had ended. Journalists weren't the good guys anymore, the Lou Grants and Mary Richardses. Now they were the whiners and spoiled brats, inhuman stick figures who acted as if they were better than everyone else. Back in the eighties, when we were still flying high, I thought it would be good for us to be unpopular for a while. But not like this.

The worst of it was that the economics of the news business had changed. Not only were we unpopular, we were unprofitable. You could see it every time a reporter went to ask Bob Marcus whether he could take a trip somewhere. In the old days the answer was always yes. It was understood that covering the news cost money, and a hefty expense account was regarded as a sign you were doing the job properly. No more. Advertising revenues were falling—you didn't need to see any numbers, you just had to look at the thinness of the paper—and circulation was down. Philip Sellinger had been saying ever since he became publisher fifteen years before that he hoped he would never have to order layoffs in the newsroom. But people were wondering whether he could keep that promise much longer. The best young reporters were beginning to drift away, to Hollywood as screenwriters, to Wall Street as investment bankers or to television as talking heads. The older journeymen reporters, like my friend George Dirk, were getting antsy, looking over their shoulders, wondering when the ax might fall. But not me. I was a rising star. Everyone said so.

One of the things I discovered when I returned home was that my exgirlfriend, Annie Baron, had become a star, too. She had a weekly column in *Newsweek* now, and appeared regularly on one of the television talk shows that had fastened around journalism like boa constrictors. I learned of her television career soon after I arrived in Washington. I was channel surfing one Friday night when I saw the face of a beautiful woman, hauntingly familiar to me, who was in animated discussion with a panel of overbearing men. They were discussing the role of the First Lady in lobbying for social legislation, and the men kept interrupting one another to talk about the political costs and benefits for the president.

"You guys don't *get it*," broke in Annie. "This isn't a baseball game. The First Lady doesn't think that way. She doesn't worry about her husband's reelection, any more than she cares whether her husband thinks she looks cute. This is a woman with larger ambitions. She wants to be *great*. That's why she's causing everyone problems." Annie smiled in that way I remembered—like the most outspoken girl in junior high—at once mischievous and sweet. The panel fell silent. The host said, "I think Annie Baron has the last word on that topic," and broke for a commercial.

I watched Annie with a mixture of admiration and astonishment. When I left America, shows like this one had been a joke—ponderous old farts sitting around gassing about the news. Annie used to call them "the fatheads." Now she was one of them, but with a powerful difference. She was smart, young, pretty. She wasn't like the politicians she covered; she was on a different plane altogether.

Annie's specialty, in print and on the air, was penetrating the public version of events to offer an inside account. Her magazine column, called *Under the Volcano,* had become something of a Washington obsession. People would read about a new outbreak of political infighting in the administration and remark, "That's just like an Annie Baron column." She had always been a facile writer, ever since her first movie review in the *Stanford Daily,* but she had gotten by for years on rhetorical tricks. Now, at last, she seemed to have found a worthy subject. She chronicled the life of official Washington as if it were a comedy of manners. She noticed the bags under the president's eyes and wondered in print what might be keeping him up at night. She observed the fastidious dress of the secretary of state and went off to interview his tailor. She went to the beauty parlor with the chairman of the Council of Economic Advisers and got her to talk about the trade deficit while she was having her nails done. The pleasure of Annie's column was that it was always surprising; you never knew what secrets she might pull out of people.

I should explain why I still felt so connected to Annie, after all those years apart. She was a reference point. It was as if she held the other key to the safe deposit box in which the valuables of my life were kept. "Only connect" had always been her line, and she meant it. That was her one requirement or expectation in a relationship. She made me read *Howards End* when we first started dating in 1978, to make sure I got it.

We had stopped living together a long time ago—after I first went overseas in 1983—but neither of us had entirely gotten over the relationship. In the first few years I was away we pretended that we could keep something going, even as we began sleeping with other people. But the edges got too frayed. When I would come back home at Christmas, there would be too much *not* to talk about, and we gradually let it slip. But she continued to live in my dreams for all the ten years I was away—making love in my subconscious, no matter who else I was seeing when I was awake. It was almost a parallel life. I went from dream to dream, weaving the secret threads together so that—truly, in my mind—it was as if we had never parted.

The very fact that I went overseas in the first place was partly Annie's doing. Nearly all my friends had argued that I should stay in New York, have fun, play the young journalist's game. Annie knew I wanted a new challenge—that if I didn't try it, I would be forever diminished—and she urged me to go, even though she assumed it would mean the end of our relationship. I was so moved by that evidence of her love that I did something I had dithered about for several years: I asked her to marry me.

But she said no. Beirut was what *I* needed to do; she needed to do something quite different. She was just starting a journalism career of her own at *Newsweek.* She wanted ferociously to succeed.

Annie had come to journalism on the rebound, too. In her case, the first love had been not tennis but ballet. She had a dancer's body: tall, slender, with arms and legs that were at once delicate and powerful. She had worked to develop that natural talent—practicing four hours a day, nearly every day of her life from the age of five to the time she went off to Stanford. I saw her onstage just once, a few weeks after we met. It was a production of *Swan Lake* by the San Francisco Ballet, and she was dancing in the corps. I fell in love the moment I saw those strong legs moving across the stage, her long neck taut as she fluttered her arms. A few months later she gave up dance, to concentrate on her studies, she said. But I always wondered if I was the real cause. Ballet, like any art, is fundamentally selfish, and when she fell in love with me, perhaps there wasn't enough left for herself.

She never lost that dancer's grace. I might be her only audience, but I was appreciative. I would catch sight of her out the window, running across the street on those slender legs—small steps, toes arched, almost prancing.

It was like watching a doe cross a clearing. In the morning, I would lie in bed and pretend to be asleep, just so I could watch her put her pantyhose on. She would bend her knee and arch those ballerina feet into the toes of the pantyhose, first one leg and then the other, and pull them up slowly over her calves—still so muscular—and then past her knees, giving them a real tug to make them smooth around the roundness of her thighs and then all the way up to her waist so that they were tight and snug all over, finally turning and looking behind her in the mirror to make sure that they were straight. How could I forget Annie Baron?

Like me, she was a Californian. Her father was a San Francisco lawyer who had built himself a big house in Los Altos Hills, overlooking the bay. Somehow the money and privilege hadn't spoiled her. It must have been the ballet, which gave her a focus other than clothes and boys and cliques. I never knew anyone who could work harder than Annie. Like so many smart women, she didn't really know how to cut corners. She had to do it the right way. She arrived at Stanford eager, unspoiled, ready for life.

If ballet was her first love, I was her second. She came to journalism only later, when she began to realize that she was sharing me with my other obsessive passion, which was newspapering. It became something of a *ménage à trois*. We would go to bars where people like David Halberstam and Norman Mailer supposedly hung out, and if any such luminaries ever showed up, we would take turns ingratiating ourselves with them. She was better at it, obviously; she was a beautiful woman. But she always went home with me.

I saw her at a book party at Bob Marcus's house, a few weeks after I started my new job. She looked lovely, as always, with those long dancer's legs and flirtatious journalist's eyes. But we both felt awkward. It's never easy for people who have been intimate to carry on an ordinary conversation, but we tried. It was like learning to talk again. She asked me what Paris had been like, and I gave her a long explanation, centering on the Maurice Costa story. She listened for a while, and then began to get bored. She didn't know anything about political corruption in France. It was an abstraction, far away.

"Don't be so *serious,* Eric," she said finally. "You sound like the national security adviser. Now that you're back home, you need to have *fun.* Live a little. Tell me something delicious and unserious."

"Like what?" I wanted to please her.

"I don't know." She gave me coy look. "Like who you're sleeping with. Not one of the copy aides, I hope. They're not worthy of you."

"No copy aides," I said. That wasn't quite true. I had asked one of the copy aides out the first week I was home, but that was purely recreational. "How about you?"

"Nobody in *particular,*" she said. She gave me a kiss and wandered off to talk to a cabinet member. I wasn't offended that she had asked about my sex life, or that she had admonished me to have more fun. It seemed possible that she was suggesting I have fun with *her,* which remained an attractive idea, even after so many years and so much scar tissue.

I thought about Annie often after that first encounter, but I didn't call her. It was too complicated. You don't put a relationship like that back together by choice. It has to be a compulsion, forced on both of you by circumstances you can't control.

10

I had been back in the bureau for about five months when I received a letter from Rupert Cohen. We had not communicated in any way since our brief contact in Paris. His letter was peculiar: very formal, carefully phrased, with no return address. It read as follows:

January 8, 1996

Dear Mr. Truell:

As you may recall, we met in May 1994 in Paris. You were seeking information, and I attempted to be helpful. While that puts you under no obligation to me, I hope you will consider this request for help.

I have served the U.S. government for more than a decade. What prompts this letter is that I have finally answered a question I was mulling over at the time we met, but did not share with you; namely, should one stay in government service when one is convinced that the ship is sinking? I have now answered that question in the negative. My organization, not in good shape when I joined, is in the process of imploding, collapsing due to its mediocrity.

Simply put, we have ceased to exist as a serious organization. We actually died, I think, quite a long time ago, but the enemy behind the Berlin Wall kept us going. It excused and camouflaged our gross inadequacies.

Here is my request: As I consider alternative areas of employment, I am drawn to your line of work. I think I am a good reporter. Gathering accurate information is, obviously, essential to what I do now—or would be doing, if I worked for a competent organization. I would like to get my foot in the journalistic door, but I don't know how. Can I presume on you for advice?

Would it be possible for someone like me to be hired by a serious newspaper or magazine? Will my employment history present an insuperable obstacle to finding work with a news organization? Is there any news organization that would find my government service an asset? If a staff job is impossible, what about freelance writing?

I realize that it may be difficult for you to answer these questions. And a response by you in any way would be an indulgence, given that we have spent so little time together. Still, I hope you might be willing to offer some help. I would be greatly indebted for any advice given. I would also be eager to share with you in more detail my thoughts about the disintegration of the concern where I currently work.

I will be in Washington in late January. I will give you a call then, in the hope that we might meet for a drink.

Sincerely,
Rupert G. Cohen

I read the letter several times over, trying to see the man in the fuzzy sweater between the lines of type. He was back, eighteen months after his invisible baton pass—and he was looking for a job! I felt that I had gotten lucky again. Out of nowhere, a serving CIA officer was asking me for help, and offering to talk about the inner workings of the agency. Things like that don't normally happen to reporters. And I was confident, as we always are at the beginning of an encounter with a source, that I was in control. Rupert Cohen might hope to use me to get a job, but I would use him to get a story. The letter promised something else. I would have a chance, at last, to resolve the question that had nibbled at me since the day I received the page of Special Intelligence: Had I been set up?

I folded the letter and put it back into the manila envelope. My new desk was neat and clean. The blank cards were waiting on my Rolodex like empty seats on a Ferris wheel; my new Federal Directory was still unmarked and ready for action. My whole world had been white. And then this spasm of color.

The presidential campaign was cranking up at the time I received Cohen's letter, and the Washington bureau was engaged in its quadrennial ritual of dissecting the candidates. I had been assigned to profile Senator James Abelard, a Pennsylvania Republican and a dark horse for the nomination. Because I was still new to Washington, I told the bureau chief I would like a partner and proposed my friend George Dirk. He was a good investigator, and it was a way of tossing him a bone. Marcus wasn't pleased—Dirk wasn't on his first team—but he agreed.

I wandered over to Dirk's messy cubicle a half hour after I received Rupert Cohen's letter. I wanted to share the news of my mysterious CIA correspondent. That is one of the characteristic traits of reporters—our inability to keep secrets for very long. It's why so many people in my business think Deep Throat doesn't really exist. If he were a single real person—rather than a composite—the secret would have been blown long ago.

Dirk was a presence, even when banished to the far corner of the bureau. He was a large man with a shock of white hair. As I approached he had his feet up on the desk and was talking conspiratorially with someone on the telephone. Dirk had many of these informants around town. Congressional aides, disgraced former officials, other reporters with information to trade that they couldn't get into their own publications, people with various axes to grind. Nobody knew who these sources were, but I had always suspected they must be mirror images of Dirk: people who felt, for one reason or another, that their careers had been sidetracked by malign powers and were determined to exact revenge. It was a network of the embittered. When Dirk saw me coming, he quickly said into the phone, "Gotta go, call you back," and gave me a guilty grin.

"I need to talk to you, Dirk," I said as humbly as I could. "Let's get a drink tonight after work."

"You must be joking. *Nobody* has a drink after work. Maybe they still do that in Paris, but here in our nation's capital it's not done. Surely you meant to say: Dirk, let's go to the health club. Or, Dirk, let's go have a papaya-juice cocktail at that swell new vegetarian restaurant."

But I prevailed on him. It was the middle of the afternoon, but that didn't matter. Neither of us had to file that night. We headed for Dirk's favorite spot, a dank, smoky hideaway called the Club Down Under that was in the basement of our building. Its proximity to the bureau added to Dirk's sense of illicit pleasure, and there was little risk of discovery—it was so dark that Bob Marcus could be sitting at the next table and you wouldn't know it.

"I got an interesting letter today," I said as we began quaffing our beers.

Dirk was instantly on guard. "Who from?" he asked darkly. Good news from anyone reminded him of his own failures, and made him depressed.

"From a CIA guy."

Dirk's face fell further. His first reaction, inevitably, was jealousy. What new opportunity did I have that he didn't?

"So what did the CIA guy want?" Dirk asked. That was another strange thing about him: however much he disliked news about his colleagues' success, he insisted on hearing all the details—almost like a form of ritual self-flagellation. It occurred to me that the more I told him, the more intensely unhappy he would become, so I began to backtrack.

"Not that much," I answered. "I met him a while ago. I think he's an analyst. He's looking for a job."

That gentle lie seemed to ease Dirk's anxieties. Lots of people knew CIA analysts; even Dirk knew a few. I decided to drop the subject. Talking about my CIA source would be a form of torture for Dirk.

"Listen," I said, changing gears, "we should talk about Abelard. I don't understand what we're supposed to do in these campaign profiles."

"Sure." He brightened. The notion that I needed help on something seemed to put him in a better mood.

"What are we looking for?" I asked. That question had, in fact, been bothering me ever since I got the assignment. Everything that was publicly available about Abelard suggested that he was a careful, thoughtful man. He was a relic of the old days; if the Council on Foreign Relations had been nominating a candidate, it would have been James Abelard.

"Dirt. Whatever we can find, in whatever hidden nooks and crannies of his life we can penetrate. And you know what? We'll succeed. Because every human being on this planet has done something wrong at some point in his life. Something he's ashamed of, embarrassed about, hoped nobody would ever discover. Something he thought the veil of privacy would surely cover. But we'll find it and strip it away. Because that's what we *do*. We are the dirt bags, into which the dirt is placed."

The level of Dirk's self-disgust had risen from what I remembered. "You need to see a shrink," I said. "Meanwhile, how do we find out about Abelard? Who should we talk to?"

"Anyone who hates him. Anyone who has a grudge against him. Anyone who has run against him and lost. His enemies, basically. And then we'll talk to his friends, to make sure the piece is *balanced*."

I shook my head. "You really are sick, Dirk. What's the matter with you?"

"I'm in a bad mood. I have this feeling I'm about to be *fired*. A human offering to appease the god of rising newsprint prices. You'd be in a bad mood, too, if you thought you were about to be fired."

"Don't be ridiculous. Nobody ever gets fired at the *Mirror*."

"That was in the old days, Eric. Things have changed. I had a very negative performance review last year. First time, ever. They're building a paper trail. They're going to get me. It's obvious. If you weren't such an ass-kisser, you would have noticed how the paper is changing."

"Fuck you, Dirk."

"I'm sorry." He was instantly apologetic when he saw that he had wounded me. "I shouldn't have said that. I'm really sorry." That was another thing about Dirk. Although he adopted the tough-guy style, he was basically a pussycat. A sort of Cowardly Lion of an investigative reporter. I decided to let it slide.

"What about Abelard?" I said. "We need to divide up the reporting."

"I'll talk to his enemies. You talk to his friends. How's that?"

"Come on, Dirk! Get serious. How about this: You do Abelard's finances—campaign contributions, financial disclosure forms, trips, honoraria, all that stuff. I'll do his personal life—who he is, what he believes, marriage, kids. And we'll split his legislative record. You do the domestic side, I'll do foreign. He used to be vice chairman of the Intelligence Committee. How's that sound?"

"Fine, fine," he said. "Don't take this the wrong way, Eric. But you sound like an editor."

11

What surprised me most about Washington was how little it was. I had become accustomed over the previous decade to capitals built on an overwhelming scale: to Hong Kong, so dense with people that they had to build skyscrapers up the sides of mountains to house them all; to Paris, built over the centuries to intimidate France and the world with its power and beauty; to Beirut, which even after ten years of civil war still had the raw power of a teeming, towering city. Washington, by comparison, was a toy town. It was a low-slung city of ornamental boxes, all essentially the same when you stripped away the stone pediments and Ionic columns, all fixed at the same height. No wonder our political culture was so uniform: it was spawned in this small city, in identical rooms in identical buildings.

The nicest thing about this little city was that I could walk to work. It took about fifteen minutes, when there was no snow, and afforded a passage through the different compartments of Washington. I would leave my apartment on California Street and set off through the comfortable old-money neighborhood of Kalorama. Several dozen of the city's leading diplomats resided here. The French ambassador lived in a mansion on Kalorama Road that backed onto the expanse of Rock Creek Park; it is said that when Charles de Gaulle visited once, he looked out from the terrace over the hundreds of acres of woodlands, which he assumed to be the property of France, and congratulated his host: "You have done well, my ambassador." The Syrian ambassador's residence on Wyoming Street was a different story entirely. It was small and dilapidated, with a big fence and a big flag and little else to recommend it. Somehow they had managed to bring the ambiance of official Damascus to Washington.

I would walk east from my building to Connecticut Avenue and the curved white façade of the Washington Hilton, famous, for those who cared, as the place where John Hinckley shot and almost killed Ronald Reagan. As Connecticut Avenue sloped south toward the White House, the urban landscape would quickly become more exotic: a strip joint on the corner of Florida Avenue, a boutique catering to leather fetishists another block down; a gay bookstore; the local headquarters of the Church of Scientology; and every few doors, a coffee bar to feed the city's caffeine addiction. Nearing Dupont Circle, I would see the signs of the city's urban pathology: homeless junkies and winos with their hands outstretched, even on the coldest days of winter; clusters of unemployed men sitting in the park, doing nothing, every day of the year; inhabitants of the city's underground economy—black men dressed in bicycle shorts, Latino men in construction boots and overalls. That was the shock, coming home from abroad: the misery and disarray of urban America. In the decade I had been away something in the fabric of the country had dissolved. America wasn't one country anymore—it was two, or a dozen, or a thousand. The extremes of wealth and color and caste felt more like Cairo or Johannesburg than any American city I remembered.

And then, below Dupont Circle, I would arrive at last at my destination, the precinct of the prosperous parasites: the lawyers and lobbyists, the trade associations, the national federations and international unions. And the journalists, God bless us, housed in the velvet cages that were the Washington bureaus of the nation's newspapers and magazines. In this neighborhood the restaurants were French and Italian; the parking lots charged ten dollars a day, and the jewelry stores gave you a careful look before buzzing open the door. But the panhandlers were here, too, sleeping in the doorways of the office buildings, charging what amounted to a tax on the city's indifference. Each morning it was the same trip, and after a few weeks it became a routine. I would pass through my air locks and arrive at the office and wait for something to happen. That was the essential, inescapable passivity of our trade. We waited—for the president to make a speech, for Congress to pass a bill, for a terrorist to plant a bomb, for *something* to happen so that we could write about it. And something always did.

My phone rang one cold, overcast morning in mid-January. I was at my desk, reading through a stack of adulatory press clips about Senator Abelard and wondering how Dirk and I were going to write anything interesting. When I picked up the phone I heard a strange, eager voice at the other end. "*Buongiorno, magnifico!* Did you get my letter?"

I had to think a moment—what letter?—before remembering Rupert Cohen's job query. My fish was on the line. "You're early," I said. "I thought you wouldn't be in Washington for another week."

"Tradecraft!" he said. "Never stick to the initial timetable. Change it before the meeting. Makes it harder to arrange surveillance."

"I'll remember that." I couldn't tell whether he was serious or not. "I'm glad you called. I did get your letter, and I'd be happy to meet with you. When would you like to get together?"

"Tonight. Seven-thirty."

"Okay," I said. Actually, it wasn't okay. I had a date to go to the movies with a woman who worked at CNN, but she could wait. "Where?"

"Adams-Morgan. Meet me at the Belmont Kitchen, on the corner of Eighteenth and Belmont."

"Fine," I said. "I'll see you there."

"Hold on, *dottore,* you didn't ask for the recognition code."

"I don't need one. I already know what you look like."

"You *always* need a recognition code. If you see a guy who looks like me in the Belmont Kitchen, ask him: 'What built Venice?' "

"Okay. And what's the answer?"

"*Fear.* I will answer that what built Venice was fear. That's why they constructed that magnificent city on a swampy island in the midst of a lagoon. Because they were so *afraid* of the barbarians on the land, who were ravaging all the other settlements on the Lombardy plain. So when I answer 'Fear,' you'll know it's me."

The Belmont Kitchen was a cozy, brick-walled café in one of Washington's few genuinely multiracial neighborhoods. It was the sort of place where people still wore berets and talked about jazz musicians. Rupert was sitting at a table in the back. The fuzzy black sweater was gone. He was wearing a blue denim work shirt and a red striped tie that looked as if it had come from Brooks Brothers. He was smoking a Camel cigarette. Since our last meeting he had grown a goatee. Otherwise, he was unchanged.

"So," I said tentatively, trying to play my role as dictated, "what built Venice?"

"Beats the shit out of me." He shook his head in wonder. "You reporters take everything so *seriously.*"

We sat down, and he called over the waitress. He looked like such a goofball, I half expected him to take out a bong and light up. But he asked for a vodka martini and insisted that I have one, too.

"You dressed up for the occasion," I said, pointing to his tie. The first time we met, he had worn that loopy black sweater and the black leather jacket. That wasn't the only difference in our interaction. Before, I had been the needy one; now, it was him.

"I'm trying to look like a journalist. What do you think?"

"You certainly don't look like a spy."

"Shhh!" said Cohen. He was looking past me to the door. A couple had just entered the restaurant—a black man with a knit cap covering a long coil of dreadlocks and a white woman who looked vaguely like Joni Mitchell. He stared at them curiously and then shook his head.

"You know what I like about this neighborhood?" he said. "It's so easy to spot surveillance. At the end of my field tradecraft course we had an exercise in D.C. to practice our surveillance detection runs. The test was whether you could identify the FBI team that had been assigned to follow you. But they had one rule. You weren't allowed to go north of Dupont Circle into Adams-Morgan. They figured that anyone from the bureau would stick out like an Eskimo in Brazil."

The martinis arrived, along with a basket of pretzel sticks. I raised my glass in Rupert's direction. "To successful detection of surveillance," I said.

"That was back in the mid-eighties, when it was still fun," he continued. "We still had the Soviets to chase. We still had Bill Casey around—I know you journalists all hated him but you were wrong about that, he was actually a *peach*—and PNINFINITE had not yet become totally obsessed with trying to stay afloat."

"Sorry, but what's PNINFINITE?"

"That was the organization's cryptonym for itself, until a few weeks ago. Before that, we called ourselves PNWORLD. Our code names demonstrated our hubris. We were *convinced* we were all-powerful. Now we're not so sure. They've just changed the crypt to NWBOLTON. Isn't that pathetic? From PNINFINITE to NWBOLTON in the blink of an eye."

Why was he telling me this? I didn't understand. I had been with Cohen for fifteen minutes and he was already divulging CIA cryptonyms. I repeated the three names to myself, in hopes of committing them to memory.

"You can write them down," he said with a wink. "I don't care. All that stuff is a joke."

Despite his offer, I kept my pen in my pocket. It was too early. I was still trying to figure him out. He looked like a hippie, he loved Bill Casey, and he seemed willing to tell me almost anything.

"That's why I want to be a journalist," he said softly, as if *this* was his real secret. "My current place of employment is in ruins. I have tried in my own modest ways to change it from within, but it is *im*-possible. The problem is mediocrity and stupidity, shielded by secrecy. Most of my colleagues are dumb as *posts*. In Rome I was the only member of the station who could read or speak Italian. The COS and the DCOS didn't read Italian newspapers, had never been to an Italian's house for dinner, could not describe any period in Italian history with confidence. I wish they were exceptions, but they're typical of the organization. These people are piston heads, really. There is no point trying to reform LA. The best solution is to blow it up. Or just quit."

"What's LA?"

"Liars Anonymous. That's my private code name for the organization. Makes it easier talking on the phone."

"And you really want to abolish it?"

"Yes, why not? Start over from scratch. Smaller, smarter, tougher. The current establishment is a stubborn but terminal cancer patient. Pull the plug! It does more harm than good. It wastes money. It perpetuates fraud. It is a product of the cold war, the bureaucratic repository of fifty years of secrecy. Sure, truth occasionally pops out—we're Americans, after all, we can't lie *all* the time. But it's a surreal world. You can't understand how bad it is, because you've never experienced it. But trust me. No other U.S. government agency is as sick inside. As exhausted by having repulsively mediocre men proclaim that the organization is more elite than Harvard, which they say to every Career Trainee class, *every* year—never mind the Howard case, and the Ames case, and a dozen other cases you don't know about. The place is *built* on lies. You cannot repair it. The Old Guard will beat you. They control personnel, they control the IG's office. They control SGSWIRL—"

"Wait! What's SGSWIRL?"

"The polygraph. And don't believe all that crap about how useless it is. With nice, middle-class Americans like the people who join the organization, it's *fabulous*. A good polygrapher can get you so nervous you're ready to confess anything. One of my worthy colleagues recently confessed to making love to a *dog*, for heaven's sake. It creates pressure, and under pressure Americans lose their minds. That's why the polygraph doesn't work with Italians, Latin Americans, Middle Easterners—because they're *always* out of their minds, bouncing back and forth between fact and fiction, they don't really register the difference. But with us, it's a weapon. By the way, do you know one of the first questions they always ask? Hmmmm? They ask: 'When did you last have contact with a journalist?' "

That seemed a pointed reminder of the risks he was taking in meeting with me. "Have you quit yet?" I wondered.

"Not yet. A few more months. I have to sign all kinds of papers. So, please, don't write anything about me. I'm vulnerable. The Brahmins would *not* be pleased to know that I was talking to a member of the press. My comments are solely for your edification. Your personal intellectual development."

"Fair enough." I was disappointed, but I could wait. He was worth the trouble. "Let's talk about your new career," I said. "What makes you think you want to be a journalist?"

"Because you get paid better for your mendacity than we do. *And,* you can get on those great TV talk shows." He smiled and stroked his goatee. "No, seriously, I want to be a journalist because I would be *fucking* good at it. Isn't that the way you people talk? *God damn fucking good!* I'm smart, I'm inquisitive, and I'm basically an anarchist. I like to cause trouble. Are those not the essential qualities of a journalist?"

"They're useful, especially when you're twenty-two and just out of college. But you have one rather large liability."

"What's that?" He was looking at me, wide-eyed, as if he could not imagine that he had any drawbacks whatsoever.

How to answer? I wanted to keep him on the line, but I couldn't mislead him. "You have spent the last ten years working for the CIA, Rupert. For most newspapers, that's a fatal flaw."

"Why? It's not as if I'm trying to keep it a secret. And I won't be maintaining any continuing relationship with the organization. Quite the opposite. I *hate* LA. So what's the problem."

"The problem is that, in the eyes of many editors, you are contaminated by your former employment. Just as they wouldn't hire an ex–bank robber to run a bank, they won't hire an ex-spy to be a reporter."

"I don't see the analogy. I really don't."

"I'm not saying I agree with them. I'm just trying to explain how most editors would probably react to you."

"Are you sure? I would be such a *good* reporter."

"I'll check, if you like. I'll run the idea by my bureau chief, without mentioning your name, and see how he reacts. How would that be?"

"*Splendid!* You are most generous. I cannot ask for more than that."

He ordered another martini, while I continued nursing the first. As he got drunker Rupert busied himself constructing a miniature log cabin with the pretzel sticks. He asked me about my job, now that I was back in Washington. I tried to explain what a 'special projects reporter' did, which only made him salivate more at the prospect of being a journalist and doing essentially whatever you wanted. I waited until he was thoroughly bombed before asking the question that had been bothering me since that afternoon in Paris when I received the sheet of paper that had allowed me to vaporize the career of a French cabinet minister.

"I have a question for you, Rupert, if you don't mind. Why did you send me that page of Special Intelligence in Paris? Were you trying to nail Costa?"

"I was trying to do you a favor. You wanted something, so I got it for you. It worked. He resigned. Next question." He went back to his pretzel logs.

"Seriously," I said. "I want to know. Was that an agency operation? What was going on?"

"It's a long time ago. I'm too drunk to explain it now."

"Stop jerking me around! I want the truth. Were you using me in an operation against the French?"

"Calm down, boy. Whoa! It wasn't a covert operation. That would have required a 'finding' and notification of Congress, and it would never, *ever*, have been approved. No, this was something different. It was informal, freelance. It was *fun*. It didn't happen, officially. So relax."

"You mean you just did it on your own? I can't believe that. Why would you do that?"

"Because I'm a crazy motherfucker, that's why. And I like the press. That day I talked to you in Paris was the first time I realized I wanted to be a reporter—*had* to be a reporter. It was my day of destiny. So it seemed only right to help you out."

"And nobody else in the agency knew what you were doing?"

"I'm not *that* crazy. Of course someone knew. Rubino sent me to see you, for God's sake. But he didn't give me a script. And he certainly didn't order me to give you the goods on Costa. That would have been *illegal*. He simply facilitated my decisions. Actually, I like to think of myself as a co-author on that story. I should have shared the byline."

He had explained it, but he hadn't, either. It was all in that murky area where Cohen liked to operate. I tried one last time to get an answer. "Why me?" I asked. "Why did you work with me?"

"Hey, lighten up! Stop asking so many questions. Have another drink. No wonder journalists are so boring. They never stop working."

I retreated. We could finish the conversation about Paris another time. And I had one more piece of business to conduct. As we were getting ready to leave, I told Rupert I was working on a profile of Senator James Abelard for a series we were doing on the presidential candidates.

"Do you know any interesting stuff about Abelard?" I asked. "So far, all I can find is people who love him." It was a throwaway. I had been asking everyone I met the same question that week. Cohen cocked his head. A sly look came over his face, as if he sensed an opportunity.

"What sort of *stuff* did you have in mind?"

"Personal, political, foreign policy. Anything that explains who he really is and whether he would make a good president."

"Let me see what I can do," he said with a wink. "Perhaps I can be of some assistance."

"Much obliged. Meanwhile, I'll talk to the bureau chief about you. Call me in a couple of days, and I'll tell you what he says."

When we were out in the street, Cohen put his arm on my shoulder. "In my soon-to-be-former line of work, there comes a time in the recruitment of an agent when you finally pop the question. We like to joke that there are three possible answers: 'Yes,' 'Fuck no!' and 'I'll call you when I get to New York.' "

I laughed, but he still had his hand on my shoulder. He wasn't smiling.

"I'm not kidding about wanting to be a journalist. I *really* mean it. So please don't play games with me. If the answer at the *Mirror* is no, don't say you'll call me when you get to New York. That would piss me off. Just tell me no. Because one way or another, this is going to work out."

12

❖

The next morning I strolled up the Corridor of the Gods to Bob Marcus's office. He was haranguing one of the copy aides about forgetting to put paper in the fax machine, and she looked as if she was about to cry. "We missed an hour's worth of incoming faxes!" he roared. "God only knows what people tried to send us!" Marcus was a stickler for details like that. He made up for his problems on the big things by overdoing the little things.

"I'll come back," I said. This didn't look like the right time, somehow.

"No," he said, glowering one last time at the terrified copy aide. "We're done. Come in, Eric. What's on your mind?" His tone had suddenly brightened to its normal managerial shade of off-white.

"I hate to bother you," I said, "but I have a question. Someone I know—a source, actually—asked me about getting a job in journalism. For the last ten years he has worked at the CIA. And he wonders if there's any way that a newspaper like ours would ever hire him as a reporter."

"What part of the CIA did he work in?"

"Operations."

"And he wants to work for *us*? For the *Mirror*?"

"Yes, or a newspaper like us. I told him I thought it was a long shot. But I wanted to check with you."

Marcus shook his head, as if he was disappointed I would even ask the question. "It's a total nonstarter. You should know that."

"Well, I thought so. But you never know."

"Totally impossible. The two professions are like oil and water. They should never, ever, mix. Never. How did you meet this guy, anyway?"

"Oh, you know, overseas. You meet a lot of people. He helped me on something once. Anyway, I'll tell him we're not the answer to his job search." I stood up to leave.

"You're going to talk to him again?"

"Sure. I promised I would tell him whether he would have any shot at the *Mirror.*"

"Well, be careful, Eric. These people are poison." He shook his head again. He was making me feel bad for even knowing Cohen. "You know, it's good you came home when you did. Stay out in the field too long and you get flaky. You stop drawing clear lines. That's probably why Weiss wants you to become an editor. He wants you to come up to New York and talk about it, by the way, when you have a chance. I told him I thought it was a good idea. You'd get the discipline and seasoning that come from taking responsibility for others."

"Adulthood," I said, backing toward the door. "What a concept!" That was the second time someone had told me Weiss wanted me to be an editor. It was obvious that I was in Weiss's gravitational force, being pulled slowly toward him.

That night, when I got home to my apartment on California Street, I found an unstamped letter waiting in my mailbox. It was printed on plain white paper, but you could see the smile on the page like an invisible watermark.

Dear Eric:

I have to leave unexpectedly today for a week with the Flying Squad, so I must postpone our next career counseling session. In the meantime, I have a piece of information you may find useful.

I believe the record will confirm (if such record can be found) that James Abelard was hospitalized for depression in 1982, and that he is currently taking a rather *heavy-duty* antidepressant medication. Whether this fact is worth sharing with the reading public, I leave to your discretion.

Your humble servant,
Brother John of Ragusa

My friends and I used to ask ourselves when we were starting out in journalism whether there was anything we wouldn't do for a story. After we ruled out things that were flagrantly, demonstrably illegal, it was hard for us to come up with things we wouldn't at least consider. Finally one of my friends asked, "Suppose somebody said you could have a great story, but you would have to eat a shit sandwich to get it." Most of us said we'd never do it, the idea was disgusting. But eventually one guy asked the essential question: How good was the story? And as we began imagining the great, prize-winning stories that might tempt us, we realized that at some level of temptation every one of us would eat the shit sandwich. That became, in my mind, one of the definitions of who were: we were the people who would do anything to get a story. For many years, I thought it was a measure of how much we loved our profession.

That long-ago discussion fell into my mind that evening, as I considered what to do about Rupert's letter. Journalistically, the right thing to do was obviously to try to confirm the information. Abelard was running for president. The possibility that he had serious psychological problems requiring medication was relevant information for voters in judging his fitness for office. But on a personal and emotional level I was uncomfortable at the prospect of reporting and publishing such information. Even a politician had a right to some privacy, especially where there was no evidence that his public performance had suffered. I was also aware that this was the second time I had received a zinger like this from Rupert Cohen. It made me nervous.

But that was all abstract, talk-show stuff. I knew very well what I would do in practice. I would "report the story out," as we like to say in the business. I would find out if Rupert's tip was true, and sort out the moral issues later. Actually, I wouldn't even do that. I would let my editors sort out the moral issues. I wondered whether I should tell Dirk or the bureau chief and decided: Not yet. I wanted to control the information a little longer.

But how to pursue the story? If I called people in Abelard's office, they would immediately push the panic button and tell the senator and his campaign manager. Everybody would go to general quarters and I would have to admit that I didn't yet have evidence of anything. So that approach made no sense. I could try some of Abelard's old friends in Pennsylvania, or people who had worked for him at the company he had founded in Erie. But that would run the same risk of premature disclosure. The answer, inevitably, was to do just what Dirk had cynically suggested back at the Club Down Under. I should talk to Abelard's enemies—specifically, the people who had run against him. If Cohen's tip had any truth, they might know about it.

Abelard's most recent reelection race had been in 1992, against a Democratic state senator named Hap Winstead, and the *Mirror*'s news-retrieval system quickly found a story that identified Winstead's campaign manager. He was a Pittsburgh lawyer named Tom DeFazio.

So I called Mr. DeFazio at his law office and told his secretary that I was a reporter for *The New York Mirror*. I have noticed over the years that almost anyone will take your call if you identify yourself that way. I don't know if it's vanity, or curiosity, or perhaps even a sense of civic responsibility. But it's touching—especially since in many cases these folks would be wiser to hang up.

DeFazio came on the line. "What can I do for you, Mr. Truell?" he asked. "You going after me, or somebody else?" He was a comedian, a regular guy.

I explained that I was working on a profile of Abelard and needed to ask about a sensitive matter.

"How sensitive is it?"

He wanted to know, so I told him. "It concerns Senator Abelard's medical history. His mental health."

"Oh, Christ!" he said. "I know what this is. The depression thing, right?"

I tapped gently on the keys of my computer, so he wouldn't hear me taking notes. It was so easy, really. You asked questions, and people told you things.

DeFazio paused a moment, realizing the gravity of what he had just said. "You aren't going to *run* that shit, are you?"

"I don't know," I answered honestly. "I'm just trying to figure out what the facts are. The newspaper will decide later what to run. I take it you have some information about his medical history."

"Look, we ran against the guy. We picked up a lot of stuff we never used. What was the point? We were going to lose. Why make Hap look like a prick? By the way, this is all off the record."

"Of course," I said. "Listen, it happens that I'm going to be in Pittsburgh tomorrow. I was wondering if I could come see you." When he said yes, I called the travel agent and booked a flight. Dirk was unhappy that I was going on a reporting trip without taking him along, but I said if I got anything good, I would share it with him.

DeFazio met me at a restaurant called the Tin Angel on Mount Washington. It was across from downtown Pittsburgh and overlooked the point where the Monongahela and Allegheny Rivers meet to form the Ohio. He was as ordinary-looking a man as you could hope to find, with a potbelly and dark curly hair that was disappearing on top. He stood up uncomfortably when I introduced myself. A manila envelope was sitting on the table next to him.

The lawyer talked plainly, chug-chug-chug, moving slowly and deliberately like the coal barges plying the river below us. He explained that like most campaigns of the 1990s, Winstead's had formed an opposition research team to gather negative information about the opposing candidate. The group had interviewed a number of Abelard's former staff people, and one of these former staffers had mentioned a 1982 incident.

"Tell me about it," I said. I wasn't taking any notes, fearing that would scare him off.

"Abelard had been in the Senate only a year. He was a very hot ticket. The Reagan people all loved him. And then something happened. The senator went away for a long vacation, and people in his office were whispering that he'd had some kind of breakdown. That was all this staff guy knew. So we asked other people."

"What people?"

"People who know things. The state police. A guy we knew at the FBI. Someone at the state agency that licenses pharmacists and mental hospitals."

"What did you find out?"

"This." He pushed the manila folder across the table. I opened it. Inside were two sheets of paper. The first was a photocopy of a prescription for an antidepressant, filed with a pharmacy in Erie. The space usually provided for the patient's name was blank. The name of the prescribing doctor was Morris Soderberg, in Pittsburgh. I looked quizzically at DeFazio.

"It's his," he said. "Don't ask how we know. We know."

The second piece of paper simply had the words "Sewickley Institute" and an address. I pushed it back toward DeFazio to interpret.

"It's a small, private clinic outside Pittsburgh. It's where the senator went in 1982."

I nodded. Looking at these most personal artifacts of a man's private life, I felt a dampness. My skin was clammy. My throat was clogged. I put the papers into my briefcase.

"What are you going to do with that stuff?" he asked quietly.

"Talk to people. Find out if it's true."

"What are you going to do then? Because I'm telling you, it's true."

"I don't know. As my executive editor likes to say, we'll jump off that bridge when we get to it. Tell me again: Why didn't you use this information in the campaign?" I wanted to know: What made him different? Why hadn't he eaten the shit sandwich?

DeFazio shook his head. "Come on. You know why. It was too dirty. And we were running so far behind, we were going to lose. Why be an asshole? I have to live in this town after the election is over. I never even told Winstead."

"Why not?" I asked.

"Because he might have wanted to use it. And I knew we shouldn't."

"Then why are you giving it to me?"

"Because he's running for president now, and it seems different. And because you're from the *Mirror,* which is a serious newspaper, and I figure you won't run a story unless it's the right thing to do."

I called Dr. Soderberg that afternoon. He was with a patient, but when I called back an hour later, he answered the phone. I gave him a spiel about how I was from *The New York Mirror* and it was an emergency and I would be in Pittsburgh for only a few hours. He asked me what I wanted to talk about, and I said I couldn't discuss it over the phone. I had to see him in person. That was really just a way to get my foot in the door, but he apparently regarded it as a positive sign of discretion, because he told me to come to his office at 6:00 that evening.

The address was in an upscale part of Pittsburgh called Shadyside, where the yuppies liked to live. The psychiatrist's office adjoined his home. I sat in the small waiting room, reading an old *National Geographic,* until his last patient emerged from behind the closed door. She was clutching a tissue in her hand. When she saw me, she must have assumed I was another patient because she gave me a faint, heartsick smile. Dr. Soderberg extended his hand. He was a thin, long-limbed man in his fifties whose face revealed nothing except weariness.

"So here you are, Mr. Truell," he said, leading me into his sitting room. There were two easy chairs and a couch. His chair had a small footrest in front of it. He motioned for me to sit in the other chair. "Perhaps now you can tell me what is on your mind."

"I want to ask you about Senator Abelard."

There was a barely perceptible tremor on his face, at the edges of his eyes and mouth. It was almost as if he had winced, with physical pain. "And what would you like to ask me about Senator Abelard?"

"About his *treatment*." It was hard to say it, but not so hard that the words didn't come. "I have been told that you treated him for depression. I have been told that he was hospitalized in 1982 at the Sewickley Institute. I have been told that he continues to take medication for depression."

Dr. Soderberg shook his head. He looked so profoundly disappointed in me, in my newspaper, in a world in which we could exist. "Why are you asking me these questions? You know I cannot answer."

"Because Senator Abelard is running for president," I said. The psychiatrist had probably heard every rationalization and self-delusion there was, but I offered him mine. "In choosing to run for president, Senator Abelard has invited scrutiny from the news media. The public has a right to know about the medical history of someone who wants to be president. Those are the rules of the game."

"Get out of my office," the psychiatrist said.

I rose from my chair. He wasn't kidding. I had one last shot. Now it was my turn to shake my head sadly, just as he had a few moments before.

"Dr. Soderberg, you know far better than I do that depression is an illness, which can be treated. I have to tell our readers about Senator Abelard's treatment for depression, just as I would have to report about a cancer operation or heart bypass surgery. It's part of his record, not a horrible secret to be concealed or lied about. Honestly, Doctor, your refusal to talk with me only reinforces the shame and stigmatization that surrounds mental illness. I think that's wrong."

He looked at me and blinked. He wanted to believe that I was sincere.

"I understand what you are saying," he said softly. "But I cannot discuss any issues involving someone who might be a patient—or might not be a patient. It would be a gross breach of ethics. So I must ask you again to leave, now."

I gave him my card. He didn't want to take it, so I left it on the chair.

As I drove back to the Pittsburgh airport I thought about the meeting with the doctor. It had aroused many feelings in me, but at that moment what I was really thinking about was a technical matter: Dr. Soderberg hadn't confirmed the story, but he hadn't denied it either, which was almost as useful.

13

❖

Arthur Bowman sat me down in his office, in the chair below the portrait of Benjamin Disraeli and next to the marble bust of the Roman historian Suetonius. I'd heard that Bowman and Senator Abelard were friends, and I had gone to see him the morning after I returned from Pittsburgh. I thought maybe he could suggest someone close to the senator to whom I could talk, but Bowman said he probably knew Abelard as well as anyone, so I should start with him.

Bowman's office was a collection of secret treasures. The walls displayed the trophies of a lifetime of reporting. Menus from the great restaurants of London and Paris, including one from Taillevent; framed invitations to the Royal Ascot Races and the Queen's Garden Party at Buckingham Palace; photos of Bowman playing tennis at the Cap d'Antibes and golf at Kapalua Bay on Maui; press cards issued by Third World militias, from Lebanon to Mozambique. And interspersed with these mementos were photographs of Bowman with the men and women who had been his companions on this promenade through the second half of the twentieth century: presidents and prime ministers, kings and emirs, Supreme Court justices and Hollywood movie stars. There was even a picture of him with Senator James Abelard.

I told Bowman what I was working on. It felt strange, enumerating the clinical details, so I talked quickly. I said two sources had told me that Abelard had been hospitalized for depression in 1982. I said I had a copy of one of the senator's prescriptions. The story felt solid, I told him, but I needed more evidence before I went with it. "Since you know him," I said, "maybe you have some ideas."

Bowman closed his eyes. They shut tight as a bank vault. His face was perfectly still, not a movement anywhere betraying any personal emotion.

"It's true," he said. "He was hospitalized, someplace outside Pittsburgh. It was very sad. I don't know anything about medication. But I do know that he got better. That was a relief to his friends. He was a basket case before."

I shouldn't have been surprised by Bowman's revelation, but I was. "You knew about his hospitalization back in 1982?" I said dumbly. "Did you tell anyone at the paper?"

"Probably not. Maybe I told Phil Sellinger. I can't remember. It wasn't a great secret among Abelard's friends."

I smiled and shook my head. It suddenly occurred to me how silly I had been, nosing around a psychiatrist's office in Pittsburgh to confirm something that one of my colleagues had known about for more than a decade. It wasn't my place, but I had to ask Bowman the obvious question.

"Why didn't you tell anyone at the paper, if you don't mind my asking?"

Bowman sighed and shook his head. He glanced absently at the photographs decorating the walls of his office. A lost world.

"Because it never occurred to me that we would publish a story about a man's emotional difficulties. Never imagined it. So, given my assumption that the paper wouldn't have any use for it, sharing the information would have been the worst kind of gossip. I don't do that. Not my style." He looked at me, sitting so earnestly across from him. "But I suppose it's different now."

"I've been wondering about that, myself. What's different, do you think?"

"Well, Jim is running for president, that's one thing. And standards have changed. We publish all kinds of things now that we wouldn't have dreamt of thirty years ago. We look at these things less as people and more as— what should I say? As journalists."

A wan smile came back on Bowman's face. "So, now that you know it's true, what are you going to do with it?"

What I was going to do with it, for starters, was tell Bob Marcus, the bureau chief. I gave him a brief memo, summarizing what I had. When he read it, he asked me to come see him right away. He had obviously gotten nervous, seeing it all in black and white. He held up the memo and whistled, a soft, sinking sound, like an incoming artillery shell. "This will destroy him," he said.

I told Marcus about my plans for more reporting and he said it all sounded fine, but that wasn't the issue right now. He had already crossed the threshold to assuming that the information was true, and was now worrying whether we should publish it. "We need to get Weiss in on this," he said. He had faxed a copy of my story memo to New York and was waiting for the executive editor to call. A few moments later the phone rang. Marcus put Weiss on the speaker.

"It's a killer if it's true," said the executive editor. "We run this, and James Abelard is revolverized, instantly, as a presidential candidate. Is Truell there? Let me talk to him for a minute."

"I'm here," I said.

"Help me out, Eric. You've looked these folks in the eye. What does your gut tell you? Is this for real?"

I thought a moment. "I think it's true. I think Abelard was hospitalized. I think he's on medication. The sources have no reason to lie to me. I'm not even sure they want us to run the story."

"Then why did they give it to us?" As far as Weiss was concerned, there were no innocent transactions. Every leaker had a motive.

"Because I asked them for information about Abelard, and they thought this might be relevant." I thought about Rupert. His self-proclaimed motivation was that he wanted a job. "In the case of one source, he may be hoping we'll do something for him down the road. But a lot of sources are like that, and I didn't promise him anything. I don't think we're being set up."

"Shit," said Weiss. "This is going to be a bitch. Have you talked to Abelard yet?"

"No," I answered. "But he may have heard something already from his shrink in Pittsburgh."

"Well, I think you have to call him right away. Go see him in his office. Today, if you can. I think you need to go over this stuff, point by point. Do the reporting. That's always the right answer, isn't it? Then we'll talk about it with the lawyers and figure out what to do."

"What should I say if Abelard asks whether we're going to run it?"

"Tell him we don't know. I mean, that's the truth. It makes us sound pathetic, but it's the truth. We won't really know whether to run it until we see how he reacts. He may admit it, say it's true, say he wants to strike a blow for open discussion of mental illness by going on the record. He may deny it, convince us our sources are full of shit. How can I say now whether we're going to run it? But we do need to talk to him right away."

"Okay," I said. "Will do."

"And we need to keep this quiet within the bureau. Please. If this gets out prematurely, we're screwed."

"We'll keep the lid on, Ed," said Marcus.

"Eric, this isn't going to be fun," said Weiss. "This is going to be pain. P-A-I-N. Remember, this is why we pay you the big bucks. So you'll have no compunction telling a beloved member of the United States Senate that *The New York Mirror* is about to blow his most private secrets. Do good. See if you can nail it."

The executive editor hung up.

I went to see Abelard the next day in his Senate office. It was the strangest, saddest encounter I had ever had as a reporter.

His press secretary, Art Snell, escorted me to Abelard's hideaway office, off the Senate floor. It was a grand room, fit for a congressional blue blood like Abelard, evoking all the history and power of the Capitol. There were heavy drapes that hung to the floor; gilt-edged mirrors on two walls; a handsome painting over the mantel of a Hudson River landscape; fine old couches and chairs that had been lent by a museum and, out the window, a magnificent view of the Mall. The beauty of the room added to my unease. I hadn't told Snell the subject, other than to say that I was writing a campaign profile of the senator, and Snell obviously expected it was going to be a normal interview, with questions about Abelard's positions on nuclear terrorism and welfare reform and tax policy. He kept mentioning position papers he wanted to send me.

Abelard received me graciously. He was a neat, compact man, much smaller in person than he seemed on television. He had close-cut gray hair, strong cheekbones and sharp blue eyes that suggested an agile mind. He sat motionless in his chair, waiting for me to begin. I had no idea, watching him, whether Dr. Soderberg had given him any advance warning. I wondered, looking at the clear, composed face, whether he was on medication.

I was very decorous, dressed as neatly as if I were applying for a job. I felt like a complete phony sitting there, pretending to be nice when I was about to go for his jugular, and I wanted to get it over with.

"Thank you for seeing me on short notice, Senator," I said. "I'm afraid that this isn't going to be an easy interview, for you or for me." I turned on my tape recorder and set it on the coffee table, between me and Abelard.

"What do you want to ask the senator about?" interjected the press secretary. "I thought you were doing a profile." He could already tell that something bad was about to happen, but he didn't know what it was.

I cleared my throat, swallowed, sat up straight in my chair. "Senator, I want to ask you about your treatment for clinical depression. I have three sources who have described your hospitalization in 1982. And I have a copy of your prescription for antidepressants."

Snell, the press secretary, was on his feet. "We're not answering your questions. This interview is over." His voice was shaking, he was so upset.

But Senator Abelard stayed in his seat. He was still calm, but the spark in his eyes had suddenly gone out and the color in his cheeks had drained. He had arrived—finally and suddenly—at the moment he had been dreading for fourteen years. He drew a deep breath, said nothing for a time, and then spoke.

"Please leave the room, Art. I wish to talk with Mr. Truell alone."

"Senator, that would not be wise." The press aide was in a panic now. "I can't let you do this." But his agitation only seemed to reinforce Abelard's calm.

"Please leave now, Art," he repeated. "If it will reassure you, I will ask Mr. Truell to treat our conversation as 'off the record.' Will you do that, Mr. Truell?"

"Yes," I said. I probably shouldn't have agreed to his request, technically speaking, but the tape recorder was still running, so I would at least have a record.

Snell retreated, closing the door behind him. Abelard looked me in the eye. It was a silent appeal.

"Mr. Truell," he said. "I would like to talk with you as a human being. Is that possible?"

I paused to consider his question, and then slowly shook my head. "I have to be honest, Senator. I'm here as a journalist."

"I see." A bit of the brightness seemed to come back into his eyes as he spoke. "Then I will pretend that you are a human being, and take my chances. What happened to me fourteen years ago—when I was, as you say, hospitalized for severe depression—is a moment for which I am everlastingly grateful. Please don't think I am ashamed of it. I truly believe that it saved my life."

"Yes, sir," I said. "I can understand that." But they were just words. My chief function that day was to turn on the tape recorder.

"For many years before that, I had been in the power of a dark force I could not control. I had suppressed it long enough to win election to the Senate in 1980, but it returned the next year, powerfully and overwhelmingly. It was an emptiness that left no room for any of the pleasures of my life. Nothing had meaning for me. My wife, my children, my friends. Even the foods I loved had no flavor. But I was a public man, to the world's eyes a triumphant man. And I could not tell *anyone* what I was feeling. In that sense I was truly helpless. I felt that to share this secret and seek treatment would destroy my career and my family. And I began to believe, Mr. Truell, that my only possible escape would be to take my own life. It sickens me now to think that I was ever so desperate, but that was the case in the spring of 1982.

"One day that spring I read a magazine article by a writer who had experienced this same sort of severe depression. It was a revelation. What more can I say than that? He was describing what I had been living. He wrote that with hospitalization and drug therapy, he was now recovering from his illness. And on that day I began to think it possible that I might survive."

I looked down at the tape, turning inexorably on its spindle. I wanted to make sure that it was still running. Abelard followed my eyes.

"Turn that damn thing off," he said.

"Yes, sir." I had no choice. By that point I was in his power as much as he was in mine.

"I found a doctor in Pennsylvania who would treat me, under the strictest confidentiality. He found my situation so extreme that he recommended immediate hospitalization. Fortunately, it was summer, and I could simply say I was taking a long vacation." Abelard paused and looked out the window toward the lone pinnacle of the Washington Monument. He was lost in time for a moment, remembering what must have been the most painful day of all—the day he dared to walk away from the capital of denial and seek help. And then he was back in the present, across the table from me.

"My friends," he continued, "the ones who had sensed what I was going through, protected me. I found drugs that allowed me to work normally— better than that, for my old 'normal' self had been a diligently constructed lie. And I began to live and share life again with others."

"I see." I was moved by what he had said, but I was also playing the words back in my mind, so that I would be able to write them down as soon as I left his office.

"But I have always known that, at some point, I might find myself in a room like this, with someone like you. This became more likely when I decided to run for president, but I chose to take the risk. I was under no illusion about the public's attitude toward illnesses such as mine. Despite my profound belief in the value of the therapy I received, I knew that my candidacy could not survive public exposure of my hospitalization and treatment. That is a reality I cannot escape.

"Mr. Truell," he said, leaning toward me. "I must ask *you* one question, and it is the only one that matters. Will you publish this story about my treatment for depression? Because if you do, I am certain it will mean the end of my candidacy."

I closed my eyes and tried for a moment to think. What could I say that would respond to the power of what he had told me? I could only tell him the truth.

"I don't know whether we'll publish it, Senator. I'm sorry. I don't know. We're going to meet tomorrow with our lawyer and the executive editor to discuss what to do."

"That means it is possible that you will run the story, even after what I have told you. That is what I infer. Am I correct?"

"Yes," I said. "It is certainly possible that we will run the story."

Abelard nodded. He made a noise that was barely audible, which began as a groan and ended as a sigh.

We never had to hold the meeting with our lawyers. That night, James Abelard dropped out of the presidential race, citing a desire to spend more time with his family.

14

❖❖

Ed Weiss must have known I would be upset. He called me the night Senator Abelard quit to cheer me up. "Abelard had no business being in the race," the executive editor said. "This wasn't a personal thing, like cheating on his wife. The guy had been in the nuthouse. Without his pills, he was a basket case. We did him and the country a favor. Don't lose any sleep over it. You saved everybody from a big mess." And that was it. On issues like mental health and gender politics, Weiss had traditional views, to put it charitably. The force of his personality had allowed him to hold on to most of the assumptions and prejudices of his youth. In his mind, James Abelard was unstable. He wasn't fit to be commander in chief. We had exposed these facts. End of story. For Weiss, it was basically that simple.

For me, it was more complicated. I knew that by the conventional standards of my profession I had done a good job, but that seemed beside the point. I felt like a silent assassin, holding a bloody knife in my hand even as my colleagues gathered around to offer congratulations.

When I got home, I made a drink and turned on the television. The late feed of the MacNeil/Lehrer show was on the public television station. They were talking about Senator Abelard's departure from the presidential race. I heard the voice first, before I saw the face.

"My only suggestion," Annie Baron was saying, "is that you should disregard the official statement put out by the Abelard campaign. It can't possibly be true. No man decides to run for the presidency and then withdraws to spend more time with his family. Men are not constructed that way. Senator Abelard is leaving for some other reason, which he chooses not to disclose." There was a controlled intensity in her eyes. She had one of those cool personalities that seem to glow red-hot on television.

"What do you think the other reason might be?" Jim Lehrer was asking, in his genial country-prosecutor way.

"I think there are secrets in his personal life which he wants to protect, perhaps involving his medical history. Things that he fears will be disclosed by the press if he stays in the race." She blinked her eyes and gave that smile of the junior high daredevil. "But that's just a guess, Jim."

It wasn't a guess. She knew. It was absolutely clear that she had the real story about why Abelard had withdrawn. You could see it in her eyes. The look that said: I know *all* the secrets. I couldn't imagine who might have told her. But that was her gift as a reporter. She could peel secrets off the backs of people—men usually—without their feeling a thing.

I called her the next morning. It was early February. A foot of snow had fallen overnight, and Washington was paralyzed. I offered to shovel her walk, which was an innocent, easy way to come see her. We had learned to be careful since I moved to Washington. There was still too much electricity moving through our circuit; if we met unexpectedly—as had happened at Bob Marcus's book party—we would crackle and spark. Our nominal dates for the evening would watch uncomfortably. What was this? should they leave? So we had learned to take precautions. It was better to meet during the day. Better to shovel snow.

She lived in a small Federal town house in Georgetown, on Twenty-ninth Street. It was a neat house, a woman's house: it smelled of clean sheets and flowers and Chinese tea. I shoveled front and back, and then came inside and lit a fire. The living room was cozy, with a love seat and chair near the fireplace. When I finished shoveling, I sat in the love seat in front of the fireplace. She took the chair.

She looked beautiful, as always: straight brown hair that she kept unfashionably long; that delicate face; the long arms pouring tea as gracefully as a geisha. Her skin was tanned; she had recently returned from a brief winter vacation in the Caribbean. As was our custom, I asked nothing about it. She knew something was bothering me—I would never have called otherwise—but she was too cagey to ask me directly.

"I saw you on television last night, talking about Abelard," I said eventually. "You know why he got out of the race, don't you?"

"Yes," she answered. "He was hospitalized a long time ago for depression. The *Mirror* was going to break the story. I know all about it. My sources tell me it was your story."

"Your sources are pretty good," I said. "Who told you?"

"Don't ask me that," she said, wagging a long index finger in my direction. "It's unprofessional. But it wasn't hard to find out. All you had to know was that the official version couldn't possibly be right. Then I just began asking his friends." She was so good at dissembling, and I understood so little.

"I'm glad you're so merry. Personally, I feel awful. I hated going to see Abelard and telling him what we had. I didn't feel like a journalist. I felt like an executioner."

"You are so *sweet,*" she said. "It's as if you've been in suspended animation all this time overseas, doing your brave deeds. You don't realize what a rotten business this is. But you shouldn't worry another minute. Abelard will get over it; or maybe he won't. Who knows? In any event, it's not your problem. He's a grown-up. He can make his own decisions. If you ask me, he had no business being in the race. You were just doing your job."

Her confidence amazed me. She seemed to know exactly where everything belonged. Perhaps it was only men who could afford the luxury of self-doubt. But I had started now; I couldn't stop.

"The funny thing is, maybe I don't like being a reporter anymore." That was the first time I had ever let that thought form clearly in my mind, and it had a surprising solidity. "I've always just assumed that we were the good guys, because we were going after the truth. But I didn't feel good when I left Abelard's office. I ran into a bathroom and scribbled down all the private things he had told me. That's what reporters do, but I knew it was wrong."

She paused a moment, to consider what I had said. "Maybe you should be an editor. Good reporters are supposed to do that, when they get tired of reporting."

"That's what Ed Weiss thinks. He wants me to come to New York. But that's the last thing I want to do right now. I'm sick of being a bystander, as it is. Becoming an editor would be like moving from the sidelines to a skybox. I still want to connect."

She smiled at my word. Her word. "Poor Eric," she said. "You know what I think? You're—what's the opposite of homesick?—abroadsick. You miss the freedom of being overseas. You want to go find another war somewhere. You're not ready for peacetime."

"Maybe I'm just lonely," I said, gazing at her.

Annie came over to the love seat and sat down beside me. I watched her walk those few feet, and let myself remember. I reached out my hand and touched her cheek. It had that downy softness of a woman's skin, warmed by the heat of the fire.

"Let's make love," I said.

"No," she answered. "I have a rule never to make love with ex-boyfriends who are in the midst of an identity crisis."

The snow hadn't been plowed, even on some of the main streets, and downtown had the desolate look of Ice Station Zebra. The bureau was empty, except for Bob Marcus and a few diehards. Everyone else who could get away with it had taken a snow day. I spent an hour tidying up my Abelard files and then began thinking about what to do next. I was still thinking when I heard the phone ring, and the now familiar voice: "Hello, *commendatore*. This is your humble servant, Brother John of Ragusa. I have returned to your snowbound capital and I want to *talk*."

The Brother John pseudonym was the same one he had used in the letter that contained the original tip about Senator Abelard. It bothered me. "Before we go any further," I said, "who *is* Brother John of Ragusa?"

"I'm disappointed in you, dear boy. That was a little puzzle for you. I hoped you'd solve it yourself. Brother John was a Venetian courtier whose specialty was *assassination*. In the year 1513, he sent a letter to the Council of Ten offering to murder various rivals and enemies of the Venetian state. He proposed a sliding scale of payments—five hundred ducats to kill the Ottoman sultan, one hundred fifty ducats for the king of Spain, one hundred ducats for the pope."

"That isn't funny," I said. "It's in very bad taste, as a matter of fact. What does Brother John want now, after he's done with Senator Abelard?"

"Brother John wants a job. But for tonight, he'll settle for dinner." He proposed that we meet for dinner that night at his favorite restaurant, a place on Seventh Street called Ruppert's. He was already memorializing himself. I reminded him that there was a foot of snow outside, but he cut me off. Ruppert's was open, and he had made a reservation under the name B. J. Ragusa. Despite my stated unhappiness with being a reporter, I couldn't say no.

15

Ruppert's Real Restaurant—that was indeed its name—was on the edge of the black belt of poverty that girdled official Washington. I approached the restaurant warily, as if I were crossing a fault line. Across the street was the city's makeshift shelter for homeless women, housed in some derelict trailers. A few blocks west was an open-air drug market. Looking north up Seventh Street, you could still see the burned-out façades of buildings that had been torched during the riots that swept the city in 1968, after Martin Luther King was shot, and never rebuilt. That night everything was covered in soft white flakes of snow.

Cohen was sitting at a table, drinking a large glass of beer. He was dressed in his black leather jacket, a blue cashmere scarf and a blue-striped shirt made of expensive cotton. Arrayed before him on the brown wrapping paper that served as a tablecloth were various vegetable dishes that were his munchies: French string beans, a grilled Portobello mushroom, thin spears of asparagus drizzled with butter sauce.

"It's been a long week," he said. "I'm babying myself."

"That's nice." I really didn't want to hear how hard his week had been. I had my own problems.

"When do I start work?" asked Rupert. "I'm sick of being a spy. I want to be a real man, like George Will."

"We'll get to the job part later, but I need to ask you about a couple of things that have been bothering me, starting with Abelard. The reason he quit the campaign is that I told him we might run a story about his hospitalization. I've been feeling weird about it, and one of the things bugging me is why you told me in the first place. You must have known it would destroy him."

"I told you because you *asked* me. You said you wanted information on Abelard, so I went out and found some."

"Where did you find it? Who told you? How did you know?"

"It wasn't hard. Abelard used to be a member of the Intelligence Committee. That meant he had been vetted for security, and there was lots of stuff about him floating around. I'm still on the 'badge table,' which means I can ask for almost anything in the registry. So I got it. I thought that was what you wanted me to do."

"It was." Everything he said sounded reasonable, but it was insufficient cause for the catastrophe that had ensued. "What did you think of Abelard yourself, Rupert? Did you like him?"

"Not much. I thought he was a wuss. Too cozy with the Froggies and the rest of the Europeans. Living in the past. But that's not why I gave you the goods on him, if that's what you mean. I'm clean. Just a freelance dirt-disher, like you."

He drained his beer and belched. "Mmmmm," he said. "Another of those and I will begin to feel like a human being again. Now, what about my *job*? When do I get vested in the *New York Mirror* pension plan?"

"I'm not done. I want to know more about Paris, too. Last time you were too drunk to finish the conversation, so let's talk now."

"Fine. At your service. What do you want to know?"

"Why did you come find me? Why did Rubino send you? You said it was all against the rules, so why did you do it? What was so special about me?"

"Because you—how shall I say this nicely?—because you had a good reputation."

"Meaning what?"

"Meaning that over the years people had found you a sensible, hard-working, trustworthy fellow. In short"—he paused—"a good journalist. And you were quite knowledgeable about France."

"But you didn't know anything about me."

"Oh, you'd be surprised. We knew more than you might imagine, even in our feeble state. We knew you had a Lebanese friend who was exceedingly well informed."

"Shit!" I felt embarrassed and angry. They'd been spying on me. Perhaps Ali had told them; perhaps they'd been bugging my phone; perhaps they had an agent in the DST who was sharing *their* taps of my phone. There was no way to know. "What else?" I said.

"Let's see . . . We knew you were working on a story about French biotechnology."

"Why did you care about that silly story? It never even ran."

"Hot topic, *professore*. Very hot. That French scientist you met is a certified *big deal*."

"Why? What are you talking about?"

He wagged his finger at me. "Naughty, naughty. You know very well that as a representative of the United States government I am forbidden to discuss classified information."

"Goddammit. You are pissing me off! You *used* me. You spied on me, and then you used me. That's against the rules. Intelligence agencies aren't supposed to do that with journalists."

"Tell that to the French, chum." He winked and sat back in his chair. He opened his mouth and dropped a string bean into it.

"What do you mean? Stop playing games."

"I mean that the French intelligence service has recruited a prominent journalist at one of America's leading newspapers."

"Which newspaper?"

"I *knew* you'd ask that. But I'm sorry. No more information until I have my job. Can we talk about that now, please. You have been stalling long enough, and I'm beginning to think it's deliberate."

He was right. I was stalling. I was still afraid that the moment I finally admitted there was no job for him at the *Mirror*, he would stop talking and the secrets would dry up. I put him off a few more minutes while we ordered a hearty midwinter dinner: pumpkin soup; yeasty, crusty bread; roast quail; a tasty bottle of Merlot. But I was uneasy. Reporters like to think they're in control of situations, but it was obvious that in this continuing encounter with Rupert I was not. It was like a feeling I remembered from tennis. Sometimes, in a tight match, I would begin to see an imaginary line traced by the tennis ball connecting me and my opponent. As long as I was moving that line back and forth, dictating the terms of play, I was winning the match. But when my opponent was moving the invisible line, I knew I was going to lose.

"All right, my friend," said Cohen as the food began to arrive. "You've put me off long enough. What about my *job*?" When do I start?" The time had run out.

"I did what I promised," I said carefully. "I talked to my bureau chief, Bob Marcus. I told him I knew someone at the agency who wanted to work for the *Mirror*."

"Right, and what did he say?"

"He said it's a nonstarter. He said intelligence and journalism don't mix."

"They don't mix?"

"Yes. He said it was an ethics issue. It would compromise the paper's reputation if we hired a former intelligence officer. People might mistrust our coverage. I'm sorry, but that's what he said."

"I see." Rupert had a strange, flinty look, as if he was trying to decide whether to tell me something. "So the *Mirror* can't hire me, because you don't hire spies. Is that it?"

"That's right. We don't hire spies." He was goading me, but I didn't understand why.

"Bullshit!" he snorted. "Of *course* you do. You just don't hire *CIA* spies."

"What are you talking about?"

Rupert paused a moment, looked at the four corners of the restaurant, and then gave me a devilish look that made instantly clear what had motivated him to join the secret world.

"My dear fellow," he whispered, "you have a foreign agent working in your Washington bureau at this *very* moment. I was speaking of him, in the abstract, a few minutes ago. He has been paid a considerable sum over the years by the very nation we were discussing earlier, our great and distinguished ally, France."

"Who the hell are you talking about?"

His eyes twinkled as he spoke the name: "Arthur Bowman."

16

❖❖

I watched Bowman settle in at his computer terminal the next morning as he began work on his weekly column on foreign affairs. It was the day after the big snow, and he was getting an early start. He looked so comfortable. His gray hair was still slick from his morning shower; his cheeks were pink and smooth. A pair of reading glasses was perched on his nose; he was looking over them to the screen. Atop his desk stood a Dundee marmalade jar containing a brace of sharpened pencils; occasionally he would reach for one and make a note on his pad. Other times he would seem to be searching for an idea, and would stare absently at the gallery of photographs along the wall, as if communing with the spirits of his departed ancestors. What was he writing about today? The inconstancy of American policy in Bosnia, the indispensability of the Atlantic Alliance, the essential American interest in free trade? I didn't have to know, to know. It was all of a piece, another few inches in the tapestry he and the ancestors had been weaving for the past fifty years.

I was hiding out at George Dirk's desk a dozen yards away, examining Bowman the way you might study a suspect in a police lineup. *Could he really have done it?* The night before, when Cohen first insinuated the idea that Arthur Bowman was a French agent, I had imagined the worst. We always do that with frightening news. If the doctor finds a lump somewhere on your body, you are instantly certain that it's cancer. Only later does a rational calculus begin.

And I had imagined the worst about Bowman. What Cohen said was plausible; the elements were there. I remembered the tone of our conversation that night at Taillevent—his curiosity about my source for the Costa story, his scorn for the CIA's new mission of economic intelligence. It was conceivable.

But now, as I watched Bowman prepare his column, the whole idea seemed impossible. Rupert Cohen was a crackpot; he was a disappointed job seeker and this was his revenge—trashing the most respected journalist at our newspaper. Arthur Bowman was our Saint Peter. If he was compromised, then so were we all.

After a few minutes Bowman emerged from his office to get a cup of coffee and noticed me, staring at him. "Young Truell," he said in his theatrical voice, walking over to shake my hand. "How goes?"

"Not too bad. I guess you heard what happened with Abelard."

"Weiss told me about it. It must have been painful, but you did the right thing. You had to report the story. Those are the rules now."

"It was awful. He looked so disappointed when I told him we might publish something. I felt I had failed his test of character."

"Part of the business," he said, looking over the top of his glasses. "Don't worry about it."

I was still at George Dirk's desk when he arrived at 10:15. He looked as if he had been drinking for the past forty-eight hours. His face had that fleshy pallor, and there were dark circles under his eyes. "Get away from my desk, you fucking snoop!" he said. "I'm still mad at you."

He meant it. Dirk still hadn't forgiven me for the way the Abelard project turned out. Part of it was his usual pettiness: I had come up with the damaging information, I had been the one to confront the senator; his own careful investigation of Abelard's finances had gone for naught. But for once, Dirk seemed motivated by deeper concerns. He truly felt that we had done *wrong*. We had destroyed a candidate, without ever giving him a chance to defend himself. What was the difference between what we had done and blackmail, he wanted to know.

"Let's drop it," I said. "I'm sick of this subject." It wasn't that I disagreed with him. I just didn't have any good answers.

"No, goddammit!" exploded Dirk. "Let's *not* drop it. I want to talk to Marcus about it, *now.*"

So we marched off to see the bureau chief, Dirk steaming like a locomotive with too much coal in the firebox. Unfortunately, Marcus was in, sitting on his couch reading the *Post* and the *Times*.

"We need to talk about some stuff!" said Dirk. His face was red.

"Not now," said Marcus. "Talk to my secretary. She'll set up an appointment." He looked at me as if to say: What is this all about? I didn't respond. I had resolved to keep my mouth shut; there was so much just then I didn't want to talk about. But Dirk was determined to make a scene.

"Excuse me, but I don't think it can wait! I waited while Eric was doing his reporting on the Abelard piece, and I waited when he went up to the Capitol to see Abelard. But I can't wait anymore. I have to tell you that I think what happened *stinks*."

"Thanks for your opinion, George," said Marcus. His eyes were shooting daggers, but George didn't see or didn't care.

"What are your *values,* Marcus? We're judging politicians by ethical standards we'd never apply to ourselves. How many people in this bureau take some kind of medication? Why don't you fire them! Why don't you include a note at the end of each article stating whether it was written under the influence of Prozac or Valium? We are such fucking hypocrites! No wonder everyone hates us."

It was a classic Dirk performance, and it was particularly ill-timed. As the tornado blew out of the office, it was obvious that my friend had not helped his career.

When I returned from lunch, the light on my phone registered a voicemail message. The voice in question was cheery, sprightly, elflike. I had suspected I might not hear from him again, but, no, I had been wrong. *"Journalistissimo!"* said the voice. "Most journalistic one. I'm leaving on another taxpayer-financed adventure, but I haven't forgotten you. Check your mailbox tonight."

Waiting for me at home was another letter. Rupert had written this one in the form of a newspaper article:

By Brother John of Ragusa
New York Mirror Staff Writer

WASHINGTON—A pending multibillion-dollar business deal in Asia could provide new evidence of the anti-American sympathies of Arthur Bowman, the senior diplomatic correspondent of The New York Mirror, according to intelligence sources.

The intelligence sources urged careful examination of Bowman's commentary on a $30 billion communications contract to be awarded next month by the Chinese government. The main competitors for the giant contract are France and the United States.

According to the intelligence sources, Bowman's articles are likely to support France in this crucial trade battle. If so, that would lend support to the thesis advanced several years ago by some members of the U.S. intelligence community that Bowman is a paid French agent of influence.

The intelligence sources, who are believed to be highly reliable and deserving of a job at a major newspaper, said the China contract calls for installation of a 21st-century communications system throughout the Asian nation. They said it will include millions of miles of high-capacity fiber-optic telephone lines, more than 200 million telephones, and other hardware.

The contract will provide an estimated 100,000 jobs to the winning country. The intelligence sources said that the French, who recently lost out to the United States on a $6 billion deal to sell commercial aircraft to Saudi Arabia, are prepared to use any means necessary to win it.

Mr. Bowman, 56, couldn't be reached for comment.

China, home to more than one billion people, is a land of contrasts.

(See Bowman, page A16)

Cohen was insane. That was certainly a possibility. Or it was conceivable that he was playing some kind of elaborate practical joke. He had taken the trouble to get the tone of his article right, especially the technique of attributing speculation and innuendo to knowledgeable sources. It was also possible that he was right about Arthur Bowman.

I called Dirk at home that night. I wanted to see how Mount Vesuvius was doing after that morning's eruption, and also to pump him for information about the China communications deal. He had already been drinking for a while and was in that exaggerated state of melancholy where you start apologizing for everything you did a few hours before. "He's going to fire me, Eric," he moaned. "I didn't realize what I was doing. I handed him the gun today, and he's going to pull the trigger. I'm a *fool.*"

"Don't worry about it," I said. "Marcus is a jerk. They don't take him seriously in New York. Keep writing good stories and he won't touch you."

"I can't believe I did it!" he wailed. "I am such an *asshole.*"

"Dirk! Stop feeling sorry for yourself for a minute. I need to pick your vast brain before it totally self-destructs. Have you been following the China communications contract?"

"Of course I have. I follow everything."

"Tell me what you know about it."

"Okay. First, it's very important to the administration. Somebody at the White House told me the president called it 'the deal of the century.' It's definitely jobs, jobs, jobs. The U.S. bidders all have factories in California, which is votes, votes, votes: American Telephone Corp., IBM, Hewlett Packard, General Science. They're all afraid that if they get shut out of the China market, they're dead. One billion consumers, and all that. They're competing against a French group that's headed by their big conglomerate, called Unetat, I think. If anything, the French want it even more than the Americans. Both sides see it as the key to Asia. It's like the founding of the East India Company in the 1700s. Whoever wins has a lock on commerce for the next hundred years. Or so they're all telling themselves."

"Who's going to win?"

"How the *fuck* should I know? But it's huge. They have a special inter-agency task force at Commerce to send memos to all the departments reminding everybody what a big deal it is. Both sides are supposedly pulling out all the stops. Haven't you been reading the stories?"

"Not very closely. But I'm getting interested."

"So you're going to steal this one now, too? You *prick*."

"No," I said, laughing. "I don't think so. Not unless it gets really good."

A few days later, Bowman opined for the first time on the China communications deal. He wrote in his weekly column that there was growing concern in Congress about the wisdom of doing the deal at all because of China's poor human rights record. He quoted an appropriations subcommittee chairman from Wisconsin as saying that signing the contract would be "craven," and he had a blind quote from an administration official saying that the White House was reviewing its options. He noted the heavy campaign contributions that had been made by U.S. communications companies and their subcontractors to the president and key members of Congress.

It was a garden-variety Washington dope story. A few titillating facts, a lot of spin. The headline helped: CHINA DEAL: A $30 BILLION BLUNDER? It was the sort of story that might lead the network news on a slow day, with the reporter standing in front of the White House saying, "A new controversy is swirling in Washington tonight, Dan, around a huge trade deal with China that some critics are calling 'craven.' " It was the sort of story that would prompt editorials in leading newspapers urging the administration to reconsider. I put Bowman's column in a file that I had started a few days before and locked it in my desk drawer at home.

I received a letter several days later. It was written on one of those small, stiff cards that are the color of butter. At the top were the embossed initials of the sender—*JLA*—in flowing script. The letter was brief, and bitter.

Dear Mr. Truell:

This letter is hard for me to write, but essential for you to read. My husband is a fine and courageous man who has done so many wonderful things for his country. But in the days since you came to see him, he has not been well. I am worried that he may take his life. I am told you are unmarried, so perhaps it is impossible for you to understand what it is like to feel so powerless to protect someone you love. But I wish you could feel what I am feeling, because it might help you to behave with greater humanity toward others. Each of us has secrets he wishes to keep private. Think of your own life, and the things you would least want the world to know. Then remember what you did to my husband, and perhaps you will feel a sense of shame.

Yours sincerely,
Joan Abelard

17

❖❖❖

The *Mirror*'s vice president for labor relations posted the buyout offer on a bulletin board in New York. Nobody thought it would come so soon, but the paper's advertising revenues had collapsed in January. It had been a bad Christmas for retailers—wasn't it always a bad Christmas?—and they were cutting back their advertising sharply in the New York and national editions. It wasn't just seasonal. Some of the business reporters in New York said that the problem was "structural." Advertisers weren't sure that newspapers—especially national papers like the *Mirror*—were the best way to reach consumers.

Everybody in the bureau seemed to know about the buyout by mid-morning. The offer had been extended to news department employees over the age of fifty-five. If they retired by the end of 1997 they would receive a special severance payment equal to two weeks' salary for each year of employment at the *Mirror*. A lot of the older reporters were gathered over by the Coke machine, next to the library, talking it over. That kind of worried gossip was something new for us. Job cuts happened to other people, in other industries—to steelworkers, foundrymen, textile workers—but not to reporters and editors.

The bureau seemed numb, as people digested the news. For years we had been able to proclaim our disdain for commerce—anyone from the advertising department had been banned from even setting foot in the newsroom—because we knew the paper was making scads of money. Weiss had encouraged his department heads to spend everything in their budgets so that accounting wouldn't try to cut the budget for next year. The notion that we should perhaps *save* the unspent money and add it to the paper's profits was regarded as heresy.

The *Mirror*'s economic situation had begun to change sometime when I was overseas, so it was hard for me to say precisely what had caused it. Readers had less time for a quality paper; advertisers had less patience with our shotgun marketing; newsprint costs were up—who knew what the reasons were? But I had felt the change as soon as I came home—the new cautiousness, the fear of offending readers, the advertising-driven sections that were being added to the paper every year. The liberality and generosity of spirit that I associated with the newspaper world was slipping away.

Perhaps we truly were creatures of economics. Reporters, despite their show of cynicism, have always been optimists at heart. They believe that the world is getting better, that human history is moving upward, that the pie is always expanding, that the truth will set people free. Everything in our own business had confirmed that view, until recently. Now, suddenly, our world was contracting; the pie was shrinking; the newsroom staff was being reduced. We weren't prepared for a world like that.

"I told you it was coming," muttered George Dirk. He was wearing his Newspaper Guild pin prominently, like an amulet to ward off the evil spirits. "This is just the beginning. They won't get enough volunteers for the buyouts, so they'll have to do layoffs."

"Never happen," I said. "Sellinger would rather fire his mother than go after the newsroom. And Weiss won't let him."

"Weiss is an *employee,* my friend, just as *you* are an employee. That means he serves at the pleasure of the publisher, who serves at the pleasure of the stockholders, who don't really exist except for the little gnomes who manage all the pension funds, who don't give a flying fuck what happens to you, me or Ed Weiss. I know you golden boys tend to forget that. But it's the truth."

Noel Rosengarten came sailing by. He had a new fifty-dollar haircut and a new thousand-dollar suit.

"I'm out of here!" he said to me. He didn't like talking to Dirk. "The future is television news. I've got a new agent, same guy that used to represent Katie Couric. He's almost ready to close a deal."

"Where are you going?" I asked. "I heard ABC might make you an offer."

"I don't think so. They want some black woman. My agent is talking to other people."

"Like who?" cut in Dirk. He was smiling from ear to ear over the fact that Rosengarten had been turned down by ABC. Noel ignored him.

"My agent is talking to a bunch of people. Something will happen. The NBC affiliate in Minneapolis wants me *bad*."

"You're going to do local news?" I asked. All I could think of were guys named Bob with blow-dried hair.

"Why not? You have to start somewhere. Learn the business. They're talking *anchor* in Minneapolis."

"Local news!" screamed Dirk. He turned to his pals standing by the Coke machine. "Hey, everybody, Rosengarten is going to become a local TV anchorman. You'll be great, Noel." He puffed his chest out and put on an anchorman's voice: *"Two people were seriously injured tonight when a bridge collapsed in suburban St. Paul. We'll have a live report later in the broadcast. And how's that Twin Cities weather shaping up, Doreen?'"*

"You are a fat, stupid hack," said Rosengarten, retreating back toward his desk. "And soon you'll be unemployed, too."

Dirk ignored this feeble riposte. He was beaming. "God, it makes me so happy to think of that guy doing lead-ins for the weather. I'll bet he changes his name to 'Skip.'"

I was invited that week to a dinner party given by Elsbeth Parsons, one of Washington's grandest hostesses, in honor of my publisher, Philip Sellinger, who was visiting from New York. I was very flattered to be asked; I seemed to be the only one of my generation at the paper who had been invited. It was a sign of something I had begun to sense in other ways, too: great expectations had begun to attach themselves to my career. In a mysterious process I didn't understand, I had been selected out from the other animals in the herd and given a special pen.

Mrs. Parsons's social secretary asked if I would be bringing someone. I thought a moment and said yes, I would like to bring my friend Anne Baron from *Newsweek*. The social secretary sounded impressed; my date was a star. When I told Annie, she was pleased, too, that I wanted her to join me, albeit a little surprised. This was big-league socializing, and we weren't a couple. But I said it was too late to say no; I had already given her name to the social secretary. Annie went out and bought a new dress by Emanuel Ungaro, a tight black sheath that unzipped across the chest to reveal a lining of cobalt blue.

Mrs. Parsons lived in Georgetown, in a beautiful old house on P Street. Annie and I rang her bell just after 8:00; we seemed to be the first guests to arrive. Mrs. Parsons greeted us at the door. She gave Annie the once-over, and then me, and seemed content with both of us. Though now in her seventies and a widow for more than a decade, she remained an extraordinarily beautiful woman—delicate, fine-boned, lovely to look at—but with a courtesan's curiosity and passion in her eyes.

"How nice that you're so punctual," she said sweetly. "We'll have a few minutes to talk before the latecomers show up."

She gave me her arm. Annie followed a few steps behind. "I'll give you a tour. Would you like that?"

The interior of the house might have been a museum of the decorative arts. Each painting and piece of furniture had been selected carefully. I inquired about the large black nude that graced the entrance hall, the voluptuous figure formed in cold marble. "Yes, that's rather nice," she said. "My husband bought it, in Paris."

Above the carved mantel was a large painting of a beautiful aristocratic lady, who bore a slight resemblance to my hostess. "Who's she?" I asked.

"Oh, she's nobody. We just bought her somewhere."

"It's such a beautiful house," said Annie. "So much history. We both come from California, where prewar means it was built before Vietnam."

"Washington is quite different, isn't it?" she said contentedly.

The doorbell rang. The other guests were beginning to arrive. Our hostess departed to greet them.

When Philip Sellinger and his wife, Barbara, entered the drawing room, he headed straight for me. He seemed almost to glide as he made his way across the carpet—I noted the silver hair, the bright blue eyes, the perfect clothes, the shine on his shoes. Like Mrs. Parsons, he was one of nature's aristocrats.

"I'm glad you're here," he said. "Elsbeth thinks you're charming, and she usually hates reporters."

I gathered that was a compliment. A waiter took orders for drinks. Sellinger had a scotch and water; I thought I had better stick to club soda, at least until I got my feet on the ground.

"How's business?" I asked the publisher. It was a simple question, but it was as if I had pulled open a trapdoor: out tumbled all the accumulated worries and frustrations.

"Business is awful," he said. "Absolutely rotten. You heard about the buyouts, I suppose. What's the Washington bureau saying about them?"

I wanted to be honest with Sellinger. I didn't know him very well, but it made no sense to start off our relationship by telling him lies.

"People are scared," I answered. "Some of them think layoffs are next. The gossips say the paper is losing money."

"The gossips are right. We may end up with a loss this quarter, just between us girls, although it may wash out on paper when the accountants are done. But the stock market already knows the truth, which is that the paper hasn't been making any money for months. That's why the damn stock price is so low. The analysts think we're so caught up in our glorious newspaper culture that we'll never cut costs the way an ordinary business would."

"Are the analysts right?" I asked warily. Cutting costs sounded like a bad idea to me.

Sellinger put his hand on my shoulder. He spoke to me in confidence, as if taking me into the club. "Listen, Eric, I don't want to run this as an ordinary business. It *isn't* an ordinary business, for God's sake. We're trying to publish the best newspaper in America, and I think we often succeed. In the old days that was enough. If the analysts didn't like our earnings in a particular quarter, it was easy to tell them to buzz off. But now it's not so easy. The people who control big blocks of stock want results, and in the marketplace, they have the votes. I used to promise we'd never have layoffs in the newsroom, but I can't anymore. We have problems you don't want to hear about."

"Sure, I do. I've been spending your money all these years as a foreign correspondent. I owe you."

"No, you don't. You're money in the bank, as far as I'm concerned. But we do have financial problems, that's a fact. We've been looking for ways to diversify, broaden the base of our revenues so we won't have to squeeze the paper. We've started up some things, and bought some things, and it's been expensive."

"That computer graphics company," I said. Everybody knew about that one. We had spent over $50 million to buy a fancy company that supposedly had a brilliant new way to produce computer graphics for the movies. But it turned out to be the second-best technology in the industry, which meant that it was worthless, and we had been forced to write off nearly all our investment.

"Yes, that. And our Internet project is costing us a bundle, with absolutely zero prospect of making any money. And there are other things I won't bore you with on this nice occasion. But the bottom line—as those idiots like to say—is that we need to raise some new capital. And that isn't going to be easy. It's a bad time for us to make a stock offering because the stock price is so low, and it's a bad time for a bond issue because the rating services think we already have too much debt."

"So what are you going to do, if you can't sell stock or bonds?"

"Maybe some joint ventures. Maybe a new equity investor from outside. We're looking at a lot of things I thought we'd never consider."

He shook his head and smiled at me. "I can't believe I've told you all this. Forget it, instantly. Now I see why Weiss thinks you're such a good reporter." He squeezed my arm and went off to talk with one of the other guests who had just entered the drawing room.

Inevitably, Arthur Bowman was one of the dinner guests. The moment I saw him I decided to put Rupert Cohen's insinuations out of my mind. This was not the evening to play FBI agent.

As it happened, I was seated next to Bowman's wife, an attractive, predatory brunette named Mara, who was full of mischievous gossip about people at the paper. She had all the tricks: an easy way of draping her hand across yours; a voice that was an invitation to conspiracy; an expensive low-cut dress that squeezed her bosom so that her breasts were barely touching, like two soft, ivory billiard balls. She was, as George Dirk liked to say, "a piece of work." I thought to myself that Bowman must have to spend a lot on upkeep—financially and emotionally.

"Don't you think that Bob Marcus is awful?" she asked me at one point.

How was I supposed to answer that? He was my boss. I mumbled something about how I hadn't been back long enough to form an opinion.

"I've heard they want to bring you to New York as foreign editor," she whispered at another point. "Would you do it? I hope not. Arthur says they need you here in Washington."

The woman was a menace, really. I had no idea whether what she said was true or not, and no idea what to say. So I changed the subject. I told her about myself. How I had grown up in northern California, and how I had hoped to play the tennis circuit when I was in college, how I had regarded joining the news business as a sort of consolation prize. She sucked it all in, with that slender hand resting on mine, gazing up at me as if I were the most interesting man she had ever laid eyes on. Superficially, it was the same technique as Mrs. Parsons's, but there was a world of difference.

Annie was seated next to Arthur Bowman. They talked animatedly through much of the dinner. The parts I overheard were about the political campaign—the Republicans who had self-destructed, the president's prospects of beating the ones who remained in the race. They were a match, those two—two thoroughbreds pacing each other down the course, teasing and charming bits of information from each other. Annie looked particularly beautiful that night, I thought. When she turned to talk to the man on her other side, someone high up at the State Department, I could see Bowman was disappointed. She had that effect on people; as much as you had of Annie, you wanted more.

When the dessert plates were cleared, Bowman offered a toast to the publisher. It was exquisite: funny, self-deprecating, sincere in its emotion. He concluded with a brief quotation from a Yeats poem about friendship—"Think where man's glory most begins and ends / and say my glory was to have such friends"—and then raised his glass.

"To Philip." All the glasses clinked around that charmed circle.

After dinner we adjourned to the living room. The fire had burned down to red coals, and Bowman was putting another log on the grate. I approached him. Perhaps it was the good food and wine, and the disorientation of being among that company, but I was feeling light-headed and playful.

"I take it you don't like the China communications deal," I said.

"Not much," he answered. He was down on one knee, poking at the fire with a brass rod. "I don't like doing business with dictators."

"Come on, Arthur! I'll bet the French paid you to write that column." I don't know why I said it, it just came out.

He looked up at me suddenly and drew his head back, just a fraction of an inch, like an animal that had been startled. The light of the fire was dancing against one cheek, but his eyes were dark and wary. "What's that supposed to mean, junior?"

"Nothing," I mumbled. "Just making a joke." A rush of heat came to my forehead. I'd said too much.

Bowman rose from the fireplace and studied me carefully, as if trying to make up his mind whether I had been serious or not, and then gave me a wink. He had concluded that I was, indeed, joking. The roguish, ex–foreign correspondent smile returned to his face.

"They don't pay me *enough,* young Truell," he said. "I should ask for more."

I laughed, of course. It was the perfect response, and the tension of the moment vanished. He took my arm, in that conspiratorial way that seemed to be part of doing business in Washington, and whispered in my ear. "The problem with that crazy China deal is your friends at the CIA. They think they've got marching orders from the White House to deliver this little thirty-billion-dollar trophy, or else. But if those cowboys don't watch out, they are going to step in some deep shit."

I was going to ask what he meant by *my* friends at the CIA, but he was already moving away from me and taking Philip Sellinger by the arm to say something conspiratorial to him. He was a force of nature, Arthur Bowman. A protean character who could change shape and color in an instant. But what I remembered later was the way he had looked up at me from the fireplace. The emotion in his eyes could only have been fear.

I took Annie home. "What did you make of Bowman?" I asked as we drove across Wisconsin Avenue to her house on Twenty-ninth Street. Her eyes went blank for a moment. She searched for the right answer. "I think he's a very complicated man. And I don't think he has a happy marriage." I told her I could understand why, after talking to Mara Bowman. She was the kind of socially ambitious woman who rode her husband like a race-horse. She had actually made me feel sorry for Bowman.

"Did you enjoy yourself tonight?" I asked. "You looked so relaxed."

"I was working every minute, Eric. I always look relaxed when I'm working. And I learned some very juicy things from my dinner partners."

"But were you happy?"

There was a faraway look in her eye, as if I had used a word that was unfamiliar. "Yes," she said. "I suppose I was happy. Lovely company."

The way she said it, I thought she meant me. When we reached her house, I asked if she felt like a nightcap.

"Not tonight," she said gently, stroking my cheek with her hand. "I've been trying to act sexy all evening, and it's worn me out." She kissed me tenderly on the mouth. Her lips lingered there, moist and full, just apart from mine. "Maybe another time," she said.

18

Arthur Bowman fired another shot a week after Mrs. Parsons's party. His story was headlined SENATE INVESTIGATES CIA CHINA PAYOFF. It reported that the Senate Intelligence Committee was investigating whether a CIA officer in China had paid a $5 million bribe to a relative of one of the top officials of the Chinese Communist Party. But that was just the beginning. The story said that the CIA man's cover job had been as a sales representative for American Telephone Corp. in Shanghai, and that the real purpose of the bribe had been to help ATC and its partners win the $30 billion communications contract.

It was, as George Dirk liked to say, a "bacon cooler"—a story so intriguing that you read it over breakfast with your mouth agape, the bacon going cold on the fork. The CIA spokesman was referring calls to the White House. The White House was refusing to comment, except to say that it was studying the allegations. In news bureaus around town, including ours, that was taken to be confirmation that the article was accurate. Bowman's sources, whoever they were, had given him a loaded M-16. For the first time since this bizarre chain of events had started, I was certain that Rupert Cohen was right.

The bureau was buzzing that morning, the way it always does when we've broken a big story. Bob Marcus called a 10:30 meeting in his blue-and-green office to discuss follow-up coverage. As the hour approached, Bowman strode up the Corridor of the Gods, accepting congratulations from other members of the bureau as if he had just hit a home run. I had been invited to the meeting, too. As a projects reporter, I was an available resource. I chose a seat as far from Bowman as I could. Interestingly, he didn't look at me once during the meeting.

Marcus's philosophy in covering a big story was to overwhelm it with a massive assault. Within minutes he had ordered up a barrage of second-day coverage: a story from our correspondent in Beijing about the Chinese reaction; a story from our business staff in New York about American Telephone's reaction; a CIA reaction story; a congressional reaction story, plus sidebars, plus graphics, plus a lede-all by Bowman, summarizing all the other pieces. As Marcus was barking out assignments, Susan Geekas ran into his office. She had just returned from the White House. "They're frantic!" she said. "They want the China contract so bad, and they're afraid this will kill it. They don't know what to do." Marcus added a White House reaction story to the budget.

"You see anything here for you, Eric?" Marcus asked. I was the only person at the meeting who didn't yet have an assignment.

"Nothing for tomorrow's paper," I said. "But I wonder what the French are up to. They want the China contract as bad as the White House does, but we haven't written anything about their tactics. I'd like to go after that."

"Okay," said Marcus. He seemed underwhelmed. "It doesn't have much to do with the main story, but if you want to take a look, fine. Maybe Arthur has some suggestions."

Bowman had been busy making notes on a legal pad. He looked up over the top of his reading glasses. "Glad to help," he said.

I wandered over to Dirk's desk. He was fuming. He hadn't been invited to Marcus's big meeting, which he took as yet another sign of his diminished status in the bureau. Unlike everyone else, he was unimpressed by Bowman's big scoop. "The guy is a phony, Eric!" he muttered. "That story is a setup. And you—you devious bastard—you knew it was coming! That's why you were quizzing me about the China contract the other night."

That was the useful thing about Dirk: he mistrusted everyone, even if his suspicions sometimes led him in entirely the wrong direction.

"I'm not wild about the story, either, if you want to know the truth," I said, "and I certainly didn't know about it in advance. But it's too late now. Marcus is going nuts with it." I described the bureau chief's manic behavior in the meeting and the fact that, by my count, we now had six different slugs on the budget. That cheered Dirk up. He always liked evidence that the paper's management was crazy.

I took advantage of his momentary good humor to ask the favor I'd wanted. "Do you have any sources at American Telephone? I told Marcus

I would try to find out what the French are up to in China, and I figured the ATC people might be angry enough to tell us something."

Dirk was cagey now, displaying his what's-in-it-for-me look. "I have a guy in ATC. A real good guy, as a matter of fact. But he probably wouldn't see you unless I came along."

"Call him up. Ask if he's free for lunch today. And I wouldn't think of seeing him without you."

We met at a restaurant in the basement of a building on K Street, the kind of place where businessmen bring their secretaries when they are trying to put the make on them and don't want anyone in the office to know. It was dark and smoky; the customers all looked like lobbyists. The American Telephone guy was sitting at a table in the corner. He was already drinking.

"Meet my friend Ralph," said Dirk. I shook the American Telephone guy's hand. Dirk had decided not to tell me the man's last name for security reasons. I found that somewhat histrionic, but it was Dirk's source, so he could set the ground rules.

We didn't have to play games; Ralph wanted to talk. He said his company was petrified. They were convinced that Bowman's story had blown their hopes of getting the China contract. Ralph wouldn't say what he did for ATC, but I guessed that he was a lawyer, since he seemed to know a great deal about the company's legal department. The general counsel had flown to Washington last night, he said, and had been meeting all morning with officials from the CIA and the White House. American Telephone had initially considered suing the *Mirror* for libel; then they had debated suing the government. Now the company's lawyers weren't sure what to do.

"Is our story right?" I asked. That was what I really wanted to know.

"It's both right and wrong," said Ralph. "That's the problem. According to my friends in the general counsel's office, the ATC sales rep in Shanghai *was* working for the CIA. It was a deal the previous CEO made with the agency, to keep a few slots abroad for CIA cover. A lot of big companies do it. Very hush-hush. Bad idea, it turns out. And yes, indeed, this CIA guy in Shanghai may have paid five million to some Chinese big shot, just like your story says. But that was CIA business, not American Telephone business."

"Are you sure?" I rubbed my eyes. There was a blue haze in the room from all the cigarette smoke.

"Absolutely. We don't pay anyone cash bribes anymore. We give them consulting contracts, or equity in a joint venture. It's all legal. Ask the Justice Department." He said it matter-of-factly, as if it were common knowledge in the business world.

"Where did this story come from, Ralph?" I asked. "Who leaked it?"

"You're asking *me*? You're from the *Mirror,* and you're asking *me* who leaked this story to you? You gotta be kidding. I should be asking *you* that, so we can go find the leaker and string him up by the balls."

"What I mean is, do you think the competition—the French company, Unetat—had anything to do with this?"

"Maybe. Probably. I really don't know, to be honest. But that would take nerve, for the French to accuse *us* of bribery. They bribe anything that walks in Asia. And that's just the beginning."

"What do you mean, Ralph? What else do they do?"

"Listen, my friend, the French have done stuff on this China deal that would tie your intestines into a bow. Sweetheart agreements with Beijing. Kickbacks to people in France. There's even a crazy rumor the French are helping the Chinese on some big weapons project. Nobody will talk about it. But even if I knew the details, which I don't, I wouldn't tell you—even if you are a friend of Dirk's, and even if you do keep calling me Ralph, which isn't my name. All I will tell you is: Look into it. Find people who really know what's going on, and ask them about it. Because this one is *nasty.*"

Late that afternoon I heard the unmistakable, singsong voice of Rupert Cohen on the other end of the telephone. This time he didn't even bother to address me by an Italian honorific. His first words were: "What did I *tell* you?" He wanted to gloat, but I cut him off. For me, this had ceased being a joke.

"I need to see you, tonight," I said. "This Bowman thing is really beginning to bother me."

"All *rightee.* Where and when? We can choose from a range of excellent restaurants managed by former LA covert-action partners: Vietnamese, Afghan, Lebanese, Ethiopian, Thai. Luckily, they all cook better than they fight."

We settled on a Thai restaurant on upper Connecticut Avenue whose chief virtue, from my standpoint, was that the tables were far apart. This time I made sure to arrive before Cohen. I wanted to control the field of play. I chose a booth far in the back of the restaurant and sat facing the door.

Eventually Rupert arrived. He was wearing a Burberrys trench coat and had shaved off the goatee. He looked less like a hippie film director and more like a spy. Or, to be precise, more like an intellectual in the costume of a spy.

"Could you please tell me what the fuck is going on?" I said when he sat down. "You've got me spooked about Bowman. Where did he get this story?"

"From the French, *sans doute.*"

"But the story says the Senate Intelligence Committee is conducting an investigation."

"Come on! You're a reporter. You know how it's done. You go to the committee with some dirt, and they launch an investigation. Then you report the investigation. But Bowman's original tip came from the French. Had to."

"How can you be so sure? He could have gotten it anywhere."

"Nope. Only another intelligence service could come up with gourmet goodies like these, *mon ami,* and it wasn't the Chinese. The French *do* this. It's a game they've been playing with us for years. We uncover their payoff in Brazil and leak it to the press. They uncover our payoff in Brazil and leak it to the press. But I must say, things are getting a bit *out of control* in China."

"How did the French find out about the payoff, assuming you're right?"

"Because our man in Shanghai got *caught.* I keep telling you the organization is incompetent, but you don't believe me. Things like this don't happen if you do it right. That's why we have *tradecraft.* So we won't get caught."

Cohen's bitterness toward his employer continued to amaze me. He was like a postal worker, ready to open fire at any moment with a machine gun. He actually made me feel sorry for the CIA. "You really hate them," I said.

"No, no, no. I am not a hater. I am a *healer.* My problem is that I'm in the wrong profession. I'm a journalist, trapped inside an intelligence officer's body. I could go on *Oprah,* but instead I'm trying to help you."

"Then help. You have to understand how risky this is for me, Rupert. Bowman is one of the most prominent reporters in the business, and I'm not going to accuse him of anything unless I'm sure about it. You're telling me he's a foreign agent, which scares the hell out of me, to be honest, but what do you really *know?* Where did you first hear about Bowman?"

"Corridor talk."

"What's that?"

"Just what it sounds like. People talking in the corridor. We're a loquacious bunch, if you hadn't noticed. An old-timer in EUR mentioned to me a few years ago that the French were a tad close to a very prominent reporter, and the organization had looked into it once upon a time, and then they had dropped it. I asked who, and he gave me Bowman's name. We were just shooting the shit, and I didn't think too much about it. But I filed it away.

"And then one morning last year I was having coffee with a French counterpart in Rome. He was a bright fellow, as evidenced by the fact that he disliked his service almost as much as I loathed the organization. We're sitting together in a café in Rome, reading the morning papers and trying to recover from a hangover inflicted the night before at an African dance club. And I come across this *absurd* column in the *International Herald Tribune* by Bowman about how tough-minded French policy had been in the Balkans, and how much better it was than anything coming out of the White House. It was a *blow job,* pardon my French.

"So I read it out loud to my French friend, and he just laughed and said, 'Our man in Washington.' And he *meant* it."

"Did you tell the agency?"

"Of course not. I don't tell them anything that's serious. They would just screw things up. No. I told *you.*"

My head hurt. I needed to know more, or I needed to know less. Where I was—in between—was the wrong place to be. "This is all very interesting, but for my purposes it's useless. We've been down this road before, you and me. I need to know real facts. I can't go to my editors unless I know who gave this China story to Bowman. Was it one of his French sources, or a French intelligence officer?"

"What's the difference?"

"You don't get it. There's all the difference in the world between someone who gives you something because you're a reporter and someone who gives it to you because you're his paid *agent.* If it's the former, then Bowman is just doing his job. He should get a Pulitzer Prize. If it's the latter, then he should be fired. I have to know which it is."

"That seems kind of strange, that the same story from the same source could win you a prize or get you fired, but I'll take your word for it. The answer is, I don't know who gave it to him. The only thing I really know is what I just told you. I doubt the organization has any details—they usually don't know *anything* that anyone would really care about—but I can try to find out. As I told you before, I remain on the exalted badge table, so I have a license to prowl. And there's the real stuff—Special Intelligence—though that would be a tad difficult to obtain in this case, since Mr. Bowman is what the lawyers call a 'U.S. person.' But I can see what's gettable. How would that be?"

I thought for a moment: How *would* that be, if Rupert Cohen prowled around the intelligence community at my request, looking for information about one of my colleagues? Not good, but what was the alternative? I felt an obligation to get as much information as I could, and then tell somebody at the paper about it.

"Do it," I said. "But be careful, and don't tell anyone what you're doing. If this goes wrong, I could get in serious trouble."

I heard from Rupert two days later. He rang me at the office and told me to call him back at a number in McLean in fifteen minutes from a pay phone. I went downstairs to Connecticut Avenue. It was a cold February day; freezing rain was falling, coating the streets and sidewalks with ice. It was miserable; even the panhandlers and sidewalk vendors had disappeared. I slipped and slid up to the Farragut North metro entrance at L Street and went downstairs to one of the phones in the Food Court. The place smelled like French fries. I dialed the number Rupert had given me.

"Listen up!" he said. "Here's the scoop, obtained with some difficulty by your intrepid colleague who had to explain more than once why he was browsing in this particular section of the local library."

"I'm listening," I said.

"The organization opened a 201 file on your esteemed colleague in the late 1960s, when he was covering the Vietnam war. Like many of your brethren in those bygone days, he met occasionally with LA officers. Your colleague passed along the kind of information journalists know: political gossip, speculation about people's needs and vulnerabilities. He probably didn't even realize what he was doing. He was an 'unwitting asset,' as we like to say. Which meant that when the LA officer finished a nice boozy lunch with Bowman at the Majestic, he'd run back and make notes of everything and send a cable back home. Just like journalists do. Ha! But I'm getting off the track.

"Cut to the mid-1970s, when the Good Ship Titanic encounters a rather large iceberg, in the form of the Church Committee. And all of a sudden the organization stops talking with its old chums in the press, including

Mr. B., and everyone's running for cover and we have absolutely nothing in the file about your esteemed colleague for almost ten years. But there's one final set of cables, and it's *yummy.*"

"What does it say?"

"Will you promise me the Los Angeles bureau if I tell you? Because I've always wanted to cover Hollywood."

"Stop it! Tell me what it says."

"There's a 1983 memo from the chief of the CI staff to the chief of EUR division. It says that a counterintelligence investigation of your esteemed colleague has been opened. No details given, except that the tip comes from a French source—cryptonym LVBLOW-1, if you care—who says Mr. B is on the books of LVKEY—that's the crypt for the French external service—and is being paid a large sum of francs for his services. The CI chief says they've looked into the possibility that it's a false-flag recruitment, and that his stuff is really being passed on to the Russkies, but they don't think so. And that's it. *La commedia è finita.* So what do you think? Am I a great reporter, or what?"

"Fuck!" I said. That was the worst possible news, because it meant I would have to do something. "That's all there was?"

"There was one more memo in his 201 saying that the case had been referred to the deputy director for operations, personally, for resolution."

"What did that mean?"

"It means they killed it, obviously. Prominent journalist. Too hot to handle. Embarrassing past history. And that was the end of it. The great glacier of the bureaucracy moved on, and now nobody knows or cares—except you and me and a few incompetent gnomes at the Culinary Institute of America."

"*Fuck,*" I said again. "Now what do I do?"

"Hmmmm." Cohen was purring. He liked making me uncomfortable. "All I can say is that if I had given you the same information about a politician, I am confident that it would be in tomorrow's newspaper."

19

I was underwater now, and I needed to breathe—to communicate what I knew to someone else. Bob Marcus, the bureau chief who had responsibility for both me and Bowman, was a possibility, but I didn't trust him. He was thoroughly intimidated by Bowman. I could talk to Philip Sellinger, who had been so nice to me at Mrs. Parsons's party, but what would he know about sources and spies? In actuality, there was only one possible solution. The man holding my oxygen mask was Ed Weiss. He had asked me to come see him, anyway, to talk about my career. I had an excuse.

I called Weiss's secretary, Peggy Moran, to make an appointment. It was her job to keep the blowhards and whiners of the newsroom—who always needed to see the executive editor *right now*—from wasting Weiss's time. "What's it about?" she asked dubiously. I couldn't give her the honest answer, so I said, "My career. It's sort of urgent." Did that mean I had a job offer from another paper, she wanted to know, and I said it was something like that, and I needed to see Weiss right away—the next day, if possible. She stuck her head in Weiss's office and came back on the phone twenty seconds later. "Tomorrow, ten-thirty. And don't be late, because I'm bumping someone else to get you in."

I didn't sleep much that night. I lay in bed worrying about so many different things. My career, Bowman's career, Rupert Cohen's bizarre behavior, the future of the paper, right and wrong. After a while it all melded into a nameless drone of anxiety—like the white noise that some people use to go to sleep, except that this was black noise keeping me awake. I felt as if I were suspended upside down in my bed, while the minutes and hours ticked off—1:48; 2:23; 4:12—each time I looked at the clock, I would get more upset about how tired I would be the next day. I finally fell asleep around 5:00 and woke up two hours later. I went to the mirror and saw what I feared: I looked horrible. The circles under my eyes were so deep they formed little crevasses. Look on the bright side, I reminded myself as I shaved: When I tell Weiss how worried I've been, he'll believe me.

I almost missed the 8:30 shuttle, thanks to a traffic jam caused by some lunatic janitors who thought the way to get better working conditions was to piss off all the commuters in Washington. The plane was full, and I had to take a middle seat between a pushy male executive and a pushy female executive, who both acted as if I had taken *their* space. They planted their elbows firmly on either armrest, so I was scrunched into the seat with my arms pressed against me as if I were in a coffin. I tried to sleep, but I was too tired.

Nothing really clicked until the cab rounded the corner from Broadway and pulled in front of the *Mirror*'s headquarters building. At that point I felt a surge of adrenaline, and I knew that it was all going to work out, because I was at the headquarters of the world's greatest newspaper, and I had come to do the right thing.

I pressed the elevator button for the seventh floor. When I first joined the paper in 1981, it was a rush just taking the ride up. The elevator doors would open onto that massive map of the world, dirty with handprints as if reporters had pawed every inch of the globe looking for news. And above the map, the familiar row of clocks, marking the different time zones of the "empire," as we referred to the rest of the world in those days—London, Paris, Beirut, Moscow, Delhi, Hong Kong, Tokyo. My only dream, back then, had been that I would someday work in one of those outposts for the *Mirror*. As it turned out, I had worked in three: Beirut, Hong Kong, Paris. I had become one of the people I dreamed about.

Now, striding past the map and the clocks, I entered the immensity of the newsroom: row on row of desks, manned by aging editors and cocky kids, each puffed up slightly from normal life size by the fact that they were part of the crew of this unsinkable schooner of the journalistic seas. In my first few years, I was excited just to cruise the room, steering my little dinghy alongside the foreign desk and the national desk and trying to make conversation with famous bylines. Maybe it's because I was a kid then and found everything about the *Mirror* romantic, but the newsroom in those days seemed to have a magnificent decay. The desks still had clunky old typewriters, with messy ink ribbons and six-ply carbon paper.

And the debris atop the desks had an epic quality: stacks and stacks of paper—the world still ran on paper back then—that conveyed the sense we knew *everything* at the *Mirror*. Every report, study and press release that had ever been issued was there somewhere in the great pile. But that was a long time ago.

This morning it just looked big. The messy old desks had been replaced long ago by spartan computer workstations. Reporters received regular admonitions to clean up their desks, just as they had in the old days, but the difference was that now people actually obeyed them. The desks and the walls and the carpets were all color-coordinated, in soothing shades that some consultant must have advised would keep the inmates *calm*. Perhaps it was my own fatigue that morning, perhaps a tiredness in the institution, but the newsroom felt a bit empty—a big, bland room, filled with frustrated people. That was what struck me, as I surveyed the rows of deskbound talent. There was so much cloistered ambition here, so many people reading their clips, marking time, remembering what it used to be like. As I walked toward Weiss's office, I passed by my old friend Fred Applewhite, who had regaled me the night I met him in Abu Dhabi with the tale of how he had blustered his way through passport control at all the miserable airports of the Middle East by thundering the name of the *Mirror* and threatening devastating consequences for anyone who defied its will. He was writing obits now.

At least he was still writing. A few yards away was Arthur Finkel, another of the heroes of my youth—a man who could write almost anything onto the front page through the sheer force of his intellect, who was now laboring in melancholy obscurity as spot-news editor on the business desk— rewriting junior reporters' rewrites of corporate press releases. "Hey, hotshot," he said as I passed by. I lingered, thinking he might want to talk to me about the latest antics in the Middle East—Finkel was part of the club, after all, he had served in Beirut—but he looked back down at whatever press release he had been reading, and that was it.

They were scared, that had to be part of it. The buyout notice had frightened everybody. Newspapers are about immortality: the permanent record of events; the transcendent power of the truth. But we were discovering that we were impermanent, earthbound, a mere business, which had to make profits and satisfy the whims of stockholders. We weren't prepared for mortality.

I rounded the bullpen and headed toward the executive editor's office.

Peggy Moran saw me coming and looked at her watch. It was 10:28. I was *almost* late. I could see through the door that Weiss wasn't doing anything, but she made me wait a few minutes before sending me in. When I finally entered his office, Weiss closed the door, sat me down on the couch and gave me a soulful look.

"I *knew* this was going to happen," he said. "I should have done something about it before."

"What do you mean, Ed?" I wasn't sure what he was talking about. Was he referring to Bowman? Then I remembered my conversation with Peggy Moran the previous day. Weiss must be assuming I was about to quit the paper, and he was launching a preemptive strike.

"I knew someone else was going to offer you a job eventually. You're too damn good for other papers not to try to hire you away. Now, there's nothing wrong with getting offers from the competition. It's flattering—to you and to us. Just so long as you say no. Otherwise, I'm going to kill you."

"I'm not going anywhere, Ed," I said, trying to think of how get the conversation back on track. Weiss continued with his pitch, oblivious to what I had just said.

"I don't know how much they're offering, but whatever it is, we can match it. *Better* it. I don't want you to leave the *Mirror* because of money. You matter to our future. I don't want to lose you." I tried to interrupt again, but Weiss kept going. This was his style when he had something important to say—he bulled through it and recited everything that was on his mental cue cards before giving up the floor.

"The point is," said Weiss, stretching out his arms as if to make room for the largeness of his message, "I've been doing a lot of thinking these past few months about the next generation of leaders at the paper. And I've decided—had decided *before* this job thing came up—that I want you to be part of that team. You're one of the brightest young people we've got, and you should begin learning how the paper works. Not from the reporting side—hell, you know that already—but from the editing side. So I'd like you to come to New York this fall as deputy foreign editor. And assuming you do well—which you will—I'd like you to take over from Lynn Frenzel as foreign editor at the end of 1997. Assuming that you aren't planning to do anything stupid, like leave the *Mirror.*"

"I'm not going anywhere, Ed," I repeated more emphatically. "I don't want to leave the *Mirror.*"

This time he finally heard me. A grin spread across his face. He reached for my hand and shook it. "Hot damn!" he said. "That's great. What about coming to New York?"

"I don't know. I'm very flattered, but I need to think about that. Right now, there's something else we need to talk about."

"Okay." Weiss nodded. He looked mildly disappointed I hadn't said yes right away to the editing job; he was the kind of person who always wanted an answer that instant, but it could wait. My head was spinning. I had come to tell him about Bowman, but it suddenly occurred to me that to do so might be a serious career mistake. He was offering me the keys to the kingdom, and I was about to piss all over one of the reigning princes. I was struggling for words when he spoke up.

"Come on, kid. What's the other thing you want to talk about? If it's money, give me a number. I'll see what we can do."

"No, it's not money. It's something pretty important that's been worrying me a lot. It's really hard to discuss with you."

"What is it?" he laughed. "Sex? Drugs? Gambling debts?"

"No." I shook my head. "None of that. They'd be easy."

"Well, what the hell is it? You don't have to worry about how I'll react. I don't give a shit about rules, and I don't believe in secrets."

I took a deep breath, closed my eyes for an instant. It was like going over the top in a roller coaster. I cleared my throat and began to speak.

"What would you do if you suspected that someone on the staff might be working for a foreign intelligence service?"

Weiss looked at me with genuine astonishment. This, truly, was a subject he had not expected. "Fire him, if it was true. But this isn't a hypothetical, I gather. Who's the suspect?"

"This is really hard, Ed. He's one of your friends. You're going to think I'm crazy."

"No, I'm not. Tell me what's on your mind. Who are you worried about?"

"Arthur Bowman."

When I said the name, he laughed out loud. "*Arthur Bowman*? I'm sorry. I don't mean to make light of it, but it's like somebody calling Ronald Reagan a pinko. I mean, Arthur is probably the most respected journalist on the paper. The idea that he's somebody's spy is—I don't know—it just seems ridiculous. But you wouldn't be raising this if you didn't take it seriously, so I want to listen. What makes you think Arthur Bowman might be working for a foreign intelligence service? And which one, by the way?"

"The French," I said. Weiss laughed again.

"The French? That's a relief. I thought it was the Russians. Well, lay it on me."

So I told him the story, more or less as it had happened.

"I have a source in the CIA," I began. "I met him overseas. He was the person who helped me nail the Costa story, actually. He's a strange guy, but very bright. And he hates the agency, which means he's willing to say almost anything. He wants to be a journalist; it's almost an obsession with him. Anyway, he contacted me a few weeks ago to ask whether we might ever hire someone who had worked for the CIA as a reporter. I checked with Marcus and then told him it was impossible. We'd never hire an ex–intelligence officer at the *Mirror*. And he said that was bullshit, because we had a spy working for us right now. And that was Arthur.

"My first reaction was the same as yours, that it was completely unthinkable. But then this guy—my source—said that if I wanted evidence that Arthur was working for the French, I should follow his coverage of the communications deal in China. And not long after that, Arthur began writing stuff that was very negative for the U.S. side and helpful to the French. He wrote a column saying we should pull out of the negotiations because of China's human rights record. And then he had the big story this week about the CIA payoffs in China. And at that point, I knew I had to come see you."

"Jesus Christ!" Weiss was trying to control his temper, but you could tell he was furious. I thought at first he was angry at Bowman, but it wasn't that. "Listen, Eric, I'm not blaming you. You were right to come to see me, but I have to say I'm not impressed with your CIA friend, who denounces one of the finest reporters in America after you tell him the *Mirror* won't give him a job, and after we publish stories the agency doesn't like. I'm not impressed with that, at *all*. Did he give you any evidence?"

I tried to think. It wasn't easy with Weiss glaring at me. What had Rupert Cohen told me, exactly? I needed to be very careful now. I didn't want Weiss to think I was being used by someone from the agency, and I didn't want him to doubt my judgment any more than he already did.

"His evidence was pretty thin," I said. "He claimed he'd heard corridor talk about Arthur at the agency a few years ago. Then he checked the agency files and found out that during the early eighties, there had been some kind of investigation of Arthur, but it was closed."

"And that's it? He blackens the reputation of one of the country's finest journalists on the basis of *corridor talk,* and some crappy investigation that even *they* decided was bullshit. That's it?" Weiss was getting angrier, the more he thought about it.

"Yes, sir." I was bailing out. I could feel the softness in my knees, hear it in my voice. "I'm sorry I brought it up. I thought you should know that somebody was putting this stuff out."

"God damn right!" Weiss stared out the window for a long time, thinking. When he turned back toward me, he looked calmer. The storm had blown out to sea.

"You did the right thing coming to me. That's the first thing I want to say. I'm not mad at you. What bothers me is that someone would be slinging this shit at a man like Arthur Bowman, and questioning his ethics as a journalist. If you knew all the times Arthur had risked his life for this newspaper, you would understand that he could *never* betray his profession. This was a man who fought to get into war zones—when all the other reporters were fighting to get out—because he wanted to do his job. Vietnam, Cambodia, Tehran, Beirut, Belfast, Bosnia. There is not one dangerous assignment Arthur hasn't volunteered for eagerly, lovingly, for Christ's sake.

"Now, I don't doubt that over the years Arthur has made some enemies at the CIA. And I wouldn't even be surprised if some of them talked about him in these famous corridors. Which is fine. Better than fine. Because if the CIA loved my diplomatic correspondent, I'd want to fire his ass! I don't doubt that Arthur has made some friends, too, and some of his friends are undoubtedly named Jacques or Henri. And it's conceivable that some of them even work for that goofball French intelligence service.

"But so what? If that convinces some paranoid at the CIA that Arthur Bowman is a foreign spy, then they're in worse shape than I thought. Understand? They are fucked up. We are not in the business of character assassination. We don't accept any wild accusation that comes our way. We have an obligation to be responsible. Do we understand each other, Eric?"

"Yes, sir."

"So, end of story. I'm glad you came, I'm glad we talked, I'm glad we understand each other. And I'm especially glad that we're going to keep this conversation to ourselves. I don't intend to tell anyone else, and I trust you won't, either. This sort of thing can hurt people. So you go ahead and chase the French intelligence service all you want—just like you did in those great stories from Paris—but leave Arthur out of it."

"I won't tell anyone," I said.

"And one other thing, Eric. Don't even think about working for another newspaper. Because if you do, I'll kill you."

I felt empty as I walked away from Weiss's office—a kind of emotional vertigo. I wanted to get away from the *Mirror* as quickly as I could. A couple of my friends shouted my name as I crossed the newsroom, but I didn't stop. No banter, no flirting with the copy aides. I wanted to be out of there. By the time I reached the elevators I was almost shaking. I thought at first that I was just worried, that I had blown it in going to see Weiss, that I had said too much, that I had made a career blunder. But that wasn't it. That way of thinking was *causing* the empty feeling. By the time I hit the street and felt the cold February air in my lungs, I knew what was wrong.

I was ashamed of what had happened in Weiss's office. I had lost my nerve. I had come on a mission to tell the truth, and I had let my ambition get in the way. The moment it became clear that Weiss didn't believe that his friend Arthur Bowman could possibly have done anything wrong, I pretended I agreed with him. I backpedaled; I dissembled. Weiss had described me as a future leader of the newspaper, but I wasn't a truth teller at all, I was a courtier. My reporting life had devoured the rest of me. All that was left was an observer, a flatterer, a passive chronicler, an ambitious young man.

I called Bob Marcus when I got back to Washington. It was a Friday afternoon. I couldn't bear the thought of going back to the office that day, but I figured I should at least check in. He'd already heard from Weiss. "I'm glad you're staying at the *Mirror,*" he chirped. I mumbled something back. He asked how my reporting on the French-in-China story was going and I said I wasn't sure, I was just getting started. "Stick with it," he said. "It's important!" Weiss must have told him to be nice to me.

Then I called Annie and asked if I could come over to see her that night. I was feeling so low. Maybe I thought that if I could understand what she had once loved in me, then I could isolate that part and act on it. She must have realized that I was in a bad way, because she just said to come by her place at 8:00. She'd fix something to eat.

It was one of those clear February afternoons when the sky is a sharp, crystalline blue and the late-afternoon sun is so low it seems almost to light the bare branches of trees from below. You never see them that color any other time of year. I walked up Connecticut Avenue toward my apartment and stopped and sat on a bench in Dupont Circle with the winos and the bicycle messengers. The sun was glinting off the trees as if they were made of metal. The whole world, in fact, had the shiny, empty look of metal. Hard, brittle, dead as winter.

Annie opened the door of her house and it was like a balm. Fresh-cut flowers were in a vase on the mantel; a pot of tea was steeping on the coffee table; there was a hint of perfume on her cheek. I still had that shattered look, from lack of sleep the night before and my ruinous trip to New York. She gave me a kiss and lingered a moment to examine my face.

"What's wrong, sweetie?" It was the first time she had used that term with me in years. "You look like you got hit by a truck."

"Bad day," I said. I rambled for a while about my trip to New York, and how strange it felt to be there, and how Ed Weiss had asked me to become deputy foreign editor. I wasn't going to tell her about Arthur Bowman, but Annie always seemed to know when I was holding something back. She took it as a provocation.

"What else happened in New York?" she asked. "There must have been something. I don't think I've ever seen you so upset." She reached out and took my hand.

"I was a coward," I said quietly. "I was going to tell Weiss something important, but I chickened out. As soon as I realized that telling him the truth might hurt me, I folded."

"Why don't you tell me?" she asked. "Then maybe you'll feel better." She said it so sweetly, as if she were offering to take a burden off my shoulders, that I had no sense that she was working me for information.

"It's very private," I said. "You can't use it in any way. It's just between you and me. It involves one of my colleagues in the Washington bureau. A CIA source told me the agency suspected this guy worked for a foreign intelligence service. I decided I had to tell Weiss about it, even though the man was one of his friends. But I backed down. When it was obvious Weiss didn't want to hear it, I played it safe."

"Who is it, Eric?" She held my hand more tightly. I shouldn't have told her, but I needed to go the rest of the way.

"The man you were sitting next to at dinner the other night, Arthur Bowman."

Her eyes widened. She stared at me and then looked away, shaking her head. She covered her face with her hands for a moment, then went into the kitchen. She said she would make me some tea. I thought she was reacting the same way Weiss had, that she thought I was crazy.

When Annie returned, she looked different. Her face looked resolute, as if she had steeled herself for something unpleasant. I didn't understand at the time how close she was to the line, or how hard she was trying to keep faith with me.

"You know what you need, Eric?" she said. "You need to grow up. If you think Arthur Bowman is a spy, then do something about it. If you're tired of being a journalist, then quit. But don't keep complaining about things and doing nothing. It doesn't become you. And it's making you unhappy."

Her words were as sharp as a slap on my face. I knew she was right. I had spent fifteen years as a journalist, trying as hard as I could to be a passive scorekeeper of other people's lives, and the disturbing part was that I had succeeded. I had become that passive person. My morals began and ended with the question of whether something would make a good story, and whether it would thereby advance my career. I wanted to make a change, to square my accounts. But I wasn't sure how to begin.

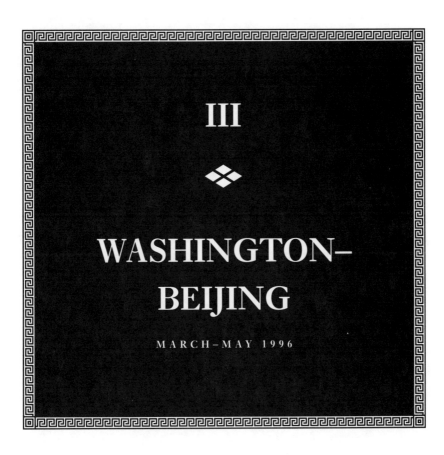

III

❖

WASHINGTON– BEIJING

MARCH–MAY 1996

20

On the far wall of the CIA headquarters building was that famous quotation from John's gospel they always mention in profiles of the agency: "You shall know the truth, and the truth shall make you free." I was standing by the security desk, waiting for my escort, and from where I stood, the only obvious truth was that the place looked shabby. The floors were dirty; the walls looked as if they hadn't been repainted since the 1960s; the most prominent decor was an electronic security gate that could read badges automatically. Lurking by the front door were a few hard-core nicotine addicts, sucking on their cigarettes. Just ahead of me at the main desk was an absurd sign listing the things that weren't permitted inside the building: NO FIREARMS OR EXPLOSIVES, NO SMOKING, NO ALCOHOL, NO SOLICITATION, NO GAMBLING. It had the feel of a classroom building at a second-rate state university.

I had called the CIA press office the day before. It was early March, and I had resolved to do something to answer the questions that had been troubling me. They had all gathered into a tangled ball, and I couldn't separate the strands without help. I wished there were someplace else I could turn, but I knew only one address. Liars Anonymous, as Rupert liked to call it. It helped that I had a clear story assignment to work on—French economic espionage in China. Marcus was waiting for it. And after some procrastination—wanting to avoid getting in any deeper, but still needing to know—I had placed the call to CIA public affairs.

I told the duty officer who answered the phone that I wanted a briefing for a story about French economic espionage. "That's a big topic," she said. "Can you be more specific?" So I explained: I wanted to know what the

French were doing to win the China communications contract. I wanted to know about French bribery of Chinese officials, about kickbacks of some of those bribes to French politicians, about whether the French were helping the Chinese develop new weapons as part of their effort to win the contract. I was fishing—mentioning every thread of suspicion anybody had ever confided to me.

When I got to the part about weapons, the duty officer cut me off. She preferred not to discuss that kind of subject on the phone, she said. Would I mind holding while she checked with a colleague? She put me on hold for a long time—it was at least five minutes—and finally returned. "Could you please come to the agency tomorrow morning at ten for a briefing?" she asked. "Someone knowledgeable will see you." She had two requests: I should come alone, and prior to my arrival I shouldn't discuss the briefing with others. I agreed; I wanted answers, and I went to Langley that morning feeling anxious, but also relieved to be doing something.

My escort eventually arrived at the main security desk. He examined my ID and then instructed the guard to give me a temporary pass. He led me to a small elevator off the main lobby, inserted a special key in a security lock, and pressed "4." When we reached the fourth floor, he steered me down a long hall to a room with a heavy metal door. A sign on the door said EUR CONFERENCE ROOM. He knocked, and then punched a code into the cyberlock.

The door swung open to reveal a windowless room. It was sparsely furnished, with a table and several chairs; the walls were painted a tired pastel blue. Atop the table was a plastic decanter of coffee and two Styrofoam cups. At the far end sat a man in shirtsleeves, leaning his chair back against the wall. It was at once chilling and reassuring to me that I knew him. The man at the end of the table was Tom Rubino.

"Thanks for coming, Eric," he said, rising from his chair and shaking my hand. The man from public affairs exited the room, leaving us alone. Rubino looked a little more tired than he did the last time I had seen him in Paris, nearly two years before. His tie was loose, his sleeves were rolled up, and he had dark circles under his eyes. He looked almost like a newspaperman. In front of him on the table was a large briefing book. He could see that I was uncomfortable, and tried to put me at ease. "How've you been? I haven't seen you since your big scoop on Maurice Costa. That was a hell of a story. Nice work." He winked.

Rubino explained that he was chief of the European division now, but that he continued to spend most of his time working on "the French target," as he put it. He had told public affairs he wanted to brief me personally, he said, because of the sensitivity of my query and the fact that I was regarded by the agency as a "straight shooter." That rang an alarm bell, I will admit, but I chose to ignore it. Rubino wanted to tell me things. That was all that was clear; the rest was fuzzy.

"So where should I begin?" he said. "With a little recent history, I guess. I'm not sure you realize how much impact your Costa story had on France Inc. I've read everything you've written since then, looking to see if you'd picked up what was happening behind the scenes, but I think you missed it."

"Nobody in France would talk to me after the Costa story. How could I have known what happened? My sources all dried up."

"What happened was that the *system* changed. Maurice Costa represented a way of doing things—a 'certain idea of France,' to bastardize de Gaulle's phrase—that had survived for fifty years. It was part of the apparatus of the French state. The system operated through state-owned companies and government contracts. It was old-fashioned graft—a whole country operating by the same rules as Chicago under Mayor Daley." Rubino was rocking back and forth in his chair as we talked; he was wired.

"What's different, now that Costa is gone?"

"The old system has been privatized. The state-owned defense companies and oil companies and banks that handled the payoffs are gradually being spun off into the private sector. It's a real power shift. This isn't what the French call *pantoufler*—the bright boys from the École Nationale d'Administration going out in their bedroom slippers to run a nationalized company. A new generation of business leaders is emerging who are half-entrepreneurs, half-gangsters. They make deals with each other. They're the new face of something my conspiracy-minded colleagues like to call the Secret Power."

"La Puissance Occulte," I said. "I heard about them two years ago from the amazing Mr. Rupert Cohen."

"Talented fellow, Cohen. A little extreme for this organization. But a creative operator. Have you seen him since Paris?"

"No," I lied. Rubino didn't seem aware I was fibbing. That eased my paranoia level. Until that moment I hadn't been sure whether Rupert's recent contacts with me in Washington had been part of some elaborate plot, with Rubino pulling the strings. But Rubino didn't look like a string puller anymore. He looked like a bureaucrat.

"From what Rupert told me back in Paris," I said, "this Secret Power sounded like the Mafia."

"They *are* a mafia. Look, Eric, the great truth of the 1990s is that the world is run by organized criminals. We don't like to admit that in the institution where I work. We still like to pretend that the world is run by governments, which have neat little boundaries, and their own currencies and stamps, and intelligence services and police forces. Those were the rules of the game during the cold war, but they've changed. Power has slipped from governments into the hands of private organizations. In New York, private currency traders have more power over the dollar than the Federal Reserve. In Russia, the mafiya has more power than the army. In Mexico, the drug lords have more power than the president. In Japan, the politicians are just a front; the real power is held by the corporations and the yakuza. And this same process is happening in France. Real power around the world does not reside with governments any longer, but with private interests. Real power is secret power."

Rubino gave me a cocky smile. He was a performer; this was his show. "Have some coffee," he said, taking the plastic decanter and pouring the oily black liquid into the two Styrofoam cups. "I'm just getting started." The coffee was dreadful. The scene in that sorry little room reminded me of an officers' club at a run-down military base. You couldn't help but sympathize with Rubino, and to think he was basically trying to do his best with the materials at hand.

"Listen carefully," he said, "because I'm getting to the serious part, where this whole story comes together. Because ultimately, Eric, this isn't about France—at least not for the agency. It's about China."

"I'm sorry, but you've lost me. What do you mean it isn't about France?"

"Just what I said. The hell with France. Let them play their games and send their Corsican thugs out to beat people up. So what? That's certainly a nuisance as far as the United States is concerned, but it's not a serious national security problem. Think of a really obnoxious little brother who does everything he can to make trouble for you—spreads gossip about you, steals money from your wallet when you aren't looking, tries to snake your dates away from you, squeals on you to the school principal—just basically goes out of his way to be an asshole. That's France in dealing with the United States. But so what?

"No, our real headache in the twenty-first century is China. The country is huge, the people are smart and industrious, and the government is run by a bunch of corrupt autocrats. Now, some Western country is going to be their main ally over the next few decades and hold their hand as they modernize. For a long time it looked like that would be the United States. But now that obnoxious little brother is trying to elbow us aside.

"That's why the communications deal is so important. Whoever helps wire the new China will control the future. I mean, it's like giving somebody a chance to build the road network in the United States back in 1950. Whoever gets the contract wins the game. That's why the French are pushing so hard. They have paid hundreds of millions of dollars in bribes—hell, our five million in Shanghai wouldn't even pay the interest on what they're dishing out. They have greased relatives of the people who run the People's Liberation Army, the Communist Party, the Communications Ministry, the Chinese intelligence service, the mayors of Beijing, Shanghai and Canton. That's all off the record, by the way."

"Hold on." I raised my hand. "At some point, I need facts. This is all very interesting, but it isn't a story. I need details about bribery. And I want to know about weapons."

"Be patient, Eric." He patted the briefing book that lay on the table in front of him, as if to reassure me that there were nuggets of gold at the end of this trail. "I'm trying to do this right. I'm getting to the weapons business now. But this part is really, seriously, no-shit off the record. I don't even want you to take any notes, so put away that notebook."

"Okay," I said, putting the notebook back in my coat pocket. I didn't care. I would make notes in the car later.

"I'll start with a riddle: What could the French offer the Chinese that we would never, ever, give them?"

"Weapons," I said. That had to be the right answer.

"Sure, weapons. But what kind? Name the weapons that will be for the twenty-first century what nuclear weapons have been for the twentieth century? Name the weapons that will give the world's most populous nation a vast strategic advantage over anybody else?"

"That's not my area. I really don't know."

"*Biological weapons.* A whole new generation of weapons that will use gene-splicing technology and recombinant-DNA technology. Weapons that will make you stupid, or crazy, or tired, or lazy. Or dead. That's what makes this so scary. We think that for the past year or two, the French have been sharing some very specialized biotechnology with the Chinese that could be used to make weapons. It's unofficial, done through a private company. But we think they're doing it deliberately, to cement the political and economic relationship. It's a sweetener. The payoff is the communications contract, and all the contracts that come after that. The price is unprecedented Chinese military power. And it scares the hell out of me."

Rubino fell silent. He leaned back in his chair again, to let me think about what he had said.

"I don't blame you for being scared," I said. "This makes everything else seem like a sideshow. What are you doing about it?"

"We're working the case, but we have our problems. The guy who got our five-million-dollar bribe was one of the top officials in the Chinese intelligence service. We'd been using him to keep tabs on this mess, but the French and the Chinese got to him and he ratted us out. I'll be honest with you, we don't have much on the ground. But we have gathered a few useful tidbits that we might be willing to share with an interested reporter." He patted his briefing book. "Are you interested?"

I should have thought about it carefully before answering. Accepting his offer would draw us closer together, and make it easier for him to ask a favor in return someday. But most reporters aren't wired that way. When we're working a source, the test we apply isn't very subtle or farsighted. We ask whether we—which we like to think means our readers—will get more out of an exchange than the source. If the answer is yes, we don't think too much about the rest.

"Sure, I'm interested," I said. "What have you got?"

Rubino opened the book. The top page was a classification sheet, bearing a string of code words. He ripped it from the binder. "From here on out, what I'm going to say is 'deep background.' It's usable in the newspaper—in fact, I'll be upset if you *don't* use it—but it's not attributable to the agency, or 'intelligence sources,' or any of that. Okay?"

I nodded. I was excited. I wanted to see the goodies he had brought along.

"Let's do it, then," said Rubino. His tone of voice was different now. It was crisper, colder, more like a military officer summarizing the order of battle. He moved the briefing book so that it was facing me, and turned to the next page, which displayed a picture of a man in a business suit. He was an elegant-looking man, with sharply drawn features and thick black eyebrows.

"This is Alain Peyron, the chairman and chief executive of Unetat. He's one of the golden boys. He went to Harvard as an undergraduate, then took a master's degree in economics at MIT. Like everyone who matters in France, he went on to the École Nationale d'Administration, and after that became an *inspecteur des finances.* He served for ten years or so in the Ministry of Defense, and then became CEO of one of the big state-owned banks. When Unetat was privatized five years ago, he was its first chairman. He is a very smart man; he even speaks a little Mandarin, which helps when he goes to Beijing. The Chinese consider him slightly less of a barbarian than the normal Western businessman. In the new France I was describing a little while ago, Peyron and Unetat sit at the very top of the pyramid."

He turned the page. The next photograph showed another man in a business suit. This one was darker than the first, with piercing black eyes, sunken cheeks and thick lips. But for the hardness, it was almost a beautiful face. He was also expensively dressed, but the overall effect was of toughness, not gentility.

"This is Michel Bézy. He has no direct connection with Unetat, but we believe he is Alain Peyron's attorney and his most important business adviser. He has an extraordinary family background. His father was a prominent French businessman in Algeria who worked closely with French intelligence. The father was killed by Algerian terrorists in the 1950s, when Bézy was studying in Paris. His mother was from one of the leading families of Corsica. He was also educated in the United States, at Stanford. When he returned home, he joined French intelligence, where he spent the next fifteen years. He was a leading member of Maurice Costa's old network. He's the link between the old world of corruption and the new. He left the government a few years ago and began doing personal legal work for Peyron. He is the bagman, not to put too fine a point on it—the fixer. He has been very active the last few years in Asia and spends much of his time out there."

"I went to Stanford," I said. I wanted him to know that I shared that biographical detail with the mysterious Mr. Bézy, but he reacted defensively.

"Big deal. I went to Penn State. Can we continue?"

The next page of the briefing book displayed another photograph. It showed a younger man, in his late thirties. He was thin, sandy-haired, wearing a blue-striped shirt and a fine linen suit. He looked like an MTV version of Peyron.

"This is Jean-Luc Gaspard. He is one of Bézy's point men. He studied computer science at Berkeley—notice a pattern here?—and then spent six years working for Apple. We think during that time he may really have been a French NOC. He quit Apple in 1989, around the time the FBI was expelling a bunch of French agents who were working in American companies.

"Now Gaspard runs a company called New Asia Development Corp., which has an office in Hong Kong and one near here, in Bethesda. It's supposedly a venture-capital firm that funds high-tech projects in Asia, but we think—scratch that, we *know*—it's an important part of Unetat's infrastructure for paying bribes in China. We can document the link through information New Asia has submitted to banks in the United States to obtain trade financing and secure leases. Those documents show that New Asia has received tens of millions of dollars in loans from an offshore bank controlled by Peyron, called Banque des Marins.

"Gaspard's m.o. is to invest in the businesses of prominent Chinese who the French want to befriend. Occasionally they're real businesses; mostly they're shell companies, and Gaspard's 'investments' are really payoffs.

"Now, we get to the goodies." He turned the page. It displayed a memorandum on the business letterhead of New Asia Development Corp. It was a copy of a payment authorization from the company, directing a bank in the Cayman Islands to pay the sum of $15 million to the account in New Caledonia of a company called NADC Ventures, Société Anonyme, with an address in Luxembourg. I was scribbling notes, trying to copy all these details in my notebook.

"You don't need to worry about taking notes. I'm going to give you this stuff when I'm done. Now, this document is basically self-explanatory. It authorizes the transfer of fifteen million dollars from Gaspard's company, New Asia Development, to this outfit called NADC Ventures. But what is NADC Ventures, you may well ask.

"We can answer that, because we have a paper trail." He turned the page to another document, this one an official-looking form written in French, under the heading *Agence Monétaire Luxembourgeoise*. "This is the incorporation certificate for NADC Ventures in Luxembourg. As you can see, it lists three principals, all by the name of Wu. The president, a Mr. Wu

Laozi; the treasurer, a Mr. Wu Pufeng; and the secretary, a Mr. Wu Yewin. The three are brothers. They are all three sons of a Mr. Wu Jingsheng. Now, who might this elder gentleman be?"

He turned the page again, to the final photograph. It showed a Chinese man: thin, sharp-eyed, dressed in a plain gray suit.

"This is Wu Jingsheng. If you do a Nexis search, you will see that until last year, he was the Chinese minister of communications. We're told that in internal discussions he was an aggressive advocate for Unetat. We think that's why he got sacked. He and his three sons got too greedy, and he pissed off colleagues who wanted a share of the loot."

He flipped over several more pages. "The rest is boilerplate. Information that New Asia has submitted to U.S. banks and local regulatory agencies. Summaries of information we've gathered about the Wu family, including addresses and telephone numbers of the boys in Hong Kong and a telephone number for the old man in Beijing."

"Fabulous stuff," I said. "How did you get it all?"

"How do you think? We *stole* it. We bribed and burgled and bled for it. We are still capable of getting the job done occasionally, when we don't have people sticking fingers in our eyes. And now you, as a representative of the American public, are a recipient of this taxpayer-financed research." He pushed the briefing book across the table. "Here's your very own copy. I hope you will use it as a basis for your own reporting."

His last comment bothered me; it made me feel like a shill. "Of course I'll do my own reporting," I said sharply. "I'm not going to run this stuff just because you told me it's true."

"Good luck. You won't be able to verify all of it, I promise you. Not unless you have an agent inside the Luxembourg Monetary Agency and someone on the cleaning staff of TRC Properties in Bethesda, which manages Gaspard's office building. But you can probably get enough to convince you it's true."

"What about the French-Chinese scheme to develop biological weapons? That sounds like the big story."

"Not now. Maybe later. Newspaper articles won't help anybody. They would only drive these guys deeper underground, where we'd never find them. I only told you about the BW angle because I wanted you to understand that this is serious business. There's a lot at stake."

"Are we done?" I'd had enough of that small, windowless room. I wanted to get out of there.

"Yes, sir. We are *done.*" He picked up a phone on the wall and punched in a number, summoning the man from public affairs.

"Just one more thing before you go," said Rubino. He removed a blank white index card from his pocket and wrote on it two telephone numbers. "If you need to reach me, here are my numbers at home and work. Call me direct, please. Don't go through public affairs. They don't know anything about what I just told you."

21

❖❖

It is a strange fact that when we become passionately involved in something, we stop "thinking" about it. My high school tennis coach was a firm believer in this concept. He was convinced that the conscious mind was the enemy of the body's natural talents. "Thinking" was what made you blow the easy volley on match point. My coach wanted us to be "no-mind" all the time we were on the court. He wanted us to be the racket, not just the person holding it. I mention this because it explains how I operated in the days immediately after my visit to see Tom Rubino at the CIA. I suppose there were a lot of things I should have been worrying about, but I was no-mind. I wasn't thinking about the story, I *was* the story. It was coming at me, racket-high, and all I had to do was hit it cleanly.

When I got back to the office late that morning, I went to see Bob Marcus. I told him I was making progress on the France-in-China story, and that I wanted to concentrate on it for the next week or two. I told him that if my reporting went well, I would be able to document that the French had paid a $15 million bribe to a former Chinese minister. That made Marcus happy. Editors are bivalves: when you have a good story, they're content; when you don't, they hate you. He didn't ask where I was getting my information, and I didn't volunteer it.

That afternoon I read carefully through the material Rubino had given me and tried to think how I should begin my own reporting. Rubino had outlined a human chain—from Peyron to Bézy to Gaspard to the Wu family. He had also described a corporate chain that led from Banque des Marins to New Asia Development Corp. to NADC Ventures, S.A. I figured my best shot was to go after the corporate chain. It was more concrete, easier to verify. I could begin at either end of the chain—in Paris or Hong

Kong—or I could begin in the middle, with Gaspard's operation in Bethesda. I liked the idea of starting close to home.

In this kind of reporting, my technique—if you can call it that—has usually been to go for the jugular. When you have a lead about someone, don't play games; don't try to go in the back door. Call up your target, identify yourself as a reporter and ask your questions. Shake the tree as hard as you can and see what falls to the ground.

So that afternoon I called the number in Bethesda that Rubino had given me for New Asia Development Corp. A young woman answered, with a pleasant trace of a French accent. I identified myself as a reporter for the *Mirror* and asked to speak to Mr. Jean-Luc Gaspard. She asked what it was about, and I said I was working on a story about companies that invest in Asia. She put me on hold while she checked with someone, who had to be Gaspard.

"I'm sorry," she came back. "Mr. Gaspard cannot speak with you. He is not available. He does not give interviews to the newspapers."

Strikeout. I left my name and telephone number, but it seemed obvious he wasn't going to call me back. As I sat at my desk, looking out the window at the morass of traffic on Connecticut Avenue, it occurred to me that my best opportunity to get Gaspard was right then, that day, in person, because I knew he was there in the office. I looked at the documents Rubino had given me. The address of New Asia Development was 4825 Bethesda Avenue. That was off Wisconsin Avenue, near Old Georgetown Road— about a half mile from the subway. I grabbed a notebook and headed for the door.

The New Asia office was in a simple three-story building in Bethesda's small commercial district. It had everything a yuppie neighborhood could want: fancy coffee bars on either side of the street, a shop selling expensive trail bikes and two bakeries. I entered the building and looked at the directory on the wall. The building was indeed managed by TRC Properties. I smiled to think of Rubino's agent, whoever he was, beavering away through the trash. There was a listing for New Asia Development Corp. in Suite 321.

A United Parcel Service deliveryman entered the elevator just after me. His brown van was double-parked in front of the building. The package in his hand was addressed to New Asia Development Corp. "I'm going up there," I said. "I'll drop it off for you." He looked at the box. It was a new cartridge for a laser printer, worth maybe twenty bucks. "Hey, thanks," he said. He handed the package over and ran back outside to rescue his truck.

The door displayed the numerals "321" but didn't otherwise identify the occupants. I knocked, package in hand. There was a delay, and then a man pulled back the door. He had a telephone cradled against his ear, and he was talking in French. He looked just like his photograph—a sleek French preppy. He was wearing a black turtleneck sweater and an expensive tweed jacket. His face looked blank, unguarded.

"I have a package for you," I said. Without being invited, I stepped inside the door. The office was just one large room. There was a big desk over by the window, and a smaller desk closer to the door for his secretary. She seemed to be out; except for me and Gaspard, the place was empty.

He held up his finger and mouthed the words: One moment. I stepped farther inside and closed the door behind me. He held up his finger again, said a few more sentences in French, and then hung up the phone. "Sorry," he said. His mind was elsewhere.

"This is for you." I handed him the package. No longer distracted by the telephone call, he now gave me a puzzled look.

"Are you from UPS?"

"No, sir, I'm not. My name is Eric Truell. I work for *The New York Mirror* newspaper. I called earlier on the telephone, but your secretary said you were busy. We're doing a story on business investment in Asia, and we're looking at some of the new players, and I wanted to ask you a few questions. It will only take a minute."

"I'm very busy." He looked uncomfortable—taken by surprise in his own office—and was obviously wondering what to do. What would be riskier—throwing me out or answering my questions? "I don't give interviews to the press," he said.

"Just a few questions, then I'll be gone." I took out my notebook. I didn't want to give him time to think about it. "You're Mr. Jean-Luc Gaspard, G-a-s-p-a-r-d, the president of the company?"

"Yes, that's right." So what? He wasn't giving anything away; that was a matter of public record.

"What does your company do?"

"Venture capital. We make investments in new businesses in Asia." That was easy, too.

"And how much money do you have invested in Asia now?"

"Quite a bit."

"More than fifty million dollars?"

"Yes, more than that." These were real questions. He was getting uncomfortable again. I would have to hurry.

"More than a hundred million?"

"No, less than that. You know, I am sorry, what was your name— Truell?—I really must go."

"Just a few more questions and I'm done. I need some basics. Where does New Asia get its capital? Are you listed on any stock exchanges?" My questions were entirely ordinary; the sorts of things that any normal company would readily volunteer. But they were also the essential building blocks of my story.

"No, we're privately held. Most of our capital comes from banks."

"I've seen some loan records that say most of your money comes from Banque des Marins. Is that right?"

Now he was suspicious. "Yes, mostly from them. I really must go now."

"Just one more question. Can you give me the names of any of the companies in which New Asia has invested?"

"No, I really cannot. I'm sorry, but now you must go." He put his arm on my shoulder and tried to push me gently toward the door. I had the advantage of being bigger than he was. I was hard to move.

"Have you invested in a company called NADC Ventures?"

With that question he lost his composure. "Out, *now*, please, or I will call the police. This is private property. I insist that you leave."

"I'm going." I handed him a business card. "Perhaps we could talk another time, when it's more convenient."

"Out," he repeated. He looked very frazzled. This was a *cauchemar*, a nightmare, and he didn't understand why it was happening. *"Salaud!"* he muttered as he closed the door. *Son of a bitch.*

I went straight back to the bureau. I wanted to begin making my own calls to Asia before Gaspard and his friends in Paris did. It was 4:00 P.M. when I got there—5:00 A.M. the next morning in Hong Kong. I dialed the number Rubino had given me for Wu Laozi, the oldest of the three brothers. A sleepy voice answered. I asked several times for Mr. Wu, but the man started screaming at me in Chinese, and I gave up. One of the brothers had to speak English. I tried the next number, for Wu Pufeng; I let it ring for a long time, but there was no answer.

The third number, for Wu Yewin, also rang a long time. I was about to give up when a voice answered. He said something in Chinese, then dropped the phone, picked it up and repeated himself.

"Mr. Wu Yewin?" I asked. I held my breath. If this number didn't work, I was out of options. The old man in Beijing would never say anything. The voice on the other end spoke again in Chinese. I repeated: "Mr. Wu Yewin, please."

"Yes," said the sleepy voice. "This is Wu Yewin. Who is calling?"

"Mr. Wu?" I was so surprised it took me a moment to think what I should say to him. "I'm very sorry to bother you so early in the morning. I work for a newspaper in America called *The New York Mirror*. I'm writing a story about companies in Asia. My records show that you are the secretary of a company called NADC Ventures. Is that right?"

There was a long pause. It was 5:00 A.M.; he had been dead asleep; some American was calling with a silly question. "Yes," he said in the soft, distant voice of someone who has just awakened. "NADC Ventures."

"My records show that your company has received investment from a company called New Asia Development Corp. Is that correct?"

"Yes, New Asia Development. Who are you?" He was waking up.

"My name is Eric Truell. I am a reporter for *The New York Mirror*. Can I ask you one more question, Mr. Wu? What does NADC Ventures do?"

"Investments. Family investment business. Thank you. I must go now."

"How much money has your company received from New Asia Development?"

"What?" he asked, a sudden sharpness in his voice.

As I was repeating the question he hung up. I called back, but the line was busy. It remained busy the rest of the afternoon and evening. By the following day all three Wu brothers had disconnected their telephones.

"You are a fool, sir." The voice was unmistakably Rupert Cohen's. He sounded very calm and utterly sincere. He was calling me at home, two nights after my visit to Langley. I was lying on my couch watching television when he called. "I am profoundly disappointed in you."

"What in God's name are you talking about?" I asked.

"I am talking about your recent visit to the Culinary Institute of America. Are you out of your mind? The gentleman you visited is an idiot. The man is a toy soldier. Haven't you been listening to anything I've been trying to tell you? I must say, I am extremely disappointed. I thought better of you."

"How the hell do you know about my meeting? It was supposed to be secret."

"Someone told me, dear boy. We are a small fraternity, a band of brothers; actually, we are a cage full of rats who would sell their grandmothers for a piece of cheese. But now that I know of your vulnerability to this sort of national-security cult propaganda, I am prepared to offer my services as a deprogrammer."

Rupert proposed that we meet for a drink at a place in Adams-Morgan called Tom-Tom. "Nobody will notice us there," he said. It turned out to be a raunchy Caribbean bar, with blue neon lights, funky music and a lot of leggy women looking down their noses at everybody. Crowding around the bar was a herd of young men in button-down oxford shirts and no ties. They looked like Capitol Hill staffers—they had to be—who had come up to Adams-Morgan hoping to score. That was the one omnipresent, irreducible fact about Washington, stretching from administration to administration, party to party, decade to decade: it was a magnet for young people who wanted to serve their country—and get laid. In the midst of this urban meat market, knocking down a mai tai, was Rupert Cohen.

"I should amend what I said on the phone," he said, taking a sip of the cocktail through a long, colored straw. "Tom Rubino is less of an idiot than many of my colleagues. He at least attempts to be professional. But he is still, at bottom, an idiot."

"He didn't seem like an idiot to me," I answered. "He seemed quite smart. And unlike you, he actually told me something useful about what the French are doing in China. He struck me as a guy who was trying to do the best he could with what he had."

"*Omigod!*" Rupert shook his head. "Has the great white case officer recruited another agent? Of course he's good at giving briefings to wide-eyed journalists. He probably even told you some *secrets*. That's part of the DO game! They pull that same routine with Congress. They send one of the witch doctors up there, who tells them how secret all the information they're getting is, and how they're in a dangerous struggle against the forces of darkness, and the congressmen think: Hey, these guys are all right! They're doing *the best they can*. We should get off their backs and let them do their job. And in the process, they overlook the fact that the institution is *incompetent*. It let Aldrich Ames stagger around drunk for ten years handing out secrets to the Russians. It's rotting from the head down. Eric, my friend, you've been *had.*"

He was beginning to piss me off. Normally, I don't get angry at people who are sources. It gets in the way of extracting information from them. So I tend to nod, and say "That's interesting," no matter how preposterous their statements are. But Rupert was making me angry.

"Look," I said, "I don't know why you hate your colleagues so much, but I have to tell you—as an outsider—that Rubino strikes me as a smart, hardworking guy. I thought that back in Paris, before I ever met you, and I think it now. I'm working on a story, and he gave me some help, which I appreciate. I take information wherever I can get it. And if that bothers you, that's your problem."

"Touching tribute. But did it occur to you to ask the great white case officer *why* he is giving this information to you, rather than using it himself? I mean, if the organization was something other than an empty shell, why would he need you, Mr. Reporter? The organization does not *like* reporters. I think you are missing the point. The fact that he met with you is further evidence he's drowning."

I had been listening to Rupert's tirades for several months now. But for the first time his assault on the agency seemed wet, lame, insubstantial.

"You are full of shit, Rupert. Rubino is working on something that actually *does* matter—how to keep China from getting weapons that are more dangerous than nukes—and you're just dumping all over him. I don't get it. The guy is trying to do his job."

"So he told you about the big biological-weapons scare, eh? You have been read into the great secret. Congratulations. You are now one of the *illuminati*. Move over, David Gergen, we have a new member of the team. The responsibles. The insiders. The former journalists."

"Fuck you. I'm no David Gergen."

"Ah, he's offended! There's hope. He's still insulted by the idea that he is selling out. Most of your confreres in the press would be flattered to be described as 'insiders' who are numbered among the 'responsible.' They would be tickled *pink*. You still have a vestige of shame, which means you are not yet a lost cause. But I have to tell you, O friend of the powerful, that I am giving up on the Establishment Press. You're all *infected*. I've been conducting my own survey, and the results are in."

"Infected with what? What are you talking about?"

"I have been contacting representatives of other respectable organs of the Fourth Estate about employment, and they all gave me the same answer you did. 'Sorry, Rupert. It's a *nonstarter*.' They all have the same aversion to employing a former intelligence officer as you do, even the magazines. You'd think that if they were willing to employ David Gergen, they would hire anyone. But no, sorry. It violates the rules; it offends the sensibilities. That's the essence of it—your profession is managed by prudes. You have given up the essential mission of journalism: afflict the comfortable and have a fucking good time about it. No, you have decided to be serious, and it's time for me to take my talents elsewhere—to the unserious."

There was no point in trying to argue with him. He was way out there in Rupertland, where the powers of ordinary argument could not reach. "So what are you going to do," I asked, "if you're giving up on the big newspapers and magazines?"

"The future beckons. You are the past—the dinosaurs. Do you know what they died of, the dinosaurs? They died of *respectability*. So the hell with all of you. I am planning to offer my services to the organs that still practice journalism in the raw. The *Sun*. The *Star*. *Geraldo*. *Inside Edition*. *Hard Copy*."

"*Hard Copy?* You're kidding me."

"You laugh, Mr. Gergen, but these people have the right stuff. They do not scruple over the rules. They are journo-anarchists, like my own humble self."

I assumed he was joking. But that was the problem with Rupert, you never really knew what the serious parts were. For the rest of that evening he gave his usual performance of Bohemian Spy, and I laughed and played along.

But that night marked a turning point in our relationship. For all the jokes, he meant what he had said about my profession, and I meant what I said about his. We were mirror images of each other—each frustrated by the limitations of where we were, each seeking a more powerful and personal connection, each racing in the opposite direction from the other.

As we were about to leave Tom-Tom, Rupert pulled me toward him, as if he wanted to confide a last secret before we went our separate ways. "Don't take all this mumbo jumbo about biological weapons too seriously, old boy. It could impair your judgment."

"It sounds pretty fucking serious to me," I said.

"In this, as in all things connected with the secret world, there is a reference point in Venetian history, if you will indulge me. In 1649, the Council of Ten received a proposal from a man named Lunardo Foscolo of

Dalmatia, who said he had a doctor friend who could draw liquid from the spleens and pustules of people who had been stricken with the plague, and then distill it. The good doctor, whose name was Michiel Angelo Salamon, proposed to use this 'quintessence of plague,' as he called it, to infect the entire Turkish army.

"And what do you suppose the Council of Ten decided? They concluded: What the hell—let's give it a try! So they authorized a nefarious plot, and the quintessence of plague was transported by ship to the Turkish army camps. And then, as always happens in the real world, the whole thing got bungled, and in the end absolutely nothing came of it.

"So the next time my esteemed colleague Mr. Rubino tries to spin you on the subject of BW, remember that you're watching a *rerun.*"

22

❖❖

Advertising revenues at the *Mirror* had continued to fall in February and March, and Wall Street analysts were projecting that the paper would post a net loss for the first quarter—the first in its history. The stock price tumbled accordingly. Investors were betting that this wasn't a cyclical downturn from which the newspaper would recover later in the year but something different—the long-term decline of a "mature business" that couldn't cut its costs fast enough to maintain profitability. Newspapers were like railroads a generation ago, argued the skeptics: a nice business run by nice people who were in love with their product and overly generous with their employees. It was almost as if the stock market were taunting the *Mirror*'s management to do something radical to improve earnings.

Reporters in the newsroom could see that the paper was drifting toward a crisis. We might not like the business side of newspapering, but we weren't stupid. We understood that Sellinger was in a squeeze, and that if he didn't cut some of our jobs, he would lose his. Rumors were circulating that the *Mirror*'s problems were so serious the paper might be vulnerable to a takeover or even forced into bankruptcy. The Newspaper Guild, eager to take advantage of the general anxiety, had mounted a new recruiting drive in February.

In mid-March the *Mirror*'s board had its quarterly meeting. The next day a memo from the publisher was posted in New York and circulated to all the bureaus. In Washington a crowd gathered to read it as soon as Marcus put it on the board.

Mirror Corp. today is announcing an important initiative to improve the newspaper's economic performance and thereby enhance its future value for readers, employees and shareholders. Because of rising newsprint costs and declining advertising revenues, we must cut expenses now. Other departments—advertising, marketing, circulation and production—have already made substantial personnel cuts over the past two years. Now, it is the turn of the newsroom.

Over the next 12 months, we will reduce newsroom staffing by roughly 60 slots, or about 10 percent. To minimize the impact of these cuts on the quality of the paper, I am asking department heads and bureau chiefs to study their operations and submit plans as soon as possible for carrying out these reductions. To the extent possible, we will meet these reductions through attrition, but this will not be possible in all cases, and some newsroom employees will lose their jobs. Career counseling will be available for all affected employees.

We are also entering today into a joint venture with Press Alert, a privately held international communications company, to produce a new financial news service that will use some of our existing resources. We hope to target this new product at the fast-growing market for electronic news and data retrieval. The new service will be called "Mirror Alert." We will also receive a substantial equity investment from our joint venture partner.

The steps we are announcing today will be difficult for many of us. But they are essential to protect the newspaper we love.

—Philip Sellinger, Publisher

Two days later the bureau chief summoned my friend George Dirk and told him, nicely, that he was being fired. Washington had been asked to cut five slots as part of the cost-reduction plan, and Dirk's was one. Because Dirk had done so many good things for the paper over the years, the bureau chief had found a spot for him—with only a small pay cut—in the Washington bureau of Mirror Alert, the new financial news service. The bureau would be based in northern Virginia, out of the reach of the Newspaper Guild, so it wouldn't offer the same benefits as a reporting job at the *Mirror,* but Dirk could have it if he wanted it.

I took Dirk out that night for a drink. He was subdued at first, still struggling to deal with the shock. He had seen it coming much more clearly than I had. Indeed, he had been anticipating his firing for so long that he was actually relieved that the paper had offered him another job. "I'm probably going to take it," he said. "What choice do I have? I've got two kids, a big mortgage on a house that's worth less than what I paid for it, a wife in graduate school who's convinced I'm going to screw everything up. If I tell Marcus I'm walking, which would make me deliriously happy for five minutes, it will take me six months to find something else. When I do, it will pay less than what Mirror Alert is offering, and it will probably be in some place like Seattle or Austin, where I don't want to live. What choice do I have, other than to take the bone they've thrown me? I'm grateful, if you want to know the truth. They're being nice to me."

I hated seeing him like that. He was like a deflated balloon, a wisp of wrinkled rubber. But as he had more to drink, a little of the air began to come back. He began raging about the perfidy of Sellinger, Marcus, the *Mirror,* the newspaper business. And then, at last, he began plotting revenge. It was a relief, really.

"You know what I'm going to do when I get to Mirror Alert?" he said, pounding the table so hard that his beer lapped over the top of the mug. "I'm going to start my own investigative unit. And we are going to *destroy* the *Mirror.* We're going to break so many stories at the Pentagon that Noel Rosengarten will fucking *surrender.* He won't even make it to Minneapolis. He's going to toddle off to law school the way he should have ten years ago and become a full-time, professional weenie. We're going to break so many stories at the White House that Susan Geekas will be demanding a transfer. She'll be asking to cover the school board in New Rochelle, or the Solid Waste Commission in Albany—anything but have to compete with me. We're going to break so many stories that Bob Marcus will *plead* with me to come back.

"And you know what I'm going to say? I'm going to say, 'Hey, Bob. Fuck you.' "

Dirk had cleaned out his desk by the end of the week; he was starting the next Monday at Mirror Alert's bureau in Arlington. There was a going-away party for him Friday. Several people, including me, made mushy speeches about what a great guy he was. Dirk saved the day with a wicked speech of his own, denouncing all the people he disliked at the *Mirror.* He actually called Noel Rosengarten a "turd."

Despite the commotion in the bureau, I continued working on my New Asia story. I still had some loose ends, starting with the former Chinese communications minister, Wu Jingsheng, who had supposedly received the $15 million payoff. I needed a Chinese speaker to help me make the call—the *Mirror* having closed its Beijing bureau two years before in a cost-cutting move. Lynn Frenzel in New York volunteered the translating services of a Chinese-American copy aide on the foreign desk. Late one night, we placed a conference call to Mr. Wu's number and managed to get him on the phone. He confirmed that he was the former communications minister, and that he had three sons living in Hong Kong, but when we began asking him about his contact with French officials, the line went dead.

I tried to reach Jean-Luc Gaspard again. Now, instead of a live human voice answering the phone in Bethesda, there was a recording. I left several messages, but no one ever called me back. I returned to his office with a photographer, who shot the company's name on the building directory and a view of the office windows from the street.

My last step was to get comment from the French government. One of my old sources in the Quai d'Orsay, Philippe Aurant, was now the chief of staff of the prime minister's office. He was one of the good guys—the new reformers who had come in after Costa's resignation. I called him and, with elaborate apologies for dropping a grenade in his lap, summarized the $15 million payoff story. Did the French government have any comment? I wondered.

"You are a very bad boy," said Philippe. "I thought you had gone home and left us in peace. This is a dirty game, and you should not be playing in it. My official comment is 'No comment.' I will discuss this with my *chers collègues*. We will call you back."

But the follow-up didn't come from Philippe; it came from Arthur Bowman. He stopped by my desk the next afternoon as I was finishing the New Asia story. He looked fluffy, as if his wife, Mara, had taken him to a spa for a makeover. His hair was cut fashionably short on the sides, and the gray color, to my eyes, seemed to have darkened a bit.

"Are you making trouble again, Truell?" he said in a loud, cock-of-the-roost voice. It had been some time since we had talked; in truth, we had been avoiding each other the past few weeks.

"I hope so," I said. "I'm certainly working hard at it."

"And what muck are we raking this week?"

His question made me instantly suspicious. He was after something. He leaned toward me and lowered his voice to the deep register that signified that he wanted to discuss serious business.

"The French ambassador called me today," he confided. "He was very upset, which is unlike him. He seems to think that you're about to run some crazy CIA fantasy about the French in China. I advised him to call you, but he said he didn't know you, so I told him I would have a word."

"Well, now you've done that. You've had a number of words, in fact. So your mission is accomplished."

Bowman took a step back. He hadn't expected that from me. "What shall I tell the ambassador when he asks me what you're doing?"

"Tell him he can read the story in the *Mirror* when it's published. It will only cost him fifty cents."

"What's the matter with you?" he said sharply. "Why are you being so rude?"

"Not rude, just careful. I'm working on a story about French bribery in China, as the ambassador undoubtedly knows. I put in a call to the Élysée yesterday asking for comment. Someone in Paris evidently called him in a panic, and now he's calling you. Take my advice, Arthur: don't get involved in this."

Bowman walked away. He seemed shaken by the conversation. It was the first time I had ever talked with him that way. In his mind I was a kid, someone who had always treated him with due deference. Something had changed, and he seemed to understand what it was.

I went back to writing my story. By that evening I had completed a draft that wove together what Rubino had given me and what I had been able to stitch together from my own reporting. I gave it to Marcus's secretary the next morning to pass on to the great man. He summoned me an hour later and closed the door. "It's certainly interesting," Marcus said, "but it has some problems. I asked Arthur Bowman to read it, too, and he agrees. I hope you don't mind."

"I do mind, Bob. I gave you the piece in confidence, because you're my editor. I didn't think you'd convene a committee. Why did you show it to Bowman?"

"Because he asked to see it." Marcus was scratching his head. He was a bureaucrat; he was just trying to keep everyone happy, that was how he defined his job. "Bowman stopped by yesterday afternoon and said he was getting complaints about something you were working on. He said the French ambassador was all bent out of shape, and that you had blown him off when he mentioned it to you, and that he was worried. He's afraid we're being used. So I told him I'd show him a copy of your piece when it came in."

"I wish you hadn't done that. This is more complicated than you realize." I stopped and reflected on whether I wanted to go any further through that door, and decided I didn't. "Anyway, it's done. What about the piece? What do you think?"

"It worries me a little, too, to be honest. I think Bowman's right. People are going to wonder whether we're carrying water for the CIA."

"Did he say that?"

"Yes, and he may be right. I mean, who are these 'U.S. officials' you're quoting in the piece. Are they from the agency?"

"Between us, the answer is yes. The CIA did help me on the piece. My assignment was to investigate what the French were doing in China to win the contract, and the agency was obviously the place to go. But the story has real reporting in it. I interviewed the French guy who paid the money, and I interviewed the Chinese guys who received it. That's a lot more reporting than appeared in Bowman's piece about the five-million-dollar bribe. That was a pipe job, all the way."

"Easy, boy. Don't start a fight with Arthur Bowman, because you'll lose. He's the publisher's best friend, and he has been around the track more times than both of us put together. So I listen to what he says. Now, I want to go over your piece again and see if I can come up with some ideas for how to strengthen it. Give me a few days to think about it, okay?"

Marcus had an icy, managerial smile on his face. I didn't say anything. I knew what was happening. My piece had become "controversial." Someone powerful at the *Mirror* had expressed opposition to running it, so Marcus was playing it safe. He was putting it in the deep freeze for a little while. When some time had passed—when it was older, staler, weaker—he might consider running it. I had seen it happen to other "controversial" stories— a project about the decay of urban school systems by our education reporter, for example—that Marcus had put in the deep freeze until they were safe, or dead.

Bob Marcus wasn't my problem. He was simply playing his role as a news bureaucrat. My problem was Arthur Bowman.

I went for a long walk after I left Marcus's office. It was still winter outside; spring hadn't yet broken through. The sky was a low overcast that seemed to hang just above the treetops like a lid. I walked down Seventeenth Street, past the gray columns and turrets of the Old Executive Office Building. Once they had been able to fit the entire executive branch into that one building; now it couldn't even hold all the White House staff. I continued down the slope of Seventeenth Street toward the Tidal Basin. In a month it would be a tissue-paper collage, as the pink and white cherry blossoms burst from their buds. Now it was just bare branches clustered around an empty, dirty pond.

I hadn't expected that Bowman would be so clumsy. It was risky to intervene to keep a story of mine out of the paper. That was stupid, and it was a sign of the pressure Bowman was under.

When I got back to the office, I called the private telephone number Rubino had given me. It was just before 5:00. He was smooth as silk on the phone. Soft, easy, gracious. I said I needed to see him urgently. When he asked what the subject was, I just said "Arthur Bowman," and he seemed to understand what I was talking about. He could see me the next morning, he said, but not at the agency. He gave me an address in a high-rise building in Shirlington, just off I-95 south of Washington, and asked me to meet him there at 8:00 A.M.

I suppose I realized that he was asking me to meet him at a safe house, but I didn't think I was doing anything wrong.

23

Josette Towers was one of the dozens of apartment buildings that were clustered along I-95 in northern Virginia, at the southern entrance to Washington. It was a land of cars and concrete and unmarried soldiers, more like San Diego or Norfolk than the nation's capital. I found a space in the parking lot that surrounded the building and walked toward the front door. A stream of women was leaving as I arrived. They were young, dressed neatly but inexpensively, heading off to work. They examined me curiously, correctly sensing that I didn't belong there. This was where Washington's secretaries lived, in modest, low-rent efficiencies and one-bedroom apartments stacked in plain brick blocks. People didn't arrive at Josette Towers at 8:00 A.M. unless they were plumbers or real estate agents.

At the front door I searched the directory for Apartment 636, punched in the assigned number and waited for the intercom. "Who is it?" asked a voice that was unmistakably Rubino's.

"This is Bob," I said, following the instructions he had given me the night before. The door buzzed open, and I walked into the building.

It was a sad place. The elevator was decorated with notices for the un-married—the Bridge Club, the Ballroom Dancing Club, the Co-ed Soft-ball League. I pressed the button for the sixth floor, and walked down a long hall to 636. When I knocked on the door, I had to say "This is Bob" again. Rubino was dressed in a business suit. He had that fresh-scrubbed, ready-for-work look. "Come on in," he said cheerily.

It was a small one-bedroom apartment that looked out on the concrete corridor of the interstate, with a glimpse of Washington in the distance. The apartment was antiseptic. You knew instantly, looking at it, that no one lived there. The furniture was bland, unmarked; the glassware in the little kitchen was lined up in neat rows. A film of dust seemed to have settled gently over the place like a light snowfall. The only sign of life was the smell of coffee coming from the kitchen. Rubino had made a fresh pot. He handed me a mug painted with yellow and white daisies.

I didn't like being there. I had thought I wouldn't mind, but now it seemed awkward, alien. I didn't feel like a reporter. Rubino seemed to sense my discomfort. He brought me into the living room, took off his suit jacket and put his feet up on the coffee table. He was trying to be my pal, but I didn't want that either. I wanted to ask my question, get my answer, and leave.

"So, what's on your mind, Eric?" he asked. It was the voice of a game-show host. "You said on the phone that you wanted to talk about Arthur Bowman. But he's your colleague. Why would you want to ask me about him?"

"Let's not play games," I said. "I want to know whether the agency has any evidence Bowman has ever taken money from French intelligence. I need to know."

"Why do you 'need to know'? That phrase has a certain resonance in my business. It's a term of art."

"I need to know because Bowman and I are on a collision course. He's trying to convince my editors not to publish my article about New Asia. I don't want to get in a confrontation with him unless I'm sure where I stand."

"But what makes you think Bowman is a spy? He's a famous journalist, one of the most respected reporters in the country. Sure, he may have written some articles that helped the French, and maybe he doesn't like the article you've written. But that's no crime. This is a free country."

He had one eye closed as he talked, as if he were sighting down the barrel of an invisible gun. I assumed he was still sparring with me, trying to find out how much I already knew. It was the kind of thing reporters did. To get anything from Rubino, I would have to tell him more.

"I have a source," I said. It sounded so coy, like a flimsy veil half covering a face. "My source told me the CIA opened a counterintelligence investigation of Bowman in 1983. He said your people had a tip from an agent in the French intelligence service, code-named LV-something. My source said that after the investigation was opened, it was referred personally to the deputy director for operations, where it died."

Rubino's eyes had narrowed down to slits, like the firing holes in a bunker. He puckered his lips. It pained him that I knew details like these. "I'd say you have a pretty good source," he said.

"So what happened? Was Bowman taking money from the French or not? Like I said, I *need to know.*"

"How are you going to use this? I could go to jail for sharing intelligence about a U.S. citizen. It's illegal. Is this for publication?"

"No. It's just for me."

"All right. I'll deny I ever said this, but the first part of what you heard is exactly right, even the cryptonym. We had a source in French intelligence we had been running for nearly twenty years. He was retiring; this was on his conscience. He said that for many years a prominent U.S. journalist named Bowman had been a French elicitational asset—which is a fancy name for a guy who tells you stuff over dinner. But during the early 1980s, the relationship had changed, and the American journalist had begun receiving money. It was obviously a very sensitive subject—a hot potato—and at that point the deputy director for operations took personal control of the case. But your source is wrong in thinking it was killed then. That was later. First we did some fieldwork. During one of Bowman's European trips, we monitored a meeting between him and a man named Salan, who was deputy chief of the French service. We figured that Salan must be his case officer. Then our French agent steered us toward a particular *banque privée* in Geneva that handled their operational accounts, and we were able to monitor the numbered accounts into which the French were making payments. And then we just had to wait until Bowman withdrew money from the account."

"You had him cold. Why was it killed, then?"

"Because the president's Foreign Intelligence Advisory Board heard about it. They wanted to know why the CIA was investigating a prominent journalist. This was the mid-1980s; the Church Committee was still fresh in everybody's mind. We shared some of what we had, but they weren't impressed. They asked if we had evidence that Bowman had ever done anything to harm U.S. interests, and we had to say no—the French were our pals back then; they were helping us roll back the Soviets, we were all on the same team. So the DDO dropped the whole investigation down the memory hole. The files don't even exist anymore. We couldn't make the case now, even if we wanted to."

"But Bowman took money from them." That was what registered for me. The money. That would be the lead in a newspaper story.

"Yes, he took money. Are you happy, now that you know?" He looked at me sitting anxiously in my chair, staring out at the Shirlington skyline. "No, of course you aren't. You're wondering what you're doing here."

I looked around the barren apartment. I hated being there. I felt as if I had strayed across a boundary line into a place where I shouldn't be. At that time I still thought I could stay on my side of the road if I just kept my hands on the wheel. "I'm not comfortable meeting in this apartment, Tom," I said. "It makes me feel like an agent."

"I'm sorry," he answered gently. "It was the quickest way to arrange a meeting. If you come to headquarters, I have to fill out paperwork and clear it through public affairs or the DCI, and I didn't want to go through all that. Next time we'll meet at my house."

It was past 8:30. The traffic out on I-95 was bumper-to-bumper all the way into the city. I had gotten what I wanted. Why was I lingering?

"There's one more thing," I said. "It doesn't have anything to do with Arthur Bowman. This source of mine says the agency is falling apart. He claims all the secrecy just hides your incompetence, so nobody outside really knows how bad it is. He thinks I'm crazy to be talking with you at all. Is he right?"

Rubino looked at me coldly, carefully.

"Your source is right that we're in trouble. We're weak, and people are taking advantage of us. You remember that big office I had in Paris? The FBI just grabbed it. Another time, when we know each other better, I'll tell you some of the good things we've done—*I've* done—that will show you we're not always incompetent. But right now, we're struggling. That's why we need help, from anyone who has the courage to work with us."

"I hope you don't mean me," I said. He was sensible enough not to give any answer.

The only way to pry my New Asia story loose from Bob Marcus's deep freeze was to enlist the executive editor. I called Peggy Moran in New York and said I needed to speak with her boss. She asked what subject, and I told her I'd rather not talk about it on the phone, which had the intended effect of goosing her to put me on top of the call list. Weiss called me back a few minutes later.

"What's up, Eric? I hope it's not another job offer." His voice was clipped; he sounded harassed.

"I just wanted to let you know I've finished that story we talked about when I was in New York."

"Which one was that?"

"The one about French intelligence. I finished it, and I think it's pretty good. But Bob Marcus is nervous about it. He's been talking to Arthur, who's been talking to the French ambassador, who doesn't like it. But I think that's bullshit."

"Of course it's bullshit. What do we care what the French ambassador thinks?"

"Right. But the story is stuck. It might help if you sent Marcus a message, saying how much you're looking forward to seeing it in the paper. Because it's good, I promise you. I'll send you a copy."

"You don't need to do that. I'm sure it's good, if you say so. I just hate to meddle in things like this. It's demoralizing for the bureau chiefs."

"I understand." I paused, to make sure he heard the next part clearly. "But this shouldn't be happening. It could make the paper look bad. And I don't want to have to raise the whole business about Arthur again."

I hoped he understood. I had never threatened the executive editor before, and I had no idea how he would respond. But of course, he didn't respond. He acted as if I had never said it.

But the next morning Bob Marcus stopped by my desk. He said he'd gotten a call from Weiss, inquiring about my story. And he'd done a little thinking of his own, as he had promised, and he thought all the story really needed was a little more background about the China communications contract, and some quotes from a few China experts, on the record.

And with those additions, and a careful reading from our lawyers, the New Asia story ran in the paper the next day. They treated it like a feature story, with an italic headline that read: *FRENCH PLAY CHINA GAME, TOO.*

My story attracted far less attention than Bowman's scoop had, but that was understandable. The fact that the French were bribing people in Asia wasn't exactly startling; it veered toward the routine. Evidently the article was read with particular interest in China. The Chinese news agency, Xinhua, moved a brief story saying that the former minister of communications, Wu Jingsheng, had been arrested.

I had won a small victory. The best evidence was that Arthur Bowman stopped by and suggested that we have dinner. He said he wanted to talk to me about my career. But I knew that it was his own career that was really on his mind.

24

❖❖

Bowman proposed that we meet at the Athenian Club, near the White House. It was across Farragut Square from the bureau, and I walked the half-dozen blocks trying to think what I would say to our senior diplomatic correspondent. I knew the truth now. I had to tell him. The game he had been playing was over. I was still trying out the words when I reached his club. It was a handsome old building on H Street with bow windows and a great blue flag with the club insignia flying over the entrance. Like so many other things in his life, it was a relic of a lost world.

The doorman met me just inside the front door with a polite but firm query: "May I help you?" When I said I was there to see Mr. Bowman, he was suddenly all smiles. He directed me upstairs, where he said Mr. Bowman was waiting. I found him at one end of a long salon, sitting in front of the fire. He had a glass of whiskey in his hand and a copy of *Foreign Affairs* propped open on his lap.

He greeted me warmly, but carefully. How was I? Did I have any trouble finding the place? What did I want to drink? When I asked for a glass of wine, he called out to a waiter in a tuxedo, who arrived to take my order. Bowman was at home here; it was obvious that this was one of his secret vices—coming to his club, calling the waiters and doormen by their first names, falling asleep in front of the fire on a wintry night.

"Weiss tells me you're the next foreign editor, if you want it," he began. "I wondered if you knew."

Yes, I said. I knew. Weiss and I had discussed the job a few weeks before. It was a strange beginning to the conversation. He had obviously been talking with Weiss. Was that how he knew I was onto him, or had he talked to someone else?

"I think you should do it," he continued. "The *Mirror* is a great paper, but it's heading into a dry spell. People are so busy now, they're time-poor, and one of the first things that go is the newspaper-reading habit. We need to rebuild that habit with a new generation. People like Weiss and me can't do it, because we're too old. Bob Marcus can't do it, because he's too stupid. We need to get the smart kids like you in place for the next lap. Let you start worrying how to keep the ship afloat."

It was Bowman's specialty: high-grade confetti. He went on for a while longer about the history of the paper, and the evolution of modern journalism and the threat to it from the know-nothings and talking heads, and why—although he, himself, had never become an editor—he thought I should go to New York. And why, even though we had occasionally disagreed about stories, he was certain I would do a good job. And how he had said that to Weiss himself, just the other day.

Everything he said was well phrased, wise, even; and in any other context I would have thanked him for it. But tonight, his charm was intolerable. It was an evasion.

"I'm very flattered, Arthur," I said. "But you didn't ask me to dinner to talk about my career."

"No, no. That's precisely what I'd like to talk about. I want to get to know you better. We haven't really talked since that night in Paris." He wasn't listening. I had been living on a knife-edge for the last several months, and he was still playing make-believe. I needed to say the truth out loud.

"I don't want to be unpleasant, Arthur, but you and I have a real disagreement about this China story. It's been obvious for weeks. You weren't happy about my reporting. And I've had questions about the sources of your stories, too."

"Let's forget all that." His voice was honey-coated. Sweet reason. "I didn't have any problem with your story the way it was published. Weiss asked me about it. I told him it was a mix-up. I don't want to be your enemy. I think you're a good reporter." He was such a manipulator. He really thought he could bury the whole thing over cocktails at his club.

"Bullshit, Arthur!" I said loudly. The word reverberated through the second-floor salon of the Athenian Club. "You and I have a problem, and we should talk about it."

Bowman was suddenly icy. His charm offensive had failed. "Lower your voice," he said. "What is this *problem?*"

"You know what it is, Arthur. There isn't a polite way to say it." I closed my eyes for a moment. I didn't know what to do, other than blurt it out. Otherwise, we would keep dancing all night.

"Go on. I'm waiting."

"You're a spy," I said slowly. "You have taken money from French intelligence."

He looked away suddenly, like a dog who has been cuffed. This was not in his universe, the possibility that a thirty-seven-year-old reporter would make such an accusation against him, in his own club.

"That's outrageous. Who told you that?"

"Wait until you hear the details, before you deny it. During the 1980s, did you meet a man named Salan, who was deputy chief of the French service?"

"I certainly know who Salan is. And I may well have met him. Why, were we being watched? My God! How stupid."

"The CIA thinks he was your case officer."

"That's *asinine.*"

"Did you ever have a numbered account at a bank in Geneva? The CIA says that a French intelligence officer put money into an account there, and that you withdrew it."

His eyes flashed. "This is *outrageous*! How *dare* you ask me a question like that? And how dare the CIA feed you such rubbish!" He was popping with indignation. It was the intense energy of a man who had been backed into a corner.

"Arthur." I reached out my hand toward his arm. He pulled back. It was almost a cringe. I could see the hurt and anger in his eyes, and something else that I had seen that night at Mrs. Parsons's when he had looked up from the fireplace. He was afraid.

"Arthur," I repeated. "Your problem right now isn't with the CIA, it's with me. I have no desire to hurt you. You're a colleague. But unless you tell me the truth, I'm going to go see Philip Sellinger, and give this same information to him."

"Oh, Christ." The look on Bowman's face when I mentioned the publisher's name told me I had made the one threat that would truly upset him. Anything else he could have handled. But Sellinger was his best friend, his windward anchor in life. And there was something else I couldn't see, deep in that bottomless lake of secrets, that he owed to Sellinger and wanted to protect.

"I'll leave now, if you want," I said. "That was what I had to tell you."

Bowman put his hand on top of mine. He looked so weary, so exhausted by his lies. I was, in that moment, the only person with whom he could share the truth. "Don't leave," he said. "Let's go upstairs, eat some dinner. Talk."

The dining room of the Athenian Club was constructed on the same vast scale as the salon below. The ceiling vaulted up more than two stories, giving it the feel of a state room in an English palace. The Pakistani maître d'hôtel greeted Arthur with the familiarity of a colonial batman. "Mr. Bowman, sir!" He almost clicked his heels. Bowman gave him a tired smile. He was not a man for grand gestures at that moment. The maître d' seated us at a table by the windows, which looked out toward the illuminated façades of the Old Executive Office Building and the White House. We were almost the only diners left in the room. We ordered quickly, desultorily. Bowman asked for a steak and a 1979 Barbaresco. The red wine seemed to pull him back together.

"I knew we'd end up like this," he said. "I felt it, as long ago as that night at Taillevent. You and I were bound to collide. And when I heard several weeks ago that you had gone to Weiss to denounce me, it was only a matter of time."

"Weiss told you about our conversation?" He didn't answer, and I wasn't clever enough to understand that there was someone else he might be protecting. He took a drink—from his water glass—and cleared his throat.

"I'm not a spy," he said. "I do not receive money from the French intelligence service, and I never have. There are reasons, perhaps, why someone would be confused. For many years I have had close relationships with senior officers of the DGSE, including this fellow Salan you mentioned. They have been among my best sources, and they have given me dozens of good stories over the years. Often, when the United States government was trying hard to suppress something, the French would tell me the truth. They're troublemakers when it comes to the Americans. That's why they're valuable.

"Another reason people might be confused is that for a number of years I have maintained a consulting contract with a French company. It's a law firm, actually. I write occasional opinion papers for them, give them advice. It's a freelance thing. Some reporters appear on television shows, some have contracts to write articles for *Vanity Fair,* some give speeches. I have my

French consulting contract. Perhaps I should have disclosed it to Weiss and Sellinger long ago, but I never did."

"Who runs the law firm?" I asked. I suspected I knew the answer.

"A Frenchman named Michel Bézy. A brilliant man, very well connected."

I nodded. Let it be, I told myself. He's finally talking. Don't stop him now.

"For many years I have been comfortable with this consulting arrangement. My French clients didn't ask much of me. But I will *admit*"—there was a sharpness in his voice that surprised me—"that recently it has become more difficult. I have felt much more pressure from them on . . . various subjects." His voice trailed off.

"Like the China communications contract."

"Yes. Like that. And it has made me feel very uncomfortable. And since we are being frank with each other tonight, it made me especially uncomfortable when my French friends pressured me recently to stop publication of your article about this New Asia company. What I *particularly* didn't like was that they threatened me—like a bunch of gangsters—when I refused to intervene in the editorial process. That made me angry, and it also frightened me. But I wasn't sure what I could do about it. That is the problem, you see, when you get caught up in something that has been going on for a long time. You aren't sure how to unwind it. And what I am afraid of, Eric, is that the pressure is about to become more intense."

"Why is that?" He was so trusting now. His whole face had relaxed, now that he had dropped the mask of rectitude.

"Because I have been invited to a conference next month in Beijing by my clients. It's a commitment that is difficult to escape. Every spring a French businessman named Alain Peyron sponsors a symposium on global economic issues. I'm sure you've heard of him, he runs Unetat. He's another old friend, for better or worse, and he's very close to my lawyer friend Bézy. Usually he holds his sessions in places like Davos, or Aspen, or Martinique, and usually I give a brief speech for which I am very handsomely paid. But this year Peyron decided to hold a special session on the future of the communications industry in Asia. He scheduled it deliberately a few weeks before the Chinese will announce the winner of the communications contract. It's his show, a chance to wave the French flag. And he will expect me to help, in ways that I cannot predict. I feel very uncomfortable about it, but I don't know what to do."

This was a strange moment for me. The intimidating figure of Arthur

Bowman had become soft, needy—almost childlike. He was caught in something he couldn't control, and he was asking me for help. Sometimes, in moments like this, we reverse roles with our elders. We become the care-givers, they become the dependents. But we need their permission.

"Do you really want my help in escaping from all this?"

He thought a moment. "Yes, I think I do. So long as it's discreet. It's far too late for me to go to the FBI. And I would die rather than let Sellinger know. I mean that. I would rather die."

I thought about his options, and mine. There might be a way we could do each other a favor. "I'm not sure how much it would help," I answered, "but you could take me with you to China. I could go along to report on the conference, and try to keep you out of trouble."

I watched his face. The reaction would tell me everything—whether he really wanted to escape, or whether he was bound up in his explanations and rationalizations and cursed to sink with them, like a deadweight. He looked blankly at me, and then smiled—and then frowned.

"I would love you to come, Eric. Truly I would. It would be a great re-lief to have an ally who knows a bit of what I've been struggling with. I think I could probably get you credentials for the conference. But even as-suming that, I don't think the paper would approve it. The financial situa-tion is so bad right now. Weiss isn't letting people travel to Chicago, let alone Beijing."

"The paper will send me," I answered, "if you talk to Sellinger and get his blessing."

"I'll call Phil," he said very softly. And then he began to shake his head, dreamily. He had come such a long way in that short evening. Something very heavy had begun to slip from his back.

25

❖

T om Rubino lived on a cul-de-sac street in a suburban housing tract in Maryland, just outside the Beltway. The development was shielded on the eastern side by a rock quarry, so that a visitor had to contend with swirls of dust and a queue of heavily laden dump trucks to reach it. Just across the river was the CIA. On a good day Rubino and his neighbors (many of whom also worked at the agency) could zip across the bridge and be at work in fifteen minutes. Once, during a visit to Moscow, I had glimpsed one of the suburban compounds where many KGB officers lived. It had its own playground, with swings, a teeter-totter, a carousel, a soccer field. The apartments were spacious, with broad balconies overlooking the countryside. The only odd thing was the enormously high fence that surrounded the place. I had wondered then whether it was to keep the KGB families in or the rest of the world out. Now, that KGB haven was undoubtedly in ruins. But the lawns in Tom Rubino's neighborhood were turning green and the first daffodils of spring were poking through the ground.

I had called Rubino after my long evening with Arthur Bowman—not to tell him anything about the conversation, which I regarded as private— but to let him know that I was going to China, and to see if I could coax more information out of him about the French-Chinese weapons project. He sounded pleased by the news of my China trip, which was fine with me.

He invited me to come have lunch with him that Saturday at his house. His tone was what you would use with an old college friend: Stop by, have a beer, see the kids. When I entered his house that day I was still, in my mind, a reporter only. I believed I could set the terms of my relationship with Rubino—get from him what I wanted, without giving him more than I should. By the time I left that afternoon I knew, in my heart, that my independence had been compromised.

Rubino greeted me at the door in a flannel shirt, blue jeans and running shoes. A little girl, perhaps six years old, was just inside the door, dressed in a baggy leotard and a ballet tutu. "Say hello to Mr. Truell," urged Rubino. She promptly ran away to hide. We went down one flight to a large family room. Rubino went to the refrigerator to get some beers. I looked through the sliding glass door and took the measure of his backyard. There was a tetherball, a Weber grill, some molded-plastic lawn furniture, a row of battered shrubs. This wasn't the world of Arthur Bowman and Elsbeth Parsons.

We drank beer and talked for a while, as if we were friends spending a Saturday afternoon together. Our careers had some obvious similarities. He had been in China in the early eighties; I had been in Hong Kong a few years later. We had both ended up in Paris in the 1990s. And the more we talked, the more obvious it was that when you boiled the externalities away, we had done much the same work. We had both been in the business of gathering information—eliciting it, trading for it, teasing it out of reluctant subjects. He called his informants "agents," and paid them money. I called them "sources," and gave them other kinds of rewards. I suppose that broke down more of the barriers—understanding that we were in similar fields.

"What's the best story you ever wrote?" he asked at one point. I had to think. They all were heaped together in my mind, like so many newspapers thrown onto a pile on the floor. I told him about a project I had done in Lebanon in 1983, when I had just arrived and wanted to understand how the place worked. I had spent a week interviewing Christians and Muslims in two villages that lay across a ravine in the Chouf mountains. The villages had been fighting for a century, and I wanted to know why. The answer, I discovered, was that the villagers didn't *know* why. They just knew that they hated each other.

"Why did they talk to you?" Rubino asked.

"I don't know. Why people tell things to reporters is one of life's great mysteries. I've never really understood it. I suppose it's because they need to tell somebody, and we're willing to listen. We use them for our own purposes, which they don't always understand."

I wanted to turn the question back to him. "What's your answer?" I asked. "Why do people agree to become CIA agents? Why do they talk to you, when it means taking such big risks?"

Rubino averted his eyes. I had asked the magician how he did his tricks. "Most good agents recruit themselves," he said. "It's not the money, or the pressure. They do it because they believe in it."

Rubino's wife brought lunch downstairs on TV trays. She had fixed cheeseburgers, with microwaved French fries. I wondered how many times she had done this over the years they had been married: brought food down to her husband while he did his spooky business with someone she'd never met before and probably wouldn't meet again.

"Tell me about the China trip," he said eagerly. I explained that I would be leaving in several weeks with Arthur Bowman—I didn't say how we had come to be such friends all of a sudden, but I suspect he had a good idea— and that I would be covering a special symposium in Beijing organized by Alain Peyron.

Rubino already seemed to know all about it; he said Michel Bézy would be there, too. I had the sense then, as I had in past dealings with Rubino and Rupert Cohen, that their possession of secret information allowed them to exert a kind of power over me. I had resisted that pull as best I could, but I was weakening. Rubino was pulling me in a direction I wanted to go, anyway.

"I want to make this trip count," I said. "That's why I wanted to talk to you. I thought about what you mentioned at Langley—the biological-weapons research—and I wondered whether I could investigate it while I'm in China."

He delayed a moment before answering. He was like a fisherman, waiting to make sure the hook was in the fish's mouth before jerking the line.

"How brave are you?" he asked.

"I don't know," I said. "Brave enough, when I have to be."

"I'm asking because there's a chance for you to do some important reporting on your trip, if you have the stomach for it. It's something only you can do. It will be hard work, and you'll need Arthur Bowman's help even to get close. But if you're interested, I'll tell you about it."

"I'm interested," I said. "Tell me what you have in mind."

Rubino was so good at what he did. I realize now that he had prepared himself so well for this meeting that he was able to make it all seem natural. We'd drunk our beers, talked about ourselves, eaten some burgers. He didn't even have to say 'This is off the record' to me anymore. I had silently accepted that we were operating under some new ground rule—premised on nonreporting in the short run, in exchange for some long-run payoff. That lure had brought me to Rubino's house. Now he was deftly opening a door, and I didn't see the surprise coming—didn't even realize it was there—until we were on the other side.

"When you were in Paris, you met a French neurobiologist named Roger Navarre. Do you remember? It was right before the Taillevent mess."

"Of course I remember Navarre. He was a sweet man, who was being manipulated by the people he worked for at Unetat. I gather your colleagues were watching him, too."

"We had him under surveillance, for reasons I'll explain. Bear with me a little longer and I think you'll understand."

"Okay. What's Navarre doing now?"

"He still works for Unetat, but for the past year he has been on loan to a private biotechnology-research center run jointly by Unetat and the Chinese government. We're convinced this is where they're doing the BW research. We think Navarre is very unhappy with what he's doing, and that he wants to come home. But his colleagues won't let him. He's too valuable."

"Have your people in China contacted him?"

"No. We've tried, but we can't get to him. We tried to pass a message a while ago through a third party, but it didn't work. That's why we need you. We think maybe you could get into that lab and see him. He knows you already; you're a friendly face, he'll trust you. You could talk to him, and find out what's going on in that lab."

"Jesus!" I shook my head. This was different from the other conversations I'd had with Rubino. The stakes were so much higher. There was so little room to maneuver. "What has Navarre been working on?"

"It's sick. They are building a weapon that attacks the human brain. It sends signals to brain cells that make them die."

"My God! They've turned his research inside out." I remembered Navarre and his mice, and how he had beamed when he talked about the miracle that had made the idiot mice smart again. "He was working on a way to heal the brain," I said, "and now they've made it into a weapon. Why did Navarre let them do that?"

"He had no choice. That's the point. He's a prisoner, and you may be the only person who can get in to see him. That's what I need from you, Eric.

If you do the reporting, you may be able to stop these experiments. Would you be willing to try?"

"Of course I would." It just came out. I didn't think about it, it seemed so obviously the right thing to do. And though I might like to pretend otherwise now, I understood what I was doing. The chief of the European operations division of the CIA was asking me to undertake a mission for him overseas, which he couldn't accomplish any other way. He was "tasking" me.

"Good man," said Rubino, smiling. He sat back in his chair. I hadn't realized how tense he had been until I saw him relax now.

"I want you to talk to someone, to get ready," he said. "She's a biologist who works for the agency. Her name is Alicia Ginsburg. She understands this stuff much better than I do. She can give you a primer on the basic science, so that you'll be able to ask Navarre the right questions."

"That's it?" I said. "You just want me to ask questions?"

"There's one more thing. If you're able to see Navarre, I'd like you to give him a message. I can't give it to you now, because it's too sensitive. I don't want to be melodramatic, but it can save his life, and maybe others', too."

Rubino's six-year-old daughter wandered downstairs. She was carrying her coat on her arm, brandishing it as a reproach to her father. "Daddy," she said. "You promised you would buy me a new guinea pig." She turned to me to explain: "Fifi is *dead.*"

"In a few minutes, sweetie. Daddy is still talking to his friend. Then I promise I'll take you to the pet store."

It was time to go. Rubino asked if I could see Dr. Ginsburg Tuesday morning. I asked if we could meet at CIA headquarters—at that point, the idea of going in through the main door was actually reassuring—but he said no, that wouldn't be wise. He would contact me Monday night with the details of when and where to meet.

He walked me to the door and extended his hand. He had a soft, moist glow in his eyes that conveyed satisfaction and pride. He was right about one thing. The best agents don't have to be pressured. They recruit themselves.

"This is going to be hard for me, Tom," I said. "It makes me nervous."

His clear, cold eyes found mine. "Of course it does. This is scary stuff. You're on the borderline now—on the edge of doing the most important thing you've ever done in your life. Of course it worries you. You're a human being, not a machine. And it will be even harder over the next few days, because you can't talk to *anyone* about it, except me. But it's the right thing. You know it."

I shook his hand, and walked down the stone steps, past his crocuses and daffodils and his daughter's bicycle, abandoned by the driveway, resting upright on its training wheels.

I stopped by Annie's house that afternoon. She was out back in her garden, clearing away the dead branches and other ravages of winter. She remarked on how much happier I looked than I did the last time I had visited, after my trip to New York to see Weiss. And it was true. I was pumped. Ever since I left Rubino's, I had felt a surge of energy. I suppose that was why I had come. I wanted Annie to see that something in me was different.

I offered to help mulch her flower beds, which was a blessedly mindless job. She handed me a rake. I was aware of Rubino's injunction not to discuss our conversation with anyone else, and I didn't really want to talk. I just needed to be with someone while I assimilated what was happening. Annie was perfect for that. She was a Zen gardener, much as I had wanted to be a Zen tennis player. Her code in the garden was no-mind, all the time.

We took a break after half an hour. Annie fixed some iced tea and brought out some Pepperidge Farm cookies that tasted as if they had been on the shelf for months. I ate them anyway, popping them in my mouth one after another. She looked at me; she could tell something had changed, but she didn't know what it was.

"How are things between you and Arthur Bowman?" she asked. "The last time we talked, it sounded like you two were going to war." Her eyes were bright with what I took to be a reporter's curiosity.

"We worked it out," I said. "Everything's fine."

"Did he convince you that you were wrong, that he's not a spy?"

"We worked it out," I repeated. "We had an honest conversation. We're friends now. As a matter of fact, we're going to China together in a few weeks."

Annie laughed aloud, almost a snort. "What a lovely couple! You two have so much in common." I laughed too, thinking I understood the joke. But the mirthful look on her face changed into something more reflective and distant; it was as if she had stitched together pieces of fabric and was now examining the whole.

"You did it, didn't you?" she said, nodding her head as she spoke. "You told Bowman."

"Told him what?" I asked. But she didn't answer. She had turned abruptly from the table and headed back to the yard, to finish her gardening.

I spread my last bag of mulch, while Annie planted the rest of her pansies in the terra-cotta pots that lined her back terrace. We worked hard, sweating together in the afternoon sun. She was wearing rubber Wellington boots over a pair of tight blue leggings, with a baggy wool sweater on top. She really was so pretty. In the years we were together I had wanted to possess that beauty, lock it up, make it mine. For several minutes I kept staring back at her as I tried to finish my mulching. I knew what I wanted. It was so close. What was I waiting for?

I finally put down my rake and walked over to the terrace. She had her trowel in her hand as she studied the different-colored pansies in her cardboard box, wondering which to plant next. I came upon her from behind and wrapped my arms around her waist. I didn't know what she would do; it had been many years since we had touched like this. I pressed my body against her. She dropped the trowel and turned toward me. She was surprised, but not displeased.

"Let's go inside," I said.

"Yes," she said. It was the sound of warmth, and desire. "You don't look so lost anymore."

"I'm not lost. I know exactly where I am. I want to make love with you."

She took my hand and led me, without a word, into the house. We never made it upstairs to her bedroom. The moment we were indoors we began pulling at each other's clothes. The afternoon sun was streaming in through the open window. The light played across the soft curves of her body the way it does across a field, so that it seems to be moving even when it's still.

It had been seven years since I had seen that body. I knew every inch of it, and yet it was entirely new and strange to me. I reached out my hand and stroked the side of her hip. I was in a trance, as if I had fallen out of consciousness into the dream life where she had been living for all these years. I wanted to see, touch, feel every inch. She whispered into my ear, "Now!" and pulled me toward her.

When I awoke on the couch, it was night. Annie's head was cradled against my chest. She fit so perfectly. As I first opened my eyes I felt as if we had been asleep for seven years, and awakened exactly as we had been before. But nothing is ever that way.

As we lay together, half awake, I called her name. I had so much that I wanted to say, but couldn't. I was wandering into territory I didn't know or understand.

"What?" she said sleepily. She nestled closer to me, her breast soft against my side. I didn't answer. The folds of sleep gathered around me again.

"Annie," I asked again a few minutes later, "have you ever imagined that you were a spy?"

"Of course," she said dreamily. "Everyone does."

26

❖

Alicia Ginsburg was a plain, thin woman with a reedy voice that croaked in the upper registers. Rubino had told me the essentials of her biography. She had come to work at the agency in the mid-1960s, immediately after receiving her doctorate in cell biology from the University of Maryland. From the start, she specialized in the somewhat obscure field of chemical and biological warfare. She had been part of the agency team that handled the major BW emergencies of the last twenty years: from the mysterious anthrax epidemic in the Russian city of Sverdlovsk in 1979 to the "yellow rain" in the 1980s to the Iraqi biological-weapons program in the nineties. She was a tough, unstinting woman; a person who had lived most of her adult life entirely within the national security bubble. She pledged absolute loyalty to that world, and had been rewarded, late in her career, with the title of division chief.

Rubino had arranged for me to meet Ginsburg at an unmarked office building on I-270 in Rockville that housed part of the agency's Science and Technology complex. It was an ordinary enough building from the outside—no different from the offices of dozens of start-up biotech companies that dotted this part of Montgomery County. But inside, the building was very different from its neighbors. It had the security regime of a place where compartmented, highly classified research was done. Everyone wore a badge, including the man buffing the marble floor of the lobby.

I parked in the lone spot reserved for visitors. A uniformed security man stopped me just past the front door and asked to see my identification. When I flashed my driver's license—rather than the CIA badge he had expected—he was instantly on the phone. Waiting for security checks had become a condition of my life; I no longer chafed at it.

Dr. Ginsburg arrived at the desk a few minutes later, accompanied by Tom Rubino. She seemed flustered by the fact that a visitor had actually come to see her. Rubino took over the task of negotiating my passage, and in a few moments I was cleared to go upstairs. Past the entry barrier, the place had the feel of a university lab complex—long corridors lined with shelves, occasional doors bearing prominent biohazard warnings. Ginsburg's own lab took up most of one wing. In addition to the lab itself she had a large office. Rubino excused himself. He said he had some business to do on the phone but would be back later.

Ginsburg sat me down in her conference room. She reminded me of one of my high school science teachers back in Davis: a woman uncomfortable with her body—you could see it in the way she held her hands awkwardly at her side when she stood—but passionate about the life of the mind. She began her briefing as if it were a college-admission interview.

"What sort of background do you have in biology?" she asked.

"None, to speak of. That's not my field."

"I see." She shook her head sadly. "Mr. Rubino didn't give me much help in preparing. In fact, he didn't tell me anything about you at all, except that you will be traveling soon to Beijing and are looking for evidence of French-sponsored biological-weapons research there. I had *assumed* you were a scientist."

"No. I'm not a scientist at all. Sorry." She didn't seem to have a clue who I was, which was reassuring.

She dimmed the lights and switched on a slide projector, which displayed a color picture of two people in white coats bending over a shallow box containing a clear substance that looked like congealed wax.

"We call this a gel box," she said. "It's the first thing you will notice in any serious biotechnology lab. Scientists use it to separate DNA strands, which is the first step in recombinant-DNA engineering. So if you should see one of these boxes, you'll know they are not making Jell-O."

"What brand names should I look for on the equipment?"

"French companies. Much of what you'd find in a laboratory in Paris is made by a company called ESI, Équipement Scientifique et Industriel."

I wrote it down. I wanted to be a good student.

"Now then, slide two shows a second warning indicator of possible biological-agent preparation." She clicked a button, and the new slide appeared. It showed a computer monitor that displayed an elaborate graphic model of the molecular structure of a particular drug compound. "This is a French system. It's called *Bio-Ordinateur.* It's used by Unetat's drug subsidiary for computer-assisted drug design. If you see this machine in Beijing, you've made a significant discovery. This is a red flag."

"Why? What can they do with it?"

"They can use it to synthesize peptides—especially the ones known as 'bioregulators,' which can, quite literally, turn the body off and on. If these peptides could be manipulated and synthesized in large volumes, they might yield very toxic weapons. It would be possible to create agents that could affect the *mood* of the target population—allowing the user to create fear, depression, fatigue, lassitude, confusion, panic. As a matter of science, this is entirely possible. So keep your eyes open, please."

She clicked for the next slide. It showed huge glass-and-stainless-steel vessels, rising up what looked like several stories. "These are called 'bioreactors,'" she said. "They are state-of-the-art vessels for large-scale fermentation of bacterial cells. The vessels can have capacities of thousands of liters. That is large enough to allow the user to create *militarily significant* quantities of specially engineered bacteria. If you see these fermentation vessels, you are not looking at a simple research laboratory."

"Wouldn't it be dangerous to get near them?" I asked.

"Oh yes, quite dangerous . . . Now here's the *last* slide." She clicked again. The slide displayed a complicated schematic drawing. It was labeled "Suicide Genes." I thought I remembered that phrase from before.

"I must warn you," she said, "that this slide contains information carrying a code-word classification. I had to obtain a special clearance, just to show it to you."

I wasn't sure I wanted to see it. Once you were read into these secrets, certain obligations seemed inevitably to follow.

"This is what the intelligence community believes Dr. Navarre is working on in China," she continued. "He is doing only a piece of the research—they haven't shown him the whole—but we suspect he understands how the parts fit together. When you met him in Paris, Dr. Navarre was working on ways to get neurotrophins into the brain with some kind of 'chaperone,' to rebuild damaged nerve cells. Is that right?"

"Yes. He thought he could cure Alzheimer's disease."

"Dr. Navarre's misfortune was that in studying what makes brain cells grow, he also had to study what kills them. One of the amazing things about the human body, you see, is that during the first years of life it must kill roughly half the brain cells it's born with. A similar process can be stimulated in adult brains by something called 'tumor necrosis factor,' or TNF. Unfortunately, some of Dr. Navarre's colleagues at Unetat realized that the same chaperone he was using to escort the *good stuff*—the neurotrophins— could be used to introduce the *bad stuff*. Once the TNF is inside the brain, it activates what we call 'suicide genes.' They make proteins that trigger a lethal cascade of events—a programmed, regulated destruction of brain cells—known as apoptosis. Scientists give these genes names like 'grim,' and 'reaper.' I suppose they enjoy jokes like that."

"What does this brain death look like, when it happens?" I asked.

"It's quite horrible. It's like the dementia people suffer in the final stages of AIDS, but worse. Disorientation, acute anxiety, loss of control of all bodily functions. It's as if the brain and spinal cord were melting away. There's nothing left. The victims die utterly alone, in pure terror."

Her explanation was careful and specific, spoken in the measured tones of a scientist. I tried to imagine thousands of people suffering in that way, unattended by doctors; to imagine children, terrified, as they watched their parents die. Nuclear war would be far preferable. "How would this weapon be delivered?" I asked.

"That's the hardest part. We think the Chinese are focusing on delivery systems. The most likely way would be to insert this TNF and its prion chaperone into a virus that is airborne, like Hanta virus. A missile warhead would release the virus in the air, over the target population. People who inhaled the virus would become infected, and many of them would die. The useful thing about Hanta virus for weapons designers is that it can survive in the soil for a very long time. Every dry and windy day, it would spread farther and infect more people."

She spoke so crisply, so bloodlessly. I didn't want to hear any more about how it would work. I wanted to know how it could be stopped.

"What if Dr. Navarre leaves China," I said, "will that end the research?"

"No, but they will have great difficulty without him. He is the only one who fully understands the biological science. He is like an Oppenheimer or a Teller. They need him."

She switched the lights back on. She looked more substantial now than before, as if she had been bolstered by her own presentation.

"Do I need to tell you how important this is? I don't think so. As a scientist, I regret to say that modern biotechnology has made possible an entirely new category of weapons. Imagine the most gruesome deaths possible. It will be possible to replicate them, on a massive scale, with these designer weapons. These are weapons of *terror*. Their mere existence may induce a target population to capitulate. Imagine such weapons in the hands of the Chinese leadership. They would threaten the security of the United States. So please pay attention during your trip. I really don't think that's too much to ask."

She called for Rubino on the intercom and primly left the room, without even bothering to say good-bye to me. Rubino arrived carrying a large map of Beijing with him, which he now attached at four corners to a cork bulletin board on the side wall. He showed me where Navarre's lab was—inside the gates of Qinghua University, northwest of the city. Qinghua was the Chinese version of MIT, and the campus was technically off-limits to foreigners. Rubino said the only way to get in would be with help from Bowman's friends at Unetat. They had an office in the laboratory complex, and their guests were allowed in and out.

He folded up the map and handed it to me, along with the portfolio of Dr. Ginsburg's slides. I took them silently. I gazed out the window and stared at the traffic sailing by on I-270. Across the highway was a fancy health club, with a big sign advertising its racquetball courts and indoor pool: GET IN SHAPE FOR SUMMER NOW! I was somewhere, nowhere, staring out the window, trying to keep from looking down.

"Now listen to me, Eric," said Rubino. "There's one more thing I have to tell you. I've had to do something a little unusual. The agency operates under an executive order that normally bars us from using U.S. journalists in any operational capacity. Because we've given you some special help today—and because we'll want to talk to you when you get back—I've decided to seek a special waiver from the director. He has agreed to let you do this. But there's a procedure involved."

"What procedure? I'm not following you."

"Technically, what we're doing is sending you under journalistic cover to gather intelligence—information that's vital to the national security, which we could not obtain in any other way. That is the basis on which we have obtained the waiver."

That last statement had the icy precision of a legal document. I had understood, in my heart, what I was doing. But I had never stated it to myself so baldly. It was like seeing your face in a mirror under a harsh light.

"What will I be?" I asked. "A CIA agent?"

"Of course not," he said gently. "You'll be a confidential source. And we'll protect you, just the way you protect your sources."

That bland reassurance didn't matter. I knew what I was doing.

"I could get fired if anyone finds out what I'm doing," I said soberly. "This is absolutely a violation of the *Mirror*'s rules."

"Nobody will find out." His voice was so reassuring. "This stuff is all technicalities. It's just paperwork, but I thought I needed to go over it with you. We have obtained similar waivers before for other reporters. I can't give you examples, but take my word. It has happened more than once, and the world never knew a thing. We're good at keeping secrets."

He shook my hand before I had a chance to say anything more, and then looked at his watch. "I have to go," he said. "Call me if you have any more questions. The guard will take you downstairs." He opened the conference-room door. A guard was waiting in the hall outside.

Often, the biggest decisions we make in life aren't really decisions at all. They're the product of habit and momentum—things that have been going on for long enough that they've built up their own speed and force and have become difficult to stop or deflect. So you let them happen. A lot of marriages are like that, and career choices, and decisions about where to go to college, or whether to have children, or where to live. We call them decisions, but they really aren't. They come to us pre-made—the sum of so many previous events and determinations that they have a *weight* that feels like a layer of time. My trip to China was like that. If there was a decision, it had been made a long time before that visit to the unmarked building on I-270.

And then the automatic reflexes took over. There were all the details of getting ready for the trip—buying my plane ticket, arranging hotel accommodations, getting shots. Bob Marcus suggested a roster of stories, but I told him I wanted to concentrate on the communications contract and the broader French commercial relationship with China. That was fine with Marcus; he had learned that in matters involving me and Bowman, it was best not to interfere.

A few days before I was scheduled to leave I received a call at home from Rupert Cohen. He sounded ecstatic, more voluble even than his usual staccato speech. *"I did it!"* he screamed into the phone *"I did it! I did it! I did it! I did it!"*

"You did what?" I asked.

"I QUIT. I fucking quit. I'm a free man! I'm a *journalist*!!!"

Rupert narrated the extraordinary procedures that had been part of his leave-taking from the agency. He'd had to sign a series of oaths, contracts and quitclaims promising in several dozen different ways that he would never, ever, violate his secrecy agreements by disclosing any aspects of his work at the agency. Violation of these promises would render him the legal equivalent of roadkill—allowing the agency to seize any and all income he had received, confiscate his property, seek recovery of additional money from his heirs and assigns. The departure paperwork ran to nearly a hundred pages. But Cohen had signed it all.

"Now that you're a journalist," I said, "where do you plan to practice the craft?"

"*Hard Copy!*" he said. "I pitched them an idea for a Washington segment I'd do every night. A sort of update on political gossip, conspiracy theories, dirt from all over. We're going to call it *The Hatchet Man*. That's the gimmick, see. I'm the Hatchet Man. I go on the air every night looking spooky as hell and I dish all this stuff out—some of it true, some maybe true, all of it interesting—and the audience sits there stoned, wondering *What the fuck is this?* It'll make fabulous television. Sort of like combining *Cops* with *Nightline*. I mean, how can that miss? That is what America has been *waiting* for. The country is *tired* of David Gergen. People are ready for the Hatchet Man. Am I right, Eric? Am I fucking right?"

Before I left, I went to see George Dirk at his new office in Arlington. It was in a modern-looking building near a metro stop. The office looked more like a trading room on Wall Street than a normal newsroom. There were monitors recording instant price movement of stocks and bonds around the world; special commodities wires that transmitted the latest computer forecasts of expected weather patterns; analytic models that mimicked the operations of government forecasters at the Bureau of Labor Statistics and the Federal Reserve.

Dirk was at one of these desks, surrounded by screens displaying obscure financial information. He had his feet up when I arrived, and he was talking on the phone with one of his confidants. "Gotta go," he said into the phone as soon as he saw me. I took him to a noisy bar across the street. A group of beefy guys were watching a basketball game on television and screaming every time someone scored. We found a table in the back.

"I *hate* my job," said Dirk. "It's a travesty. Mirror Alert is not to be confused with journalism. A. J. Liebling would not be pleased to see where his profession has ended up. Do you know what we *do*? We compile a tip sheet for Wall Street. We exist to provide a few thousand asshole clients with a five-second beat on Reuters in reporting the earnings of Micron Technology or a dividend cut by General Motors. A big scoop for us is an exclusive on what the Agriculture Department will report about expected soybean production in September. We have four people covering the Bureau of Labor Statistics and nobody covering the State Department. How do you like that? We have so many people covering the Federal Reserve that Alan Greenspan can't take a shit without one of our guys handing him the toilet paper. I mean, this is not a life."

"It's a job," I said. I didn't want to hear about his problems right then.

"Yes, jobness is the principal virtue of this job. No doubt about it. And payness. But other than that, it's pathetic. The managers—they want you to call them that, by the way, not 'editors'—are all from our beloved joint venture partner, Press Alert, ownership unknown. And believe me, they know absolutely nothing about the news business. Most of them are Wall Street washouts, as near as I can tell. I wonder if Sellinger knows what second-raters our new partners are. I can't believe he made a deal like this. I used to think Sellinger was a smart guy."

"Maybe he didn't have a choice."

"We all have choices, buddy boy. And I'm telling you, these Press Alert guys are weird. In fact, I am conducting my own quiet examination of who they are and where they came from. It's the only thing that is keeping my mind alive at present. And I'm telling you, there is a *story* here. I'm never wrong about these things." His eyes glinted with the fire of revenge. "How about you? What's up with you?"

"I'm going to China for a week with Arthur Bowman."

"You're shitting me. You and Bowman? That can't be healthy."

"I'm chasing the best story of my life." The force of that statement left even Dirk momentarily speechless. "The reporting has been weird, and the story scares me a little. It's dangerous, in a bunch of different ways."

"What are you talking about? I'm really not tracking you at all."

"I can't explain. But I need to ask you a favor. That's why I wanted to see you before I left."

"Me? A powerful, globe-trotting journalist like Eric Truell needs a favor from me?" Dirk's self-loathing had returned with gale force. "Me? The guy who spends his days analyzing whether leading indicators will be lagging and whether cattle futures will be rising faster or slower than hog bellies. You need help from *me*? I find that hard to believe."

"Shut up, Dirk. This is for real."

I removed a key from my pocket and handed it to him. "This is a key to the center drawer of my desk at home. Inside the drawer is a sealed envelope with a file inside marked 'LA.' If anything happens to me in China, I want you to get the file. Annie Baron has a key to the apartment—she's watering the plants for me—and she can let you in. The file will explain what I've been working on. Take it to Ed Weiss."

"What does LA stand for?" asked Dirk.

"Liars Anonymous," I said. "Don't ask what it means. I'm not sure I know myself."

The night before my plane left from Dulles a courier dropped off an envelope at my house. The courier wasn't from one of the commercial delivery services. He made me show identification before he would give me the package, and he made me sign a receipt. Inside the envelope was a one-page letter from Tom Rubino:

Dear Eric:

I mentioned two weeks ago that I had a special favor I would ask you to perform during your trip to Beijing. Because of its sensitivity, I didn't want to give you the details until you were about to leave.

Here is my request: If you are able to see Roger Navarre and talk to him in confidence, I want you to judge his state of mind. If my information is correct and he wants to come home but is unable to do so, I would like you to give him this message.

Please tell him that the United States government is prepared to get him out of China and bring him to the United States, where he will be offered a generous resettlement payment and a stipend to support his research. Tell him that if he is interested, he should *not* go to the U.S. embassy, but to the following address: "Australia Shipping Desk, Gloria Plaza Hotel, 2 Jianguomennan Dajie, Beijing." He should identify himself as Bob Thorpe. They'll do the rest. If he asks, tell him that we're *very* good at this. We do it with shipping crates, and it always works.

There are many reasons you might not feel comfortable with this request, and you are under no obligation to fulfill it. But I hope that you will. I cannot imagine a greater service you could do—an act that would make more of a difference for good. I know you well enough to be confident that is the business you are really in.

Good luck.

27

Arthur Bowman met me at Dulles Airport. He was carrying a traveling bag that contained his red velvet bedroom slippers, a CD player with a selection of Bach cantatas and a small shaving kit. I will say this for Bowman: the man knew how to travel. As always on his overseas trips, he was flying first-class. That was part of his understanding with Philip Sellinger. They had concocted some rationale involving the likelihood of meeting important sources, but the truth was that Bowman liked big seats and fine food and wine, and he felt these modest perks were a small price for the *Mirror*'s stockholders to pay to keep him happy and productive.

When they called for the first-class passengers to board the plane, I reached out to shake Bowman's hand farewell. I was flying coach and would be spending the next fourteen hours back in steerage, doubtless surrounded by children with earaches who would howl all the way to China. But instead of saying good-bye, Bowman handed me a first-class boarding pass.

"I got you upgraded," he said. His explanation had something to do with frequent-flier miles and a friend who worked at a travel agency. I didn't really understand it, but I didn't quarrel. I just followed Arthur past the stares of envious travelers who parted to make way for us.

Somewhere over Pittsburgh, the stewardess served cocktails and the two of us began to talk. We hadn't spent much time together since that night at the Athenian Club, and I wasn't sure what the balance was in our relationship anymore. We had known each other for years as stereotypes—Bowman the all-knowing veteran of a thousand deadlines and me the brash kid. Those roles had come crashing down in one evening, but I wasn't sure what had replaced them. The truth was, we didn't know each other very well.

"This trip is costing Phil Sellinger $5,758," announced Bowman, raising his glass of Glenfiddich in homage to the publisher. "And that's just my ticket. Isn't that extraordinary? Not simply the money, but as a statement of journalistic principle. I had to scream at Peyron's people. They wanted to fly both of us first-class on Air France, gratis. I gave them a speech about newspaper ethics and told them to piss off. We were flying United."

"How did you persuade Peyron to let me attend the conference? He can't have been pleased."

"He was less than thrilled about your trip, as you surmise. The New Asia story did not amuse him and Bézy. But I made it a *point d'honneur.* I told them you were the best young reporter at the paper. I said that unless they allowed you to cover the conference, I would refuse to participate. I also pointed out that you were likely to be in Beijing regardless of what they did—since the Chinese had given you a visa. At that point, logic prevailed. They concluded that they couldn't stop your trip, so they embraced it. Peyron says he wants to meet you. He'll give you an interview if you want."

"I'd love to talk to him, and Bézy, too. And I'd like to see some of the technology projects Unetat is doing with the Chinese. Do you think they'd go for that?"

"Why not? They want everybody to know how friendly they are with the Chinese. They think it will help them win the contract. What do you want to see?"

"I gather they're doing a joint biotechnology project," I said, treading as lightly as I could. "Maybe we could look at that."

"No harm in asking," he answered. He held his glass of whiskey up to the window. The crystal filtered the bright sunlight like a prism, casting a dozen different shades on the golden liquid. "No harm at all."

I wanted to tell Bowman the truth—to describe the chain of events that had put me on that airplane next to him, to recount the meetings with Rubino and Ginsburg—to draw him into the web of obligations that I had incurred, so that I could turn to him later if I needed help. But I knew that was unwise. I was beginning to like Bowman, but I still wasn't sure that I trusted him. And he had enough problems of his own. People who had paid him a lot of money over the years thought they owned him, and he was about to default on their investment.

"Are you worried about what might happen in Beijing?" I asked. I was curious about what he might answer. Bowman was one of those people who make a point of not registering emotion.

"I'm always nervous before I start something new," he said. "But the minute we arrive in Beijing, it will go away. It's the anticipation I don't like. You've heard the saying: A coward dies a thousand deaths, a brave man only once. That's corny, but it's true. I remember trying to get into Iraq in 1980, after the war with Iran started. I had flown to Kuwait and told Ed Weiss that in twenty-four hours I'd be in Basra, where the heaviest fighting was. The Iranians were bombing the city, and the Iraqis were attacking across the river toward Khorramshahr. I'd done this sort of thing in Vietnam, but it took me a whole day to get up my nerve. I drove up to the border the first day and chickened out. I was so ashamed I went back to my hotel in Kuwait City and got stinking drunk. Even with all the booze, I barely slept that night, because I knew that the next day I'd *have* to do it. Weiss was clamoring for copy. But the minute I was across the border, it was easy. I was doing what I knew how to do. I was so high after a few weeks in Basra they had to drag me home."

Bowman was a pro, but I wondered if even he had any idea of what might lie ahead. "Arthur," I said, "when we talked that night at the Athenian Club, you said you were afraid Peyron would try to pressure you in Beijing. What did you mean? What would he want you to do?"

"Cook a story, probably. I don't know. Maybe more. You never know with these guys. But if he leans on me, I'm going to lean back."

"How are you going to do that? What's your leverage?"

"You, young Truell. I'll tell them that if they don't back off, you'll write a story that will blow them sky-high—two weeks before the Chinese announce the contract. Why do you think I let you come along? You're my insurance policy."

Cocktail hour seemed to last until we were over Denver. Bowman and I were, as the therapists like to say, "self-medicating." But for all the boozy talk, he remained a mysterious figure to me. Above all, I didn't understand what had led him to accept money from people he must have known were connected with French intelligence. When you're drinking with someone, you eventually lose the normal inhibition about asking questions that might be offensive. So I asked.

"How did you get involved with Peyron and Bézy and the rest of them in the beginning? What made you do it?"

The question took him by surprise. He drew back into the vastness of his first-class seat and closed his eyes. I thought I had lost him, but a moment later he began talking.

"It sounds so predictable and pathetic. But I didn't realize what I was getting into. I had known French intelligence officers since I first went to Vietnam in the mid-1960s. I spoke the language, I liked the culture, and I found them useful. They knew things about Vietnam the Americans didn't understand. I used to see a man in the French embassy in Saigon regularly, and when visiting big shots came in from Paris, I would talk to them, too. There was one man named François Salan who became a special source. He was the guy you mentioned that night at the Athenian Club. He was a fabulous operator; that was what impressed me. He knew what he was doing.

"We stayed in touch after I left Indochina. He was a rising star in the French service, and he arranged for me to see his people when I traveled. They were very useful in the Middle East. The French were the only ones who really understood Lebanon. The Israelis thought they did, but they were seduced by their own agents, the Maronites. The French were too cynical for that. They knew that Lebanon was a sack of shit. Salan helped me in lots of ways: he gave me stories; he introduced me to people; once, when I got kidnapped by some crazy Alawites in Syria, Salan arranged my release. And when I could, I did Salan a good turn. Mostly little things: making sure the French got a chance to put their spin on events, playing up some of the themes that mattered to them. I didn't tell the paper about my contacts with them, but let's face it, there are lots of things a foreign correspondent doesn't tell the home office. Right?"

"Right," I said. We were coconspirators, members of the secret society who knew how to hide our bar bills as telex charges, who paid our hotel bills with cheap money we changed on the black market but got reimbursed at the inflated official rates of exchange. I understood all that. But taking money from a foreign intelligence service was different. I needed to comprehend that, too. Bowman was getting to it, in his own meandering way.

"When I came back to Washington in the mid-1970s, something was different. I wasn't going to be a roving wild man anymore. I met Mara, and she got pregnant, and I got married, and that was fine. I was ready to settle down, and she was a great beauty. The talk of the town. Suddenly we had a life to support. She wanted to entertain, so we needed a fancy house in Georgetown. She wanted to raise perfect children, so we had private-school bills. She wanted to take holidays in fashionable places, so there were travel bills. It cost a lot of money, and it was very hard for me to tell her to slow down, to remind her that I was just a journalist.

"So we began to operate close to the edge financially. You don't understand what that's like, do you, Truell? You're a kid. The biggest expense you've got to worry about is dinner after a movie on Saturday night. But when you're married and have kids, the bills add up. I went to Sellinger after I had been back home awhile and told him the numbers didn't work—I was going to have to quit unless he could find some way to supplement my pay. He did his best, but it wasn't enough.

"And then one spring about fifteen years ago, I did something stupid. I was having dinner with my friend Salan in Washington, and I was complaining about my midlife crisis. That's always a tip-off for spooks, you know, when middle-aged men start whining about how tough things are. I told him I was broke, and that Mara was demanding that we go somewhere exciting that summer. Maybe I was asking for it. Probably I was. That night Salan mentioned that a friend of his had a place on the Riviera, at the Cap d'Antibes, that would be empty for part of August, and maybe I would like to use it.

"So I said sure. I figured it would be a little condo near the beach. But it was an estate on a hill near the Hôtel du Cap, overlooking the sea. It had a pool, and a guesthouse, and a half-dozen servants who came with the place. Mara and I were there for most of the month. All our neighbors were oil sheiks and movie stars and zillionaires. I made a feeble attempt to pay when we left, but Salan's friend wouldn't hear of it, and who was I kidding? To rent that place for the month of August, for real, would have cost a hundred thousand dollars. So I just said thank you.

"And after that, the slide downhill was easy. Salan knew that I would take money, so he offered it. And I took it. Washington had become so expensive, and the more Mara had, the more she wanted. You buy the dress, so you have to buy the shoes and the handbag; then you have to buy the pearls, and the diamond earrings, and the coat. And then you can't drive up in the same old car, so you need a new BMW.

"Salan proposed the consulting arrangement with Bézy as a cutout. But what you said at the Athenian Club about a numbered account in Geneva was right. They paid the money in, and I withdrew it to pay my bills. And guess what: as I took more and more of their money, they began to expect something for it. I tried to cooperate. And I did some other things—to help Sellinger—that I'm not going to talk about, even with you, even as drunk as I am. But I thought I could handle it, Eric, until this China business came along. And you came along. And here we are."

28

Bowman and I parted company at the airport, which was just as well, because I feared that if I had any more to drink, I would die. He was staying at the fanciest place in town, naturally, a place called the China World Hotel, where Unetat was holding its conference. I was lodging at the humbler Great Wall Sheraton on the Third Ring Road. We said our good-byes like two old drunks and pledged to meet in twenty-four hours, after we had slept off the effects of the trip.

The last time I had visited Beijing was in the late eighties. Back then, the loudest sound on the main boulevards had been the gentle whirring of bicycle wheels; now the streets were clogged with cars, motorcycles, trucks and buses. It was rush hour all day long. The trip in from the airport had once been a soothing passage through parklands and fields shielded by neat rows of trees. Now it was a long traffic jam, past acres of new construction being thrown up in the race to make money. Seeing the frantic pace of commercial activity, I understood better why the French and Americans were at each other's throats over the communications contract. China was the future of capitalism. It was that simple.

After a long sleep and a visit to the hotel health club, I wandered over to the China World to check out the conference. The lobby was as lavish as that of any hotel in New York or London: rich Chinese carpets; gleaming brass and stainless-steel fixtures that had been polished and buffed so well they were like mirrors; teakwood furniture that had been oiled and stained to a deep, lustrous red. At the Unetat hospitality desk, a lithe young Frenchwoman handed me my credentials. Her name was Lisette, and she seemed to know all about me.

"I *knew* you would come," she said.

Her eyes were a sharp cerulean blue, and her blond hair was gathered up on her head, exposing a beautiful neck. I gazed at her appreciatively. Somebody at Unetat had taken the trouble to assign her to me. Don't even think about it, I told myself. My life over the coming week in Beijing was already complicated enough.

Lisette gave me a conference program. Most of the sessions sounded numbingly dull, on topics like "China and the Fiber-Optic Future." But one item caught my eye. It was a breakfast discussion of "Biotechnology and Pharmaceutical Manufacturing in the New Asia." I asked Lisette to reserve me a place.

"Do you have plans tonight?" she asked. "We have tickets for the Beijing opera. Perhaps you and I could go, and then have a late dinner afterward?"

Fortunately, in this instance I did have another engagement. Before leaving Washington, I had made arrangements to have dinner with an old friend from Hong Kong, a Chinese-American lawyer named Michael Wee. He had worked for many years with one of the big New York firms and then launched his own legal business.

"I'm sorry," I said, "but I've made other plans."

"Then, we will do it another night," she said. She looked so tempting. There was a way her blue eyes caught the light—you wanted to look more closely, to see what made them sparkle so.

"We'll see," I said. "It's going to be a busy week."

Michael Wee picked me up at my hotel in a chauffeured Rolls-Royce. I didn't recognize him at first. He was dressed in a beige Armani suit and a black cashmere turtleneck; his hair was pulled back in a ponytail, and he was wearing a pair of round tortoiseshell glasses that made him look like a Chinese owl. The man I remembered had been a hardworking associate in his firm's Hong Kong office, a geeky Chinese-American kid who was great at managing the legal minutiae of international joint-venture agreements. Now he was a superstar.

"Hey-hey-hey, Eric," he called out to me through the window of his Rolls. He shouted something in Chinese to his driver, who hopped out to open the door for me.

"You look like you won the lottery," I said, registering the suit, the car, the man himself. This was a guy who a few years before had trouble picking up the tab when we got drunk with some of his Japanese clients at a nightclub in Hong Kong. I'd had to lend him three hundred dollars to pay the bill.

"I couldn't help it," he said. "I put a big bet on China, and my number came up. I got rich."

As the chauffeur navigated the crowded streets of Beijing, Michael explained how this miracle had happened. It had started with the fact that he was a smart lawyer who spoke Chinese and English with equal fluency. Those attributes made him a valuable adviser for Western companies that were considering launching joint ventures in China. His white male partners had continued to take him for granted, but as the Chinese economy began to explode in the late 1980s they realized that he was a profit center for the firm, and made him a partner. At that point, Michael said, he began taking revenge for the years he had been treated as a doormat. He demanded an ever-larger share of the pie, and in 1991, when his partners finally balked, he walked away and started his own firm, taking most of his old clients with him. His business had continued to expand in step with the Chinese economy.

"I'm a conglomerate, Eric," he said. "I've opened law offices in Beijing, Shanghai, Guangzhou, Hong Kong, Taipei. I have so much business, I've had to refer some of it to my old firm."

Michael had booked a table at a restaurant in the Beijing Hotel, a vast Stalinist edifice next to the Forbidden City and Tiananmen Square. The chauffeur once again scrambled to open the door. Leaving the car, I remarked on the unusual Hong Kong license plate: "8222."

"The numbers mean 'Prosperity-Easy-Easy-Easy' to the Chinese," he said. "That license plate is worth a thousand referrals."

"How did you get it?"

He pressed his thumb and forefinger together. "The same way you get everything in China, Eric. I paid someone some money."

The restaurant was on the seventh floor. The maître d' welcomed Michael deferentially and escorted us to a table by the window overlooking Raise the People's Consciousness Cultural Palace and, beyond that, Tiananmen Square. The food began arriving almost immediately. Michael had ordered a banquet: bears paws, hot Szechuan shrimp, a whole fish fried in spicy oil, Beijing duck. I felt as if I were in the company of a visiting mandarin. As we ate, Chinese politicians and businessmen stopped by the table and jabbered away at Michael in Chinese. He would listen to each of them and then offer a few words of advice. He was evidently the Chinese superlawyer—the man to see in Beijing.

"I need some help, too, old friend," I said when the waiters had cleared the last of our food. "I'm working on a great story, but it's one that could get me in real trouble if I make a mistake. That's why I need your advice."

"Whatever I have is yours, within reason."

"My excuse for coming to Beijing is to cover the Unetat conference and all the hullabaloo surrounding the communications contract. But what really interests me is French business corruption."

"I know," he said, tapping his nose. "I read your story about New Asia Development Corp. It was faxed to me a few hours after it was published in New York. It was very accurate."

"I'm glad you liked it."

"I didn't say I liked it. It caused serious indigestion among some of my clients. A lot of them do the same things—the Germans, the Brits, the Japanese, the Taiwanese; it's a cesspool, here, really—and they were all wondering where you got your information, and whether they were next. Where did you get your information, by the way?"

"I can't tell you. I think the story referred to 'U.S. officials.' "

"Okay, that's an answer. But it doesn't matter where it came from, because it was *right*. And it was a classic example of what the French do here. That's why they're going to win the contract."

"You think so?"

"It's a lock. I told my American clients that, months ago. I represented American Telephone, General Science and some of the other companies in the U.S. consortium. They wanted me to help them make the right contacts, find the right joint-venture partners. So I asked them flat out, 'Are you prepared to break the law? Because otherwise you're going to lose. The competition has greased every palm from here to Guangzhou.' "

"How does the game work?"

"It's just like what you wrote about New Asia, multiplied a hundred times. A thousand times. You find the people in government who can stop the deal from going through; then you find some way to pay them enough money to keep them from making trouble. Usually, it's through their kids. The children of the senior cadres are all very rich, if you hadn't noticed. The old man may still be wearing a Mao suit, but the kids are buying up beach property in Malibu. This is still a Confucian society. It runs on respect for elders, and the basic business unit is the family. The kids are out shaking down Western businesses on behalf of Dad and Granddad. That's for ordinary deals. But the communications contract is bigger."

"How will it work, precisely? Where will the French payoffs go? I hate to push you, but I need to know."

Michael Wee lowered his voice. "Okay, there's an organization in Beijing called the Military Industry Committee of China, known as MICC, for short. It's connected to the military, and it's run by a three-star general. On all the really big national deals—like commercial aircraft or the communications deal—you have to go through MICC. You negotiate the basic price with them—let's say it's ten billion dollars. Then their guy comes back and tells you they will pay thirteen billion. The extra three billion is MICC's share—a lump-sum bribe, which they will distribute to all the palms that need to be greased. It's a way of converting the public treasury to private use."

"How do you know where to send the three billion?"

"MICC tells you exactly where it should go—to accounts in Hong Kong or the British Virgin Islands or New Caledonia or wherever. They tell the seller which agents will handle the money. I know a recent deal where the Chinese were buying a billion dollars' worth of airplane parts. The leading bidder was a subsidiary of a big U.S. company. MICC told them where to pay the commission, but they refused. So the contract went to another company. That's the problem for American companies. They can't play the game by the Chinese rules."

"But the French can—" I said.

"Yes, indeed, and the money begins to add up. Take the communications deal. On most Chinese business it's safe to assume that the payoffs amount to at least five percent of the deal. Often it's a lot more, but let's be conservative. On a thirty-billion deal, that amounts to one and a half billion in bribes! Now, when you have that much graft, some of the money is going to stick to the fingers of the people handing it out."

"Kickbacks, you mean. People keep dropping hints to me about money that will be kicked back to France as part of the communications deal, but I haven't found anyone who really knows anything."

"Now you have." He smiled, like a ponytailed Buddha. "I know because I've counseled some of the people that are involved. But I'm not talking." He held a finger to his lips.

I looked around the restaurant. Most of the other diners had left. Some waiters were standing a dozen yards away. Had they been listening to our conversation?

"Is it safe to tell you what I'm working on?" I asked.

Michael thought a while. "No, it isn't safe to tell me, and I don't want to know. It's dangerous here. People don't play by American rules. The French don't, and the Chinese certainly don't. If you get in trouble, I'll try to help. But my best legal advice is: Don't get caught. The Chinese show no mercy to people who are unlucky."

My jet lag kept me up most of that night. I couldn't help wondering whether I would have been more comfortable with Lisette in my bed. I was finally sound asleep at 6:30 A.M., when the alarm rang. The pharmaceutical breakfast would be starting in an hour. I showered and shaved and caught a taxi to the China World Hotel. Lisette was waiting for me, dressed in a tight black miniskirt.

"How did you sleep?" she chirped. "Not so well? Too bad. But I have good news for you. Monsieur Peyron will see you this afternoon, at three, here at the conference center. He will give you an interview. Are you happy?"

"Yes," I said, "I am extremely happy. As we like to say in America, 'I owe you one.' "

"One what?" she asked. It was hard to know whether she was acting the coquette or just being stupid. She led me toward a small meeting room where the pharmaceutical session was about to start. The discussion was moderated by a Unetat executive named François Minart, who identified himself as the company's group vice president for pharmaceuticals. He talked for ten minutes or so about the size of the Chinese market for pharmaceutical drugs. The gist of it seemed to be: one billion sore throats, one billion earaches, one billion cases of acne. Then the three panelists gave their spiels—all wildly favorable to the Chinese. Lisette watched with her usual dewy-eyed enthusiasm. At last, the moderator asked if anyone had any questions. I stood up and identified myself as a reporter for the *Mirror*.

"What about biotechnology?" I asked. "Does Unetat have any plans to work with the Chinese on genetic engineering?"

The three panelists looked at one another. None of them had a clue as to what the right answer was. Eventually Mr. Minart, the Unetat man, spoke up.

"We have a small research effort under way with the Chinese, to acquaint them with some aspects of modern biotechnology. But there are no plans at present for any joint production."

After the session ended, I went up and introduced myself to Minart.

"I'm here with Arthur Bowman," I said, hoping the name would register with him. "We'd love to talk more with you about what you're doing here. Perhaps we could even see the biotechnology-research project you mentioned. That sounded interesting."

"I don't think so, really," he said. "It's very small. Not worth the trouble."

"Maybe we could meet for lunch some time this week, then." I handed him my business card, with my hotel and room number written on the back.

"Perhaps," he said. He looked over to Lisette and raised one eyebrow, as if to say, Who is this clown? "Our public relations department will contact you if it is possible."

"How many people are working in your biotechnology project?" I asked.

François Minart looked at his watch. "I must go. I am sorry. I am late." It was obvious I wasn't going to get anything out of him. He walked off, leaving me standing there with the lovely Lisette.

"Was it good for you?" she asked.

"Oh yes. Very good. I'm interested in anything about the pharmaceutical industry."

We walked back to the press center together. On the message board was an envelope with my name on it. I assumed it was probably Lynn Frenzel from the foreign desk, wanting to know whether I would be filing anything that day. But it was from Arthur, and it was very brief. "Need to talk. Come to my room, ASAP."

29

Arthur Bowman was pacing like an animal in a cage when I reached his suite. He couldn't stay still. He'd sit for a few moments in the living room, wander into the bedroom to fetch something, then bolt out to the balcony. I told him that Peyron had agreed to see me that afternoon, but he barely paid attention. He wasn't talking so much as snarling: "What assholes!" he'd mutter, and then stalk off. "Who do they think I am?" he'd say, pointing his finger at me angrily. "I am not going to play their game anymore." I still had no idea what he was talking about, except that he was very upset. I'd never seen him quite like this. He was normally a man who prized decorum and self-control, and here he was spinning his wheels, without enough traction even to explain to me what had happened.

"Let's take a walk," he said finally. "I need some air."

We were soon out on Jianguomenwai Dajie, the crowded main street that led toward Tiananmen Square. I looked back toward the hotel to see if anyone was following us. "Don't!" Bowman said sharply. "If they see you looking for surveillance, they'll only be more suspicious. Just keep walking and talk quietly, and make sure nobody's too close."

"What in the hell happened?" I asked in a voice just above a whisper. "Why are you so upset?"

"They went too far. Just like I told you they would. Fuck them! Who do they think they're dealing with? Those cocksuckers." He was boiling over again.

"Calm down, Arthur. Just tell me what happened."

"Last night . . ." he began, and then stopped. He was so angry he was still having trouble getting the words out. He took a deep breath, which seemed to help. "Last night, I was invited to a dinner party given by the French ambassador here. Peyron was there. Bézy was there. Some other people from Unetat. It was very French, very civilized. After the dinner, Bézy asked me to stay. He took me to a room upstairs that was like a bubble. I figured it must be where they talk about secrets. Inside, it was like a little conference room. I really didn't want to be there with him. Bézy is a *shit*." His voice was rising again.

"Not so loud. What did Bézy say?"

"He gave me a document, which he said came from the National Security Agency. He said it was the specs for a plan the NSA and CIA had drawn up that would allow them to capture whatever Chinese communications traffic they wanted, if the U.S. consortium wins the contract. He claimed it was like a trapdoor; with it, the Americans could read encrypted Chinese stuff. He wanted me to write a story about it in the *Mirror*. A big exposé that would end any chance for the Americans to win the contract."

"What did you tell him?"

"I said no. I wouldn't do it."

I was surprised, I will admit. For months I had watched Bowman write whatever the French gave him. Now he was refusing. "Why?" I asked. "Because the document isn't true?"

"No, not that. It probably is true. Hell, I *hope* it's true. It sounds like a good idea. No, I said I wouldn't do it because I knew it was wrong. Bézy made me feel like a whore, taking me into his secret room and trying to use me to screw my own country. It made me sick, Eric. I love my newspaper. It's the thing I care about most in the world. I'm not going to turn the *Mirror*'s pages over to them. I won't do it anymore. And that's what I told him. I gave him a loud 'Fuck you,' to his face, in his bubble."

"What did he say?"

"All the shit you'd expect from someone like that. He said it was too late for me to back out. He said it was the last thing they would ever ask me to do. He said if I did it, I could name my reward: an apartment on the Île St.-Louis; that villa I liked so much in Cap d'Antibes, whatever I wanted."

"Did he threaten you?"

"Not really. I think he knew that would backfire—exposing me publicly as a French spy. No, he didn't try that. He tried something nastier." Bowman looked away, in embarrassment.

"Well, what did he do, then, if he didn't threaten you?"

"I really don't want to say. This whole thing makes me sick. It disgusts me."

"Come on, Arthur. Tell me. I need to know."

"Okay. You asked, so I'll tell you. Bézy threatened *you.*"

I felt a sudden, sharp chill. "Me? What can he do to me?"

"Aw, a bunch of crap. You don't want to hear it. It will just upset you."

"Yes, I do. What did he say?"

"He said you were working for the CIA. He had a list of stuff, going back to Paris. A whole bunch of things. I didn't even listen. He said if I didn't write the article, he would do everything he could to hurt you and the *Mirror* by making it all public."

"Oh, Jesus," I said. I stopped for a moment to get my bearings. "What did you tell him?"

"I told him to fuck off! I said it was outrageous bullshit, that you were one of the best young reporters in America, and they could say whatever they wanted, because nobody would believe it. I told him if they tried anything like that, you'd sue them for libel, and I'd testify for you and describe everything Bézy had said to me. *Everything.* That seemed to shut him up. What an asshole, thinking he could pull a stunt like that."

I didn't respond. So many different thoughts were firing at once in my mind, I couldn't follow any single one through to its conclusion. I thought about Ed Weiss, Rupert Cohen, Tom Rubino, Arthur Bowman—each holding a tether attached to me at a different point. And I was standing on a dusty street in Beijing, pulling them all toward something very messy.

"What an asshole, right?" Bowman repeated. He wanted some confirmation, some signal that his ordering of the world was correct. He was waiting for me to answer. I knew I had to tell him something.

"I don't work for the CIA, Arthur."

"Of course not, for Chrissakes! The whole thing is outrageous." He wanted to leave it there, but I hadn't quite finished.

"I've talked to them, sometimes. I met with their people before this trip."

"So what? I've talked to them plenty, too, over the years." He looked carefully at me. I think he must have seen on my face the same thing I'd seen on his, that night at Mrs. Parsons's. I was afraid. His own expression changed. He looked perplexed at first, then gentle, almost paternal. "Is there anything you need to tell me, Eric, about what you're doing here?"

I tried to think, but all I heard in my mind was the roar of the traffic. "No," I said.

He stopped, turned away from me for a moment and then looked me in the eye. "Is there any *reporting* you need to do in Beijing? Anything sensitive? Because I think you should get it done as quickly as possible. In another day, you won't be able to move in this city without a parade following you."

He knew. I hadn't told him, but he knew anyway. We were going to play it out, like a pantomime. In that moment, I loved Arthur Bowman. He was strong enough not to ask any more questions.

"There's one thing," I said. "I need to visit a joint French-Chinese biotechnology project that Unetat is sponsoring. They have a lab out at Qinghua University. I want to go out and take a look at it. I asked the Unetat people this morning for permission, but they put me off. Maybe we could ask them again."

"Don't ask, just do it. That's Bowman's first law of reporting. If you ask, they have a chance to say no. Where is this place?"

"North of the city, next to Beijing University. But it's closed to foreigners. We may have trouble getting in."

"Nothing is ever closed. That's Bowman's second law. You get us there, and I'll get us in. I can bluff my way past anybody. Plus, I have credentials." He opened his wallet and displayed a Unetat identification card. "The official French get-out-of-jail-free card. I got it for services rendered. How nice to have an opportunity to use it."

Bowman was cruising now. Back in Washington, watching him ply the dinner-party circuit, it was easy to forget what a good reporter he was. He loved figuring out how to do something he'd been told was off-limits. He studied his Beijing map and concluded that our best bet was to take the subway to another part of the city—away from the tourist areas—and take a taxi from there. We did just that, catching the subway at the Beijing railway station and riding it 180 degrees around the city to the Fuchengmen stop. From there, we found a taxi that took us to the gates of the university.

A man in the brown uniform of the Public Security Bureau was slouching against the university gatehouse, watching people come and go.

"Just act like you belong here," said Bowman. "If he says anything, let me handle it." He strode off grandly toward the gate. I followed a step behind. As we approached, the PSB officer stared hard at us. Bowman nodded his head and gave him a little wave. The guard hesitated and then called out something in Chinese. Bowman flashed his identification card and said "Unetat"—pointing to himself—and kept walking.

We were inside the gates now. The PSB man would have to create a scene to stop us. Bowman kept going; the guard fell back into his slouch. We melded into the flow of students and faculty crisscrossing the quadrangle. The campus was like the rest of Beijing: crowded with people; dust and concrete blurring together in a tan-brown landscape.

"Now where the hell is this lab?" asked Bowman. I pointed to where Rubino had said it would be, near the back of the campus, in a building marked N-16.

Bowman led us there, walking deliberately, but not so fast that he seemed to be in a hurry. We passed classroom buildings and laboratories; after perhaps ten minutes, we reached our destination. Building N-16 was a large two-story structure with bars on the windows and a guard booth just outside the front door. It appeared to be brand-new.

Bowman turned to me. "This is it, buddy. This is your show. Are you looking for anyone in particular?"

"I need to see a French biologist named Roger Navarre. He has a lab here. And I want to take a tour to see what kind of equipment they've got."

Bowman went up to the guard, greeted him in guidebook Chinese and asked to see the French scientist. "*Ni hao. Wo yao Roger Navarre.*"

"*Bushi,*" said the guard sternly, shaking his head. That obviously meant no.

"Roger Navarre," Bowman said again. He removed his ID and pointed at the company name. "Unetat," Bowman said loudly. "*Unetat.*"

The guard went inside to fetch someone more senior. A minute or so later a Chinese man in a white coat emerged. "Yes, please," he said. "Can I help you?"

"My name is Arthur Bowman." He extended his right hand in greeting while displaying the card in his left hand. "I'm in Beijing with Unetat for the Asian Communications Conference. I was hoping that we could see Mr. Roger Navarre. I was told that he works in this building."

"One moment, please. Could I have your identification card, please." He took the Unetat card and disappeared back into the building. We had another wait, this time for several minutes. I took the opportunity to tell Bowman about the breakfast meeting that morning and the conversation with François Minart, the Unetat group vice president for pharmaceuticals. Eventually, a tall blond man emerged and shook Bowman's hand. He was formal in his manners and spoke with a French accent.

"Hello, Mr. Bowman. Welcome to Qinghua. How may I help you?"

"Are you Roger Navarre?" Bowman asked.

"No. My name is Antoine Seraut. Roger is busy in the lab right now. I'm afraid this is a closed facility. We do not normally have visitors here."

"Yes, yes," said Bowman. "I know—we were talking with François Minart this morning, and he said you had a marvelous biotechnology-research project going here, and we thought it would be a good idea to come visit while we were in Beijing."

"You talked with Minart?"

"My friend Mr. Truell did." He nodded in my direction.

"That is very nice, but Monsieur Minart doesn't have authority to send people here. This facility is not under his control."

"Yes, I know," said Bowman. He was running out of cards to play, but he still had one on the table, facedown. "I'm familiar with the situation here. I work with Michel Bézy."

The Frenchman took a step back. "You know Michel Bézy?" That name was obviously powerful magic.

"Bézy and I work together. We were at the ambassador's residence last night, with Alain Peyron. If you have any problems, just call Bézy. He should be at the French embassy. He'll explain."

Seraut retreated back into the building, apologizing as he did so. It was a magnificent bluff. Bowman whispered to me that he knew Bézy wasn't at the embassy that morning.

The Frenchman returned, looking uncomfortable. "I could not reach Monsieur Bézy. But Alain Peyron's office said it's true—you are a special friend of Unetat—so I suppose I can give you a brief tour. A few minutes, only. Is that all right?"

He opened the front door and led us down a long hall. A bulletin board displayed biohazard signs like the ones I had seen at Dr. Ginsburg's lab on I-270. I stopped at the first door and peered through a glass window. I saw a gel box; beyond it was an array of fermentation vessels, which were like the ones Ginsburg had shown me but much smaller.

"We do some of our cell cultures here," the Frenchman said brusquely. He wanted to get us in and out, as quickly as he could.

We continued down the corridor. I peered through another window. Inside was a cluster of computer equipment like the system Ginsburg had said could be used to design the molecular structure of new biological agents. I searched until I saw the brand name: *Bio-Ordinateur.*

"What do you use this for?" I asked.

"Design work," he answered.

"Design of what?"

Seraut ignored my question and continued walking down the corridor. I lingered behind, looking carefully through the window and trying to take a mental photograph of the room. It was like seeing evidence of a crime that was unfolding in real time, with me and Bowman the only witnesses. I felt as if I had been interposed in history, given a chance to stop something terrible from happening. Imagine that you had visited the Wannsee Conference in Nazi Germany as the Holocaust was being planned. What would you have done? How could you have stopped the machine of inevitability? Simply to witness—to report—would not have been enough. You had to act.

"Is Mr. Navarre here?" I asked. Our host continued to ignore me. Arthur picked up the cue.

"Yes, what about Roger Navarre?" he pressed. "You mentioned earlier he was in his lab. We'd like to just say hello to him, briefly, if we could. I would hate to tell Michel Bézy that we came all the way out here without at least shaking hands with him." I was awed by Bowman's performance. With those few words he had backed Seraut gently into a corner. Each time Arthur invoked Bézy the same look of anxious deference came over the Frenchman's face.

"I will see if Roger can be interrupted," he said. He walked to the end of the corridor, where he unlocked a large metal door.

I turned to Bowman. "I need to talk to Navarre alone, for thirty seconds, if you can find any way to distract our host." Arthur nodded; he understood.

The door of the laboratory swung open, and a small man with a shock of black hair emerged. He walked slowly toward us, accompanied by Seraut. He was the same man I had met before, but his complexion was much more sallow, and there were deep circles under his eyes. It was the haggard look of a prisoner.

"How do you do?" said Navarre, shaking our hands. "I am pleased to meet you. I do not have many visitors here." He studied my face. A flicker of recognition came into his eyes, but he said nothing.

Bowman took Seraut aside. "Let me explain about Bézy," he said in a confidential voice. "He pays me a great deal of money. I can explain it to you, *entre nous*." Bowman steered our host a few yards down the hall for a private conversation, giving me an opportunity to talk in confidence with Navarre.

"I *know* you," whispered the Frenchman. His eyes were dancing now.

"You came to my laboratory in Paris." There was a look of wonder on his face. Someone from his old life had come to see him.

"Yes. I have to ask you some questions, Mr. Navarre. How is your research going here? Do you have any concerns about it?"

"The research is very bad. He lowered his voice. "I am not happy here."

"Why not?" I didn't have much time. I needed to keep pushing. "Are you worried that it could be used the wrong way?"

"Yes, exactly that," said Navarre. His face was becoming more animated. He looked over at Seraut, still talking with Bowman. "They are taking my work and twisting it, to do terrible things. I did not realize when I came, what this project involved."

Arthur made a sudden loud noise, a kind of pained grunt, as if something were stirring in his gut. "I'm terribly sorry," he said to Seraut, taking him by the hand, "but I have been having a bad stomach. Something I ate. I must get to the bathroom right away. Can you take me there, please." Seraut was looking back anxiously toward Navarre, but Arthur tugged at him.

"Right now!" said Arthur. The Frenchmen led him down the corridor, glancing back every few steps to make sure we were still there.

I spoke quickly and quietly to Navarre: "I have a message for you from the United States government. If you are unhappy here and would like to leave, they can help you escape. They will offer you money to start a new life in America. Would you like to leave? Do you want help?"

"Yes," whispered Navarre. His eyes were clouded with a combination of fear and relief. "I want to leave. What we are doing here is wrong."

"The U.S. government will help you. They have ways to get people out. Listen to me carefully and I will give you the instructions. Stay away from the U.S. embassy. As soon as you can, go to the Australia Shipping Desk at the Gloria Plaza Hotel and tell them your name is Bob Thorpe. Can you remember that?"

He nodded. I looked down the hall. Seraut had left Bowman in the bathroom and was already hurrying back.

"Say it back to me, to make sure you have it right."

"Australia Shipping Desk," he whispered. "Gloria Plaza Hotel. Bob Thorpe."

"That's right," I said. "Leave as soon as you can. I think they will become suspicious soon about my visit here. Good luck."

"Thank you, sir." He was looking up at me with his eyes wide; his expression was worshipful. He could not believe what had just transpired. I was his deliverer. I had arrived from nowhere on a spring morning to release him from this nightmare. "I can leave at lunchtime," he whispered. "The guards go away for a few minutes then."

Seraut was nearing us. He was looking at his watch. "I am very sorry," he said. "Mr. Navarre must return to his work now."

"I understand," I said. "Well, thank you very much, Mr. Navarre. I'm sorry you can't discuss your research, but I understand you have rules. At least I can tell François Minart I saw the laboratory he was so excited about during his presentation this morning."

We shook hands; Navarre's palm was moist with sweat. Seraut walked him back to his laboratory. Then he escorted me down the corridor, toward the main entrance. "What was your name?" he asked as we walked. "I didn't get it before."

"Eric Truell. I work with Mr. Bowman."

We stopped near the door and waited for Arthur, who soon emerged from the bathroom looking embarrassed. "Whoa!" he said. "I'm sorry, fellas."

He shook the Frenchman's hand vigorously. "Thank you again, Monsieur Seraut. I will tell Michel Bézy about our visit. He will be grateful, as I am, for your help. Best of luck here. À bientôt."

He strolled off jauntily, back toward the gate. He maintained an amiable patter of conversation as we retraced our steps and transited the campus. When we were outside the gate, he turned to me.

"I don't want to know any details, but I trust this is all in a good cause."

"The best," I said, smiling.

I looked at him, dressed in his fine tailored suit, his sharp eyes scanning the pavement, that princely demeanor intact on the other side of the world from home, playing every point to win. Arthur Bowman was the real thing.

30

Bowman wanted to disappear for a little while; stay away from the China World Hotel for a few hours; go to some tourist attraction so we could say we had just stopped off at Qinghua on our way there. He proposed the Great Wall, but that would take the rest of the day, and I had my interview with Alain Peyron that afternoon. We settled on the Lama Temple, a Buddhist monastery near the university. We wandered through the gaily painted buildings, looking at happy Buddhas, mischievous Buddhas, Buddhas past, present and future. Arthur quickly exhausted his patience, but he wasn't yet ready to go back to the China World, so we stopped at my hotel to eat lunch and pick up my tape recorder.

I was decompressing. I felt as if I had been through a bizarre rite of passage. I had accomplished a task I had been dreading, and I knew in my heart that I had done something important, and that by any ordinary measure I had done something good. My life had intersected momentarily with history, and I had been an actor, not a watcher.

Arthur did not share my sense of release. If anything, he was becoming more tense. He ordered the most expensive bottle of wine on the menu and then, peevishly, sent it back. I asked him if he had any suggestions for what I should ask Peyron. "Ask him whatever you want, but he won't say anything useful. The only reason he's seeing you is that he wants to know what you're doing."

We returned to the China World a little before three o'clock and went to the press center. The Unetat staff quieted down as they saw us approach. Even Lisette looked away. We were clearly on someone's shit list. A message was posted on the board for Arthur. As he read it I could see the tension on his face.

"This should be fun," he said. "Bézy wants to see me, right now."

"What are you going to do?"

"Go see him. I don't really have a choice, do I? Unless I want to run away, which I don't. Nope, young Truell, you and I get to play this one out."

I was already feeling guilty. I had drawn Arthur into something he still didn't fully understand. "Let's meet later," I said. "Five o'clock, back at my hotel. We can take a walk, figure out what's up."

He took me by the elbow. "Watch out, Eric," he said. He was worrying more about me at that moment than about himself. "You have just kicked over a rather large hornet's nest, and unless you're careful, you're going to get stung."

Lisette escorted me upstairs to Peyron's suite. She had a look of disappointment on her face. I was a bad boy; I had not performed as she had hoped.

Peyron was waiting for me in his sitting room. He was dressed in a smoking jacket made of embroidered Chinese silk and was smoking a Gitane through a long black cigarette holder. His face was dominated by thick black eyebrows; they were heavy and Mediterranean, almost menacing; the eyes and mouth were lighter, sweeter, finer. It was a face that combined, in these different elements, the contradictions of his country—the face of a virtuous bandit. He looked at me quizzically as I introduced myself; his eyes, under the weight of those eyebrows, seemed to be asking: Can this lanky young man actually be the person who is causing us so much trouble? He dismissed Lisette, but a security man remained in the room, sitting in a chair by the door.

I took out my tape recorder, but he immediately waved me off. "You'll have a much better interview if we do this off the record," he said. His English was flawless, almost without accent. Fine, I answered. I wasn't sure how to begin. It had been a while since I had been a reporter. I felt rusty.

"Back in America, most people seem to expect that Unetat will win the China contract," I said. "Are they right?"

Peyron smiled and shook his head. In his world, reporters were fools, and I had just added further evidence. Instead of answering my question, he asked one of his own. "Why did you come to Beijing, Mr. Truell?"

"To attend your conference. If you win the contract, your company's relationship with China will be one of the biggest stories in the world. I want to understand it—by investigating what you're doing here."

"I see." He nodded, took several puffs on his cigarette and then stubbed it out. "Why did you go to our research facility at Qinghua University this morning?"

I waited for words to come. I didn't feel fear so much as uncertainty about what would happen next. Of course he knew I had been to the lab. We had given our names to Seraut, who had called Peyron's office. The only thing that reassured me was that he couldn't know what had transpired during our visit—otherwise he wouldn't be asking me questions.

"Biotechnology is a hot topic," I said. "I heard you had a project at Qinghua, and I wanted to see it. I talked to your group vice president, Mr. Minart, about it, this morning. Ask him. He'll remember me."

"Please—" He waved his hand dismissively, as if I was wasting his time with an answer like that. "Why did you want to see Roger Navarre?"

"Because I knew that he was a prominent biologist who was doing interesting work. I'd met him before, in Paris, to talk about his research. Check your records; you'll see. I was curious about what he was doing here, so I wanted to see him. That's what I do. I'm a reporter. I talk to people who are doing interesting things, and then I write stories."

He put his hand up, palm out. "Enough," he said, arching one of those big eyebrows. "Who told you about Navarre? You say you 'heard' that he was doing interesting work, and you 'heard' that we had a research project. But where did you hear these things. They are not widely known, I assure you."

"From sources. From people back in the United States who follow your company."

"From the CIA." Both of his black, bushy eyebrows were now angled upward. "Is that the answer?"

"From sources," I repeated. "I'm a journalist. I talk to people who have information. That's my job."

Peyron put his lips together and made a contemptuous sound, which was something between a kiss and a cluck. "Nonsense," he said. "What did you say to Mr. Navarre when you were talking to him?"

The fear came now in a sudden surge. I tried to talk, but nothing came out. My chest felt tight, as if a corset had been cinched around it. I closed my pad and put my tape recorder back in my briefcase.

"This isn't an interview," I said. "You're asking all the questions. I want to leave now." I stood up to go. The security man was on his feet instantly.

"Sit down," said Peyron, motioning to both of us. "Nobody is going to hurt you, Mr. Truell. I understand you have a job to do. But I do need to know what you said to Mr. Navarre. Tell me, please."

"I asked about his research," I lied. "Navarre said he wasn't allowed to tell me anything. That was it."

Peyron was looking at me sadly. The Sun King was unhappy. His genteel approach was failing, and he would soon have to call on the forces of darkness. "You make a great mistake in telling me these lies, Mr. Truell. We are in China. I wish you understood how powerless you are here."

I could feel the tightness returning. I needed to escape this box, to reverse roles somehow with him. All I had was the reporter's weapon—the ability to ask questions. That was my secret power.

"What *about* Roger Navarre?" I asked softly.

"Excuse me?"

"What is Navarre doing in that laboratory that he couldn't talk about? Why are you so worried about what he might have said?"

"Stop this game, Mr. Truell," he said, waving his hand again. His dismissal made me feel bolder.

"No, I mean it. Why is this biotechnology-research project so sensitive? You keep asking me about it, so I have to wonder why. It only makes me more curious." I felt that I was recovering my balance; I knew the ground I was standing on.

"All right," said Peyron wearily. "We'll play the reporter game. Turn on the tape recorder, if you like. I want a record of this meeting, too, to show that I have cooperated and answered your questions. And then we will say good-bye to you." He called to the security man to bring him a tape recorder. "What do you want to know? I will be as frank with you as you have been with me."

I pushed the "record" button, but I knew this was a useless exercise. An interview is valuable only to the extent that a person is prepared to answer questions. Otherwise, it is simply a cover for lies. But if Peyron wanted a record, I would fill it with as much damning information as I could.

"What is Unetat doing at Qinghua University?" I asked. "Does it involve biological-weapons research?"

"Of course not. That is absurd and libelous. The Qinghua project involves pharmaceutical research. Ask Mr. Minart. He'll give you a statement."

"If you win the communications contract, will you work with the Chinese military on developing new weapons systems?"

"Absolutely not. Our involvement in China is entirely commercial. I just told you. We have no role in military research whatsoever. Next question."

"What's your relationship with Michel Bézy?"

"He's my attorney. Beyond that, I have no relationship with him."

"If you win the communications contract, how much of the thirty billion dollars will be paid in commissions to Chinese agents?"

"None. Next question."

"How much money will be kicked back to French politicians if you win the contract?"

"Really, Mr. Truell, this is pathetic. Is this how journalists conduct themselves in America? If you print any aspect of this, we will sue your newspaper and win a very large judgment."

I had one more question, and I wanted to ask it to protect my friend: to give him some cover, to separate him from me. "What is your relationship with Arthur Bowman? Some of his colleagues at the *Mirror*, including me, are worried that he's too close to your company."

"We have no relationship with Arthur Bowman," answered Peyron. He removed his cigarette holder from his lips and pointed it at me as he repeated the words. "We have no relationship with Arthur Bowman."

I took a taxi back to my hotel. This time the surveillance was obvious. One car driven by a Chinese man was on our rear bumper the whole way, and I thought I saw another tail, driven by a European. I went up to my room and waited for Arthur. Five o'clock passed, and I tried to convince myself that nothing was wrong. The old pro had figured out a way to manipulate this new situation, just as he always did. But by 6:00 I was genuinely frightened. I called his room and left messages. I called the press center and left a message there, too. I even called the overnight editor on the foreign desk in New York, thinking they might have heard from him. But there was silence in every direction.

Just before 7:00 P.M. I heard a feeble knock on my door. I rushed to open it, and Arthur stumbled into my room. He looked awful. His face was ashen, a color paler than white, like the color of bones. He was stooped over in pain. I helped him to my bed and laid him down.

"My God, Arthur! What happened to you?"

"Turn on the radio," he said. I turned the knob and the tinny sound of Chinese pop music filled the room. He told me to make it louder, until the sound covered our voices.

"You need a doctor. Let me call the embassy."

"Don't call *anyone*. Just bring me some whiskey from the minibar. That's what I need right now."

I poured the whiskey into a glass and handed it to him. He drank most of it down in one gulp. "What happened?" I asked again.

"You owe me. Big-time." He managed a half-smile.

"What happened?" I asked a third time.

"Bézy went crazy. Roger Navarre escaped from the lab today. They don't know where he is. They're trying to find him."

My heart leaped. "My God. He did it. He ran away!"

"Shut up!" Bowman said sharply. "Don't say another fucking word."

"And they think you know where he went?"

He nodded. "They beat the crap out of me. Quite literally. Bézy wanted to know what you told Navarre."

"What did you answer?"

"Nothing. I didn't know anything, so I had nothing to say. It took a long time before he believed me."

I winced, imagining what he must have gone through. "What did they do to you?"

"I don't want to talk about it, Eric."

"Tell me something. It was my fault. I need to know something. Where did they take you?"

"Bézy took me to the cellar of a building near the embassy. A foul place, smelled like death. He strapped me to a chair and asked me questions. Some Chinese helpers did the unpleasant stuff."

"What? You have to tell me."

"Electricity. Water. Anything that wouldn't leave a scar."

"Oh, Jesus. I'm so sorry, Arthur. This was my fault."

"No, it wasn't. And don't think I was brave. I told them everything I knew. I would have betrayed you, believe me, but you hadn't told me anything. That was what saved my life. They realized I didn't know, so there was no point hurting me anymore. You're the brave one, Eric, for keeping the information to yourself. But this is your problem now. You're the one who has what they want."

There was a loud knock on the door. "Hotel security," called a voice outside.

I opened the door a crack but kept the chain bolted. A Chinese man in plain clothes was standing just outside. Behind him were two uniformed PSB officers. "What is it?" I asked.

"Turn the radio off," said the man in plain clothes. "Too loud. You must turn radio off, please, or these men arrest you. No TV. No noise."

"Okay," I said. "I'll turn it off." I closed the door.

"We have to get out of here," Bowman said. "They want the music off so they can hear what we're saying. Grab some more bottles from the mini-bar while I'm in the bathroom cleaning up. Then let's go."

Bowman took a quick shower and emerged looking a little better. He was still walking with difficulty, but the color was returning to his face. We took the elevator down to the lobby and called for the first taxi in the queue. A Chinese security man waved away that driver and called for another, who was idling nearby.

"Be careful what you say," said Bowman. "He's a cop, and he understands English." Bowman asked the driver to take us to Tiananmen Square. We could talk there, and when we had figured out what to do, we could get some dinner. We passed the journey in silence. On the way, Bowman polished off a vodka and a gin.

When we were out in the vast open area of Tiananmen, Bowman resumed where he had left off. "You're in trouble, Eric," he repeated. "Bézy will come after you, now that he's convinced himself I don't know anything. He's pretty worked up about Navarre. He seems to think you're responsible for his running away today. And he's absolutely positive you work for the CIA."

"Maybe that will protect me." It was a strange thought—after dreading for so long that anyone would guess at that connection—to consider that it might actually do me some good. "Maybe they're afraid of the agency."

"Maybe so, Eric, but that's a risky bet."

We were nearing the giant obelisk in the middle of the square, known as the Monument to the People's Heroes. Standing on its stone steps was a man with earphones on his head and a parabolic dish pointed toward us. About fifteen yards behind us was a pair of men who'd been tracking us since we left the taxi. The Chinese were not subtle about surveillance. We turned our backs to the man with the dish. Bowman lowered his voice.

"Bézy is careful about picking fights. He had his Chinese friends work me over today because he thinks he owns me. You're different. He may be afraid of messing with you, but don't bet your life on it. These people are seriously upset. I don't know what you wandered into at Qinghua—and I don't want to know—but they act like it's the Manhattan Project."

"That's exactly what it's like."

"Will you shut up! Jesus! You are such a . . . *kid*!" That was the worst thing Bowman could think of to say. He actually smiled as he said it, and he meant it. I was a kid, and he had to protect me from my inexperience. "How are we going to take care of you, Eric? How do we get you through the next few days? What about going to the American embassy?"

"No. I can't do that. That's what they're expecting me to do. It would confirm everything they already think."

"So what, if it saves your life."

"No," I repeated. "This is not a negotiable item, so drop it."

"Okay. What about leaving China on the first flight tomorrow?"

"Will you come with me?"

"No. Can't do it. I have to make my speech to the Asian Communications Conference, don't forget. And I want to talk to Peyron before I leave. I want to tell him, in my own words, what his sadistic friend Bézy did to me. Peyron pushes the buttons. I want him to know what comes out the other end. Besides, what can they do to me they haven't already done?"

"You know their secrets, Arthur. They won't let you walk away with them."

"Don't be so melodramatic. I'm not going to blow their secrets, and they know it. I have as much to lose as they do. I could go to jail if all the details come out. No, you're the one with problems. We can't do anything tonight except be careful. But if things look dicey tomorrow, we'll put you on a plane."

"I won't leave China until you do, Arthur."

"You're a fool," said Bowman. "Let's go eat."

We headed back toward the red-tiled roof of the Gate of Heavenly Peace, with its familiar photograph of the Great Helmsman, Mao Tse-tung. Bowman was walking slowly, still leaning on me occasionally. The booze seemed to have helped ease the pain, and Bowman was a fighter; anger had a medicinal effect on him. He steered us to the right, toward the area known as Wangfujing, which was full of narrow lanes and small restaurants, where Bowman figured it would be safer to talk.

It was past 8:00 now, but the streets were still crowded. Down Chang'an Street, you could see a line of people outside McDonald's. We headed toward what we hoped would be the safety of Wangfujing and its alleyways. Bowman remembered a Szechuanese restaurant down one of these hutongs. We still had our watchers, trailing behind. We turned left onto a street called Chenguang Jie. Bowman thought his place was nearby. I looked behind. It seemed to me that our entourage had grown; there were perhaps half a dozen people following us now.

We turned into the hutong where Bowman thought he remembered the restaurant. It was a narrow street, only one lane wide. When we had gone perhaps fifty yards, I heard Chinese talking animatedly at the top of the lane, their singsong voices announcing that something unusual was happening in their tiny block of Beijing. An instant later I saw why they were babbling. A large truck had turned into the lane. It barely fit, it was so wide. It accelerated down the lane, sweeping away some of the laundry that hung from second-floor windows. As the truck gained speed, the driver switched on his headlights.

"What the hell is this?" said Bowman, staring into the light.

I will not forgive myself for what happened in the next few seconds. Arthur stood motionless in the middle of the lane, arms outstretched, calling out to the driver to slow down. I stood and watched, immobilized. The truck was still gaining speed.

"Arthur!" I cried out, running toward him. "Get out of the way!"

The truck was coming faster. The headlights were shining directly at Arthur. There could have been no mistaking who it was. His arms were still outstretched; he wasn't moving. It was almost as if he were beckoning the truck toward him. He didn't try to escape; this *was* his escape.

"Arthur!" I screamed a final time.

I heard a horrible sound as the truck hit him full on the body. It was like the noise you hear when your car hits a dog in the road—so much louder and more solid than you expect, and then that softer, juicier afternoise, as the soft tissue bursts and the life spills out. I am ashamed to say that I didn't see the moment of impact—only heard it—because I had ducked into a little doorway, desperate to save myself. Arthur might have found a doorway, too, if he hadn't been so hobbled by pain, and if he had truly wanted to live.

The truck passed over Arthur's body and kept going, down the lane and out the other end. When it had gone, I left my hiding place and went to Arthur's side. His body was splintered on the pavement. He was broken and torn in so many places, he was like a bloody rag doll. His face was bleeding from a dozen rivulets, but you could still see the features. The mouth was trying to move. He was still alive.

"Arthur!" I wailed. "My God!"

"Eric," he said. The voice was tiny, almost a spirit voice, there was so little life left in his body. "Eric," he repeated.

I bent down, my ear near his mouth. I heard him whisper, the words coming in thin broken bundles. "Take care of me."

"Breathe, Arthur. Don't die." I wiped the blood away from his mouth and eyes with my shirt. "Please don't die."

He began to speak again, but the words died on his lips. I took his hand. It was wet with blood.

An ambulance arrived almost immediately. It must have been ordered in advance. They said Arthur died on the way to the hospital. He was so battered and broken that I believe he must have died of his wounds. But I think they would have killed him if he had survived the crash. They wouldn't let me ride in the ambulance. A plainclothes cop pushed me away, and then I ran. I was afraid they would kill me, too, and I didn't want to die.

When I reached a phone, I called the U.S. embassy. The duty officer sent a car for me right away. When he asked me to describe what had happened, I wasn't sure how to begin. The truth was so complicated. I thought of Arthur's last words to me, not really sure what he had meant, and resolved I would try to take care of him better in death than I had while he was alive.

The Chinese informed the embassy later that night that Bowman's death had been an accident. The driver of the truck had been drinking, they said. He had been arrested and charged with the killing. It was a great tragedy. The embassy duty officer asked me if the Chinese account was right. I said I didn't know. That first night I wasn't ready to tell the story. It was too strange, leading outward in too many directions, hurting too many people. So I concealed the essential elements of what had happened.

After fencing for an hour with the duty officer and giving a brief statement to the Chinese police, I asked to talk to the ambassador. I might have blurted everything out then. But he was such a dolt—a well-meaning but vacuous political appointee—that I decided it would be smarter not to tell him anything. He kept telling me how painful this was for him personally, how Arthur had been a close friend. They had probably met at a cocktail party. I thought of asking to see the station chief but decided against it. I was a public actor that night. I was writing a script I would have to live with. I had to be careful which doors I opened.

Then a kind of journalistic autopilot took over. I called Ed Weiss, the executive editor, who had just seen the story on the wires and broken the news to Arthur's wife, Mara. I called Philip Sellinger, the publisher and Arthur's closest friend. Sellinger began to cry on the phone. It was after midnight when I sat down to write a story for the *Mirror* about the tragic death of our diplomatic correspondent in a road accident in Beijing. Unetat issued its own statement that night, calling Arthur "the greatest American journalist of his generation" and expressing sorrow at his death.

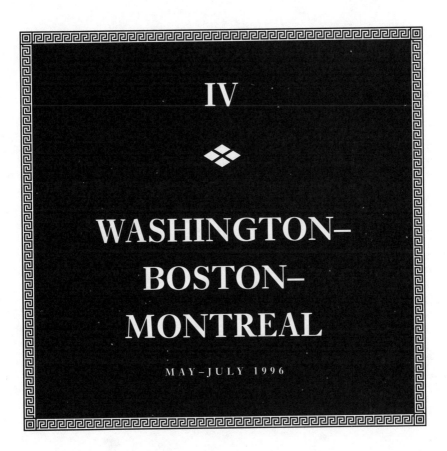

IV

WASHINGTON–
BOSTON–
MONTREAL

MAY–JULY 1996

31

❖

I brought Arthur's body back to Washington on the airplane the day after he died. Before leaving Beijing, I went to his hotel and gathered up his fine suits and shirts, French silk ties, socks and underwear and packed them into his suitcase. I also collected the few papers lying on his desk, along with his laptop computer. The Public Security Bureau took a formal statement from me that morning. I described what had happened the night before in that narrow lane. The truck had killed him, I said. That was a fact. They knew the rest. The Chinese seemed relieved that I wasn't making trouble. They cleared the normal bureaucratic hurdles so that Arthur's body could leave on the United flight back to the United States. They wanted us both out of the country.

The long flight home was like passing through a dark tunnel. The airline upgraded me to business class as a gesture of sympathy. I sat in the big seat with my eyes closed, thinking about the events of the past few months and how they had converged in Beijing that week. The flight attendants kept offering me drinks, but I didn't want any softening of the disaster I had set in motion. I wanted it to hurt.

Phil Sellinger was at the airport to meet us, his arm around the grieving widow, Mara Bowman. When she saw the coffin, Mara began to sob, violently, like a woman at an Arab funeral. Sellinger tried to comfort her but it was impossible. She needed to cry. Arthur must have flown overseas a hundred times in his life, to wars and revolutions and earthquakes and massacres, but he had always come back. Someone like that begins to seem immortal. When it finally happens, your defenses are gone. At the back of the crowd, standing apart from Sellinger and the Bowman family, I saw Annie. She was wearing dark glasses. She came up to me and kissed me on the cheek, so softly. We embraced, and I felt her body tremble in my arms.

Reporters were waiting for us, too—mostly local TV reporters who regarded Arthur as a minor Washington celebrity. I held an impromptu press conference just past the customs' arrival hall. I told the official story.

After the funeral service was over, I stood outside St. John's Church, shaking hands with mourners as they emerged. It was a spring day, and a soft breeze was blowing across Lafayette Park, filling the air with petals from the dogwood trees and azalea bushes. In the slow march out of the church were friends and colleagues I hadn't seen in years, people who had been touched in some way by Arthur. Henry Pelt, the news aide on the foreign desk, who'd had to put up with Arthur's requests and diatribes from overseas for so many years; Chuck Marsh, the technician in the communications center who had received Arthur's telexes from a score of war zones; Erin Shaw, the dictationist who transcribed stories from Arthur when he was in some remote place and there was no other way to get his copy into the paper.

The Washington bureau emerged in a cluster. Bob Marcus made a little speech when he saw me, about how bravely I had represented the paper. Susan Geekas said the president had promised her, personally, that he would be at the funeral and she didn't understand why he hadn't come. George Dirk gave me a hug and didn't say a word.

A gray-haired man approached me on the sidewalk. It took me a moment to recognize him, he had aged so visibly since the last time I saw him. It was Senator James Abelard. I could not imagine that he would want to talk to me, after what had happened, but he was walking directly toward me. He reached out his hand.

"You spoke well," he said. "You all spoke well."

"We all loved Arthur," I answered.

"I know you did. So did I. He was an unusual man."

I looked at his face. He had spent a season in hell since I saw him in his office in the Capitol. I needed to say something to him, to tell him that I was not the same brash young man he had met.

"I'm sorry for what happened between us, Senator. I've thought a lot about it since then. I'm not sure it would happen the same way again."

He didn't answer. He shook my hand again, and walked away.

A reception was beginning at the Athenian Club, a few blocks away, where official Washington was gathering to assert its claim on Arthur with

more speeches and testimonials. Arthur was one of those people who had
helped define a social circle: journalists, members of Congress, foreign service officers, professors. Arthur had given this unwieldy group an identity
over the years—they were all his friends—and they must have wondered
how they would survive collectively now that he was dead. Without
Arthur's charm to animate their proceedings, they were a group of rich,
well-educated windbags.

The church had almost emptied now. A few mourners who had been sitting in the upper balconies were still trickling out, but the show had ended.
A feeling of loneliness came over me. I hadn't loved, or even liked, Arthur
until near the end, but now I felt devastated by losing him. I had joined the
long list of people whose secrets Arthur knew, and kept. I wasn't sure I
could share them with another human being. Indeed, I wasn't sure where
my future led, on the road away from that church.

I was trying to decide whether to go to the reception at the Athenian
Club when I felt a tap on my shoulder. I turned around and saw Tom Rubino. He was dressed in the funeral outfit: blue suit, white shirt, blue tie.
Unlike the other sad-eyed mourners, he looked radiant. He shook my hand
firmly.

"We need to talk," Rubino said. He handed me a slip of paper with a
date, time and address written on it.

32

❖

I suppose I could have said no. I could simply have crumpled Rubino's message into a ball and tossed it into a trash can outside the church. And, in theory, I could have walked away from the whole mess, kept the secrets to myself and prayed that nobody would find out. It might even have worked, for someone who was more self-contained than I and better at keeping secrets. But I was a walking example of one of Bowman's laws of journalism: I needed to talk, I needed to share my experiences with someone who knew what I had been through. Unfortunately, the only person who fit that description—the *only* one—was a senior officer of the Central Intelligence Agency. As the day of the meeting approached I found that I was actually looking forward to it.

The address Rubino had given me was the apartment building in Shirlington. It was the same safe house that had made me so uncomfortable during my earlier visit, but this time it seemed natural and appropriate. I would have been upset if we had met anywhere else. Even the silly recognition codes were welcome.

When Rubino opened the apartment door, he was beaming. I remember a similar look of pride on my father's face the day I graduated from Stanford. Rubino embraced me, then sat me down in that cheesy living room, poured me a cup of supermarket coffee, offered me a glazed doughnut. He couldn't stop smiling.

"You did it, Eric," he said.

"Did what?" All I could think of was the mayhem I had left behind in Beijing.

"Roger Navarre made it to America. He arrived yesterday. We got him out in a shipping crate, through Guangzhou. You saved his life, my friend."

"He made it?" I shook my head. The scientist had escaped his prison at Qinghua. It was a thrill, the idea that I had helped save his life. "That's fantastic! I was sure the Chinese would get him."

"They tried. They shut our embassy down tight. But the operation at the hotel worked. We had him on his way within an hour after he showed up at the Gloria Plaza. He was upset when you weren't there. He thought you'd be the one to take him out. At first he didn't trust our guys. You're his hero. Other people's, too."

Rubino reached into the briefcase beside his chair. He pulled out an envelope with my name on it. "Read it," he said. Inside, on thick bond paper, was a letter on the embossed stationery of the director of Central Intelligence. Rubino asked me to read it out loud, so he could hear.

"Dear Mr. Truell:

I am writing to express the profound thanks of the President of the United States for the courageous service you have rendered to your country. The assistance you provided the Central Intelligence Agency in our recent operation in Beijing, China, made an important and lasting contribution to the nation's security.

Some patriots have the opportunity to serve their country openly, in public view; others must do so in secret, in ways that can never be disclosed. But their service is no less important for being secret. We can never express our gratitude to you openly, but the few who know what you did will always celebrate your achievement."

When I finished reading, Rubino extended his hand. I thought he wanted to shake, but he actually wanted the letter back. "Sorry, Eric, but you can't keep it. We'll hold it for you in a secure vault at the agency. If you ever want to look at it, let me know, and I'll get it out."

"Thanks," I said. He could keep it locked as deep in the vault as he liked. Burning it would be all right with me, too. "What will Navarre do now?" I asked. I thought of that dark little troll in his laboratory at Qinghua, and the look on his face when I told him the U.S. government could get him out. What would he do with his freedom?

"First, he'll have a nice, long debriefing. In exchange for being released from hell, he gets to tell us what he knows about Chinese biological-weapons research. Then, he's a free man. If he likes, he can work for us. Or we'll set him up at a good university. Whatever he wants. We've already put aside two million dollars to buy him an annuity."

"Can I see him? That would mean more to me than the letter, frankly."

"Not right now. We're trying to build him a new identity. If we aren't careful and they find him, they'll kill him."

"Then can I write about him? Do a story saying that he defected? That would make me feel better about everything, if I could get some journalism out of this."

"At some point, sure. It's your story. But I'd be happier if you waited awhile. Right now, anything in the newspaper would be dangerous. It might push people to do stupid things."

I nodded. It made sense, and he was at least pretending that I had a choice. I closed my eyes. My stomach hurt. I remembered the way Arthur looked on the ground, the way the bones were breaking through the skin, the way the blood poured from the wounds on his face, the way his nose had been crushed, like the pulpy rind of an orange.

"I appreciate the letter and everything, Tom. But I'm still struggling with all this. Bowman was ten yards from me when he died, and I didn't do anything to help him. I put him in danger and then I couldn't save him. I have a feeling the only reason the Chinese didn't kill me, too, was that they assumed I was working for the agency. That bothers me. And now I'm sitting in this safe house reading a thank-you letter from the director of the CIA— and I can't talk about any of it with the people I really work for. I don't have a sense of closure yet. There are too many loose ends."

"I can understand what you're feeling." Rubino nodded his head. He was all sympathy.

"The worst of it is that the people who killed Arthur are getting away with it. They even issued a press release saying what a great journalist he was. Did you know that? It makes me crazy. I want to get even, but I don't know how."

Rubino listened, stared out the window, then turned back. There was a sly crease on his lip. "You know, we could help you with that," he said.

"Come on! You can't help anyone. And I don't want to play any more spy games. I want to go back to being a journalist."

"Suppose we could arrest Michel Bézy and try him in a U.S. court. With your help, we could lock him up for a long time. Would that seem like a good way to get even?"

"Of course it would. It would be fantastic, after what he did to Arthur.

But how could you arrange that? And how could I possibly help? That's ridiculous."

"You hold the high cards, Eric. You're the only one who knows the truth. That gives you leverage over Bézy, and we can give you more. I'll make you a promise: if you can get Bézy to America, we can arrest him here on a terrorism charge."

Rubino was scary, he was so good at it. He never told me to do anything; he just opened a door, letting the idea take hold. I tried to push it shut.

"Tempting," I said. "But I'm not interested. I did what you asked in China, and I'm glad if you think it did some good. But I want my life back."

"I understand." Rubino didn't argue with me. He sat there silently, knowing that I would argue with myself. "I knew it would be a long shot," he said after a while.

"The whole idea is crazy. I mean, how would we get him here? Bézy isn't an idiot."

"You'd have to do it straight, to make it work. You'd have to ask him to come to the U.S. for an interview. He's scared of you; he has to be. You'd play on that. Tell him that if he doesn't come, you'll print a story he won't like."

"But what could I possibly have that would be so threatening to Bézy that he'd come to America to talk me out of printing it?"

"Ah!" Rubino smiled. "That's where we come in." He was so pleased with himself, having led me along his carefully prepared trail to the precise spot where he wanted me to end up. "We can provide you with information."

He removed another envelope from his briefcase and handed it to me. Inside was a plain piece of paper with the name "ALF Orient, S.A." and an address in Luxembourg. Below that were the words "PanAsia Credit P-20-52-D."

"Sorry, Tom, but I don't have a clue what this means."

"This is Bézy's greatest secret. It's the name of the shell company he uses, and the number of its offshore bank account. In a few weeks, assuming the French win the China contract, more than one hundred million dollars will flow into this account. If you are in possession of this information, you will have a great deal of power over Mr. Bézy."

"Wonderful! Then he'll have to kill me, the way he killed Arthur."

"He may want to—frankly, Eric, that's part of the lure—but he won't be able to. He'll be playing on our field. We'll have him in our sights the moment his plane lands."

"God damn you." I loved his proposal and I hated it; it was what I wanted and what I feared. "Suppose it works out just the way you say. He comes to the United States, and you arrest him. What happens then? Do I have to testify in court?"

"If you want to testify, you can. It would be a very complicated story to tell, and parts of it would have to be handled *in camera,* out of hearing of the public. It might cause some problems for your newspaper, too. But if you want to tell the story, we're willing. A safer course would be to prosecute him on other crimes. We wouldn't be charging him directly for the murder of Arthur Bowman, but it would be payback, just the same."

Why did I even consider it? These guys had been on a twenty-year losing streak. They were so mired in failure that a whole generation of them had done nothing but spin their wheels. They were collapsing of their own weight, in Washington and around the world. Most of what they did nowadays was make-believe. They pretended to recruit people, wrote phony cables dressing up lunchroom gossip as secret intelligence. They were losers. They couldn't even protect themselves or their agents. How were they going to help me exact revenge? But Rubino wanted it so badly. The ferocity was in his eyes. He was playing on a losing team and he needed a win. My problem was more complicated: I needed to keep faith with myself.

I took the paper with Bézy's bank account number and told Rubino I would let him know. I asked him to destroy the letter from the director of Central Intelligence.

33

I still had Arthur Bowman's laptop computer at home. I had brought it back with me from Beijing and meant to return it to the office, but there had been so many things going on in that first week I had simply forgotten about it. One night while I was paying some bills, I noticed it propped against the wall of my study, and I admitted to myself that I was curious about what it might contain. Bowman had kept so many secrets while he was alive. Now that he was gone, whatever he had left behind in the computer constituted a kind of electronic afterlife. I plugged the machine in and turned it on. The screen glowed up at me, listing the files that were the last remnants of Arthur's life.

Most of the files were junk: drafts of stories, notes from interviews, lists of phone numbers. But there were several items that roused my curiosity. There was something called PHIL.DOC. It turned out to be a memo Bowman had written to the publisher, Philip Sellinger, in early March, a few weeks before that month's decisive board meeting. Headed "Possible Investors," it made clear that the *Mirror*'s financial situation had been far shakier than most members of the staff had realized:

Dear Phil:

Here's an update on my conversations with international investment groups that might be able to provide the quick infusion of capital the board of directors thinks the *Mirror* needs. Unfortunately, I don't have any breakthroughs for you:

*The Jamil Group in Riyadh is prepared to invest at least $100 million and maybe more. They publish a newspaper in Saudi and some magazines in London, and have a very profitable advertising business throughout the Middle East. They'd love to have a vanity showcase in the U.S. But they're not right for us. Despite their claims of independence, they are ultimately a captive of the royal family. We don't need these headaches.

*My Korean friend Jaehoon Park, from the Horizon Group, paid a visit when he was in Washington last week. He says Horizon is looking for media properties in America, but they're thinking mainly about electronic, not print. I can continue the conversation, but I don't think it will lead anywhere. Anyway, I don't trust Horizon Group. They'll only invest if they think they can take advantage of our weakness.

*I talked with our old college classmate Shigehiko Watanabe and several other Japanese who know and respect our journalism. They would like to help us out. But Watanabe cautions that most of the potential Japanese investors have been burned on U.S. equity deals. That means they won't invest without the certainty of a good return, or the prospect that they'll eventually get control of the company. Since we can't promise either, this route probably won't take us anywhere.

*I called Chris Ricks at Cloward's in London, to see if any British or Dutch media companies might be interested in an investment in the $500 million range. He said he would check, but he'd already been contacted by our investment bankers in New York and had told them it was a nonstarter. Quality newspapers are cratering in the U.K., and they assume the same thing is going to happen to us. So they're out.

*There are other prospects in Asia, Latin America, the Middle East and Europe. Some of them wouldn't be suitable. But if you're running out of options, let me know.

I appreciate the terrible pressure you're under right now to save the paper. Don't let the bastards get you down.

As ever,
Arthur

Another file was slugged ABEL.DOC. It was a brief letter Arthur had sent to the wife of Senator James Abelard. The letter was dated a week after my visit to see Abelard at the Capitol, which had prompted his sudden withdrawal from the presidential campaign.

Dear Joan:
I know this is a bitter time for you and Jim, and I don't blame you for hating the newspaper business in general and the *Mirror* in particular.

But what happened may have been for the best. Nobody's secrets ever survive a presidential campaign. The fact of Jim's hospitalization would have come out eventually, perhaps in a way that would have been far more damaging to Jim. I wish we lived in a world where a politician could still have a private life, but we don't.

You're understandably furious at the young reporter who visited Jim and "threatened to destroy him," as you put it. But in asking those questions about Jim's experience with depression, he was just doing his job. He may have come on a little strong, but he's basically a good kid, one of the best at the paper. I have no doubt he regards me with the same suspicion as does toward Jim, if that's any consolation. Journalism is a murder-and-create business, and the murderous ones are also the creative ones.

What distressed me most in your letter was the possibility that Jim's withdrawal from the campaign had triggered a new bout of depression, and your worry that he might try to injure himself somehow. I was so glad for your call last night with the news that Jim had checked himself back into the hospital. That was the right thing to do, and I will do everything I can to protect his privacy.

Mara sends her love. If there is anything we can do to help you now, please let us know. You and Jim are in our thoughts and prayers.,

> As ever,
> Arthur

Another glimpse into the life of Arthur Bowman was a document titled BUDGET.DOC. It recorded his expected income and expenses for the year, and offered a bleak summary of his precarious financial situation. Reading it, I understood better the financial pressures that had driven him toward his alliance with Bézy and Peyron.

1996 ANTICIPATED EXPENSES:

Mortgage	$34,000
Housekeeper	$18,000
Harry—Amherst tuition, etc.	$30,000
Sarah—National Cathedral School tuition	$12,500
Martha's Vineyard house—August rent	$10,000
Winter vacation	$7,000
Food, etc.	$9,000
Mara's clothes	$10,000

AB clothes	$3,000
Kids' clothes & sports equipment	$2,000
Sarah's allowance	$1,250
Mara's therapist	$7,500
Athenian Club dues	$3,000
AB lunches and spending money	$5,000
Mara—Hairdresser, manicure, etc.	$8,000
Car payments	$8,400
Insurance, etc.	$3,000
Utilities	$6,000
Money for Mara's mother	$10,000
St. John's pledge & charities	$4,500
Gardeners	$4,000
Grand Total	$196,500

1996 ANTICIPATED INCOME

Mirror salary	$142,000
Special compensation bonus from Sellinger	$30,000
Speeches, etc.	$10,000
Pretax gross income	$182,000
After-tax income	approx. $110,000

NEEDED FROM 1996 BÉZY CONTRACT

If held offshore and untaxed	$100,000
If declared	$180,000

I came upon a final item. It was slugged AB.DOC. At first, I thought the AB stood for Arthur Bowman, and that it was set of personal notes. But it wasn't that. AB.DOC was a love letter Bowman had written in February to a woman, recalling a trip they had taken earlier that month to the Caribbean. I had to read it twice before I realized who "AB" was.

Dearest Annie:
  I hate being back. I can still feel you on my skin, taste you on my tongue. I don't usually think of my life as a prison, but I do now, because it keeps me apart from you. Running away to Antigua was sublime, and I don't think M. realized a thing, but I hate to live this way. I don't know

which is worse—falling asleep without you, or waking up without you.
Do you love me just a little?

I love you with all my heart,

A.

When I finished reading the letter, I drove to Annie Baron's house in
Georgetown. I didn't call first, because I knew she would tell me not to
come, and I was too angry to wait for answers. How could she have done
it? It seemed such a profound infidelity, not simply to me but to herself.
How could an attractive, smart woman in her thirties have had sex with
him? A self-important man in his fifties who ate too much and drank too
much, whose entire career had been an act of betrayal. How could she?

It was like a hidden pattern in a drawing: we can stare at it for hours and
see nothing, but once we finally get it, it's *all* we can see—it's so obvious. I
began running the scenes back in my mind. The intimate way Arthur and
Annie had talked at Elsbeth Parsons's dinner. The way she had leaned
toward him, laughed when he made a joke, touched him gently. I hadn't
thought to look under the table. Were they touching there, too? And that
beautiful tan? Now I knew where it had come from—the "sublime" visit to
Antigua. And Annie's questions to me when I had returned from New York
after trying to tell Weiss that Bowman was a spy. She had obviously told
him about it later; *that* was how he knew I was onto him that night at the
Athenian Club. She had snitched. And Abelard. Bowman must have told
Annie about my confrontation at the senator's office; that explained why
she had been so clever on television.

She had betrayed me in so many big and little ways. I remembered her
mocking laughter before we left for China. "You two have a lot in common," she had said. And the image of her at the airport when I returned
from Beijing with Arthur's body, the way she stood away from Mara and
the family, hiding her eyes behind those sunglasses. And at the church during the funeral, those tears streaming down her cheeks. And all those years
when I had been away overseas, trying to become a foreign correspondent
like Arthur Bowman. No wonder she had been so coy during my appren-
ticeship. She already had the real thing.

I pounded on the door of her town house. There was no answer at first,
so I kept my hand pressed on the buzzer until she came downstairs.

"Who is it?" she asked warily, peering out through the peephole.

"It's Eric," I said, my voice still trembling with anger. "I need to see you."

"It's late. I'm not dressed. Can it wait until tomorrow?"

"No, it can't wait. I found out about you and Arthur."

There was a long pause, perhaps twenty seconds; then she opened the door. She was in her bathrobe, wearing her furry bedroom slippers. Her hair was up and fastened loosely with a barrette. Her posture was stooped, like that of a Degas ballerina at rest. She led me silently into her living room. She looked disoriented.

"What did you find out?" she asked carefully. Bowman was dead, and she was still covering for him.

"I brought his laptop back from China. One of the files was a love letter he wrote you last February, after your trip to the Caribbean. I couldn't believe it. I felt like a fool. How could you have done it? Why didn't you tell me?"

"You snoop," she said coldly. "Reading other people's mail. It was none of your business. It was a secret."

I was furious all over again, listening to her. "How *could* you have slept with him?" I asked bitterly. "It's unbelievable."

She put her hand up. "Stop it!" she said. There was deep anger in her voice. "You have no right to interrogate me, especially now, after Arthur's death."

"What's that supposed to mean?"

"I have this feeling, Eric, that Arthur would still be alive if he hadn't gone to China with you. That wasn't any accident in Beijing. He was murdered. I've known it since the moment I heard the news. Tell me the truth."

"Yes," I said. "He was murdered."

"Who did it?" Her voice was blue ice.

"The French and the Chinese." She was the first person to whom I'd told that secret. Instead of being lightened, my burden felt heavier now. "You can't tell anyone," I said.

Tears filled her eyes suddenly. Her lip trembled for a moment; she bit it, hard, to keep from crying any more. "Why did they kill him? What had he done? Was it because he was a spy?"

"Yes. Something like that."

"Why did you let him go to China? You knew! I told Arthur you suspected he was a spy—I had to—and of course he said it was all nonsense. But you knew he was in danger."

"He understood what he was doing, Annie. He wanted to be free. His life had gotten so complicated. At the end, I'm not sure he wanted to live anymore. When that truck came down the alley toward him, he didn't move."

"Oh, Arthur!" It was a wail, a call to the dead. "Oh! Oh!" She burst into sobs that shook her body. She cried the way children do, a sound like a moan underneath the tears. I tried to put my arm around her, but she resisted. In her mind, I was part of what had killed Arthur. I went to the kitchen and made her some tea. When I returned, she had stopped crying. Her eyes were red; the remnants of her mascara were traced on her cheeks. She needed to talk now; so did I.

"How long were you lovers?" I asked. Despite her tears, I was still angry. I needed to know the details.

"A long time . . ." Her voice trailed off. "Years."

"How did it happen? I don't get it. He was so much older. He was married to another woman. He wasn't really attractive. That's the part that's hardest for me. I thought I knew you."

"Eric." She shook her head sorrowfully. "You don't understand. *I loved Arthur.* This wasn't a mistake, something Arthur made me do. I loved him. I'm devastated. I don't know what I'm going to do without him."

I suppose that was the one answer I hadn't expected. It put me in another place. What was the point of feeling jealous?

As Annie sipped the tea, she explained the story of their love affair, delicately at first, then bluntly. It had begun ten years before, not long after I had left for Beirut and she had moved to Washington. Bowman was the dashing war correspondent back from his adventures. He was already married to Mara; after he met Annie he had wanted to get a divorce but Annie hadn't let him. She was just starting her career, and she didn't want to marry anyone. She was a young climber, and he was Mount Everest. "I just wanted to sleep with him," she said. "That was why it lasted so long. Arthur stopped playing his act when we made love. He was just there, with me."

"But he was so old," I said.

"I know. It's strange. It's just, he knew things; he taught me things. He already was what you were trying to become. I didn't threaten him. He just wanted me to be myself. I don't know. We all want to be adored, and Arthur adored me."

"Why didn't you tell me, a long time ago?"

"Because it was a secret. Have you ever had a real secret, Eric? Probably not. You're so normal. The all-American tennis star. You've probably never had an awful secret in your life."

"Yes, I have." I said it so quietly, I'm not sure she even heard me.

"I loved you, too, Eric. That made it so hard. I always thought we would get married in the end. That was the thing. I knew you'd slept with other women. And you knew I'd slept with other men, even if you didn't know about Arthur. But I just assumed someday we'd find a way back to each other—get married and have children. I thought we were almost there when we made love again, that time before you left for China. Arthur seemed so distant then. And you were so strong, and you wanted me, and I loved you."

"Is that why you never married anyone else? Because you thought we'd get married someday?"

"Yes. Partly that. I don't know, partly that. And I liked my secret life."

At the door, as I was leaving, Annie asked me a last question. "What are you going to do about Arthur?" Her voice was stronger now; she was looking directly at me. "You have to do something, if he was murdered. You can't do nothing. You have to write an article, or tell the CIA, or file a lawsuit, or something."

"I know," I answered. "But this is so much more complicated than you realize. That's why you can't tell anyone about it. You could hurt me and other people if you say even a word. But I promise you: I'll do something about Arthur."

34

❖

The *Mirror* continued to operate normally, despite the trauma that surrounded Arthur's death. That was one of the likable things about newspapers: they published every day, so they had to pull up their socks and get on with it. We produced a special commemorative section about Arthur in our Sunday magazine, with excerpts from some of his famous stories and pictures of him in Vietnam and Lebanon, wearing safari suits and looking cool. And that was the end of it. The janitors cleaned out Arthur's beautiful office and packed all the photographs and testimonials in a box and sent them home to Mara.

I figured that the best therapy for me would be to get back to work, too. I told Bob Marcus I wanted to do a long explanatory piece on the China communications contract, pulling together the reporting I had done while I was in Beijing. That was fine with Marcus. Everything was fine with him. He was in permanent management mode these days, sending out a stream of memos about readership surveys and high-impact stories and diversity workshops and circulation penetration. The office grapevine had picked up the rumor that I would be going to New York soon as deputy foreign editor, so everybody was being extra nice to me—especially Noel Rosengarten, who still hadn't left. The TV deal in Minneapolis had fallen through, and there was a rumor that he might be axed.

I worked hard on the China story, but it bored me. My actual experience in Beijing had been so powerful, yet what I wrote seemed bloodless and unreal. Partly that reflected the unusual constraints I was operating under, but it also demonstrated the process of denaturing and compression that goes into writing any news story. We need to squeeze enough life out of events to make them lie down flat on the page. We need to chop up the immensity of human experience into pieces that will fit. We are the scorekeepers of life, not the players. We like to imagine that virtue and merit lie with us—the scribes who stay clean on the sidelines—rather than the dirty wretches out on the field.

The truth was, I hated being back in the office. I sat at my computer, trying to concentrate while the usual circus went on—Susan Geekas whining about how awful they were to her at the White House, Amory Small telling his lame sexist jokes, the ceaseless churning of office politics. Ordinarily this was just background noise, but I now found it grating and unpleasant.

My friend George Dirk exploded my balloon of self-disgust with a telephone call. "Hey, asshole!" he said. Unlike most colleagues, Dirk made no effort to be nice to me. "I know you probably don't have time, what with getting ready to go to New York and take over from Ed Weiss. But you might be interested in talking to us peons over at Mirror Alert, because there are some extremely strange things going on here. One of you Master-of-the-Universe types should probably know about them. The others won't take my calls, so you're the lucky one. If you're not too busy negotiating a book contract or something."

We met for dinner that night at a run-down steak house in Arlington. There were yellowing autographed pictures on the wall, of Hollywood has-beens and low-life politicians who had visited the restaurant. There was a glossy photo of Rosemary Clooney; a grip-and-grin shot of Congressman Wayne Hays of Ohio; a picture of Chuck Bednarik in his football uniform—all of them bearing messages to the owner, written in the magnanimous style of people who know they will be famous forever.

George eased his large body into a booth. Even though the restaurant was nearly empty, he talked so quietly I could barely hear him. He was at his most conspiratorial that night. He had even made the reservation—for this empty restaurant—under a false name.

"You know me, Eric," he began. "So you know I'm not the kind of person to make hasty judgments." Actually, I knew him to be *exactly* that kind of person, but it didn't matter. "I have now been working for Mirror Alert for more than a month, and I have to tell you, there is something *wrong* there. The operation does not pass the George Dirk smell test. You follow me?"

"No, I don't follow you. What's wrong at Mirror Alert?"

"Okay. Point number one: What does it *do*? Basically, it exists to provide inside financial information to traders in the market. Advance tips about trade statistics, or unemployment numbers, or crop forecasts, or what the Fed is going to do at its next meeting. Or lists of companies that have recently retained investment bankers, which means they may be involved in tender offers or takeover bids. It's all boring stuff, but if you're even twenty seconds ahead of the market, you can make an enormous amount of money. Mirror Alert is trying to get some of this stuff twenty-four or forty-eight hours early—before the numbers are even washed and dried. This stuff is totally inside information—it would be illegal to trade on it, normally, but because Mirror Alert is regarded as a legitimate news organization, we're allowed to put it out. And you know what? We're pretty good at it. Not us old farts who were brought over from the *Mirror,* but the kids from Press Alert. Some of their information is so good, in fact, that we actually have to tone it down before putting it out, so it will look like a prediction and people won't know that we've actually *got the number.* These kids are getting this stuff from somewhere, and don't ask me how. Actually, *do* ask me how. Go on."

"Okay, George, how are they getting this stuff?"

"I'll tell you how. They pay for it. I mean, they have to. I've been a reporter for fifteen years, and I know what you can get from sources the ordinary, straight-up, no-money-changes-hands way. You get tips, leads, maybe once in a while you get some documents. But this stuff is in a different category. It's privileged information. People can go to jail for leaking it. Cash has to be changing hands somewhere. Somebody is bribing the people who take out the trash, or the bike messengers who carry messages around town, or the FedEx clerks, or the night clerical staff at the law firms, or whatever. It's *ugly.* Anyway, that's point number one.

"Point number two is that even if you're prepared to swallow Mirror Alert's basic mission, somebody is playing games. The operation isn't like anything I've ever seen. The editors are weirdos. They're all from Press Alert—that was part of the joint-venture deal, it turns out—and they're like robots. We reporter-peons go out and collect the information, and then we send it into a special 'editors' basket.' That turns out to be a black hole. We can't access the stories we filed, once they go to the editors. They claim it's a security precaution, but Eric—*they sit on this stuff.* It stays in their basket. Sometimes a few minutes, sometimes hours, sometimes days.

Think about it. We send the editors market-moving news, and they sit on it. What does that tell you?"

"That they're trading on the information themselves, before putting it out on the wire."

"Exactly. Or maybe they're making it available to a few special clients for a ton of money. But the point is, they're using journalistic cover to acquire information, and then using that information to make money. They're *laundering* information—making it look clean but using it to do dirty deals. Or so I hypothesize. I'm still gathering evidence, but what do you think? Should I blow the whistle?"

"Not yet. It's scary stuff, but it's just speculation. You don't really know anything. As Weiss would say, it's a little thin." Thinness was the quality the executive editor liked least in stories.

"I'm working on it. I'm trying to find some way to put a marker on a piece of information, so I can track it through the system, and see who trades on it. What do you think of that?"

"Good idea. As soon as you pin it down, you need to go tell Sellinger, right away."

"I dunno, buddy. How can you be sure Sellinger isn't part of the problem?"

"What's that supposed to mean?"

"Mirror Alert is his deal, Eric. If people are making dirty money on this stuff, Sellinger has to be part of it."

"That's ridiculous, Dirk. Even for a paranoid like you."

"Oh yeah? Well, then, you tell me: Who the hell owns Press Alert? Your pal Sellinger left that out when he announced the partnership. All we know is that they're an international communications company that's willing to invest five hundred million dollars in a sweet, money-losing newspaper company. So I did a little checking, and Press Alert is not *normal.*"

"What do you mean? What's abnormal?"

"It's not in any of the business directories; it isn't listed on any stock exchange; it has never registered a bond offering; the only mention of it in the *Financial Times* or *The Wall Street Journal* over the past five years was when they did the deal with us. In normal corporate terms, *they don't exist.* They say their corporate headquarters are in Geneva, but I asked a buddy of mine at the AP to check it out, and it's basically just a fancy mailing address with a nice office on the Rue du Rhône and a few secretaries to answer the phones. So my buddy pulled the Geneva corporate registration records to see who controls the stock of Press Alert, S.A. And it turns out to be a shell corporation with an address in the Bahamas. You want to explain that to me, Mr. Hotshot Friend of the Publisher? How did the *Mirror* get in bed with a company like that?"

"Because Sellinger needed money," I said. "That's the only thing I really know. Back in March, before the Press Alert deal was announced, he was so desperate he had Arthur Bowman out beating the bushes, looking for the five hundred million. Bowman talked to investors from Japan, Korea, Saudi Arabia and Britain, but he didn't get anywhere. But Sellinger obviously got the money from somewhere."

"How do you know that, Eric? I'd hate to think you actually are a friend of the publisher."

"Because I brought Bowman's computer back with me from China. One of the things he left on the hard drive was a memo to Sellinger, describing the contacts he'd made with all these investors."

"You sneak. That is so un-Truell-like. You are showing encouraging signs of going to seed."

Behind George on the wall was a picture of Edd "Kookie" Byrnes on the set of *77 Sunset Strip*. The inscription read: "Great dinner, Emilio! Thanks a million, Baby!"

"Just promise me one thing," I said. "You'll tell Sellinger if you find out anything important."

"You're missing the *point,* Eric." His eyes were glinting. "It may be Sellinger's scam."

The lady on the phone said she was calling from the Washington bureau of *Hard Copy.* She asked if I could hold one moment for Mr. Cohen. Jesus! I thought. He'd actually done it. The mad Venetian scholar had found a job as a reporter.

"*It's me!*" announced Rupert. "It's the Hatchet Man. I'm getting ready to do my first live segment next week and I'm looking for material. And you are on my list, Mr. Gergen. Most definitely on my list of news suspects."

"I have nothing for you, Hatchet Man. You're a competitor."

"I *am* flattered. Can it be that a great newspaper like the *Mirror* really considers a dirtbag sleaze TV magazine show like *Hard Copy* competition? My, my, my. But don't worry, Dave. I don't want to steal your stories. I want to *interview* you."

"About what?"

"What really happened in China, dear boy? How was Arthur Bowman killed? I mean, I read that shit you wrote about a runaway truck, but it was *not* believable. Not to a former trickster like me. All your sleepy, responsible newspaper friends swallowed it just fine, but the Hatchet Man doesn't work for the Establishment Press. And the Hatchet Man wants to know what happened."

"I wrote the truth. We were in a little alleyway in Beijing looking for a restaurant. A big truck came roaring down the street. Arthur jumped in front to slow it down, and he got hit. That's the story. That's how he died."

"Eric, babe, those are the *little* facts. I want the meta-facts. Nothing happens in Beijing without the Chicoms putting it in motion. So why did the Chinese want to kill Arthur Bowman, bigfoot journalist of the century? What was his game? Or maybe the culprits were his French friends, with whom—as we know—he was a tad chummy? Either way, it's a *story.* So tell me, what's the poop?"

"Are you recording this, Rupert?"

"Of *course* I am. The Hatchet Man records all his interviews. Why? Is that considered impolite by you celebrity journalists?"

"Fuck you, Rupert. I thought we had a relationship of trust. I protected you for months while you were still at the agency. You should treat me better."

I heard an electronic click. "You're right," he said. "I should treat you better. I owe you one. And I should stop referring to myself in the third person, I realize that. I'm just very wired right now. I *need* copy, and I thought maybe you could help me out. But the bottom line is, you're not going to tell me anything I can use next week. Is that right?"

"That's correct, Rupert."

"Crap! I'm really nervous, Eric. I've never done this. I want to be a star, but I don't know what I'm doing. I'm sorry to be such a jerk. I know I owe you a favor. You listened to all my ranting and gave me *encouragement,* when everybody else just wanted me to go away. I realize that. I shouldn't call you David Gergen, either. I don't know why I do that. You can trust me. And if you're ever in a jam, you just call on the Hatchet Man. Okay?"

"Okay, Hatchet Man. Break a leg. Do you have anything else for the first show, now that the item about me has fallen through?"

"Just one thing: I have a source in the White House who tells me the president has herpes. Serious, full-blown oozing-dick herpes. The lawyers want another source before they let me go with it, but how are you going to confirm something like that? Really! And the president isn't going to *sue.*

Can you imagine getting discovery in that lawsuit? But my producers are worried. Do you know what they said? They said it would be *irresponsible* to run the story. Can you believe that? This isn't the *New England Journal of Medicine,* for God's sake. It's *Hard Copy.* Does *everybody* on this fucking planet have to be responsible?"

35

❖

The Chinese government announced on Wednesday, May 15, that it would award the communications contract to the French company, Unetat. Because the Chinese would be purchasing what the announcement described as "upgrades, product enhancements and long-term technical support," the total value of the contract would be increased to $38 billion over seven years. The deal also included a complicated financing package: the European community agreed to underwrite the deal, allowing China to borrow the $38 billion from European banks at low interest rates. I could only assume that $8 billion of that total would find its way to the commission agents, consultants and other intermediaries—French and Chinese—who had been swimming around the deal. In effect, the citizens of Europe were lending money that would be paid out as bribes to the deal makers.

The White House issued a statement congratulating Unetat but expressing regret that the U.S. consortium's bid had been rejected. White House political aides were privately telling Susan Geekas that the president was relieved, because he had never been comfortable with the idea of America's getting so close to the dictators in Beijing. The politicos apparently didn't get the message to the assistant secretary of state for East Asia, who opined on background that the new French-Chinese alliance was "a potential disaster" for the United States.

The next morning, the *Mirror* carried my backgrounder on the China deal across the top of the front page, twinned with the day story about the contract award. We destroyed the other papers: none of them could match my account of the seamy side of the deal. Ed Weiss was in heaven. He lived for stories like this. The producers of *MacNeil/Lehrer* asked me to be a guest that afternoon, and Linda Wertheimer interviewed me on *All Things Considered.* The editor of our Sunday "Mirror on the World" section asked me to write an essay on the Bowmanesque topic of what the China deal would mean for global economic and political stability.

I was momentarily part of the great national dialogue—in which the big newspapers, television and radio all vibrated at the same pitch—discussing the same topic, beating it to death and then moving on. It was like a huge dinner-table conversation where only one person was allowed to speak at a time, and it was briefly my turn. It was fun, having people say they'd seen me on television or heard me on the radio. That sort of celebrity is the compensation for the passivity of being a reporter; it makes you feel like you're somebody, even if you don't really do anything.

That Thursday afternoon, the day my story appeared, I also received a call from a *Nightline* producer. He said they were doing the show that night on the China contract and asked me a lot of questions, but his assistant called back later and said they had booked someone else as a commentator. I turned on the show that night with some curiosity. To my surprise, I saw the perfectly poised face of Annie Baron. Nothing would have suggested to a reviewer that a few days before, she had been sobbing uncontrollably. Tonight, she was cool, clear-eyed. The usual host, Ted Koppel, was away, and the guest host was asking Annie what had gone on behind the scenes in the China deal. That was her specialty: tales of life under the volcano.

"The French are playing a dirty game," she began. My heart stopped. I thought she was going to blow the whole thing right there, on national television. But she had a different purpose. "To win this contract, the French have done some terrible things. Bribery, bullying, even violence. I've only heard hints, so I can't give you any details. But there are people who know the whole story—including people in the U.S. government— and I wonder whether they'll do anything to make the French think twice about the tactics they've used. You know how tough guys in movies are always saying, 'Don't get mad, get even!' Well, this may be one of those situations."

The host pushed her to explain what she meant about the French and their dangerous game, but Annie had said all she intended to. She darted away on another vector, saying that in the wake of the China debacle, there were new rumors that the secretary of state would be replaced if the president won a second term in November. But I understood Annie perfectly.

She was telling me to do something; and perhaps she was also warning me that she would take action herself if I failed to do so.

I called Rubino the next morning, two days after the Chinese had an-nounced the contract award. I still had the private work number he had given me. I said I had thought a lot about the matter, and I was interested in talking more about how we could bring Michel Bézy to justice.

"You just want to talk about it?" asked Rubino.

"No, I want to make it happen. But I need to know how we'd lure Bézy here, if I agreed to help."

"Give me a few hours," he said. "I'll show you."

Late that Friday afternoon, an envelope arrived at the bureau with my name and the word "Urgent" on it. The envelope had no other markings. I was sitting at my desk when the receptionist dropped it off. I didn't pay any attention at first. Public relations people always mark their press re-leases "Urgent," and I put it aside while I finished writing a thank-you let-ter to Michael Wee, my friend in Beijing. When I finally opened the manila envelope, I found inside a smaller letter-sized envelope with my name on it, marked "Personal and Confidential," enclosing a brief note:

From sources familiar with the details of the China contract:

On Thursday, May 16, $120 million was wired to Account P-20-52-D, at PanAsia Credit in Vanuatu, the New Hebrides Islands. The money was paid from the account of a French-Chinese joint-venture company called Inter/Orient, which has been established to disburse progress pay-ments for the communications contract. This morning (Paris time), Fri-day, May 17, $40 million was withdrawn from the Vanuatu account and transferred to bank account 5371-77-244 at Organisation des Banques Suisses. Swiss banking records identify the beneficial owner of this ac-count as a French national named Michel Bézy.

Rubino had delivered the instrument of revenge. The material had the rock-hard certainty of fact. I could only admire the technical competence of the people who had collected the information. They had Bézy, cold.

My phone rang at home that night at 10:30. The caller didn't identify himself, but I recognized the voice as Tom Rubino's. He asked me to call him back from a pay phone. I put on my bedroom slippers and a pair of jeans and went downstairs to the phone in the lobby of my building and dialed the number Rubino had given me.

"Get any interesting mail lately?" he asked.

"Yes," I said. "It's nice work. Our man would not be happy to know that information is in the hands of a reporter."

"So are you in or out? We need to know."

"I'm interested. But what happens if I can't get our man to come to America. Can I still use the information in a story?"

"Absolutely. The information is yours now. You can do whatever you want with it."

"And if I say yes, what happens then? Will you have to get another special waiver for me, and tell the president and all that?"

"No. This is different—it isn't an intelligence mission, it's law enforcement. It's really an FBI operation, since it's inside the country. You'll still be a confidential source for us. But basically, you'll just be doing your job as a reporter, arranging an interview with someone. We'll do the rest."

"I want my life back after this. I just want to be a journalist again."

"That's your problem," Rubino answered, "not mine."

On Monday morning, I went to Bob Marcus and told him I had a blockbuster. A French lawyer named Michel Bézy—who was the personal adviser to Alain Peyron, the CEO of Unetat—had received a $120 million kickback on the China plane deal. He had already transferred $40 million to his own Swiss bank account. I had the numbers of both accounts, I said. Marcus loved it. It was "the next shoe dropping," he said, documenting the allegations I'd hinted at in my front-page piece a few days before.

Marcus immediately called the *Mirror*'s general counsel in New York. The lawyer advised that we needed to talk to Bézy. Unless we were able to interview him, we couldn't run the story. So there it was: the planets were all in alignment. The requirements of *The New York Mirror* and the Central Intelligence Agency were identical.

I had a number for Bézy's law office in Paris, which Rubino had given me in that first pack of material back in March. It was 10:30 A.M. in Washington—early enough that Bézy might still be in his office. A Frenchwoman answered the phone in the singsong *"Bon-jour, mon-sieur"* voice favored by Gallic shopkeepers and secretaries. I gave her my name and told her I was calling from *The New York Mirror*, and that I wanted to interview

Michel Bézy for a story. "*Ne quit-tez pas, mon-sieur,*" she said. She put me on hold for so long I thought we'd lost the connection, but eventually a man came on the line. His voice was clipped, perfectly controlled.

"This is Jacques Alessi, Mr. Bézy's confidential assistant. How may I help you?"

"I'm a reporter for *The New York Mirror.* I would like to speak with your boss for a story I'm working on."

"We know who you are, Mr. Truell, you can be assured of that. What is the nature of your story?"

"It's kind of sensitive. I'm not sure whether Mr. Bézy would want me to talk about it with you on the phone."

"As you like. We cannot answer your question unless you tell us what it is. I handle all of Mr. Bézy's sensitive matters. If you would like, we can use the procedure Mr. Bézy follows on important international calls. I will call you back on another phone. You will give me another number in your office—not your usual extension—where you will receive this call."

I gave him Dirk's old number. The desk was still empty, and the phone hadn't been removed. Alessi called back five minutes later.

"This is Mr. A, from Mr. B's office," he said. I assumed that Mr. B himself must be listening on an extension. "If you're ready, please go ahead with your question."

"Fine. As you know, I have been reporting on the business activities surrounding the China communications deal. Now I have another story. Are you listening?"

"Yes, yes, we are aware of your stories, Mr. Truell. Go ahead."

"I have documentary evidence that on May 16, the day after the China contract was announced, a hundred-and-twenty-million-dollar payment was sent to an account at PanAsia Credit in Vanuatu controlled by Mr. Bézy. The next day forty million dollars was transferred from there to Mr. Bézy's numbered account at Organisation des Banques Suisses in Geneva. I have the account numbers, but I don't think you'd want me to mention them over the phone."

"No, that is not necessary." There was a long pause—long enough to allow a hasty consultation in Paris. "And what are you going to do with this information, Mr. Truell?"

"I'm going to publish it in the *Mirror,* unless Mr. Bézy can tell me why I shouldn't. I'd like to interview him, as soon as possible, in the United States. Unless he agrees to meet with me in one week's time, I will assume he has no comment and we will go ahead with the story."

There was another long pause. "You said you are prepared to discuss this with Mr. Bézy. Does that mean you might *not* publish the information?"

What was he asking? Did he think I could make the problem go away? It didn't matter to me. He could think whatever he liked. "That's right," I said. "We might end up publishing nothing. My information could be wrong. I could be misinterpreting it. That's why I need to interview Mr. Bézy."

Again, there was a pause. It was like talking on a ship-to-shore radio, waiting for the response to be formulated and sent. "Could you meet Mr. Bézy in France, Mr. Truell?"

"No. It has to be in the United States. After what happened in China, I think that's a reasonable request."

"Where in the United States?"

"That doesn't matter to me. You choose anywhere you like."

"Very well. I will speak with Mr. Bézy and get back to you as soon as I can."

Alessi called back thirty minutes later. He said that Bézy had agreed to my request for an interview. He would meet me in one week, on Monday, May 27. Alessi said he would call me the night before the meeting to propose the specific time and place. I wondered if that would give Rubino and the FBI enough time to get ready.

"Can I call you back?" I asked.

Alessi said no, his boss needed an immediate answer. Otherwise there would be no interview. I said the arrangement sounded fine. The train was coming through the station, and I wanted to be on it.

When I called Rubino's private number that afternoon to tell him the news, he was formal, almost stiff, lacking his usual recruiter's enthusiasm. At first I thought he was upset that I had agreed to the short timetable for meeting with Bézy, but that wasn't it. The FBI had field offices in every major city in the country, he said, and he would let them worry about making arrangements. No, Rubino's new tone reflected something more fundamental. I was his guy now. He didn't have to be nice to me.

"You're going to need some training," he said. "You almost got killed in China, and we can't expose you to those risks again. The agency will be in real trouble if anything happens to you."

"But I don't want any training. I'm a reporter. I'm going to interview the subject of a story. That's it. No one needs to train me how to conduct an interview."

"It's not an option, Eric. I'm sorry, but that's the way it is. It's not my call. I am operating under orders. I need at least two days. That isn't much, but we'll be able to run through the basics of tradecraft."

"One day," I said. "Two days is too much, but I'll give you one day."

That's how I was operating at that point—taking anything that made me uncomfortable and dividing it in half.

36

My tradecraft class was held in a nondescript office building at a strip shopping mall in Falls Church. Rubino told me to arrive at 9:00 sharp. From the outside, there was no hint it had any connection with the United States government. Above the front door were the words INSUR-ANCE BUILDING, and on the first of its six floors there was, indeed, a small insurance underwriting business to maintain the illusion. The building was on the edge of seediness: rusting metal pillars, venetian blinds askew, peeling paint. Out front, there was a small parking lot, but I had been instructed to park in the underground garage so my arrival would be invisible. The building was used to shield the identities of people under deep cover, but it seemed to embody the inner decay of the agency itself. These people had no trouble, nowadays, passing for insurance agents.

The elevator had buttons for only the first and second floors. I pushed "2," as instructed. The door opened a few moments later onto a bleak hallway, with faded yellow walls and a gray linoleum floor. At the end of the hallway was a closed door; sitting in a chair by the door was a security guard.

"I'm here for an appointment," I said awkwardly. "My name is Truell. They're expecting me, I think."

He took my driver's license, punched a code into a lock and disappeared behind the door. As I waited, another elevator arrived from the parking garage. A man wearing a government security badge around his neck emerged. He inserted the card into a security device next to the elevator buttons. Another car arrived promptly to carry him to the upper floors. The second floor of the "Insurance Building" functioned like an air lock, shielding the real work of the building from contamination.

The security guard returned and handed back my license. "This way, sir," he said, holding the door open.

Beyond the door was a bustling village. There was a bulletin board with notices for the CIA credit union; a reminder for people traveling overseas to get their malaria shots; announcement of a support group for new mothers; even a sign-up sheet for the office yoga class. The people in the corridors defined American ordinariness: women with frumpy hairdos, men with potbellies, a diverse mix of faces that were dignified, reserved, like those of people you see at a military base. These people were not "club-bable," to use an expression beloved by the CIA old boys of an earlier era. One of the ordinaries approached me. He was short and fat, with thinning white hair. He was wearing an old gray suit. The fabric of his white shirt was straining at the buttons, and the zipper on his trousers had begun to pull apart. He looked like a guy who might be the ticket taker for a Celtics game at Boston Garden.

"Hi there!" he said. "I'm Frank, from the Office of Security. I'm going to be your instructor for this one-day forced march. I told them it was impossible, and they told me to stuff it, so here we are. Come on in my office. We only have eight hours, so let's not waste time. You want some coffee? A doughnut? They're right over there—delicious, especially the jelly ones. Take two. You have a long day ahead of you."

I took two doughnuts—plain and powdered sugar. This Frank, whoever he was, seemed like the kind of person whose suggestions you obeyed. On his desk was a stack of back issues of *Guns and Ammo* magazine. The books on his shelf included *Shadowing and Surveillance, How to Disappear Completely and Never Be Found, Sneak It Through: Smuggling Made Easy* and *The Complete Guide to Lock-Picking.*

"Do you know anything about tradecraft, son?" he asked.

"No," I said. "Sorry, but I really don't."

"Ever been in the military, or the police? Or maybe the ROTC in college? The Boy Scouts, even?"

"No, sir."

"Why, you little shit!" He wagged his finger at me. "Why the hell not? What's the matter with you, for Chrissakes?"

"Nothing's the matter with me. I just never did those things." For a short, fat man in his seventies, he was intimidating. I looked at my watch, and then at the door. "Maybe I should go, if my background bothers you."

"Hell, no. Calm down. I'm just kidding around. Having a little fun. My son is useless, too. It's nothing to worry about. Because after one day with Frank, you're going to know everything that's worth knowing. Am I right?"

"Yes, sir."

"Now, we're going to skip a lot today. In fact, we're going to skip almost everything, because we only have one fucking day. We're going to skip the crash-bang, high-speed driving stuff, because you're not going to be doing any driving. And we're going to skip flaps and seals, because you're not going to be steaming open any letters. And we're going to skip agent recruitment, because you're not going to be recruiting anyone. We're gonna skip covert communications, and how to evade radio jamming, and parachute drops, and coastal landings at night in rubber rafts and a whole lot of other crap that you don't need. Am I right?"

"Sounds right to me. I'm not planning any rubber-raft landings anytime soon."

"Don't be a smart aleck, son. It's not becoming, and it wastes time. We're going to concentrate today on just three things: how to detect surveillance, how to protect information, and self-defense. That's all. You learn that, and Uncle Frank will give you an extra doughnut."

"Sounds good," I said. Life here seemed to be measured out in doughnuts.

"Let's take a ride," said Frank. He strode out of his office toward the elevators, grasping me by the elbow and pushing me before him like a shopping cart. When we reached the basement parking garage, he steered me toward an old Chevy Impala, opened the door and told me to get in. He drove a few miles to Tysons Corner Mall, the largest shopping mall in the region, and parked in front of Nordstrom's department store.

"Here's the drill, son," he said. "In this shopping mall there are five people who have been assigned to tail you. Your assignment is to identify any three of them. If you do it, you get to have lunch. If you fail, no lunch. Tough shit. And don't try to cheat on me by chowing down in the mall. Is that clear?"

"But how am I going to know who's tailing me? I don't have a clue how I'm supposed to do this."

"Good boy! When you don't know something, always ask questions. Now there's three types of surveillance. There's your loose tail, where you're following the target from a distance; there's your close tail, when it's essential not to lose the target, so you run some risk of detection; and there's your rough tail, where you don't care if the target knows you're following him. To make it easier, the five folks following you have been instructed to maintain a close tail. So you have a chance of catching them.

"Now, on a surveillance-detection run—which is what this—you want to look for the odd man out. The person who speeds up when you do and slows down when you do, even though everybody else is walking at normal speed. Or the person who follows you outside when everybody else is going inside. Or the person you saw in Nordstrom's, and then in Crown Books, and isn't it a coincidence he's now in the doggie hair salon, too? Am I right?"

"You're right. Look for the odd man out."

"Here's a few more tricks of the trade from Uncle Frank, some things you can use to help spot a tail. Elevators are good, because they force the hand of the people tailing you. Somebody's got to get on the damn elevator with you or they won't know where you got off. Empty spaces like parking lots are good, because you can see who's coming behind you. Escalators are good, because you can see the whole line of people, and your tail almost has to be one of them. And here's one of Frank's extra-special secrets, known only to a few discriminating members of the surveillance fraternity: when you're moving, drop a piece of paper into an unlikely spot, and then watch to see if anybody picks it up. The tail will sometimes think you're filling a drop, and he'll stop to look. And you got him!

"Okay, son, that's it." He pushed me out the car door. "You're due back here in two hours, at eleven-thirty on the dot. Don't fuck up."

I stood on the curb and watched Frank roar off. It was still fairly early in the morning, and the mall was relatively empty. I figured that worked to my advantage. Somewhere out there were five pairs of eyes, watching me intently. I walked into Nordstrom's and headed for men's clothes. I tried to be aware of everyone around me. I saw a full-figured blond woman in her fifties enter the store. She was dressed in white Capri pants that were a size too tight, and she was heading slowly in my direction. From the other direction a young man in jeans was ambling toward the men's section, too. A dark-haired man in a neat business suit hovered nearby; I thought at first he was a salesclerk and walked over to ask him a question, but he turned and walked away. In the shoe department a neatly dressed black man was trying on a pair of wing tips.

How could I get the watchers to make themselves more obvious? I found some corduroy pants on a rack and went into one of the fitting rooms. I sat there, watching the entrance. Someone had to be waiting for me. After several minutes I popped out of the fitting room suddenly. Standing just out-side was the woman in the Capri pants, looking at a selection of overcoats. Why was she looking at them in late May? She had to be one of the peo-ple following me. I took out my reporter's notebook and wrote "Blonde in tight white pants."

Next I tried Frank's parking-lot move. I left Nordstrom's and walked out across the wide-open space of the lot. I figured only one member of the sur-veillance team would follow me, but which one? Off to the left, I saw a big truck that would shield me from view. I ducked behind it, waited a few moments, and then sprinted toward the distant corner of the lot. Behind me, far in the distance, I saw the black man who had been trying on shoes, walking quickly in my direction. He had to be one of them, too. I headed back toward the mall, passing him on the way. "Howdy," I said. He glow-ered at me. I wrote a brief description of him in my notebook.

The third was the hardest to identify. I crisscrossed the mall, stopping in bookstores, pet stores, optometrists, lingerie stores, toy stores. I kept look-ing for the odd man out—the person who didn't fit, or whom I'd seen else-where. But I was striking out. I even tried Frank's trick of dropping pieces of paper into possible hiding places, but nobody fell for the bait. It was past 11:00 and I was already hungry. A Taco Bell was up ahead, and I thought how good a burrito would taste, especially if I failed to meet my quota and was denied lunch. But as I was standing in line I considered how Frank would berate me for breaking the rules, and decided to order a cup of coffee.

While I sipped the coffee it occurred to me I hadn't tried Frank's eleva-tor trick. I found the main elevator block and pressed the "up" button. By the time the car arrived I had been joined by a half-dozen people. One of them had to be shadowing me. I studied each of them carefully, trying to match them with people I'd seen elsewhere in the mall. My eyes settled on a dark-haired man standing in a corner. He was wearing dark glasses, a red windbreaker and jeans. I sensed I'd seen him before, but not like that. And then it was obvious: he was the man in the business suit I'd approached at Nordstrom's, asking directions. He'd changed clothes. I made a third nota-tion in my book and went outside to find my instructor.

Frank was waiting in his Chevy Impala. He was reading the racing form and circling horses he liked at Charles Town that night. "Come on!" he barked. As soon as I was in the car, he popped it in gear and drove off.

I described the three surveillants I'd been able to discover during the exercise, and gave him a brief explanation of how I'd spotted each of them. He wasn't as enthusiastic as I'd hoped. In fact, he seemed angry. "So where are we going to lunch?" I asked. But he was still glowering at me.

"You piss me off," he said. "You know that?" He pulled the car off the road and parked it behind a warehouse. He pulled the trunk release and the lid popped open behind him. "Get out!" he snarled.

"What did I do?" I asked anxiously. "Where are we going?"

"Shut up!" He removed a snub-nosed revolver from a shoulder holster. "I'm famous for two things in the agency—always carrying a gun, and hating smart-aleck kids from Ivy League schools. None of my colleagues would be the least bit surprised if I actually shot you. Now get out of the car and get into the trunk."

"This is a joke, right?"

"Wrong!" He whipped the barrel of his revolver across my cheek, leaving a red welt. "Get in the fucking trunk, now!"

The trunk was dirty and dusty and smelled of gasoline. I climbed in carefully, trying not to rip my pants on the tire iron. "Don't close the top, please. I won't be able to breathe."

"Shut the fuck up."

He closed the trunk and suddenly it was tight and dark. I heard him get back in the car and head off. He was singing loudly to himself, a Broadway show tune. We drove for perhaps twenty minutes. Finally the car stopped, and the lid of the trunk popped open. We were in a dark place that seemed to be underground. It felt damp and chilly.

"Get out, pretty boy," he said. My legs were stiff and I had trouble standing at first. He laughed and pushed me to the ground. "Pathetic," he said.

"Fuck you!" I swung wildly at him. He danced away nimbly, despite his age and girth. He pulled the gun out again and began waving it at me.

"Don't even think about it," he said. "If I didn't like you, you'd already be dead. Now get in there." He pointed to a wooden box a few feet away, not much bigger than a coffin. I did what he said, afraid of provoking him any more.

I was in that box at least two hours, maybe three. The cold, the wound on my cheek, the ache in my legs combined to make me feel miserable. I had no idea why he'd put me there, or when he would let me out.

When Frank finally opened the door I fell out of the box onto the concrete floor. I was thirsty, faint, sore. It was all I could do to keep from crying. Frank pushed me into a small room illuminated by a bright fluorescent tube. There were two chairs. Frank shoved me into one and sat down in the other himself.

"You're not really a reporter, are you?" he said.

"Yes, I am. I work for *The New York Mirror.* I've worked for them since I got out of college."

"Bullshit!" he said. "You work for the agency. Why else would they have me train you? They don't do that for reporters."

"They did in my case. I can't explain why, but they did."

"Who's your case officer, then? It has to be that asshole, Tom Rubino."

"I don't have a case officer."

"It's Tom Rubino. This would be typical of him, this kind of half-baked Twinkie of an operation. I'm not letting you out of here until you tell me it's Tom Rubino."

We went on this way for another twenty minutes, with Frank badgering and me struggling to keep him at bay. The more he asked about Rubino, the tighter I became. I had a powerful desire not to tell him anything. I didn't know whether he was crazy, or playing games, but I felt as if I were fighting for my life.

And then it was over. Frank stood up, kicked his chair back and walked out of the little room. I was deliberating whether to run away, when I smelled the aroma of food. Frank reentered the room carrying two bags, one from Pizza Hut and one from Burger King.

"Congratulations," he said. "You have now completed hostile-interrogation training." He handed me the bags of food. "I didn't know which you liked—pizza or burgers—so I told them to get both."

"You fucker! That was a game?"

"It was a simulation, junior, not a game. And it wasn't half as nasty as The Farm, where they put you in the box for twenty-four hours. But it had its moments. Sorry I got a little carried away with the pistol. Is your cheek okay? Your mother would be proud of you, son. You did a good job today. I thought you'd be peeing in your pants by the end, but you toughed it out. Put 'er there."

He stuck out a meaty hand and gave me a shake.

"Thanks," I said. "You're a very believable homicidal maniac."

"Damn straight! The lesson here, my boy, is: Stick to your story. Don't change it as you go along. If you're telling them a cover story, think of real people and places. If you should actually be tortured—God forbid!—don't give it all up right away. Let it go in pieces. Think of it like undressing. Give 'em one piece of clothing at a time, maybe you'll still have your jockey shorts on at the end, who knows?"

Frank looked at his watch. It was after 3:00. "We have one more session," he said. "Let's go back upstairs." He led me up a stairway and across a catwalk and we soon found ourselves back at the basement elevator. All that time we had been in the bowels of the Insurance Building.

The self-defense class was held in a small gym on the fifth floor. Short, fat Frank was not the instructor. Instead it was a compact woman in her early thirties, dressed in a warm-up suit with the CIA crest on the chest. She showed me the Kung Fu pressure points on a chart—the points which, if attacked, could kill or cripple an opponent. She demonstrated some basic moves that could be used to ward off a deadly assault—the kick to the groin; the push of fingers toward the eyeballs; the disabling kick that could shatter a joint in an instant. I had studied karate when I was a kid, and I had tried to keep fit in the years since. But when it came time to do exercises on the mat, she overwhelmed me.

"Don't use any of these fighting techniques unless you have no other option," she said. "If you use them against a skilled opponent, there's a good chance he'll kill you. Quite often, the best defense is not motion but time."

When the self-defense lecture was over, Frank took me back to his office. "Are you going to be carrying a firearm?" he asked.

"No," I said.

"Mistake. I've got some nifty pieces for you to look at in the armory." He opened a copy of *Guns and Ammo* atop his desk and flipped through pictures of various 9 mm automatic pistols, all shot in the lurid colors of cheap pornography. "Hubba! Hubba!" he said, pointing to one of the guns. "Sure I can't interest you in one of them?"

"Nope. I wouldn't know how to use it. It would only put me in more danger. I'm a reporter. That isn't my cover, it's what I do. Reporters don't carry automatic weapons."

"Maybe not, but you need *something*. I've decided I like you. I'm not going to send you out there buck naked. No way."

He took me down the hall to a moldy storeroom lined with metal shelves. He pulled something down from a box and handed it to me. It appeared to be a fancy Mont Blanc fountain pen. "Now this is perfect for yuppies. You assholes actually buy these three-hundred-dollar pens. This one shoots out a chemical that's like Mace, but better. It will incapacitate a couple of guys. The gold clip is the trigger. Pull it toward you and it fires. You arm it by twisting the barrel—like so. Use it in good health."

I took the pen from Frank and pointed it directly toward his eyes.

"Ha, ha. Funny boy!" He pulled another item down from the shelf. It appeared to be a plastic Bic lighter. "Do you smoke? No, you're a yuppie. Of course you don't. It's *bad* for you. But bring this along anyway and pretend. It's a stun grenade. You arm it by pulling down on the gas jet and turning the flint wheel, just the way you'd light it normally. Three seconds later, it detonates. So throw it and turn your back, quick. You don't want to have this in your hand when it goes off, I promise you. And cover your eyes; it puts out a lot of light. Here, take a couple. What the hell?"

I took the exploding lighters, and put them in my pocket, next to my Mont Blanc assault fountain pen.

"Don't you love this shit?" said Frank. "Isn't this what it's really all about? What else do you want? Do you need any disguises? I have wigs, glasses, all that stuff. Voice-alteration devices? False documentation? Uncle Frank has the whole candy store, right here."

"Nothing," I said. "I'm just a reporter, going on an interview. With any luck, the fellow I want to talk to is going to end up in jail."

Frank looked at me—a lean, cocky, thirty-seven-year-old at the end of my one-day encounter with the black arts. He put his hand on my shoulder.

"Are you scared, son? About what's going to happen, I mean."

I thought a moment. "Yes," I said. "I'm quite scared."

"Good. You had me worried for a minute. But as long as you're scared, you won't do stupid things. Now come to Papa."

He embraced me and gave me a kiss on the cheek.

Rubino was waiting for me back in Frank's office. He was neatly dressed, looking very bureaucratic in contrast to Frank's disheveled attire. He asked me to join him in a nearby conference room. "Well, now. How did it go?"

"Pretty good, I think. I learned a lot. I have to ask you, who was that guy Frank, my instructor?"

"His name is Frank Jones. That's his work name, at least. I don't know his real name. He's an old washout from the Near East Division. He made a lot of money in the Middle East after he retired from the agency, but then he lost it all. He's broke, basically. We give him a small contract to help him get by, but I'm not sure he's worth the trouble. This may be his last month on the payroll. Funny old guy, isn't he?"

"I liked him a lot. I got a sense, talking to him, what it must have been like in the old days, when you guys were waving guns around and barking orders and the whole world was going your way. It must have been fun."

"Ancient history," said Rubino. "We have work to do." It was obvious he wasn't a big fan of Frank's. It was after 5:00, and I was exhausted. I asked if it could wait, but he said no, we had to do it then.

He went over the operational plan he had prepared with the FBI. The National Security Agency would be monitoring Bézy from the moment he left for the airport in Paris. They would know when his plane took off and would track it over the Atlantic, collecting any in-flight communications sent along the way. Once the plane landed, the bureau would take over. They would have people on the ground at the airport, and a small army at the designated meeting site. It all sounded smooth and seamless, as he described it, but Rubino still seemed worried about the possibility of a "flap"—the agency's all-purpose term for anything that went bad in public. Anything was better than a flap.

"If we run into any problems," he said, "we abort the whole thing. Are we clear on that?" That was the message he really wanted to convey. It was obvious that someone at the agency had gotten nervous and screamed at Rubino, making him nervous, and now he was making me nervous. I felt sorry for him: he had to worry about an inspector general, congressional investigating committees, federal prosecutors. "Listen to me, Eric!" he said. "This is serious. If anything goes wrong—*anything*—that's it. Coitus interruptus. We don't try to be heroes. We bail out. Understood?"

"Sure. I don't want to get in trouble. But why did Frank give me the poison pen?" I showed him the armed Mont Blanc.

"Shit! Did he give you that? Well, he's crazy. Just don't use it. Now when you get the call Sunday night, I want you to meet me at the safe house so we can go over the details one last time."

"Not there. I hate that place. Can't I go to your house?"

"Oh, I suppose so. It's not secure. I could get in trouble. So don't tell anyone."

It was the first time I had seen Rubino look so nervous. He was running a complicated interagency operation, with multiple layers of paperwork and coordination and ass-covering. And he was clearly afraid that I was going to screw it all up.

37

❖❖

On Thursday night, four days before I was supposed to meet Bézy,
I received an agitated call from George Dirk. I was sitting on my balcony,
reading a book and watching the sun go down. I was trying to chill out—
to avoid "thinking" about what I would be doing on Monday. Dirk was
red-hot. "*I got it!*" he screamed into the phone. "You wanted an example
that their operation is crooked? Well, I got it. It's going down tonight. You
have to come over to my office and watch it happen."

"I'm about to smoke a cigar," I said.

"Bullshit. This is important. Come over here right now or I will perma-
nently write you off my Christmas-card list."

Worrying about Dirk's problems was better than worrying about my
own. And it was a beguiling spring night; the city was garlanded with the
blossoms of the flowering trees and shrubs that lined every street. I drove
down Seventeenth Street to Memorial Bridge and crossed the Potomac as
the last light lingered over the broad, gentle river. The trees along the banks
were etched in black, like photographic negatives. The river itself was
painted in the imaginary colors of nightfall—inky blues and greens. If this
were any other city, poets would sing of its beauty. Instead, it was fated to
be the home of journalists, who regarded beauty as a conflict of interest.

Dirk escorted me up to the Mirror Alert office. The place was almost
empty; a sole figure was sitting in the editors' area behind the partition.
Dirk led me back to his small cubicle, which contained two computer ter-
minals: one was a PC with the Mirror Alert news system; the other was a
Bloomberg terminal that carried news from financial markets around the
world.

"Do you know what's on the front page of the *Mirror* tomorrow?"

"No," I said. I was far from the daily flow of the paper at that point, wound in my own cocoon. "What have we got?"

"A blockbuster. We will carry a story saying that the chairman of the Federal Reserve has heart trouble and will announce his resignation next week. Look at it, I have it right here on the screen." He pointed to the story displayed on his PC. It led with the expected resignation of the Fed chairman.

"Do you have any idea what the markets will do when this story hits, Eric? They think the Fed chairman is God! They're convinced that if anything ever happens to him, the president will appoint a moron. This is market-moving news, no?"

"Definitely. The bond market will go nuts. When do we put it out?"

"Aha! That's the issue. The contents of the *Mirror* are embargoed each night until nine-thirty. But the major stories are all made available to us at Mirror Alert at seven-thirty, so that we can prepare our own electronic versions to release when the paper hits the streets. That's why I can get it on my screen—because they've already moved it to us. It's part of the joint-venture deal between the *Mirror* and Press Alert. Right now, it's almost eight-thirty, which means we've had the information for nearly an hour. If Mirror Alert is airtight, the markets shouldn't begin to move until nine-thirty. Correct? But guess what?"

"They're already trading on the news?"

"You got it. And what's even more scary, the heavy trading began a little after we got the feed at seven-thirty. Here, I'll show you."

Dirk took the keyboard of his Bloomberg terminal and punched in some symbols. "Check it out," he said. "This shows trading in U.S. Treasuries in Tokyo over the last hour. Notice anything strange?"

"Yeah, prices are falling off a cliff." The Bloomberg price chart showed a steep fall that began just after seven-thirty P.M., New York time. Prices for thirty-year Treasuries had fallen a full two points in the last hour. That was a huge drop. Bond prices are measured in one thirty-second increments, each of which is called a "tick." That meant prices had fallen sixty-four ticks in an hour, as traders at each of the major bond houses began to revalue their huge inventories. Bond yields—which are the effective interest rates the bonds pay, based on those prices—were shooting up, correspondingly.

"Look here!" said Dirk, pointing to a new screen with quotes from other Asian markets. "The same thing is happening in Singapore, and in Hong

Kong. And the dollar is getting hammered on all those exchanges, too." He called up another screen that summarized trading on Asian monetary exchanges. "Check this out!" he said, pointing to the bottom of the screen to a headline for a Bloomberg Business News bulletin on the bond market. The headline read: BOND SELL-OFF SPARKED BY FED RESIGNATION RUMOR.

Dirk punched another button and the lead paragraph of a news story flashed on the screen: "Analysts attributed a sharp slide in prices of U.S. Treasury securities in trading early Friday in Asian markets to rumors that The New York Mirror will publish a story Friday saying that the chairman of the Federal Reserve will resign next week." I studied the two flickering screens: cause and effect.

"Bingo!" said Dirk.

"Strong circumstantial evidence," I said, "but it doesn't prove that the leak came from our colleagues at Press Alert. It could be any doofus copy editor in New York."

"If this was an isolated example, Eric, I might agree with you. But it's not. I've been collecting others. Last week, Mirror Alert had a story predicting that the April unemployment number would be a lot lower than people had been expecting. God only knows who our sources were for that story, but it turned out to be right. We ran it—officially—at ten in the morning. But the night before, there was heavy selling of U.S. Treasuries in Singapore. Now, I can't prove to you the traders were basing their moves on an early look at our story, but I am morally certain of it."

I looked over to the editors' bull pen. The lone editor in residence was at that moment picking his nose. "Who are these guys, anyway?"

"Shitheads. They call themselves journalists, but they're mostly ex–bond traders and Wall Street scum. A lot of them are European. You want another example of their thievery?"

"Sure, if you have one."

"Okay. Two weeks ago, The *Mirror* carried a story saying that J. M. Sedgwick Securities would be firing its chief investment strategist because of trading irregularities. Market-moving news, sent over to Mirror Alert at seven-thirty, as per our arrangement. Guess what? Heavy selling of J. M. Sedgwick Securities begins immediately in Asian markets, where they're sold. It's a pattern. They take the information here and trade on it overseas, where they think the SEC won't notice. It's corrupt! These people are thieves. We are in bed with a bunch of con men! And the worst of it is, we still don't know who they are."

"You have to tell Sellinger, Dirk. Call him tomorrow."

"He's away. I already checked. He won't be back until Monday. And I still think he may be one of the bad guys."

"Call him Monday. You have to. This could destroy the *Mirror*. You have to blow the whistle. If Sellinger doesn't listen, go to Weiss."

"I don't know. That's not my style. I need to be sure who owns them, before I go to war. I have a buddy in the Bahamas who's working on that. He thinks he's close to getting some names of the people who own the Press Alert shell company down there. I would love to wait until I have that, before I go to the big shots."

"You can't wait much longer, Dirk. If you're worried about seeing Sellinger alone, we can go together. How about that? I'll be away Monday, but we could go see him Tuesday. We'll tell him what you've found out."

"Gosh, a hotshot like you, joining a nobody like me. I'm so flattered. He'd think it was dogshit, coming from me, but he'll know it's *serious* if someone important like you comes along."

"Fuck you, Dirk. I was just offering to help."

He looked sheepish; he knew he had overdone it. "I apologize, Eric. Really. Sometimes I can't help myself. I just don't feel centered unless I say something offensive. But I'd like your help. We'll go up Tuesday, stop at Radio City Music Hall, see the Rockettes. Then send the bill to Sellinger."

Annie knocked on the door of my apartment Saturday afternoon. She was dressed in loose jeans and a cashmere sweater. She had her hair pulled back in a ponytail. There was a gentleness in her eyes, a vulnerability. I had known Annie long enough to sense that she wanted something.

"What are you doing here?" I asked. After our last meeting I had assumed that she was a page in my life that had finally turned.

"I thought maybe you'd like to take a walk," she said. "It's such a pretty day."

And it was. The sun was shining. Spring was still all around us. We strolled through the embassy ghetto of Kalorama, where the European diplomats' children were out walking with their South Asian servants, and down into Rock Creek Park. I thought she must have come to push me again to avenge her beloved Arthur. I wanted to tell her the whole story of what was about to happen, but that was impossible. So I said just a few words.

"I'm going to get the man who killed Arthur," I said. "If everything works out, he'll go to jail. At the very least, I'll be able to write about him in the paper."

"That's good," she said. "I'm glad. I knew you would." That was it. She looked pleased, but she didn't press me for any more details. I began to wonder if perhaps she had come to see me for some other reason.

I was happy enough to be out walking and didn't need any explanation for her visit. But after we had gone a mile or so, she stopped and looked at me earnestly, fiercely. "I just couldn't bear ending it the way we did," she said. "It seemed wrong to part like that, after so many years. I felt empty afterwards."

"I did too, but I thought that was probably the right feeling. I mean, we are empty, aren't we?"

"I guess so. But then, why do I still want to see you?"

"Force of habit. Fear of the future. Genuine affection. All good reasons."

We walked awhile longer in silence. The bicyclists and joggers rushed by us, on their way to somewhere. I was relaxing, in her presence. I had always loved to watch her walk, the way her feet barely seemed to touch the ground.

"Do you ever want to have kids?" she asked. She took my hand in hers as she said it. That was an unfair thing to do. I held it for a moment and then let it go.

"I don't know. Finding someone to marry is proving to be harder than I thought."

"For me, too."

A tall black man sailed by us on Rollerblades, his muscles rippling as he pressed into each turn. He was dressed in spandex bicycle shorts and wrap-around blue-tinted sunglasses, listening to music on his Sony Walkman. He exhibited a perfect solitude, lost in the pleasure of his body and the music and the day. In the wake of the Rollerblader pedaled three small girls on bicycles, followed by a man who appeared to be their father. Each of his daughters needed help with something: a push, an untied shoelace, a horn that wouldn't honk. Annie watched this pageant attentively.

"What about us?" she said. "Do you think it's too late for us to have kids?"

I stopped and looked at her. "Why are you doing this, Annie? You know I still love you. But we've hurt each other so much over the years. Not just about Arthur, but other things. There's so much scar tissue now, I don't know if anything real can grow."

"Yeah, I suppose. I don't know. So what are you going to do?"

"Keep looking. I'd love to be able to start over again fresh. I'd love to look in that other person's face and see nothing but a clear reflection. Maybe this time I'd be more careful not to damage it."

She fell silent again. We walked a few minutes, and then she took my hand again. This time I let it stay.

The path we had been traveling beside Rock Creek Parkway was opening to a broad meadow at P Street. Couples, gay and straight, were lying on the grass necking. Annie looked at one boy and girl wrapped around each other. They couldn't have been much older than sixteen. He had his hand under her T-shirt. Her eyes were closed in rapture.

"Let's rest," she said. We found our own patch of grass, away from everyone else. It looked out on an array of daffodils, spread along a hillside. Annie looked at me coyly. "I saw this cute thing on TV. They were asking famous couples what they found sexy about each other. And it made me think about us."

"Go on."

"Well, one of the questions was what was sexy about the other person. And I wondered what you'd say about me. What's the sexiest thing I ever did when we were together?"

"Mmmm." I smiled. She was outrageous. "That's tough. There were so many things. But probably what I liked best was when you weren't trying to be sexy. Just watching you put on your clothes, when you didn't know I was looking. You were so graceful. I always thought about that when I was away from you."

"Eric! That's embarrassing." Her cheeks were blushing. She tilted her head back and shook her ponytail in the wind. "Anyway, that doesn't count. I couldn't help it."

She slipped her arm around my waist and pulled me toward her. "We could try to start again," she said. "We could see if it works this time."

"We've had enough of trying, Annie. I can't be tentative anymore. I need to start over. I need to make a relationship count this time, so it's for real. Since the day I met you, I've been straddling somewhere between being married and being single, and I don't want that anymore. It wore us down. We can't go on trying."

Her eyes widened. "Do you want to get married?"

"I don't know what I want. I need to think. I've been trying to get some balance, and now I feel all wobbly again. There are so many things going on in my life that you don't know about. That's part of what makes it hard to think about you and me right now."

"Tell me about the other things. You can trust me."

"God, I'd love to. In a few days I hope it will be over. Then I'll tell you everything, maybe. But right now I can't. I'm overloaded. Any more weight on this truck and it's going to break down."

"Okay," she said. "You're probably right. We don't need to try anymore. We need to do it, or not do it."

We picked ourselves up off the grass and tucked ourselves back in, so that we didn't look too obvious. I walked her the rest of the way to her house in Georgetown. When we reached the door, she kissed me on the lips, softly at first and then passionately.

"I love you," she said.

For once, I let it lie there, rather than hitting it back. I kissed her, again, on the cheek. "I'll call you next week," I said. As I walked back to my apartment I had a strange thought. The reason she wanted me now was that she was afraid I didn't want her. We were caught in the perpetual-motion machine of unhappiness. There were easier ways to be unhappy, it seemed to me.

At 6:30, Sunday night, my phone rang. It was Alessi, calling from Paris. He said the rendezvous with Bézy would take place the next morning in Boston. I should be on the 11:00 A.M. water shuttle from Logan Airport to downtown Boston. Someone would meet me at the Boston side. I should come alone. If anyone accompanied me, the meeting would be canceled. He said that Mr. Bézy was looking forward to meeting me. "He hopes it will be a fruitful discussion," Alessi said.

Rubino's family was just sitting down for dinner when I arrived. His daughter recognized me from before. "We're *eating* now," she said. Rubino took me out back, to his derelict garden. The tetherball was blowing in the breeze, clanging against the pole. Rubino punched it hard—too hard, I thought—wrapping it tight.

I told Rubino the details of my conversation with Alessi: Boston, the 11:00 A.M. water shuttle from Logan Airport, Bézy waiting on the other side. Rubino shook his head unhappily. "That gives them a lot of control," he said. We hadn't even started the operation yet, and he was already worrying. He went off to call someone at the FBI, so they could begin moving their people into place in Boston. "The bureau will get some boats," he said when he returned. "That will help."

He had a legal pad in front of him, with a checklist. He told me to take the 8:00 A.M. USAir flight, which would get me into Boston at 9:30. The FBI would have someone on the flight, someone at the airport, someone on the water shuttle and a small army on the other side.

"Will I know who they are?" I asked.

"Not unless they're incompetent. But if anything doesn't feel right to you, pull the rip cord. Don't get on the water shuttle. Don't get off at the other end. We're counting on you to exercise good judgment. Here. This is for emergencies."

He handed me a box. Inside was what appeared to be a bulletproof vest.

"It's made of Kevlar," he said. It's light. Police wear them. It will stop almost anything. It was Frank's idea, after you left. He was worried about you."

"Journalists don't wear bulletproof vests."

"Grow up, will you. I can't order you to wear the damn vest, but you'd be stupid not to."

Rubino looked back at his legal pad. I went over my own mental checklist, trying to remember any final worries. "Suppose Bézy isn't there?" I said. "What do I do then?"

"Abort, immediately. That means you've been double-crossed. Get away, however you can."

"What if I can't?"

"You mean if you're kidnapped?"

"Yeah, I guess that's what I mean."

"We'll do whatever we can, but it will be tricky. We only have authority to go after Bézy, and the bureau will stick to its rules of engagement, no matter what. But it's silly to worry about things like that. This is all going to go fine. Tomorrow night, Michel Bézy will be in a federal prison cell in Boston."

I looked at my watch. It was getting late. "I should let you have dinner with your family," I said.

Rubino made me try on the bulletproof vest before I left. It fit perfectly. He shook my hand.

"I'm proud of you," he said. "You're a tougher person than I expected."

When I got back to California Street, I called Bob Marcus, my bureau chief, from the pay phone in the lobby. I told him I had good news. Michel

Bézy, the $120 million fixer I wanted to write about, had agreed to see me the next day in Boston. I'd be able to ask him about the money, as our lawyers had insisted I should. Then we could run the story. Marcus kept repeating "Great story!" I think it was still cocktail hour at his house.

"It may get a little messy up there," I said. "I think the FBI may be interested in this guy, too."

"Great story!" he said one more time. "And, hey! Be careful!"

38

The 8:00 A.M. Monday USAir flight to Boston was nearly full with its normal cargo of lawyers, bankers and bureaucrats, all in their boxy business suits. I looked up and down the aisles wondering who the FBI agent in the crowd might be. In 1996 that was an impossible task. The cultural icons had become confused. Nearly everyone looked neat, had short hair, was toned from workouts at the gym. We were becoming a nation of FBI agents. It didn't matter. I had brought along a magazine, one of the glossy new breed that alternated lefty articles about America's cultural sickness with fawning articles about Hollywood movie stars. I was too nervous to read much of anything—even the article about Demi Moore's new star power was heavy going—but the advertisements were nice.

We all like to maintain the illusion, when we're in stressful situations, that we know what we're doing. The problems arise when we have more than one answer. I was going to Boston to interview a corrupt international lawyer who had been involved in the death of my colleague, so that my newspaper could publish an exposé about him. I was going to Boston to help the CIA and the FBI arrest this same man and bring him to justice in the United States. The first explanation sat better with me than the second, but they were bound together with invisible but unbreakable knots. I wondered if I would ever get back across the line I had crossed in April, when I had agreed to deliver Rubino's message to China. I wanted the clarity of being just a reporter again, but at that moment I didn't know how to get there.

The flight was twenty-five minutes late arriving at Logan Airport because of air-traffic delays. That was a blessing; it meant less time on the ground to be nervous. After leaving the plane, I hunted for an uncrowded men's room. I had brought the Kevlar vest along in a travel bag and needed somewhere to put it on. The first two lavatories near the gate were packed with travelers, but I eventually found a deserted one downstairs, near the car-rental desks. The vest still felt bulky, but with my raincoat buttoned, I looked almost normal. The Mont Blanc pen was in one pocket; the cigarette lighters were in another.

I boarded the bus for the water shuttle at 10:40. I was looking twice at everyone now: I felt as if I were surrounded by angels and devils, all invisible, attending my every movement. After a ten-minute ride, the bus stopped at a simple, gray dock. The metal gangway swayed and clanked as I made my way down. Three other passengers were already waiting under a gray awning: a heavyset man reading a thick novel about Nazis; a woman in a neat business suit reading *The Wall Street Journal*; a man in dark glasses and a double-breasted suit gazing out at the harbor. I reckoned the last of these must be Bézy's man.

The ferry slowly churned toward us. The sky was overcast, heavy with dark tufts of cloud, and the wind was blowing up whitecaps on the water. I felt as if I were standing at a three-dimensional intersection. Behind were the runways of Logan Airport; overhead was the regular roar of jet airplanes, taking off and landing; a mile ahead, across the harbor channel, was the wharf where I would finally meet Bézy. The ferry neared the dock a few minutes before 11:00. The crew slipped bow and stern lines over the cleats, put down the gangplank and dropped the chain so the passengers could board. As I moved toward the boat, the man in the double-breasted suit came up behind me.

"I am Alessi," he said. "Let us wait for the next boat."

I stepped back from the gangplank. It was a reasonable move, right out of Frank's textbook, and it made no difference to me. My problem wasn't the water shuttle, but what lay on the other side. The other two passengers had already boarded the boat. One of them—the woman who had been reading *The Wall Street Journal*—looked back at me anxiously, and then turned away. The crew cast off the lines and the boat slipped off from the dock.

Alessi removed his sunglasses and shook my hand. He had a thin face with hooded eyes that gave little away. He was a functionary, an arranger, a procurer. "We are glad to see you," he said.

"How's Mr. Bézy?" I asked.

"Good," he said. Not a word more. He didn't want to talk; he was busy scanning the harbor for whatever might go wrong. We waited in silence for the next boat. Soon another bus arrived with more passengers. I figured at least one of them had to be from the FBI.

"How was your flight?" I asked, breaking Alessi's shroud of silence again. I'd always asked that same question to arriving guests when I worked as a bellhop at a hotel in Palo Alto one summer. The theory was that if you could get someone talking on the elevator up to the room, he would give you a bigger tip.

"Fine, thank you." He resumed his surveillance, studying the watery field of play. A half-dozen boats were visible in the Inner Harbor: several sleek launches, a Boston police harbor patrol; a few larger boats. I wondered what sort of naval support the FBI had managed to scare up.

The next shuttle boat was approaching the pier. It was a gray tug: broad-beamed, with an open rear deck and a small enclosed cabin. The wind was rising, adding more chop to the water, and it took the crew longer to bring the boat alongside the dock and secure the lines. The gangplank went out, and the chain was lowered.

"Let's go," said Alessi.

We boarded the little boat. Five or six passengers clambered on behind us. Alessi and I each bought a one-way ticket. When everyone was aboard the crew cast off and we nosed out into the channel, toward the skyscrapers of downtown Boston. Alessi stood on the forward part of the deck, scanning the waterline. A Boston whaler skimmed toward our starboard bow from the direction of Chelsea and the Mystic River. Our boat slowed to let it pass. On our port side, far in the distance, were the old brick wharves that had survived from the nineteenth century, now gussied up for tourists.

We were heading toward Rowes Wharf on the Boston side, in the shadow of the new office buildings, apartment towers and hotels that lined the waterfront. Dead ahead was a huge archway, perhaps a hundred feet high, draped with a giant American flag. Down the wharf, to the left, stood a rusted metal bridge. As we came nearer I could see several cruise boats and private yachts tied up along the dock. I scanned the faces onshore, looking for the FBI men.

The wharf was perhaps fifty yards away now. The waves slapped against the hull as the ferry began to slow. We were close enough now that I could see the faces clearly. There was a line of men gathered on the terrace of a hotel that fronted on Rowes Wharf, pretending not to watch us. They formed a taut spring, ready to uncoil instantly the moment someone spotted Bézy and gave the order to move in. They were not of my world, these robotic FBI men. It was strange to think of them as my allies and protectors.

We neared the wooden piers of the wharf. One of the crew jumped off and secured the bow line and the gangplank went out. The other passengers went first; Alessi and I waited. Up on the dock I could see the strain on some of the faces. I felt the hardness of the vest against my chest. I tapped my pen, my lighters. I was grateful now for all this silly gear. Alessi motioned for me to come. I looked for Bézy on the dock, but didn't see him.

"Where are we going now?" I asked.

He pointed to a sleek yacht, thirty yards away down the wharf, in the shadow of the rusted bridge.

"Bézy is there?"

"You'll see Mr. Bézy soon."

That wasn't an answer. Alessi was pushing me now, gently, toward the gangplank. I resisted. "Come with me," he said.

"You lead the way. I'll follow." I didn't understand what was happening. Was this a trick? Was this the moment to abort, as Rubino had insisted I must do if anything went wrong? I couldn't know without going further.

Alessi walked up the plank to the wharf and turned left. This was my moment to flee. I could bolt off to the right and run, and keep running. But where would I be then? What would be my destination? It seemed to me, in that instant of decision, that the only thing I would prove in running away was my own cowardice. The impossible ambiguity of my position—half-reporter, half-spy—would remain with me.

I followed Alessi, walking several steps behind. As I moved off the dock onto the stone walkway that girded the wharf, several men fell in behind. I saw flickers of recognition from faces up ahead, in the direction we were heading. It was like watching a slight breeze blow through a field of grass. The blades barely moved. Theirs was a world of precision and discipline. They had their rules of engagement written out, neat and clean, telling them precisely what to do. I didn't have any rules.

Alessi and I walked briskly down the stone walkway toward the waiting cruiser. I could see the name of the boat on her stern. She was the *Serendipity*, a fifty-footer rigged with radar and other gear for ocean navigation.

"Slow down," I said to Alessi. We were almost there. There were more ripples of movement along the line of the dock. People sitting in outdoor cafés were poised in their chairs; loiterers in doorways were moving out of the shadows. Up ahead was a bus with smoked windows, its doors opened.

Alessi stopped. We were alongside the boat now. A steward was on deck, extending his hand to help me down.

"Time to go," said Alessi. The boat was waiting. The engines were idling; the crew, fore and aft, was ready to shove off. Inside the cabin, I imagined, sat Michel Bézy, waiting for his moment to dicker with a reporter from *The New York Mirror.*

I took a step toward the boat, then turned back for a last look at the wharf. A man had emerged from under the arches and was looking directly at me. He was dressed in a trench coat, belted at the waist. He had the intense manner of a unit commander who had reached H-hour. As I stepped toward Alessi's boat he began signaling me urgently with his hand. Alessi was already on board, talking to the captain; he didn't see this bit of pantomime.

"Be careful!" the man onshore seemed to be saying, or maybe it was "Don't go!" I didn't respond at first, but when he did it a second time, I put my thumb in the air. It's okay. I'm going. He's on the boat. I'll be all right.

I saw the man lift his sleeve toward his face. I guessed he was speaking into a microphone, relaying information and asking for guidance. Perhaps he was talking to Rubino. How would Tom explain my lapse? I was already ignoring orders; I was unreliable; there might be a flap. The commander let his sleeve drop; he was listening now to someone speaking in his earpiece. The whole tableau on the dock seemed frozen in time for an instant: the men and their guns immobile, waiting for instruction.

I stepped onto the *Serendipity.* The steward steadied me as the boat surged away from the dock. "Welcome aboard," he said.

Alessi had gone into the cabin. I looked back toward the shore. The man in the trench coat was boarding a launch that had been idling a little farther down the wharf. He must be the agent in charge. Out in the harbor channel, a larger boat was moving toward us. The welcoming party had put to sea.

The *Serendipity* churned out toward the channel, its screws biting into the dark water of Boston harbor. We had the breeze in our faces now, and there was a hard pounding against the hull as the boat struggled against the wind and the tide. Alessi called to me from the cabin. He wanted me inside. I rehearsed what I wanted to say to Bézy: *The New York Mirror* has obtained information that you received a $120 million payment as part of the communications contract. What was the money for?

I entered the deckhouse and walked down a few steps. It took my eyes a few moments to adjust. The main cabin was opulently furnished, with sofas and chairs and a gleaming mahogany table in the center. I looked for Bézy at the foot of the table, but he wasn't there. Except for Alessi, the cabin was empty.

"Where is he?" I said.

Alessi's face colored. Finally he had something to say.

"I am very sorry. Mr. Bézy was forced to change his plans last night. He would like you to meet him in Montreal this afternoon, where he has other urgent business. He will be happy to give you the interview there. We have a private plane waiting at Logan Airport to take you. This boat will take us back to the Logan dock. Mr. Bézy asks me to apologize to you for this inconvenience. He cannot see you here."

"That's not what we agreed on," I said.

I suppose all the sirens should have gone off at that point—I should have been angrier or more frightened—but I had been in this situation so many times in my life: an appointment broken, a meeting rescheduled, a change in plans. Reporters are always regarded as movable parts. It's assumed that they can accommodate themselves to the schedules of the real people who do the work.

"Why did you lie to me and pretend he was on the boat?" I asked Alessi.

"I apologize for the deception. But I needed the opportunity to talk with you privately. Out there it would have been impossible. It's quite obvious we are not alone."

"I'm not sure I should go to Montreal," I said. "That wasn't the plan."

"Mr. Bézy is expecting you. He wants very much to talk."

"What if I don't go to Montreal? Can I still talk with him?"

"No. He wants to see you in person. He says it is important that you come. There are things you may not understand, which he wants to talk about—secrets he would like to share with you."

What did that mean? Was it another trick, or was there an additional layer to Bézy's activities I hadn't understood? I looked out the windows. The two boats that had been shadowing us since we left Rowes Wharf were coming closer. Alessi saw them, too.

"I see we have an escort," said Alessi. He didn't look surprised or angry. He seemed almost pleased to see them, as if they confirmed his expectations.

"If I go with you, will I be safe?" It was a dumb question, perhaps, but often that's the kind reporters ask.

"Of course you will be safe. If Mr. Bézy wanted to hurt you, he could do it at any time. He could do it now."

I looked out the portholes again. The boats were only twenty yards off, now. The larger boat was on our port side; I saw a few men on deck and assumed there must be several dozen more below. Off our starboard side was the smaller launch. The man in the trench coat was talking into a phone, having another conversation with his superiors. They had their arrest warrant; they had probable cause to believe that Bézy was on board the yacht; they were prepared to board, if someone gave the order. They were about to make a mistake.

"What is your answer?" said Alessi. "It appears they will be alongside in a moment."

I thought another moment, but I knew that I would say yes. In the instant of decision, something automatic takes over in most people: it's hard-wired. In me, the automatic reflex has usually been: Yes. I want to stay at the table, finish the game, play another set. And in this case, there was something more powerful at work. The CIA had ordered me to say no, but the reporter's answer had to be yes. It was a clear, unambiguous choice. This was my opportunity to move back across the line, to leave Rubino's team and rejoin my own.

"I'll go to Montreal," I said.

"Good. Mr. Bézy will be pleased."

We heard the sound of a siren, then the sharp pop of a flare across our bow.

"I think we should go up on deck," said Alessi.

The man in the trench coat had a bullhorn in his hand. "Ahoy, *Serendipity*. What is your destination?"

"The airport," Alessi shouted back. "We will dock at Jeffries Yacht Club, next to the dock for the water shuttle."

The commander stepped back into the cabin and picked up his phone to relay this latest bizarre fact. He came back on deck and bellowed again with his bullhorn. "We will escort you to the dock, *Serendipity*. Are you prepared for us to search your boat when we get there?"

"Do you have a warrant?" asked Alessi.

"Yes, we do," barked the commander.

"Then of course you may search. We have nothing here that you want."

Alessi went up to the captain of his boat and spoke to him in French, then retreated back to the cabin. I went to the rear deck. The commander's launch was a few yards off our starboard side. I could see him beckoning to me again, as if to say, Come, jump, get away. I gave him another thumbs-up signal, in response: it was okay, I was safe. But in my mind, the connection between us had been severed.

"Get off the boat now, Truell," he called out.

"I'm all right," I said. "I know what I'm doing."

The commander shook his head. He didn't understand. I was screwing up the plan. He returned to his telephone and more conversations with his colleagues. After a few minutes his launch peeled off and sped toward the Logan dock to prepare for our arrival. The larger boat shadowed us the rest of the way.

We docked a few hundred feet from where the water shuttle had departed forty-five minutes earlier. It had been a very long round trip. As the crew was making fast the *Serendipity*'s line, Alessi approached me. "I hope this search will not take long," he said. "The plane is waiting."

"Maybe I can help," I said. The commander was standing just back from the dock. Behind him were several dozen men in blue jumpsuits, ready to board the boat and search it. I jumped off the stern of *Serendipity* and walked toward him. He moved toward me at the same time. Alessi remained back on the yacht with the captain.

"What the fuck is going on?" the FBI man said. "I'm the special agent in charge. I work with Rubino. Are you okay?"

"I'm fine. There's no point in searching the boat. Bézy isn't here. He's in Montreal. I'm going to interview him there."

"That's against orders."

"I don't have any orders. Anyway, I've made a decision. I'm going."

A dark look of consternation and confusion came over the FBI man's face. He turned away from me and began speaking into the sleeve of his trench coat again, and then listening through his earpiece. The conversation took several minutes, back and forth.

"We're searching the boat," he said. "Those are our orders."

I looked back at Alessi. He was looking at his watch, impatient to go.

"Search whatever you want," I said. "Bézy isn't there. Meanwhile, that gentleman and I are going. We have to catch a plane."

The FBI commander had one more frantic conversation into his sleeve. When he turned back to me, his eyes were on fire. He was furious, but he couldn't do anything about it. He couldn't arrest me; he couldn't order me; he couldn't detain me. He moved so close that we were almost touching and spoke into my ear.

"If you go to Montreal, Truell, you're on your own. That comes from Rubino. He's pissed at you. He says you fucked him."

"I know. Tell him I understand how he feels. But I'll be okay, and so will he."

I walked back to the yacht, where Alessi was waiting. He had a camera in his hand. Evidently he wanted to record this scene for his files.

"We can go now," I said. "They're going to search the boat. I told them Bézy wasn't aboard, but they want to make sure."

"Why did they think Mr. Bézy would be here?" His expression was almost a smirk.

"Beats me," I said. "They must have had bad information."

A limousine was waiting above the dock to take us back to the airport. I walked stiffly up the long ramp. The bulletproof vest had all the suppleness of a tree trunk. I had to get rid of it before boarding their plane. I assumed I could find a men's room back at the terminal and ditch it there.

As we walked toward the limousine I looked back at the FBI commander and his unhappy little army. I could almost hear him say the words: You asshole. I was undoubtedly a reminder for him of what every cop knows in his soul: reporters always screw things up. I gave him a little wave, good-bye.

Alessi and I got into the backseat. "There's one detail about the flight to Montreal," I said as the car pulled away. "The *Mirror* will have to pay for my share of the cost. We have rules about that."

The chauffeur drove in the direction of the main terminal, but then took a separate ramp toward General Aviation, where private jets boarded their passengers. I felt the vest, still tight against my chest. I had to get rid of it.

"I need to find a men's room," I told Alessi.

"We don't have time now," said Alessi. "There is a toilet on the plane."

"But I really need to use the men's room now."

He smiled blandly. "No time. You'll have to wait."

The plane taxied away from the General Aviation terminal five minutes after we arrived, and it was airborne soon after that. When we reached cruising altitude, I got up and went to the toilet. As quickly as I could, I removed the Kevlar vest. It felt bigger in my hands than it had on my chest. Where to discard it? I found a cabinet under the sink, where they kept extra paper towels and toilet paper, and stowed it in there. With luck, nobody would find it for a few days. I put my shirt back on, tucked in my trousers. I examined myself in the mirror. All things considered, I didn't look too bad.

39

❖

Michel Bézy was waiting for me in his suite at the Ritz-Carlton Hotel in Montreal. It was late in the afternoon when we arrived, perhaps 5:00 P.M. He sat in a leather chair, smoking a cigarette, in a small library that adjoined the main living room. He was thin and wiry, with sunken cheeks and dark, radiant eyes. He was different from what I had expected: younger, smoother, better dressed, looking more like an international lawyer than a thug. He was a hip gangster—Jean-Paul Belmondo in a business suit. He appeared to be utterly relaxed. He was on friendly turf, in a fine hotel in the second-largest French-speaking city in the world. I was at a disadvantage—tired after a long day of travel, unsure of what lay ahead. His first words to me were a provocation.

"Mr. Truell," he said. "I have been waiting many months to ask you a question. Who do you work for? Are you a journalist, or a spy?"

"I work for *The New York Mirror*," I answered. "I've worked for them for more than ten years."

"Yes, yes, I know. But who do you really work for?"

"I told you. *The New York Mirror.*"

"I knew you would say that, and I don't mind. You may answer as you like. I am happy that you were willing to come to Montreal. It is a mark of courage and respect. Those are qualities I like."

"I came because I want to interview you for a story."

"Of course you do. Would you like a drink? Some whiskey? Champagne? You must be tired. Alessi said there was quite a show in Boston."

"A Diet Coke, thanks."

"How delightful! A Diet Coke. Americans are so wonderful. A Diet

Coke it is." He called out to Alessi, who went to the bar and fixed my drink. "So, we will have a conversation, you and I. You will ask me questions, and I will ask you questions. I may have a proposal for you, but we can get to that later."

"I'll go first." I took out my notebook and a tape recorder, but he waved his hand for me to put the machine away.

"Don't be silly!" he said. I put it back in my pocket.

"My question is about money," I began. "I know that you received a hundred twenty million dollars a week ago from Inter/Orient as a kickback on the China deal, and I know that forty million dollars has already gone to your account in Switzerland. I'd like to give you a chance to comment before we publish it in the *Mirror*."

He extended his arms, palms up, like a supplicant.

"What can I do? Your people are so good. How did they do all that? The wire transfers and account numbers were all encrypted. Supposedly the ciphers were unbreakable. It's all very impressive, I must say. Hats off."

"Is that your comment?" I asked. We were speaking on different frequencies.

He laughed at what he regarded as my obfuscation. "Obviously you're not going to tell me how you did it. But this is a mark of America's power, that you can get this information and use it so ruthlessly. No other country can do that. And if you can find these accounts, you can find others. And if you can intercept encrypted communications, you can penetrate the banks and steal my money. That is the message you are sending me, and I understand it. Message received. So what is it that you want from me? What can I do that will convince you to stop this pursuit?"

"Nothing. We're going to run the story unless you can show me that it's false."

"Enough about the story. The information is true, obviously! The story is my little problem; there are many ways to solve it. My big problem is the CIA. What can I do to solve my big problem?"

"I don't know. You'll have to talk to the CIA."

"This is tiresome. We have known for two years that you work for the agency. That's the reason I wanted to talk with you. You told Alessi on the telephone that we would meet and talk, and then, perhaps, the *Mirror* would not run the story. That's why I agreed to meet you. So I want to know: What is the price? How do we get the CIA to stop this campaign?"

"I keep trying to tell you, Mr. Bézy, I don't work for the CIA. I am a reporter for *The New York Mirror*. I'm sorry if you're confused about that, but it's really not my fault."

Bézy shook his head. He was trying to be reasonable, but I was frustrating him. He stood up, went into the bedroom of his suite and returned with a lit cigarette in his mouth. "Why are you so difficult with me, Mr. Truell. I have the greatest respect for you. The way you used Arthur Bowman was very clever. The way you arranged Roger Navarre's escape was more than clever. It was brilliant. We know who you are. We know what you did to Maurice Costa. We know about the campaign you and Mr. Rubino have organized against us. We want to make peace. That is the question: How do we make peace? Please. You have come so far. It is time for us to be honest."

"All right. Let's be honest. Why did you kill Arthur Bowman?"

"We didn't. Our Chinese partners did, but I suppose we encouraged them. Bowman was a nuisance, bringing you out to the biological-research facility, helping you get Navarre out. We could applaud you, but not Bowman. He was ours. We bought him, but he did not stay bought. When I finally realized that poor Arthur didn't know about the Navarre operation—that you had simply manipulated him—I had no more use for him. The Chinese insisted on his removal, and I said all right. Many people were pleased to be rid of him. But they did not dare go after you. That is an honest answer. Are you happy?"

"I'm glad to have the truth. But I should tell you, since we're being honest, that Navarre's escape wasn't my doing. The agency did it. I simply delivered a message."

"I know, I know. I come back to my question: What is your price, Mr. Truell? How do we obtain your support?"

"I don't have a price. I'm a reporter for *The New York Mirror*."

A smile came over Bézy's face. My repeated invocation of the *Mirror* had emboldened him to share the real secret he had been holding in reserve. He leaned toward me.

"You keep repeating that you work at the *Mirror*. All right, I believe you! And I'm glad of it. So how would you like to work for me?"

"I wouldn't. I'm a journalist."

"But I'm a journalist, too, Mr. Truell, in my way. I'm the best friend *The New York Mirror* has. And I repeat: *How would you like to work for me?* If you say yes, you can run Mirror Alert tomorrow, and perhaps someday soon, you will run the *Mirror*, too."

"What are you talking about?" I was struggling to fit the pieces together. They were all there—I had seen each of them separately—but I hadn't assembled them.

"Mr. Truell, I *own* Mirror Alert. Through my company, Press Alert, I have invested five hundred million dollars in your newspaper. With luck and good management, someday I will own it. And I want you to be part of my team. Your connections would be of enormous value. You are a man of the world. You are a journalist in the tradition of Arthur Bowman, but a cleverer man. So I ask you, will you come work for me?"

"Absolutely not." I was trembling, like an animal whose hiding place has suddenly been ripped away. I had known for months that an international investor was backing Press Alert, and I'd known that Bowman had been scouting for money. But I had not imagined that a share of my newspaper had been delivered into the hands of a killer.

"Please, Mr. Truell. You are too hasty. This is a serious proposal. Mirror Alert is a very profitable business, and it will become more so. Our special competence lies in knowing what information is valuable, and selling it to people who need it. That is the soul of journalism. As the world gets bigger and more complicated, people will have greater need for the specific information that Mirror Alert can provide. The mass audience is the past. We are the future. And you are the right man to run this business—with the CIA's backing or without it, I don't care. You have shown courage and skill. And as you are so fond of telling me, you are a 'journalist.' So will you please think about it?"

As I looked at Bézy, sitting so confidently in his leather armchair in his $1,500-a-night suite, it occurred to me that he might be right. The future of the news business might indeed belong to people like him. That only made his offer more unattractive.

"The fact that you are connected in any way with *The New York Mirror* disgusts me. The idea of working for you is repellent. Is that an answer?"

"Be careful, Mr. Truell. This is not an offer you can turn down."

"Why not? I just did."

"Because if you say no, I will have no more use for you."

"I'm not afraid of you. Too many people know we're meeting here today. The CIA knows. The *Mirror* knows. If anything happens to me, you will lose your hundred and twenty million, and a lot more."

Bézy smiled. He had been playing in this league for so many years, and I was such a rookie. "I admire your courage, sir. Truly I do. But you must be more careful. I have the power to destroy you, in a way that will also destroy the credibility of your newspaper."

"How will you do that?"

"I will expose your relationship with the CIA. You will deny it, in the same tiresome way. But I have the evidence. Would you like to see? Alessi!" He called to his assistant, who was in the adjoining sitting room. "Alessi! Bring the Truell file."

Alessi emerged with a manila envelope with my name in bold letters on the cover. Bézy opened the flap and pulled out a half-dozen photographs and a long explanatory memo. Bézy spread the pictures out atop the glass coffee table.

"Here they are," he said. "These will be on the desk of Ed Weiss tomorrow if you refuse. The executive editor of the *Times* will also receive a set."

I looked at the pictures that stared up from the coffee table. They had the grainy quality of celebrity photos that are shot through telephoto lenses, like the pictures of Princess Diana in bikini bathing suits that appear in the supermarket tabloids. The first was a shot of me and Tom Rubino in a café on a Paris street corner; the second showed me and Rupert Cohen leaving Au Cochon d'Or in Paris; the third caught me and Cohen at a bar in Adams-Morgan; the fourth showed my car parked in front of Tom Rubino's house in Maryland; the fifth had been taken by a security camera in the hall of Building N-16 at Qinghua University, showing me talking with Roger Navarre; the sixth showed me and Frank Jones sitting next to each other in his Chevy Impala; the last was of me talking with the FBI commander on the dock at Logan Airport a few hours before. It was an impressive dossier, cataloguing my contacts with the agency. The only spot they seemed to have missed was the safe house in Shirlington.

"Good work, wouldn't you say? We are not so good as the CIA, but we are not so bad, either. We have a great advantage, which is that everyone underestimates us. We have worked hard on the written explanation that will accompany the photographs, too. And we have one more piece of evidence. Alessi! Bring the vest."

Alessi entered the room again, this time carrying the Kevlar vest I had discarded in the toilet compartment of the airplane. He laid it on the table, next to the pictures.

"They do not ordinarily give these to journalists, I think. Alessi tells me it is an unusual model, made especially for the FBI. That will be helpful. We'll add it to our report."

Bézy sat back in his chair, supremely content. He had done a careful job. There was no disputing the fact that he had the evidence to destroy my career and severely embarrass the paper.

"Perhaps you would like some time to think about it," he said.

"Yes," I answered. "I need some time."

The Frenchman said he would give me until the next morning. He had to speak to Peyron in Paris before he did anything, and it was too late to call him now. He said he had booked a nice room for me in the hotel—fit for a future editor! But he warned that I shouldn't imagine I would gain anything from the delay, or from any foolish attempt to escape. The documents would be in New York the next day, regardless. They would be delivered to the *Mirror* and the *Times* at noon if I refused Bézy's offer.

"From your situation, there is no escape," Bézy said slowly. "We would like you to be our colleague, but if we cannot have that, we are indifferent to your fate."

Alessi took me down the hall to my room. It was decorated in the same lavish, modern style as Bézy's suite. Pastel walls; heavy curtains in rich French prints; fine hardwood furniture; armchairs covered in raw silk; a minibar stocked with goodies, a view of the garden behind the hotel. It was the sort of deluxe room I would never have stayed in as a reporter for the *Mirror*. That was part of Bézy's challenge: a proffer of my future life. But for now, a guard stood watch in the hall outside, halfway between Bézy's suite and my room.

40

I lay down on the bed and closed my eyes. Of all the revelations of that long day, the most upsetting had been Bézy's threat to the *Mirror*. A newspaper is like a church: it is built by ordinary sinners, people who in their individual lives are often petty and corrupt, but who collectively create an institution that transcends themselves. A newspaper in that way achieves a kind of divinity. It embodies the quest of its reporters and editors for an absolute—the truth. What is holy about a newspaper is the struggle of these imperfect human beings to connect with something perfect. I could not bear the thought that I would defile my church any more than I already had.

I've often thought that people who go into ordinary professions like business or law lack sufficient ambition. Even the most successful of my Stanford classmates have made this mistake. One man is now an investment banker in New York—already, at thirty-seven, the man to see about mergers and acquisitions in the movie business. I'm told he made close to $5 million last year. But he lacks ambition. He wants to be rich and powerful, to live well, to take care of his children. I decided to become a journalist because I wanted more than that.

What would my future be if I said yes to Bézy? Money, power, protection from scandal—bought at the price of absolute dependence on my protectors. It would be my role to maintain the public appearance of respectability, even as Bézy moved privately to subvert it. If I rebelled at any moment at this corrupt bargain—sought to exert even the slightest independence—I would be caught in an even more devastating web of scandal and blackmail. Beyond humiliation, I would face the prospect of legal prosecution. The deal Bézy was offering was the essential Faustian bargain: prompt relief and pleasure in the short run, in exchange for a very long run of misery. What he was proposing, it occurred to me, was that I join the Secret Power.

And what was my future if I said no to Bézy? Acute danger in the short run; the likelihood that my "career" as a journalist would be ruined; beyond that, stretching to infinity, the opportunity to strive for things of ultimate value.

The question Bézy had put to me was not really a choice. My ambitions lay in a different direction from what he proposed. If I'd seen more clearly what lay ahead, I might have made a different choice, but I don't think so. Even the most grievous sinner, facing excommunication, doesn't wish for the certainty of damnation.

I knew I should call someone at the *Mirror,* to warn them of what was coming. There was a telephone in my room, but it was undoubtedly monitored. I should go outside to make any calls. After a few more minutes lying in bed, making sure I knew my own mind, I got up. I needed to get organized. I found a guidebook with detailed maps of Montreal and the province of Quebec. I studied them for a few minutes and then tore them from the book and put them in my pocket. The hotel was on Rue Sherbrooke, the main street of the old Montreal neighborhood known as the Golden Square Mile. Just east of the hotel was the campus of McGill University. Surely there would be public telephones there.

I opened the door of my room and peered down the hall; the guard immediately began whispering into his walkie-talkie. He followed me to the elevator and rode down with me in silence. In the lobby, two other men picked me up. I didn't have to use any of Frank's tricks to discover them; they simply fell in behind me.

I walked out the front door of the hotel, onto Rue Sherbrooke and turned right toward McGill. It was a pleasant May evening; the streets and sidewalks were filling as Montrealers made their way to the downtown clubs and restaurants. After several blocks I came to the great stone gates of the university. The watchers stayed close as I entered a telephone booth; one of them stood at the door, as if he were waiting to use the phone next.

My first thought was to call George Dirk. The man outside the booth watched me dial Dirk's home and punch in my credit-card number. I opened the phone-booth door and asked him to leave, but he just moved closer, so he could hear better.

Dirk's wife answered the phone. She said George had gone to New York that afternoon. He was hoping to see the publisher of the *Mirror* the next day. She didn't know where he was staying in New York. Was there any message, if he called in later that night? "Just say Eric called, and that George should tell Mr. Sellinger everything he knows," I said. "Tell him that Sellinger isn't the problem."

My next call was to Tom Rubino. I felt I owed him that. I didn't want him to worry, and it didn't matter now if Bézy knew I was contacting a CIA officer. I rang his home number. The daughter answered. "Ru-bi-no res-i-dence," she said, pausing at the end of each syllable to make sure she got it right. Her father came on the phone a moment later.

"This is Eric," I said. "I'm in Montreal. I'm fine."

"You really fucked up today!" His voice had a hard edge of anger. "I am in real trouble because of you."

"I'm sorry. I just called to tell you I was okay."

"Glad to hear it. Hope you stay that way. Because I have nothing for you. You disobeyed an order. You left me and a lot of other people hanging. We don't do things that way. There is *serious* flap potential here, my friend. The inspector general, congressional committees. This is a real mess you've handed me."

"Sorry," I said again. "I did what I thought was right."

"Well that's pretty damned selfish. Anyway, you're on your own now. I am under direct orders from the DCI to stay out of this. There's nothing I can do to help you now. You understand that? Nothing."

"I got it. Best to your wife and daughter." I hung up.

I felt sorry for him, actually. He was an apparatchik, a prisoner of a bureaucracy that was so bruised and battered, it couldn't afford any mistakes. He was in an impossible bind: his business required him to take risks, but he faced severe punishment if any of them went bad. He spent so much time protecting his flank against the FBI, he had little energy left for operations. He and his colleagues had held a series of supposedly clandestine meetings with me, and most of them had been photographed by Bézy's men. Mediocrity, shielded by secrecy. That was the culture my friend Rupert Cohen had rebelled against. It was what had created the world of make-believe intelligence.

Bézy's watcher was rapping on the door of the phone booth. He was getting impatient.

I knew I should call Ed Weiss before he got the documents, but I didn't want to talk with him yet. What would I say to him? How would I explain? I dialed his office number in New York, hoping I would get his voice mail; otherwise I would hang up. I heard the familiar mock-tough voice, telling me to leave a message at the beep.

"Hello, Ed." I cleared my throat. This was going to be hard, even talking to a machine. "This is Eric Truell. I'm calling you Monday night. You're going to get some material Tuesday that will upset you a lot. The documents will show that I have been working closely with the CIA on some things. This has all been very complicated. You've been so good to me, I owe you an explanation. I'll give it to you when I see you, which I hope will be soon. I love the *Mirror* and don't want to hurt it."

The watcher pounded the door again. That was all I had to say. I didn't have anyone else to call.

I didn't feel like going back to the hotel yet, so I lingered inside the gates of the university for a few minutes, and then walked back down Rue Sherbrooke. Bézy's men were still tagging along behind. I was looking in the window of a Gianni Versace boutique—gazing at a long-legged mannequin who reminded me of Annie—when one of Bézy's men ran up behind. "Monsieur Bézy wants you back in the hotel," he said. "No more walking tonight."

Back in my room, I ordered an expensive dinner from room service. If I was Bézy's prisoner, I would at least make him pay for it. The meal arrived on an elaborate cart: smoked salmon, grilled sea bass with crushed tomatoes and tarragon, a hazelnut torte for dessert and a bottle of Chablis. The waiter laid out this feast with care. I wrote a twenty-five-dollar tip on the bill.

But I only picked at the food. The reality was dawning on me that I was a prisoner. I had to get away soon. Already, Bézy was preventing me from roaming the city at will. The next morning, after I refused his offer of employment, he would have to take harsher measures. Certainly he would carry out his threat to send out the dossiers about me and the CIA, but he would want a tidier solution, one that would stop me from making more problems. It seemed impossible that he would allow me to survive as a free actor.

I needed to flee, but I didn't know how. I wished now that I had spent more time with Frank. I had the fountain pen and the other toys he had given me, but I wasn't sure I knew how to use them. Fighting my way out of the hotel sounded suicidal; slinking away would be more my style.

Or jumping. I looked out my window. We were on the fourth floor. Fifteen feet below was the roof of the hotel ballroom and beyond that, a green-striped awning covering part of the garden restaurant. At the back end of the garden was a green wooden fence that looked low enough that I could climb over it. It seemed a possible escape route: out the window, jump to the roof, slide down the awning, jump to the ground and over the fence. There were still a few diners in the garden lingering over their coffee, but perhaps later. I would need some way to distract Bézy's men so they would relax their guard.

I took the elevator downstairs. One of Bézy's men picked me up in the corridor and rode down with me, stone-faced. I crossed the lobby and entered the hotel bar, a cozy place done up in red and blue velvet. I motioned to the bartender, a white-haired, red-faced man who looked to be everybody's pal. I crumpled twenty dollars into his palm and asked him if he knew any women who might like a date with a lonely American. I pointed to a voluptuous redhead sitting alone at the far end of the bar. The bartender shook his head.

"She's a dead fuck," he said. "Fuck her and you're dead." She belonged to someone else. The bartender said he'd see what he could do for me.

I took a seat at a table in the corner and waited, sipping a ginger ale. My watchers sat nearby, popping cashews into their mouths. Fifteen minutes later a blond woman in a blue dress with a slit up the leg ambled through the front door. The bartender pointed toward me and whispered something in her ear. She cruised over to my table. Her treads were a little worn, but she was okay.

"My name is Jacqueline," she said. "The bartender said you wanted some company." I bought a bottle of champagne and charged it to Bézy. After twenty minutes I took her hand and led her upstairs. For the first time, the watchers looked seriously unhappy.

When we got to my room, Jacqueline took off her blue dress and laid it neatly on the chair. She had big, billowy breasts that spilled out over the top of her brassiere and a big ass. I excused myself and went to the bathroom. "I'll be back in a minute," I said. "You get in bed and see what's on TV."

When I got in the bathroom, I locked the door and opened the window. Below, I could see the flat roof of the ballroom and the green stripes of the awning. The garden looked deserted now. I eased myself out the window, put one foot on the ledge below and then the other, steadying myself with one hand on the window frame. I was about to jump when someone emerged from the shadows of the garden below and shined a light on me. He shouted something in French and another man came running. I climbed back into the bathroom, closed the window and sat down on the toilet seat. I was shaking.

After a while, Jacqueline called out to me. I went back into the bedroom, bitterly disappointed to have missed my chance. She had taken off the rest of her clothes. We petted for a while. She was really quite pretty, but my heart wasn't in it. I asked her to give me a back rub, and then I gave her some money. When I refused her offer of a blow job, she got upset. I had hurt her feelings.

I lay in bed with my clothes on, glancing up occasionally at the Expos game on television. But mostly I just lay there with my eyes closed. In my whole life I had gotten into a fistfight only once, when I was in high school in Davis and a classmate called me a "nigger-lover" because I invited a black girl to the junior prom. Other than covering wars and mayhem, that was the sum total of my combat experience. I had seen lots of weapons at close range, but never used one myself. This time I would have to fight. My only hope was to get away from the hotel, however I could. I didn't want to kill anyone, I just wanted to run away.

I took the Mont Blanc pen from my pocket. It was a beautiful object, the gleaming black barrel wrapped with four gold bands. I twisted the safety as Frank had demonstrated, and put my finger on the gold clip that acted as trigger. It felt so solid in my hand, I thought I could do it. The exploding Bic lighters worried me; I still wasn't sure how quickly you were supposed to throw them, after turning the flint wheel. But I would figure that out later.

Around two in the morning I rose from my bed. I took one of the hotel's fancy terrycloth bathrobes from the bathroom and put it on over my clothes, hoping it would offer some sort of a disguise. I looked at myself in the mirror; my condition had deteriorated noticeably from a few hours ago. My face was tired, drawn, marked by stress. I stood by the door for almost a minute, summoning my courage.

I grasped the Mont Blanc pen in one hand and turned the doorknob quietly with the other. The guard was slumped in his chair. I made it almost to the stairwell before the guard jerked awake and shouted for me to stop. I bounded down the stairs ahead of him, but I knew he would catch up with me by the time I reached the ground floor. *Use the pen!* I told myself. After descending two flights, I stopped suddenly and turned back to face him. The pen was still heavy in my hand; I turned the safety.

He was almost on top of me when I pressed the gold trigger. A cloud of gas roared out of the barrel. It was louder than I expected. He fell back with a sudden scream and slumped on the stairwell. Amazing! It worked. I hoped he wasn't dead. I left him there and continued down the stairs in my bathrobe, past the lobby floor to the basement.

At the bottom of the stairs there was a corridor leading to some shops and a door that led back toward the kitchen and service area. I raced through the door. A sleepy old waiter saw me run by in my white bathrobe and asked me in French if I needed anything. I kept running down the corridor, toward the loading dock at the back. As I reached the back door, another of Bézy's men was entering the service area, screaming for me to stop.

I was in the alley now. My pursuer was behind me, coming fast. My last hope was the crazy exploding lighter Frank had given me. I reached into my pocket for it and turned the wheel—stared at it for a terrifying moment—and threw it toward him, falling to the ground and covering my eyes. The grenade made the sound of a Roman candle on the fourth of July—a loud *pop!* accompanied by a dazzling explosion of light.

"I can't see!" screamed Bézy's man. I raced down the alley and out onto Rue Drummond, which ran south from Sherbrooke toward the St. Lawrence River. I didn't see anyone behind, but I knew they would be coming soon, in force. I removed the bathrobe and folded it over my arm.

I walked quickly toward the district known as Ste.-Catherine, which the guidebook had described as the center of Montreal's night life. There were people on the streets, emerging from the bars and strip clubs. I needed to leave the area, quickly, and find somewhere safe to spend the night. Hotels were a bad idea. Bézy's men would be notifying the police soon, and a ragged guest with no luggage would arouse suspicion even if they didn't.

My best chance, I decided, was to seek the refuge of the powerless—sleeping in the park. Above the city loomed the round peak of Mont-Royal, surrounded by dense woods. A taxi driver took me up to the Avenue des Pins, which bordered Mont-Royal Park on the south. I trotted up a winding road, into the woods; after a few hundred yards I ducked into lush foliage and traversed a series of narrow trails toward the summit. High up, near the top, the forest seemed to close around me. The path opened to a small clearing, framed by a stand of birch trees. I lay down under the tight canopy of trees, pulled my hotel bathrobe over me and slept peacefully, for the first time in nearly a week.

I'm sure I looked wretched when I awoke at dawn. I hadn't bathed or shaved or brushed my teeth; my mouth felt mossy inside. But I figured my ragged appearance was useful cover: Bums are just bums; nobody pays them any attention. I relieved myself in the woods, scouted the area to make sure I was safe and then returned to my burrow and fell back asleep for another two hours. I awoke the second time feeling hungry and knowing that I needed to plan my next moves carefully: today would be more dangerous than last night.

My goal was to get to New York as quickly as I could, so that I could talk to Weiss and Sellinger and help them deal with the bomb Michel Bézy had dropped on the *Mirror.* Flying there seemed out of the question. Bézy's men would be at the airports, perhaps aided by the Quebec police. Renting a car would also be risky, since I would have to produce identification. The best way out would be to take a bus south, to upstate New York; once I was safely in the United States, I could fly to La Guardia.

I studied the Quebec maps I had torn from the hotel guidebook. The most direct route to the United States was due south to Plattsburgh, New York, along Canada's Route 15, which crosses the border just west of Lake Champlain and becomes I-87. That was the easiest way—but I suspected it was also the most dangerous. Bézy would assume that if I was running south, I would take that route. The next quickest way would be to travel southwest from Montreal along Route 20, which skirts the St. Lawrence River, and cut south at Cornwall—crossing into New York at Massena. A third alternative would be to continue along the St. Lawrence all the way to Kingston, and then head south to Watertown, New York. That route had the virtue of being indirect.

I ventured from my woods about 8:00 A.M. and headed east toward Plateau Mont-Royal, a bohemian neighborhood that sounded from the guidebook like a local version of Adams-Morgan. I found a cash machine that would give me Canadian money and then bought myself a big breakfast at a neighborhood diner. After breakfast I went shopping for a new outfit—blue jeans, a leather jacket, an Expos baseball cap. I also bought some deodorant and a toothbrush at a drugstore, then found a public bathroom where I could clean up.

Feeling more like a human being, I headed off to a museum, then to a movie and finally to a restaurant for a late lunch. By 4:00 P.M., I thought it might be safe to go to the Voyageur bus station downtown, on the Boulevard de Maisonneuve. When I got there, I took a seat in the waiting room and surveyed the place. The buses that headed south toward Plattsburgh and the United States were all departing from the right side of the station. On Gate 1, where the next U.S.-bound bus was about to depart, several men were examining the boarding passengers. I had been right; that route was dangerous. But I didn't see any police at Gate 11, the departure gate for the next Toronto Express, which stopped in Kingston.

I approached the ticket window cautiously, head down, cap pulled low on my head. I paid $41.42 Canadian for a one-way ticket to Kingston. The ticket seller peered at me through the window, studied my unshaven face for an instant, and then handed me the ticket. I had an hour to kill before the bus left, so I went back out on the street and browsed in a local bookstore for something to read on the trip. I settled on a recently published account by four Hollywood prostitutes describing the sexual tastes of their clients.

As I was standing in line to board the bus I saw a team of Montreal police officers moving toward us. They were now examining each bus before it left the station. The good luck I had enjoyed all day seemed to be running out. I waited until they were almost to our bus and then left the line, telling the man behind me I needed to go to the bathroom. I stayed in the toilet until just before the bus's 5:30 departure time. When I returned, the driver had started up the engine. The police had moved on.

I found a seat in the back and began reading my Hollywood book. About an hour out of Montreal, we entered Ontario. It was probably a silly notion, but I believed that Bézy's powers diminished the moment French was no longer the official language. As we crossed that provincial border, some of the fear inside me began to ease.

It was almost 9:00 P.M. when we arrived in Kingston. I figured my best bet would be a cheap hotel near the bus station. When the desk clerk asked where I was from, I said Toronto. He gave me a room with a nice bathtub and a clean bed, where I had another good night's sleep.

Early the next morning I went back to the bus station and bought a ticket for the first bus to Watertown. The bus rolled south, past the green-ribbed shores of Lake Ontario. We stopped briefly on the U.S. side after we crossed the border into New York State, and I had to show my driver's li-

cense. But if anyone was looking for me, the news hadn't reached this remote border crossing.

I went shopping for another change of clothes in Watertown and bought
the most penitent costume I could find—a gray business suit, a white shirt,
a modest tie—and took a taxi to the airport. I caught the 1:05 P.M. flight
to La Guardia and was in New York an hour later. I didn't call ahead to tell
Weiss I was coming. What was the point? He could start screaming at me
when I got there.

41

The New York Mirror Building had a look of magisterial shabbiness that afternoon, like an old stately home whose heirs could no longer pay the upkeep but couldn't bear to sell it. The brass fixtures in the lobby downstairs, once polished daily to a bright shine, were dull and worn. The doormen in their blue uniforms, who for generations had welcomed visitors to the building, had been replaced by rent-a-guards from Wackenhut. I flashed my identification card for one of the security guards; he barely looked at it. He was making little more than the minimum wage: what did he care who walked into the Mirror?

Even the elevator looked ragged. Graffiti had been etched onto the wood and metal—not clever jokes about Ed Weiss or Lynn Frenzel, but ordinary vulgarity on the order of "Denise sucks dick." I pushed the button for the seventh floor. As the doors closed and I rode up toward the newsroom, I had a clammy feeling, like what you get when a fever is coming on. I hated what I was about to do. The doors opened onto that immense map of the world and all those clocks, recording the local time in all the bureaus of the *Mirror* I would never see again.

The moment I entered the newsroom I sensed a buzz out among the desks—as people saw me and whispered to one another that I had arrived—and then a terrible hush. As I made my way toward Weiss's office, the whole place seemed to stop working. It was a long distance, past so many staring faces. I was powerfully ashamed. "They've been looking for you!" whispered Lynn Frenzel as I rounded the foreign desk. "What did you do?" asked one of the news aides. Everybody in the newsroom seemed to know I was in some kind of trouble, and that the paper had been trying to find me for the past twenty-four hours.

"Oh my God!" said Peggy Moran when I neared Weiss's office. "He's here!" She called into the office for Weiss, who stuck his head out the door and thundered: "Get in here!"

I had seen Weiss angry at other people many times over the years. He had a famously explosive temper, and it was not uncommon for him, when he was truly angry, to scream at people and even throw things. I'd heard that the assistant managing editors sometimes had to hang up on him when he was shouting at them over the phone about something he didn't like. But I had never seen Weiss angry at me.

As soon as I entered his office, he slammed the door shut. Bézy's photographs were laid on top of his desk. Weiss's face was red; the muscles around the sides of his eyes were twitching. He was glaring at me.

"How the fuck could you do this?" He picked up one of the photographs and waved it at me. "How, God damn it?"

"I don't know," I said. "At the time, I thought I was doing the right thing."

That brief response only pushed him to a higher level of fury.

"*The right thing?* How could working with the CIA be the right thing? Are you out of your mind? Do you have any idea how much this is going to hurt the paper? Do you know that the editor of the *Times* is already calling me, asking me about this god-awful mess? The right thing! Jesus Christ. You're worse off than I thought. You are pathetic, Truell."

"Calm down, Ed."

"Fuck you! I want your resignation, now. The hell with that. I'm not going to let you resign. This is a firing offense. It says so in the style book. You're fired!"

"Do you want to hear my explanation, or do you just want to scream at me?"

That did it. He grabbed the closest thing he could find on his desk— which happened to be a bronze paperweight he'd received as an award from the American Society of Newspaper Editors—and hurled it across the room. "You arrogant prick!" he shouted. He grabbed a framed certificate from Columbia University awarding us the Pulitzer Prize a decade ago and threw it against the far wall, shattering the glass.

This explosion of anger seemed to calm him a little, or perhaps he was just embarrassed to be so out of control. He lowered his head. "You fucker!" he muttered. He picked the battered Pulitzer Prize award off the floor and put it on his desk, then collected the shards of glass and threw them in the waste basket. He gestured for me to sit on one of the couches. He sat in a leather chair.

"All right," he said. "How did it happen? I want to know."

The gravity of the situation was sinking in, now that his tantrum was over. He really was firing me. I had betrayed my newspaper. My career was ending, right now, there in this office.

"I'm sorry, Ed. I feel so bad about what happened. Honestly, I want to cry."

"Don't. That's the one thing that would make this worse. Now tell me how this happened."

I had to think. How had this chain of events and circumstances, now wrapped so tightly around me, actually begun? "There are a lot of ways to answer that, but the serious part began the last time I was in this office, the day I came to see you about Arthur Bowman."

"So it's my fault? I made you do it! That is really lame, Truell. You *are* pathetic!"

"No, it's not your fault. But you asked how it happened, so I'm trying to tell you. I tried that day to get you to understand that Arthur was in serious trouble—that he was taking money from people he shouldn't have. But you respected him so much, you didn't want to hear about it. So I went to other people, who *would* listen. They were at the CIA. That's how it started."

"Remind me what terrible things Arthur had done. I've forgotten."

"Arthur Bowman took money from French intelligence. It probably added up to millions of dollars over the years. That's how he managed to live so well. He worked for gangsters, who leaned on him to cook stories, which you ran in the *Mirror*. You remember all those stories he wrote about the China contract? His French friends bought those stories. If Arthur were alive, he'd tell you the same thing."

"Bullshit! How do you know that?"

"Because Arthur told me. When he realized I knew he had taken money from them, he was almost relieved. These people were leaning on him to do more and more for them. He hated it. That's why he wanted me to come to China. He thought I would provide some protection. He wanted out. He was so tough in China, I began to understand why you all loved him so much. But they got him. The people he had been working for killed him."

"What are you talking about? You said Arthur's death was an accident. A truck ran over him. You wrote it in the paper. We published the story."

"I wanted to protect Arthur's reputation, and the paper, and myself, but that story wasn't true. A truck did run over him. But the Chinese government sent the truck, and somebody told them to do it."

"Who, God damn it?"

"Those pictures?" I pointed to the pictures atop Weiss's desk of me and my various CIA friends. "The people who sent you the pictures were the ones who killed Arthur."

"I have no idea who sent them. They were anonymous."

"So I'm telling you. The man who sent them is named Michel Bézy. He's a former French intelligence officer. Arthur had a contract with him for more than ten years. He paid Arthur a lot of money, and Bézy thought he owned him. When Arthur tried to fight back, Bézy got him."

"Come on! You're making this up."

"The hell I am!" I wanted to blurt out the rest. To tell Weiss that Bézy had his hands around the throat of the *Mirror* itself—that he had a $500 million investment in corrupting everything Weiss had built. But I held my tongue. I felt I owed it to Philip Sellinger to tell him first. Sellinger had formed the alliance with Bézy, and it was Sellinger who had to decide what to do.

"Prove it!" said Weiss. "Prove to me that you're not making it up."

"I will, if you'd just listen to me. I know Bézy had the Chinese kill Arthur because Bézy told me so himself. Monday night in Montreal. And I know he sent you the pictures because he showed them to me before he sent them, to try to scare me. I called you that night and left you the message on your voice mail, for God's sake. How would I know the photos were coming unless I was with the guy? Didn't you hear the fear in my voice? Bézy wanted to kill me, too. His guys were beating on the phone booth, trying to get me to hang up."

Weiss cracked a thin smile, the way he used to when I told him about some outrageous story I had been working on. "Shit!" he said. "This is the craziest yarn I ever heard. Have you lost your marbles, Eric?"

"It's all true. It will take a while to really explain all of it. And there's more that I haven't told you, that I need to tell Mr. Sellinger about first. But you'll see. It's all true. You may not agree that I did the right thing, but you'll at least understand how it happened."

"Maybe so," said Weiss, "but right now we have some business to do."

Weiss summoned the lawyers, and I went through the story again. The only part I left out was Bézy's role in Press Alert, and his $500 million investment in the *Mirror*. Weiss and the lawyers listened carefully enough to what I said, and made notes. But they didn't really seem engaged until we began going over the pictures of me and the various CIA officers.

It was quite a gallery: Rupert Cohen, Tom Rubino, Roger Navarre, Frank Jones, the FBI commander in Boston. They held up each picture and asked me to identify the other person and explain what I was doing with him. My answers seemed to track Bézy's written explanation closely, picture by picture. He had done a good job in writing it up, but, then, he'd had good material to work with.

When we got to the picture of me and Navarre, the French biochemist, Bézy's explanation apparently had been skimpier, leaving out any mention of the biological-weapons research. When I described my role in the CIA operation that had helped Navarre escape from China and brought him to the United States, Weiss shook his head.

"You did that?" he said. "You've got balls. I'll say that much for you."

The lawyers looked uncomfortable, as if they didn't want him to say anything nice to me. They were negotiating my departure.

When we'd finished going through the pictures, I handed Weiss one more nail for my coffin. It didn't matter to me anymore—I was halfway out the door—but I wanted him to know. I said Rubino had told me, before I went to China, that he had obtained a special waiver from a presidential executive order that bans the use of U.S. journalists in intelligence operations.

"Jesus, Eric!" said Weiss, shaking his head. "Why did you do it?" He wasn't angry anymore. He was tired, and sad. He'd always liked me. I had been his favorite, his hope for the future. And now I had fucked up so totally that I was, professionally speaking, a dead man.

"At the time," I repeated, "I thought it was the right thing."

This time Weiss didn't throw anything, or even raise his voice. He knew what would come next, and he was blaming himself. "Why didn't you tell me?" he asked quietly. "Maybe I could have helped."

"I wanted to tell you. But I knew you would make me stop. And I felt I had to do it."

"Nothing more to say?"

No, I said. That was it. Now Weiss got very serious. He spoke slowly, looking directly at me.

"I told you before, Eric, that working for the CIA is a firing offense, and I meant it. It's a gross breach of professional ethics. It violates the most basic obligation of a newspaper reporter, which is to be independent of any private or government organization that we cover—especially an intelligence agency. Our readers cannot trust us unless they have confidence that we adhere to these standards. When they are violated, the paper must defend itself by punishing the person who has broken the rules.

"So I must ask you to leave the paper, effective today. The lawyers have these papers they want you to sign. I hope you'll do that, and not jerk us around. You owe us that, I think. I'm told you have a lot of accumulated sick leave and vacation time, which should keep you going until the end of the year. And you'll get the money in your 401(k) plan, and whatever else we owe you.

"Assuming you agree, I will put out a statement this evening saying that we have asked you to leave the paper, for cause. As has been our practice with other serious discipline cases, the paper will not make any further public comment about the reasons for your dismissal. A newsroom is a gossipy place, and people will be making all kinds of guesses about what happened. But I have no interest in seeing the details of this mess get out, and I assume you don't either. I will also try hard to dissuade the *Times* from writing a story. I can't promise you, but the editor over there owes me a favor, and he knows it."

The lawyers handed me the papers. I read Weiss's announcement—it was as bland a firing notice as he could have written under the circumstances—and then signed the papers. That was my last gift to the *Mirror*. The modern approach would have been to retain a lawyer and negotiate a more generous settlement. But I had no stomach for that.

When the papers were all signed, Weiss shook my hand, told me how sorry he was it had come to this and said he hoped I would find some other work that would give me satisfaction. He pointed me toward the door.

"Can I ask one favor?" I said. "I can't bear to walk back across the newsroom, where everyone can see me. It would hurt too much. I need to go upstairs and see Mr. Sellinger now. Can you take me up the back stairs?"

"Sure, kid," said Weiss. "You want me to come along?" I said I would rather talk to Sellinger alone. Weiss buzzed the publisher and told him I was coming up, and then escorted me to the stairwell outside his office door.

I didn't see Sellinger at first, the office was so big and the view was obscured by a huge vase of cut flowers. Where Weiss's office was full of journalistic trophies, Sellinger's was filled with the trophies that money can buy. The walls were hung with large abstract expressionist paintings—a big bold composition of slashing colors by Michael Heizer and a luminous blue canvas by Richard Diebenkorn. It was a grand office, suitable for the gentle man who had tried so hard to keep our ship afloat.

His secretary had left the door open, but I asked him to close it. Sellinger looked haggard. The sparkle in his blue eyes was gone; the trim, elegant body looked as if it had been crumpled into a ball and then straightened out again.

"I've been fired," I said.

"I know," he answered. "Ed just told me. He said he had to do it, to protect the newspaper."

"He's probably right. I didn't try to talk him out of it. But there are some things he doesn't know—no one knows—that I have to tell you."

"I can guess at some of them. But go ahead. You tell me the story, and I'll listen."

"Before he died, Arthur Bowman was trying to help you find enough money to keep the *Mirror* afloat, wasn't he?"

Sellinger gave a thin smile. "Yes. He used all his contacts to try to help find us some additional capital."

"Arthur didn't have much luck at first," I continued. "He tried Arabs, and Japanese and Koreans and Brits, but nobody wanted to buy a piece of a failing old newspaper. But one day he called and said that if you were really desperate, he knew a French company that could help."

"That's almost right," Sellinger said. "Actually, I was the one who called Arthur. I said I had exhausted all my options. If we couldn't find five hundred million dollars in two weeks, a syndicate of our creditors was going to be formed, and they were threatening to force us into bankruptcy. We were close to the end. Arthur said he knew one group in Europe that might be able to help, and I asked him, please, to do what he could."

"So Arthur called his friends," I said, picking up the narrative. "And their company was called Press Alert. And they were prepared to put up the five hundred million."

"That's right. Arthur said they wanted to invest in media businesses in the United States. They had an idea for this financial news service that would use the *Mirror*'s name to attract customers and offer very specialized information. That's how we got started with Mirror Alert."

"Did you know then who was running the company?"

"Arthur told me it was run by a Frenchman named Bézy, who was the personal lawyer for Alain Peyron. I knew Peyron, of course. I'd met him at meetings around the world. Arthur might even have been the one who first introduced us. I got the impression that some of the Press Alert money came from Peyron. But the source wasn't really clear, and at that time we weren't in a position to ask any questions of investors who had five hundred million to spare. We were grateful. It saved the newspaper."

"Did you know that Press Alert was a corrupt company?"

"No. I had suspicions. It was obvious this man Bézy made Arthur uncomfortable, though he wouldn't explain why. But as I told you, we were desperate. We did not perform our 'due diligence' with much vigor. We couldn't afford to."

"Do you understand, now, that they are a corrupt company?"

"I'm beginning to. A strange young man named George Dirk came to see me yesterday. He said he was a friend of yours, and that you had urged him to come talk with me. He laid out the most appalling evidence of what these people are doing—how they are using our reporting and our good name to cheat the markets. Is it true?"

"Yes, it's true. Bézy asked me to run this business for him, two days ago. I refused. That's why he sent the photographs to Weiss and the *Times.*"

"Mr. Dirk claims Press Alert is violating the securities laws. He thought I might be involved, too, but I think I convinced him otherwise. I knew nothing about this, Eric. I obviously made a dreadful mistake in taking their money, but I did it to save the *Mirror.*"

I believed Sellinger, but that wasn't enough. He needed to act quickly or the paper *would* be destroyed. "What did you tell Dirk you would do about the insider trading?"

"I told him I'd look into it. I asked him to leave whatever evidence he could with me, and I would look it over and get back to him. I don't think he was very impressed with my diligence. He seemed a somewhat angry man, with a bit of a chip on his shoulder."

"Dirk is a lunatic. But he's right about Press Alert. These people are poisonous. They will wreck the paper. You've got to get them out, as quickly as you can."

Sellinger's eyes went wide, almost as if he were about to cry. "You don't seem to understand, Eric. We have no money. The *Mirror* is hanging by a thread. If we push out our only new source of capital, we will be forced into bankruptcy. The paper will be sold. Your friends will all lose their jobs. This ship will sink."

"Mr. Sellinger, these people killed your best friend, Arthur Bowman. Do you realize that?"

A ghostly look came over Sellinger's face. His skin lost what little color it had; his eyes turned hard and bitter. "I suspected it," he said. "I didn't dare ask you, after you returned from Beijing. But I knew how apprehensive Arthur had been about Bézy, and I wondered if he might have played a role in Arthur's death."

"Bézy will kill the newspaper, too. You don't have a choice, Mr. Sellinger. You must go to the board and tell them what you've learned from Dirk, and then go to the SEC. These people are doing illegal things. If you don't act quickly, they'll take the *Mirror* down with them."

"What should I do?" asked Sellinger.

"I'm just an ex-employee, and not renowned for my good judgment," I said. "But I'd suggest that you start by calling George Dirk and telling him to come to New York right away—to brief the board of directors about what he has discovered."

42

❖❖

Ed Weiss summoned all his journalistic powers to keep the lid on my story. He called the editor of the *Times* and invited him to lunch. It happened they were old friends from Southeast Asia, too. He and Weiss and Bowman had once shared the same faithful translator, who turned out to be a Viet Cong agent. Over lunch, Weiss leveled with him—that was the essential bond among journalists, that we would tell each other the truth, even when we couldn't inform the wider world. He told the *Times* man so much about me and Arthur and the CIA that the poor fellow was in an impossible situation. Before, he hadn't known enough to publish a story. Now, he knew too much.

For insurance, Weiss added a kicker: he reminded his editor friend of the case of a former *Times* columnist who for many years had been helpful to the CIA. The problem, Weiss observed, was the fact that the agency had continued to use journalists for cover in operations, even when there was an executive order nominally forbidding them from doing so. The wisest course, Weiss said, would be for the two of them to meet privately with the director of Central Intelligence—and the president, too, if it came to that—and demand that the rules be changed so that a journalist would never again be subject to the intolerable risks and temptations that had destroyed Eric Truell's career.

The *Times* editor called back a day later to say that he had talked with his publisher. The *Times* agreed that the Truell story involved sensitive national-security issues, and that it was probably best handled by internal disciplinary action at the *Mirror*. That was the end of it. The *Times* story died. Weiss called me on the phone to let me know. He was so pleased with himself. "I saved your ass," he said. "I got the *Times* so tied up in knots they won't be able to piss for a week." Nothing pleased Weiss more than outsmarting the *Times*. For that moment, he was the meanest, toughest dog on the block.

I was happy for the paper, though it didn't do me much good. The rumor circulating in New York and Washington was that I had been fired for plagiarizing material from the French press while I was a correspondent in Paris, and that Weiss had only recently discovered it. I suspected Weiss himself had set the rumor in motion. It deflected attention from my real transgressions—for which Weiss himself arguably bore some responsibility—while ensuring that I would never work for a major newspaper again.

Weiss was a master player. He might have been a buccaneer in another life, or an army general. He had that essential bloody-mindedness that is part of being a leader—the ability to persuade the troops to go over the top of the trench shouting "Die, you bastards!" just for the glory of it. A Union officer wrote a memoir after the Battle of Gettysburg in which he remarked that the single most important attribute of a good officer was that he must never show fear in the sight of his troops when his unit was under fire. That commendation applied to Ed Weiss. Even after what he'd done to me, I would still have followed him into battle.

Philip Sellinger had the far harder task of trying to save the *Mirror* from bankruptcy, and he rose admirably to this challenge. The day after I left his office, he did indeed summon George Dirk to brief a secret meeting of the *Mirror*'s board of directors. With Sellinger at his side, Dirk laid out his evidence that Mirror Alert's editors—all employees of our partner, Press Alert—were profiting from inside information gathered through reporting. They were selling the information to a few crooked customers and trading on it themselves. At Sellinger's urging, the directors voted to turn the information over to the Securities and Exchange Commission.

That same day, Sellinger had Dirk deliver a briefing on the Press Alert problems to Ed Weiss. Weiss decided to rehire Dirk on the spot and assigned him to write an exposé of the *Mirror*'s ruinous relationship with its European partners. That was easier for Weiss—exposing the mistakes of the business side of the paper. Sellinger was uncomfortable at first with the idea of the paper washing its dirty laundry in public, but Weiss convinced him that we were better off exposing ourselves than waiting for others to do it.

Sellinger moved with remarkable speed to disentangle the *Mirror* from Press Alert. He hired the best corporate lawyers and investment bankers in New York to study the contract. They found language that would allow Mirror Corp. to dissolve the partnership unilaterally, because of the evidence it had discovered of criminal wrongdoing.

Late Friday afternoon after the stock market had closed, Sellinger issued a press release terminating the partnership with Press Alert. It was just two days after I had been to see him and one day after Dirk had briefed the board. The release also announced that we would be filing a lawsuit in federal district court, accusing our former partners of fraud. Press Alert countered with its own late-night press release, announcing that it was withdrawing its $500 million equity investment immediately and countersuing the *Mirror* for fraudulent misrepresentation of its business prospects.

That Sunday morning, the *Mirror* published George Dirk's lengthy exposé of the fraudulent trading by Press Alert employees. The story was mentioned on several of the Sunday talk shows as a model of responsible self-examination by the press. In the jury of opinion, the *Mirror* had won: the plaudits for exposing the corrupt joint venture far outweighed the embarrassment of having gotten into it in the first place.

But when the financial markets opened Monday morning, the *Mirror*'s stock plummeted. Trading had to be halted, as Sellinger and the investment bankers struggled for some way to replace the $500 million in equity and shore up the company's crumbling balance sheet. After frantic discussions through that night and into the morning with the paper's top management, union representatives and investment bankers, a plan for a leveraged buyout was drafted. The *Mirror*'s employees would purchase the newspaper, using money borrowed from banks. The banks agreed to lend the money on the promise that *Mirror* employees would accept sharp cuts in their salaries until the paper was profitable again. George Dirk was part of the negotiating committee. Because of his reputation at the paper as a malcontent, he was beloved by the unions. His recommendation to accept the deal was decisive in making it happen.

I called Tom Rubino just once, and we met for lunch at a restaurant in McLean. I wasn't sure what I wanted from him; perhaps it was just a chance to say good-bye in person, or maybe I was hoping he would thank me again for my role in Navarre's escape. But Rubino was still angry with me. The flap I provoked had gotten him into serious trouble, just as he had predicted. The inspector general's office was conducting an investigation, as was the House Intelligence Committee. Miraculously, nothing had leaked. But Rubino said his career at the agency was probably over. Despite the success in getting Roger Navarre out of China, any hopes he might have had of moving up from division chief to deputy director for operations had been destroyed.

I asked what had become of Navarre, now that he had a new identity in the United States. "He's working for us," Rubino said. "On BW counter-measures." I knew what that meant. The unthinkable would continue to be thought, but for our side now. Rubino was eager to end our lunch. It was an embarrassment.

"I should have known better," he said as we parted. "You were a reporter. I was a fool to think it would work."

I had cleaned out my desk in Washington the morning after I was fired. I thought some of my old colleagues might call me, if only to pump me for gossip. But I was instantly an unperson. With the exception of George Dirk, who called regularly, my phone didn't ring. In the eyes of my colleagues I was a ruined man. In a way, it was a liberating feeling. We all dread making the ultimate mistake, slipping off our spot on the greasy pole and falling into the abyss. But it turned out there was no abyss. There was simply the experience of living inside myself and trying to understand what had happened. I suppose I could have sued someone. That's what people do, nowadays, when something terrible happens to them. But I couldn't imagine doing it.

Annie Baron called me the day after I was fired. "I'm proud of you," she said. She seemed to understand, without my saying a word, that I had lost my job in the same war that had taken Arthur's life. She offered to come visit, but I wasn't ready to see her. Several weeks passed and I kept thinking the next day I would call her. But I never did. I had been thinking, since that lovely May day we went out walking, what answer I would give to her question: Could we truly begin all over—marry and have a family and start our life clocks again? But as the days and weeks passed, I knew that starting over in this way was impossible. We are the sum of our choices and decisions, chances and accidents. Our personal history is built up in layers that contain our history as surely as sediments of rock contain the history of our planet. I couldn't undo my previous life with Annie any more than

I could undo what had happened at the *Mirror*. It was all woven together in one fabric, which was my life.

One evening, out walking along M Street, I saw Annie on the arm of another man. She was glowing. She looked up at him with the spark of love in her eyes. He was a guy in his mid-thirties, handsome enough, sure of himself and his entitlement to happiness in the simple way that people are, until their expectations have been confounded. She didn't see me, and I let her walk by. I didn't feel pain so much as finality. She was starting afresh, and so eventually would I.

It was a hot morning in July, a day when the canopy of summer had settled over Washington, trapping the heat and the bugs and the car exhaust. I was coming out of the coffee bar in Dupont Circle where I went each morning to drink my cappuccino and read the newspapers. Just outside the door I saw the familiar face of Rupert Cohen. He had a stylish new haircut, short on the sides and moussed on the top; the scraggly beard was gone, and so were the goofy bohemian clothes. He was dressed in a well-cut Italian linen suit, slightly baggy at the knees; his shoes were the kind you buy in New York for four hundred dollars. Rupert had a microphone in his hand and I saw, to my horror, that a cameraman was following him.

"What are you doing here, Rupert? Is that camera on?"

"This is the Hatchet Man, coming to you from Dupont Circle in Washington, where the fat-cat journalists live," he said into the microphone. "The man who just walked out of the fancy coffee shop—where they charge two dollars for a cup of java!—is Eric Truell, former reporter from *The New York Mirror.*"

"Turn the damn camera off, Rupert!" I thought this must be another of his pranks.

I began walking up Connecticut Avenue toward my apartment building. Rupert and the cameraman followed close behind, calling out for me to stop so they could interview me. It was hard to break free, because a small crowd had formed. They wanted to watch the ambush interview. It was like a sporting event; some of the onlookers were razzing me, asking me what I was afraid of.

"Why are you running, Mr. Truell?" shouted Rupert. "The Hatchet Man wants to ask you some questions. What happened to you in China in May?"

"Nothing happened. Stop this! I can't believe you're doing this, Rupert. You're my friend."

"What happened in China?" he repeated. "Is it true that your colleague Arthur Bowman was murdered by the Chinese government? Why was he killed? What had he been doing?"

"I have to go. No comment." I pushed at the people in front of me, opening a hole in the circle of onlookers, and dashed through it. People in the crowd began to boo me, and cheer on the Hatchet Man. I ran up a block, where I had to stop for a traffic light. Rupert caught up with me again.

"Why are you running away, Mr. Truell? Isn't it true that when you were in China, you were conducting a secret intelligence operation for the CIA?"

"God damn it, Rupert! This is private. How can you do this? No comment."

"Why is the *Mirror* covering up what happened? Why aren't the other newspapers reporting anything? Why is there this conspiracy of silence?"

"Go away, Rupert. Leave me alone. My career is ruined. Isn't that enough?"

"The Hatchet Man doesn't play the Establishment game. We just report the news, we don't make it. Answer the question! The public has a right to know!"

The light had finally changed. I sprinted across the street. He ran after me, still shouting his questions.

"When did you first start working for the CIA? It was in Paris, wasn't it?"

"Rupert, how can you do this? It's inhuman." I was running harder now, up the slope of Connecticut Avenue, but he was still behind, microphone in hand.

"How could you betray your profession? The Hatchet Man wants to know! The Hatchet Man wants to know . . ."

I ran for a long while. When I stopped, no one was behind me.

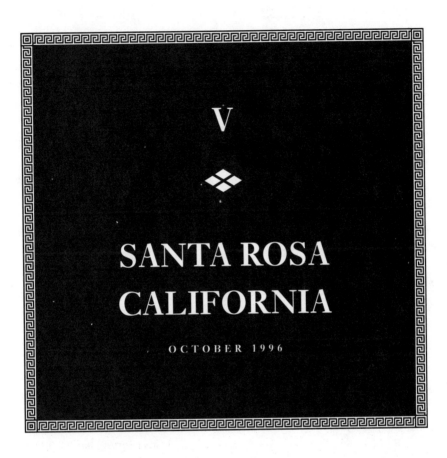

V

SANTA ROSA
CALIFORNIA

OCTOBER 1996

43

❖❖

I left Washington late that summer. There was nothing left in that city that mattered to me. Inevitably, the details of my secret activity began to trickle out. Rupert Cohen's ambush interview ran on *Hard Copy,* but nobody paid much attention to that. The serious problems began after the media reporter at *The Wall Street Journal* got wind of the informal understanding between Ed Weiss and his counterpart at the *Times* to suppress details of my case. Then all the dogs began to bark. Nothing excites the news media like transgressions involving the church elders. For nearly a week, various publications took turns speculating about the nature of my dealings with the Central Intelligence Agency. The only thing that saved me from total destruction was that Weiss steadfastly refused to comment. My departure from the paper was a personnel matter, he said, and as such, the paper wouldn't discuss it. Period. Reporters could badger him as much as they liked, but he wasn't budging.

As I said, you had to love Weiss. He was probably the last captain who would ever sail a journalistic ship as grand as *The New York Mirror,* and in that sense he had it easier than the people who would follow him. But still, he knew how to stand up there on the bridge and make the damn thing run.

The problem with staying in Washington was that I couldn't just tell everyone to piss off and go away. I was a public person now, stripped of any privacy. People called me at 2:00 A.M.—reporters, cranks, who knew who they were?—until I got an unlisted number. I was an official bad guy; my job was to act contrite. My former friends in the media, now as earnest with me as they would be in talking to a cancer patient, counseled that I should go through the ritual of public confession and absolution—on

Nightline, preferably. But that was the last thing I wanted to do. I still wasn't sure, in my heart, that I had committed any ultimate sin. I knew I had violated the rules of my profession, and that I deserved to be fired. But the rest, I didn't know. I was never going to survive in that ambiguous position in Washington, where people actually whispered behind my back in the checkout line at the Safeway in Georgetown that I was "the CIA reporter." I knew I had to leave. I needed a job, for one thing, and in Washington I was untouchable.

I am happy to report that bad things happened to Michel Bézy. His mistake was that he had made too much noise. His power was truly of the secret variety, and it turned out he couldn't survive long in a public fight. When Sellinger called in the Securities and Exchange Commission to investigate Press Alert, he set in motion a formal process of investigation. Unlike most of what Bézy had encountered in his previous dealings, the SEC could not be bribed or tortured or intimidated into submission. The agency was like a giant, lumbering animal; once it started, it was very hard to stop. Worst of all for Bézy, the SEC requested assistance from Paris. The French authorities, after several weeks of indecision, agreed to comply.

It was as if Bézy had suddenly lost the mandate of heaven. The new French government had been looking for ways to signal that it would not tolerate the same outrageous degree of corruption its predecessors had accepted. Now Bézy had given them an opportunity. My old friend Philippe Aurant at the prime minister's office paid me an urgent visit in early August and asked for details about Bézy's activities. I told him the story as it had happened. A month later Aurant called to say that Michel Bézy had been arrested on a charge of tax evasion. That sounded like a joke—cheating the tax man was France's national sport, after all—but Aurant said the game really was up for Monsieur Bézy. The evidence against him had come chiefly from his old patron Alain Peyron, who was said to be indignant—indignant!—to discover his former attorney's transgressions. A settlement was worked out quietly with the SEC; Bézy settled in for a long prison sentence in France. That gave me a moment of satisfaction, but it did nothing to address the problem of what I should do with my life.

I decided to go back to northern California, not just because it was home but because I truly loved that part of the country. I returned in September and stayed the first few weeks with my parents in Davis. I felt better the moment I stepped off the plane in San Francisco. It was as if the air had been washed, it was so clean and fluffy. You forget back East how unpleasant the weather is; it begins to seem natural that the climate has a soggy heaviness, like the kitchen in a greasy-spoon diner. You think you'll always have to live like that. But then you walk out the door and find that on the other side it's sunny, with the temperature in the seventies and low humidity, thank you very much. I began to play serious tennis again, for the first time in years, with some of the guys on my high school team. I was in better shape than most of them, which made me feel I hadn't completely wasted the past twenty years.

The nicest thing my parents did was not ask me any questions. It didn't seem to matter to them what I had done or not done; they loved me anyway. I went camping one weekend with my dad at Yosemite, something I'd always tried to avoid when I was a boy. It was bliss. We drank beer and went fishing and cooked our meals over a campfire. One night after we'd eaten, he asked me in that sweet, serious way I remembered from when I was a kid, whether I had given any thought to what I'd do for a living now. It didn't matter to him, he said. But if there was any way he could help, I should just let him know. I answered that I was thinking about it.

What I was trying to decide was whether I still loved the craft of journalism. That was the only thing I really knew how to do, and despite my recent troubles I was pretty good at it. I tried to think of other kinds of work I might enjoy, in professions where my firing from the *Mirror* wouldn't be such a liability. I could still go to law school, but then I'd have to be a lawyer. I could try to open a bookstore or a restaurant, but I imagined sitting in the place all alone, waiting for customers to come, and how depressed I would feel. I wanted a job in which I would be helping people in some way, but I knew I didn't have the temperament for something really serious, like being a social worker or a cop.

The more I thought about it, the more obvious it was that my best opportunity to help people—and make a living at it—was by giving them accurate information, in a newspaper. Journalism was my profession, and I had always loved it, even when it didn't love me. Unfortunately, I was radioactive as far as most newspapers and magazines were concerned. I stood even less of a chance of getting hired by most of the reputable journalistic organs than Rupert Cohen had when he left Liars Anonymous. Even a former spy was more hirable than a defrocked member of the news priesthood.

I knew of only one newspaper in the world that still had any reason to be nice to me. It was the *Santa Rosa News-Herald,* located in a small town about fifty miles west of where I had grown up. I had worked there the summer after my junior year at Stanford, covering the Elks Club and the school board and Little League baseball and anything else they asked me to do. I had over a hundred bylines in the paper that summer—an average of over one a day. One Saturday I'd had three stories on the front page. As local papers went, it was pretty decent. Santa Rosa was on the edge of the Sonoma Valley wine country; its readership was relatively upscale for a small town, and its news hole hadn't shrunk as much as those of the other small papers. The publisher had tried to keep in touch with me after I went overseas for the *Mirror.* He'd sent me letters in Beirut and Hong Kong, which always closed with something to the effect of: Don't forget your old friends in Santa Rosa, now that you're a big star.

I made an appointment to see the publisher of the *Santa Rosa News-Herald.* I wasn't a big star now. I was an unemployed reporter—quite possibly an unemployable one. I felt guilty even calling him. I hadn't bothered to answer the last letter he sent me in Paris, after my great exposé of Maurice Costa. In truth, I *had* forgotten my old friends in Santa Rosa. But he didn't seem to hold any grudge; bad behavior is expected of people who become famous. The publisher's office had changed very little over the years. He still had testimonials on the wall from the American Press Institute and the California Press Association, along with some rinky-dink journalism awards.

The publisher was much nicer to me than I deserved. He sat me down on one of his big couches, where advertisers used to hold forth in the old days when they came to complain about our stories. He didn't seem to know much about what had happened to me recently, except that I'd gotten into some sort of trouble with the media elite, which was a plus as far as he was concerned. I said I needed a job, and he smiled the biggest smile I had seen in months. An old friend was asking him for a favor, and what makes a man happier than granting a favor?

The publisher arranged for me to see his managing editor. She was a quiet, tough-minded woman in her late fifties who had gotten her start as a copy editor at the *Chicago Tribune.* She seemed embarrassed when I arrived for the interview. The publisher had leaned on her to see me, but it wasn't that. I was a famous journalist from the East; I had won a Polk Award. I had gotten into trouble—yes, she was certainly aware of that—but I was still a news celebrity, and it was hard for her to understand why

I would be applying for a job at a small paper with a daily circulation of under fifty thousand.

"This is what I know how to do," I said. "And, frankly, I need a job. The big papers won't hire me."

She had two openings. One was an entry-level job for a reporter-trainee who would cover local education. It paid $17,500 per year and was, as she said, "not appropriate." The other was for business editor, a relatively senior job that paid $42,000, with eligibility for an annual profit-sharing bonus. The old business editor had quit a few weeks before to start a public relations firm, and she was looking for an experienced journalist to take over.

"I could do that job," I said, without thinking about it a great deal. Editing sounded like a job for a grown-up. People at the *Mirror* had been telling me for several years that I should become an editor; perhaps they had been right. She asked me a bunch more questions and eventually said that if I truly wanted the job, I could have it. My biggest problem, she said, was that I was overqualified to work at the *News-Herald*.

I was elated. But I thought I needed to raise the unmentionable subject. "You know why I left *The New York Mirror,* don't you?" I said gravely.

"You did something for the CIA that you weren't supposed to. Isn't that it?" She was trying to remember the details of what she'd read in the newsmagazines. "I certainly don't approve of that. But I gather you feel now that it was a mistake and you'd never do it again—in the unlikely event that the CIA was bent on infiltrating the nerve center of northern California agriculture." She laughed, and that was it.

So I started again, to the extent that we can start anything fresh, back at the newspaper where I had received my first paycheck. My title was Assistant Managing Editor. I had three reporters, all in their twenties; an assignment editor in his late fifties who had run the section once but gotten fired; and a part-time copy editor. My staff, such as it was, seemed excited. I was a star, a prizewinner; the other things that had happened to me were so far away. They sensed that someone smart, who had played on a larger stage, had arrived at their sleepy little newspaper with something to prove. But what was it? I gathered them the first day in our corner of the newsroom and made a little speech. The room was messy with paper and broken furniture and the remnants of people's half-eaten lunches. The *News-Herald* wasn't prosperous enough to be neat.

I said I wanted to make two promises. I would help them be the best reporters and editors they could be. And I would never do anything that violated journalistic ethics. They listened politely enough to me; they must have wondered why the new guy sounded so earnest. When I was done, one of the young reporters raised his hand. He looked like a smart kid, cocky even. He reminded me a bit of myself at that age, to be honest.

"I have a question about coverage, Mr. Truell," the young reporter said. It was the first time a colleague had ever called me Mister. He tilted his head back, looking me in the eye, sizing me up. He said he was working on an exposé of the leading auto dealer in town. He'd spent weeks looking at court records and discovered that the auto dealer had been sued more than a dozen times during the last five years by unhappy consumers. He thought he had a great story about a dishonest local businessman, but the dealer was a big advertiser and the *News-Herald* had never run a critical article about him. He was a friend of the publisher.

"Will you run my piece?" the reporter asked. The little group gathered around my desk went dead silent. "I need to know," the young man said. "Because I don't want to do any more work on the story if you're just going to kill it the way they did the last time."

There it was. I closed my eyes and listened to the sound of the traffic out on Highway 101. I had ended up in this little California town, trying to save what was left of my career and my self-esteem. I wasn't trying to be a crusader. I just wanted to be a journalist again. And I knew the answer to his question. I had lived with ambiguities all my life, but this one was black and white.

"Of course I'll run the piece," I said. "You get the facts right, and I'll run it."

The kid reporter was still squinting at me. He had heard promises like this before, and he wasn't sure he believed me. He must have heard the rumors. I was the guy who'd gotten too close to the CIA. I had been corrupted. How could he trust me to protect him from this auto dealer, and all the other people who wanted to manipulate newspapers. "What if the publisher says you can't run it?" he asked. "That's what happened the last time, when I wrote a story about the supermarkets. The publisher said it was irresponsible, and full of innuendo, and the *News-Herald* wouldn't run it. Suppose he says that again. What will you do then?"

I thought a moment, but no more than that. They were watching me, waiting to see what the rules would be. These kids didn't have any money.

They needed their jobs. But they were willing to put themselves at risk for the power of an idea, which was that a serious newspaper fights for its independence. It doesn't let other people push it around. And they needed an answer from their new editor.

I turned to my staff and smiled, a smile less of confidence a of simple experience. "What's the worst thing the publisher can do?" I said. "Fire me?"

They all laughed, even the cocky kid. That's the wonderful thing about being fired. It gives you a kind of immunity. You don't have to be afraid of the things that frighten most people. They've already happened to you.

"So what should I do?" persisted the kid reporter. He was so hungry, so needy, so pumped with ambition, just as I once had been. What to tell him, to temper his fear and arrogance just enough to do the job?

"Suck it up!" I said. It was a phrase Weiss had often used to rouse the troops. I had never been sure what it meant. Did it mean suck up your gut? Or suck up your breath? Or perhaps, suck up your courage? I'm not sure Weiss himself knew what it meant. It was just one of the things he said to get us all juiced up, but in that moment the meaning of the phrase suddenly seemed obvious. It meant: *Suck up life.* Take it in whole, taste it, experience it, make sense of it. Tell the truth about it. That was the only lasting satisfaction in our business. The rest was the ordinary part, the news.

ACKNOWLEDGMENTS

This book wouldn't exist without the help of five people: my editor, Jonathan Karp; my literary agent, Raphael Sagalyn; my friends Lincoln Caplan and Garrett Epps; and my wife, Eve Ignatius. The book emerged out of discussions with them over the past several years and their comments on early drafts. I am especially grateful to Jon for his counsel. I owe special thanks to my cousin, Dr. Michael Ignatius, an assistant professor of neurobiology at the University of California at Berkeley, for his help in understanding the world of prions and neurotrophins; to Richard Drezen for his research help; and to my colleagues Don Graham, Len Downie and Doug Feaver for giving me time and support.

ABOUT THE AUTHOR

DAVID IGNATIUS is assistant managing editor for business news at *The Washington Post*, where he has also served as foreign editor and editor of the Outlook section. Before joining the *Post,* he was an award-winning reporter for *The Wall Street Journal,* where he spent three years chronicling the collapse of Lebanon and the rise of terrorism. He has written for *The New York Times Magazine, The Washington Monthly,* and Foreign Affairs. He is the author of a trilogy of novels set in the worlds of intelligence and the Middle East: *Agents of Innocence, SIRO,* and *The Bank of Fear.* A graduate of Harvard and Cambridge, he lives in Washington, D.C., with his wife and three children.

ABOUT THE TYPE

This book was set in Garamond, a typeface designed by the French printer Jean Janson. It is styled after Garamond's original models. The face is dignified, and is light but without fragile lines. The italic is modeled after a font of Granjon, which was probably out in the middle of the sixteenth century.